DETECTIVE QUINN ISAACS:

IMPERFECT
THE ^ WEB OF CRIME

JACQUE JACOBS

An imprint of
Drellag Press, LLC

Acknowledgements

With continued gratitude, I extend thanks to Susan Lovelace and Dr. Dondra Maney for their commitment in reading every word that I first write in a story. Support and encouragement from friends Ruth Jackson Johnston, Dr. Bill Johnston, Paula Van Hooser, Dr. Ann Alexander, Michelle Wheeler, Charlene Tardi, Dr. Rosemary Green, Denese Gray, Judy Hunter, and Dr. Lance Curlin keeps me going on the days when it would be easy to wonder if anyone is interested in the stories I weave. I give special thanks to Andrea Adamcova, Victoria Wlosok, Natalia Wlosok and Karolina Wlosok for their love and encouragement on this writing adventure.

While writing is a solitary endeavor, the feedback from readers of the many drafts and edits, and the willingness of others to tell me the bald truth, keeps me going. I hope the fun I have in crafting a story is equally fun and interesting for you to read. Thanks for coming along on the journey.

The final steps in bringing this book to print and e-book could not have happened without the amazing photographic work of Bill Johnston, Awesome cover design by PixelSudio at http://www.Fiverr.com and book formatting by Arkonna at http://www.Fiverr.com

Dedication

With love and deep affection, this book is dedicated to my Goddaughters: Victoria, Natalia, and Karolina.

Other Works of Fiction by Jacque Jacobs

Love is a Cabin Series

High on a Mountain – Book 1

Life on a Mountain – Book 2

Settled on a Mountain – Book 3

New Beginnings on a Mountain – Book 4

Community Unites on a Mountain – Book 5

Holidays on a Mountain – Book 6

Love is a Cabin Series

The Almost Perfect Crime – Book 1

Table of Contents

Part I
Crime Comes in Many Forms

Chapter 1

*Come with me into the woods. Where spring is advancing, as it does, no matter
what, not being singular or particular, but one of the forever gifts,
and certainly visible.*
Mary Oliver

A Mountain Hike

"How much farther to this waterfall?" Quinn looked back over her shoulder
at Billy. She lifted her foot; it felt weighted in lead in the hiking boots she
hadn't worn since last fall. Her five foot-nine inch frame was fit from her
daily workouts in her home gym, but hiking—well, that was different. Four
busy months into her new job as lead detective in Round City she hadn't
had many breaks and not much time outdoors, so she was excited about
the hike—and her developing personal relationship with Billy.

"Patience is part of the journey to discovery." Billy Williams smiled at
her determination to beat him to the Falls. He was lead detective from the
Sheriff's Station in the next county over. He and Quinn had worked several
cases together when she was in Immigration Enforcement.

"Going philosophical on me, now?" The lilt in her voice belied the pain
she felt from the blister she'd likely be nursing tonight. *I should have worn
heavier socks.*

Billy loved sparring with her. "Good detective work requires patience, a
bit of philosophy, and more determination than climbing this mountain."
He stepped up behind her and tapped her shoulder.

She turned her head toward him. "I thought we were out for a hike to
clear my head of detective work."

"You're right. I'm sorry." Billy leaned in and kissed her lightly...then more passionately. He tilted his head back and looked into her hazel eyes. "Forgive me?"

She pulled him back to her and returned the kiss holding it long enough they both had to gasp for air. She gently bit his lower lip as she stepped back. "You're forgiven."

She took two steps away from him and looked up the trail. Taking in the chartreuse and pale green leaves of the new growth on the sugar maple and hickory trees, dwarfed by the tall evergreen pines, she bent her knee and took off in a sprint. "Last one to the top..."

"Carries the other one down?" Billy laughed. He took a giant step and slipped on a loose rock. He toppled forward and instinctively put his hands out to break his fall. He rolled over and groaned.

Quinn moved toward him, squatted down, and gently rolled him onto his back. "Your shoulder?"

He nodded his head and rolled his eyes. "Please don't tell Doc Smith I was horsing around."

"Billy, look at me." Her eyelids squinted and her brow furrowed.

The pleading in her eyes was clear to him even in his pain. "I think I can move my arm. Just give me a minute." He turned his hands so that his palms were facing up; the scrapes were superficial.

She sat on the ground, crossed her legs, and leaned in to check his pupil reaction. "Well, the good news is it doesn't seem to have damaged your brain."

"Ha! That happened long ago...owww, my shoulder...my back."

Quinn knew the seriousness of the injury to his shoulder several months back when his vehicle was run off the road in a multi-state criminal case which they had both investigated. She shook her head and drew on their customary, often light-hearted, banter. "You know, Billy, you could have just asked me to carry you down instead of being a showoff."

Billy slowly lifted his left arm. "See. My shoulder will be fine. My back from rolling over on my service weapon—well, that will hurt for a while."

Quinn reached down, touched his face, and stroked his cheek.

"Thanks." Billy's smile carried a bit of the impish grin she loved. "I needed that—the power of your touch."

"Happy to oblige." She took his Yeti off his hip and opened the lid. "Think you can drink some water?"

"Sip, maybe."

She lifted his head and put the Yeti to his lips. "I see there's a good size flat spot up ahead. I can call for a helicopter and medivac you out of here."

Billy leaned on his right shoulder and pushed himself up. "I'd sooner let you carry me down." His grin was huge in response to her scowl. "Relax, I don't need that either. Just a bump, a scrape, and a jarring to remind me of my messed up shoulder." He was sitting straight up now and lifted both arms over his head. "Good...as...new." He took a sharp breath. "Soon."

"Okay, brave guy. I'm going to check out the flat area ahead. I'll be back."

"I'm not going anywhere. Look for the waterfall off to the right."

Quinn finished the last fifty yards of their intended hike and surveyed the flat surface; she was sure a helicopter could land here. She lifted her head and caught her breath as she took in the clear blue sky and the shade of the trees on the rocks beyond. She heard the continuous running of the falls and turned to see the water being funneled down a crevice in the mountain. Her head turned quickly when she heard a moan.

"Billy, are you okay?"

She saw him heading toward her. "Right as rain. Nice view?"

She heard the moan again. It wasn't from Billy.

Finding Her Way

Angela leaned against the broad trunk of a pitch pine, one of the largest trees in this part of the Smoky Mountains. *It looks like a giant Christmas tree.* Her head hurt each time she tried to sit upright; she was sure she could feel the earth spinning.

In the early morning light, she had stumbled upon this path. Unable to see anyone in either direction, she started climbing. She didn't know if she would find shelter, but hoped someone would come along who could help her. *Air, I need air.* The warmth of the spring day and the sight of wildflowers blooming gave her hope. She tried to pull her sweater tighter around her.

Why didn't I call cousin Peter on my way to Grandmother's? She'll be furious because he'll call her and push until she tells him I didn't get there. She took several short breaths. *Sorry, Peter. I know you wanted to finish that land deal. I'll call you as soon as I can.* She leaned her head back against the tree—her breathing was shallow and her asthma well on the way to making her panic—she had lost her inhaler climbing the mountain. *Where is my phone?* She gasped for air again.

In the quiet of the morning, she strained to hear what she thought was a woman's voice; it was clear and sounded concerned…for Billy. *Is that what she called him? Billy?* Then she heard the man's voice. *Billy? That's a nice name. He sounds kind.* She struggled through shallow breaths for air and now was wracked by short gasps as she tried to get oxygen into her lungs. She put her head against the wide breadth of the tree as she burrowed into the deep gnarly scar at its base.

A Hike Diverted

Quinn put her finger to her lips.

Billy stopped. He heard the noise. He nodded and pointed.

They both turned and moved in the direction of the large pitch pine.

Quinn stepped up beside him and held her hand up for them to stop. She whispered, "Do you hear anything now?"

He shook his head.

They waited. Then they heard the gasps and both pointed at the base of the tree.

Quinn nodded and they stepped out.

Billy spotted the body and raised his hand to signal Quinn to stop. Keeping his eyes fixed on the person, he pulled his service weapon, and aimed it at the ground. He signaled Quinn he was taking the lead.

Quinn nodded. She knew Billy needed to be in front. She had not brought her service weapon as they had agreed it was important to the purpose of this hike to get her out of work mode.

"Hello. Do you need help?" Billy raised his voice keeping it calm and clear.

There was no response. It was difficult with the shade under the tree to tell whether the huddled body was male or female.

Billy moved closer and saw a young female in black jeans, a t-shirt with something printed on the front of it, and a lightweight gray sweater. The clothes appeared of good quality, but not new. He didn't see blood anywhere or any sign of injury or assault. He looked at the ground around her and there was no sign of a struggle—nothing visible other than the forest floor.

"Hello. Do you need help?" He was right beside her now.

Angela opened her eyes. In a voice more dreamlike than awake, two words spilled out: "Cuz? Billy?"

Quinn had been scanning the area looking for signs of anyone else. She moved off to Billy's right and was equal distance from the figure. She knew by the Prada jeans and Gucci loafers it was highly unlikely this young woman was out for a hike. She looked carefully at the young woman. She whispered to Billy, "Did she say, 'cuss?'"

He shrugged his shoulders and looked back at the young woman. "I'm Billy. Who are you?"

"Help me...my head hurts..." Her voice trailed off into silence. Her breathing was irregular.

Quinn quickly moved in and felt for a pulse in the young woman's neck—it was faint. "She's burning up with fever. We have to get her to a hospital. Do you know her, Billy?"

"Never saw her before in my life. We'll have to riddle that out once we get her down the mountain. We have no first aid...nothing to help her up here."

Quinn leaned in towards the young woman. "I'm Quinn. You're going to be okay. We are police officers and we're going to get you to the hospital." Quinn stood up and looked from him, over to the flat ground, and then down the trail. It had been more than a three hour hike up the mountain—carrying a body down would lengthen the time. *Billy's shoulder couldn't bear up under the weight even if we could fashion a stretcher from limbs and vines.* She watched the young woman carefully. "We need to get a helicopter here."

Billy moved toward Quinn. "Want me to call for help?"

"Thanks. I've got it." Quinn lifted the hand-held police issue digital radio she carried on hikes in these mountains; phone service in the mountains was too unreliable. She moved toward the flat top on the mountain. "See if she has any identification on her, please."

"Detective Isaacs," the Round City Police dispatcher responded immediately. "How may I direct your call?"

"Need a helicopter rescue. *My* party is fine. We found a young woman at Indian Flats Falls who is running a high fever and struggling to get air. We need to get her to the hospital."

"I've got your coordinates. With the trail, we might get an ambulance most of the way up there. Anywhere for a helicopter to land?"

"I don't think we have time for an ambulance. There is a flat area about 200 feet by 200 feet without any trees. I think you'll need the mountain copter out of Maryville or Knoxville."

"No problem. Back with you in a minute."

Quinn called over to Billy while she waited. "Any ID on her?"

"None. Not a thing on her. No jewelry, watch, phone, nothing. I've scanned the area and nothing seems to have disturbed the pine needles other than our footprints."

Quinn nodded and held up her finger. "ETA?"

"Eighteen to twenty minutes, Detective. One HELO on the way coming from Pigeon Forge."

"10-4." She ended the transmission and walked back toward Billy. "Guess you heard that?"

"I did. Hope they make it in less; she's struggling to get air."

HELO

Time seemed to stand still in the quiet—save the running of the waterfall. Quinn pulled her hair into a knot at the nap of her neck and stood in the flat area watching the sky. She squinted as she pointed toward the sound of the helicopter she heard coming from the northeast. Her radio signaled an incoming call.

"Isaacs."

"Detective, the HELO pilot notified he has spotted you. Please move back."

"10-4."

She moved toward the trees. Within a minute the helicopter pilot easily landed. The EMT hopped out of the co-pilot seat and moved quickly toward Quinn and Billy.

"Thanks for coming." Quinn stepped forward and extended her hand. "This is Detective Billy Williams from the Valley." Quinn noticed it wasn't a trauma helicopter.

"Oh, hey, I'm Becky. Hey, aren't you the guy that…Sorry. That was inappropriate." The red flush rose on her face. She had a medical bag and was moving toward the young woman under the tree.

"No problem. Yep, I'm the guy who went flying through the air in a Camaro. You must be based in Maryville."

"I am. Ya'll okay?"

"Fine." Quinn pointed toward the large pitch pine. "We were on a hike, heard a moan, and approached. The young woman muttered a few words and then nothing. Her breathing is shallow and she seems to have a fever—at least to my touch."

Billy looked at the slow moving rotors. He knew it was protocol to keep the blades moving. "Do you have a stretcher on that HELO?"

"Yep. The trauma chopper was already in use, but we can get her out of here. There's a SKED© in the helo. If you could grab it, we can head out."

Quinn turned and called loudly. "I'll get it. Room in there for all of us?" She was already moving toward the helicopter.

"One of you will need to ride up front with the pilot. We'll be a bit tight, but we should be fine."

Billy watched as Quinn sprinted to the helicopter, stuck her head in, and put on the headset the pilot handed her. She listened, nodded to the pilot, climbed in the back, and pulled out a litter. Billy recognized the oblong orange plastic which he had always thought looked like a shallow bathtub with hand holds.

Quinn left the back door open as the pilot had instructed and pulled the litter close to her body holding it tightly with two hands.

Billy watched in admiration as she moved in spite of the rotor blades stirring up more than a gentle breeze.

The EMT was still bent over the young woman. Quinn placed the litter on the ground. "I'll help lift her and carry her to the chopper." She saw Becky look up at Billy. "Let's show this male cop what two women can do." *No way I'm letting him try to lift this litter.*

"You got it." Becky showed Quinn how she wanted to move the young woman. She looked up at Billy. "Got the pictures you need?"

Thanks, Quinn. I don't think I could stand the pain of lifting her. Billy held up his phone. "Got them: her and the area." He watched the two women start to move.

"Humor him. Desperate need for attention, that one." Quinn used the bantering to break the tension but was totally focused on getting the young woman to the chopper and the hospital.

Billy took pictures as they lifted the body and put a sheet on her. He took photos where the young woman had been tucked in against the tree. He stepped back and took pictures of the surrounding area, but there were no footprints other than hers and theirs; footprints being an exaggeration as it was only the movement of pine needles that showed depressions of someone walking here. He did a quick search around the tree, but there was nothing that didn't belong on the forest floor. He pulled his handkerchief from his pocket and tied it to small seedling next to the tree. *We'll get a team up here as soon as we can.*

The litter was locked onto clips on the floor of the helicopter. Quinn squeezed in on the far side of the litter while Billy got in the front. Becky continued to monitor the vitals of the young woman. It was clear the pilot had patched through to the emergency room at the hospital: "BP 88 over 48; Pulse..." She finished giving the young woman's vital signs.

The headsets crackled as the pilot announced they were moving out. He lifted off the mountain and headed for the hospital in Round City.

Quinn found herself staring at the face of the young woman. She felt her heart rate accelerate and her hands go clammy. *Stop! Stop! It's not Eliza. This isn't the shooting. You are saving this young woman. Focus.*

Six minutes later they were on the roof of the hospital where a medical team was waiting and took over. The pilot spoke to Billy and Quinn through the headphones. "Need me to fly you over to the Station or want someone to pick you up here?"

Quinn spoke up. "We'll let you and Becky head back. We can get a ride. I want to check on the young woman before we leave. Thanks for the ride and the quick service."

"Here to serve."

Quinn and Billy headed for the door being held open by a hospital staff member. They waved as Becky exited the same door and moved toward the helicopter.

"Happy to be off the roof before those blades start up again." Billy ducked even though he was already inside the building.

Quinn showed her ID to the hospital staff member.

"Yes, Detective Isaacs, I know who you are."

Billy held his up for the woman to see.

She nodded. "This way, please."

They rode the elevator down to the first floor and headed toward the emergency room. The staff member took them to the check-in desk and left.

"Detectives, if you'll wait here for a few minutes, I'll let you know when the doctor can speak to you." The woman at the desk was friendly—but firm.

"Thanks." Quinn turned and saw the vending machines. "Buy you a cup of coffee, Billy?"

"Sure."

They sat in a far corner of the empty waiting area.

"Billy?"

"Yes." He looked up from the magazine he had picked up off the side table.

"Never mind." She turned and stared out the sliding glass doors.

He turned to look at her. "Hey, what's up?" He brushed the top of her hand.

She turned towards him. "It's nothing. Just a little flashback."

Billy sat up straighter. He knew she had been in a school shooting her senior year in high school.

Quinn saw the admissions clerk stand and started to stand, too. *Good she's coming to get us.* Then she saw her sit again.

"It's nothing. It's just on the helicopter I was looking at our Jane Doe and..." she turned back to the sliding doors as they opened and then shut as someone left.

This time Billy held her hand and squeezed it gently. "Look at me, Quinn."

She did.

"It's a natural reaction to severe trauma. There was likely something in this young woman that reminded you of one of the girls with you at the time. You can always talk to me or tell me. I'm here for you."

She squeezed his hand and let it go. "Thanks, Billy. It's just that after seventeen years I still can't get used to the flashbacks." She sipped her cooling coffee. "Ugh."

Billy flinched.

Quinn chuckled. "Sorry. It was the coffee, not the flashbacks—although they are ugh, too."

"Agreed—on both counts. Want to talk about it?"

"No, not really. I'm okay now. I just wanted—no, needed—to tell you."

He leaned close to her ear and whispered, "I love you." He knew how she felt about public displays of affection during professional time—and agreed with her although he struggled at times not to take her in his arms.

Another thirty minutes passed as they both flipped through old magazines. They had given up on the really bad vending machine coffee. Quinn looked up when the doors from the ER opened and a young man in scrubs approached them.

"Detective Isaacs?" He looked from one to the other.

Quinn was on her feet and extended her hand. "Yes, I am."

"I'm Dr. Scott."

Quinn turned to Billy. "This is Detective Williams from the Valley Sheriff's Station."

Billy shook Dr. Scott's extended hand.

"Were you in pursuit of this young woman for something?"

Quinn and Billy looked at each other. Billy stepped back; this was Quinn's jurisdiction.

She shook her head. "We weren't and there was no sign of anyone else. We were out on a hike to the falls and heard her moaning. Is she going to be alright?"

"Do you know her name?"

"No idea. She had no identification on her."

"I'm sorry to inform you she coded just as we got her in the ER. We did everything we could to save her but we were unsuccessful."

Quinn watched the physician's face. "Any idea what caused her death?"

"Afraid that will be for the Medical Examiner to determine."

Without hesitation, Quinn extended her hand. "Thank you for your efforts, Dr. Scott. She's ours now. We'll do everything we can to find out who she is. Dr. Walters, our ME, will do his due diligence to determine the factors that contributed to her death."

"Yes. Yes, he will. If you have nothing else for me, I'll leave you to make the arrangements." Dr. Scott turned to walk away.

Quinn saw the sadness in his eyes.

"Dr. Scott…"

He turned around.

"Thanks for all you did to try and save her." Quinn looked into his eyes.

"When you find out who she is, I'd like to know." He walked back through the doors into the ER.

Quinn turned to Billy. "Do we need to get your shoulder checked while we're here?"

"I'm good. Thanks for asking."

"Okay." She studied his eyes for any sign of pain. Satisfied she turned to walk over to a corner away from the person who had just come into the waiting area. "Let me get arrangements made with the ME and to have someone pick us up."

"I'm with you." Billy threw his half-full paper cup in the trash.

Mystery to be Solved

Quinn sent a secure message to the Chief while they waited to be picked up. The response from Chief Hansen was immediate: "CU on arrival w/Det. Wms."

"10-4." *Why does she want Billy there?*

Quinn and Billy took the elevator straight to the morgue when they arrived at the Station. "Chief Hansen would like you to come with me to see her."

"Sure." Billy stepped off the elevator after her.

The ME, a retired physician, was in his office and waved them in.

Quinn entered first. "Morning, Dr. Walters. I regret we have a young woman coming in for your table."

The ME nodded his head slowly. "Never know what a day will bring."

Quinn turned back and looked at the elevator. "Doc, I still can't get used to the elevator being fixed."

"Yeah, didn't you hear? New Chief in the house."

"I know. Lucky for me." She smiled. Quinn noticed Dr. Walters' new assistant, Sue, was standing to the side. *Big change from the last assistant. Wonder how things are going?*

"Just wanted to give you a brief on what we know at this point." She gave him an overview of how they found the young woman and what the physician had said.

"I know Dr. Scott. I'll call him once they deliver our Jane Doe."

"Thanks, Doc. We need to try and figure out who she is as soon as we can. Once we do, can you take care of letting Dr. Scott know her name?"

"Sure thing, Quinn. I'll get with Chuck on prints and DNA as soon as we can get them. You know they may not be in the system."

"I know." Quinn was somber. *Given the clothes she had on, it's highly unlikely she's in the system, but she's not going to be a Jane Doe—I promise that. Chuck is a great forensic tech—he'll find out who she is.*

"You'll do right by her, Quinn."

"We will. Thanks, Doc. Now we need to go see the Chief..." She turned to Billy. "Detective Williams, Chief Hansen awaits."

Billy raised his eyebrows. "Yes, ma'am."

She turned back to the ME. "So, unless you need me at the moment, Doc, I'll check in with you later."

"Later is fine, Quinn. Sorry your hike got interrupted." The ME gave them a slight wave of his hand.

"Oh my gosh, Billy, the hike...your SUV is at the base of the mountain."

Billy turned back to the ME. "Good detective, this one." He pointed to Quinn. "She might make lead detective one of these days."

"Could happen." The ME smiled at both of them. *Something tells me there is more to this relationship than two detectives working across jurisdictions.* He nodded. *Well, good for them.* "I'll be in touch, Quinn."

The ME turned to Sue. "Let's get ready."

Quinn started for the stairs which she usually preferred and turned back to the elevator. "I vote for the ride. My feet are killing me." Quinn pushed the button. The doors slid open quietly. She smiled.

Once inside the elevator, Billy was tempted to pull Quinn into an embrace, but he respected her role in this police station and didn't know where there were cameras. "Quinn, thanks for taking the litter. Hard for a mountain boy to watch two women do the work..."

"But you could get used to it?" She smiled. "I wouldn't have let you pick it up if I had to do it by myself—and not to make a gender point." She looked straight at him.

"Thanks. I got the message. My shoulder thanks you, too."

"Now, about your SUV?"

"Well, there's a problem to figure out, Detective Isaacs, since I believe both of your vehicles are at your home." His mischievous banter was back.

She threw her head back and laughed—as much a tension breaker as anything. The elevator doors opened. Captain Brown, second in command in the Round City Police Department, was standing there.

"Must have missed a good one. Good morning, Detective Isaacs. Williams."

"Captain." Billy nodded.

Quinn smiled. "Good morning, Captain Brown. A little humor at my expense, nothing more."

Captain Brown, normally all business, turned stern eyes toward Billy while a smile crept across his lips. "Do I need to arrest this man for harassing a police officer?"

Quinn had to keep herself from making a joke. She stood up straighter. "Not this time, Captain. Thank you for coming to my aid though. Have a nice day."

"You, too." Captain Brown's eyes now twinkled.

Quinn and Billy stepped off the elevator and let the doors close. They looked at each other and shrugged—both of them suppressing a laugh.

"Caught by the Captain." Billy's banter was in full force.

She gently tapped him on the arm and frowned. "Enough, already."

"Yes, ma'am." He gave her a mock salute.

She tried to change the tenor of their interaction. "I didn't know you knew Captain Brown."

"Everyone knows Captain Brown. We've had a few joint cases in our day. He's alright. He may have lightened up a bit with your new Chief."

"Could be." Quinn opened the door to the Chief's outer office. "After you, Detective."

Chapter 2

Falsehood is so easy, truth so difficult.
George Eliot

Location, Location, Location

Andrew Culbert III sat at his polished walnut desk and looked out the glass of his corner window on the fifth floor overlooking the city where he and his father had amassed a fortune in real estate. *How did he get my private number?* He logged out of his computer and headed for his administrative assistant's office.

He talked as he walked past her desk never turning his head to look at her. "Lee Ann, I'll be out for several hours. If you don't hear from me, clear my calendar for Monday." He knew she'd clear his calendar, even over the weekend.

"But, sir..."

The main office door slammed behind him. He didn't even hear it. At the front of the building, his driver pulled up in the large black SUV. Andrew stepped into the back and shut the door with a bang.

"Where to, sir?" Startled, the driver looked through the glass; Mr. Culbert had never slammed the door.

"My club. Then I won't need you the rest of the day."

"Sir?"

"You heard me. My club." Andrew turned off the communication between the front and back of his SUV and slunk down in the seat. *It wasn't supposed to be like this. Make use of that mountain acreage my great-grandmother got in the late 1800s, don't ask any questions, and stay out of the way.* He had done that. He felt the SUV slow. He stepped out as soon as the vehicle stopped and never looked back at his driver. He took the steps into the private club two at a time.

"Good morning, Mr. Culbert. Dining with us this noon?"

"No, Frank." He kept walking toward the elevator.

Ten minutes later he was in his personal dark blue Ford SUV, dressed in jeans, a navy t-shirt, and plaid shirt hanging loose to cover his Ruger GP 100 pistol; he long ago decided his gun of choice would not make him look like a gangster. This one certainly fit the bill. His Italian designer suit of light weight cashmere hung in the closet of his private room at the club. He headed east on I-40 and decided against texting his wife. *No need to get her engaged in a long series of questions; where are you going...how late will you be...She'll be fine. I'll be home by supper.*

A text message signaled on his display screen on the dashboard. "Take Exit 407. Await instructions."

Andrew slammed his fist against his steering wheel. *I don't take orders from anyone.* He swerved to miss a deer crossing the highway. *Slow down. Want to end up dead?*

Station Activity

Ms. Leonard stood as Quinn and Billy entered. "Morning Detective Isaacs, Detective Williams. The Chief is expecting you. Coffee? Tea? Water?"

Quinn shook her head. "No, thank you. Detective Williams?"

"I'm good. Thanks."

Ms. Leonard opened the door to the Chief's office and stepped aside. "Chief..."

"Thanks." Jill Hansen approached the door and nodded at Ms. Leonard and pointed to the table for the two detectives. Her administrative assistant closed the door behind them.

Need to ask the Chief how she managed to tame Ms. Leonard...no more snarls.

"Thanks for coming, Detective. I know it's your day off. Detective Williams, I appreciate your time."

"No problem. Happy to be of service." Billy smiled at her.

Quinn immediately knew the formality meant this was not a social call. Chief Hansen was much more relaxed than the previous Chief of Round City, but she followed protocol when business was involved.

"Am I correct that the young woman you encountered on the mountain did not survive?"

Quinn's response was quick. "Correct, ma'am. She did not."

"Any identification on her?"

"No, ma'am." *This is not like the Chief. She doesn't normally get so involved in a case.*

"Received a call of a missing young woman, but as you know, our current policy is we don't investigate adults until they've been gone forty-eight hours unless there is a report of foul play." She handed Quinn a piece of paper with a name, address, and phone number.

"Yes, ma'am." Quinn studied the address. She handed the paper to Billy. "Looks like it's in your jurisdiction."

He nodded. "Would appear to be in The Mountain Villages."

"It is." Jill Hansen studied Billy's face. "When I was informed you were bringing in a female, I talked to Sheriff Oliver about the missing person's report since the call came from your jurisdiction. Turns out the same person called your Station, Detective Williams. The Sheriff said he'd have you follow-up."

"Any idea why it was reported here and also in the Valley?" Billy kept eye contact with the Chief of Police.

"Fact or speculation?" Hansen matched his tone.

"Perfect response. May I quote you on that in the future?" Billy grinned.

Hansen nodded and smiled. "The death of the young woman in our morgue, who may or may not be the missing young woman, appears to have occurred in our jurisdiction. Our lead detective, who herself misses nothing, can decide on someone to accompany you if you like…in case it relates to the body in our morgue."

Quinn looked from one to the other. *When did I first hear someone talk about me saying, 'She's very observant. She misses nothing.'* She swallowed a gulp of air. *It was long before the shooting in high school.* Quinn gave a light shake of her head and refocused on the Chief's comment and noted Billy had been given an out not to have anyone from Round City with him, but it was clear the Chief wanted someone there.

"Yes, ma'am. Detective Isaacs can decide."

Hello, I'm here. You don't need to talk about me like I'm a child to be seen and not heard. We'll be talking about this, Detective Williams. She had to tighten her lips so as not to frown and show her frustration.

"I'm sure she will." Jill's tone was matter-of-fact. "Questions, detectives?"

"No, ma'am." Billy stood and extended his hand.

Quinn started to stand.

Chief Hansen put up her hand to stop Quinn as she looked at Billy. "May I have a moment with my detective?"

"By all means. Great to see you again, Chief. Sorry for the circumstances." Billy walked out.

The Chief turned to Quinn. "Didn't intend for you to be blindsided by inviting Detective Williams."

"Wasn't. No problem, ma'am."

"Seemed expedient in the moment to invite you both. Just want to clarify that I wasn't trying to take control. I also have no concerns about your ability to manage this. A loss of life is always tragic; let's hope this one isn't a criminal case."

"Thanks, Chief. I hope it doesn't become a criminal case, too. I'll send a team out to where we found her to make sure we didn't miss something." She paused. "I'll have someone accompany Detective Williams."

Jill stood. "And, Quinn. You didn't ask for my two cents, but might be good to have a female with him. The woman who called it in is in her seventies if my information is accurate."

Quinn stared at her. The Chief knew that Quinn was the only female detective. "Yes, ma'am. I'll check on female officers."

"Quinn, are you okay?" Jill looked at her. "You did just learn a young woman you were trying to help didn't survive." She studied Quinn more closely. She knew about Quinn's role in trying to protect three girls in a high school shooting.

"Yes, ma'am. Not my first, and I'm sure it won't be my last. I'm just trying to sort out the options for the follow-up. I'll keep you informed."

"Thanks." Jill opened the door, shook hands with Quinn, and watched her walk out of the office. *Guess I should have been more direct—I don't have a problem with her being on the investigation with Billy Williams. One of the mistakes I made in my career was thinking I wasn't capable of having a personal relationship with someone I worked with; it cost me the love of my life. Quinn can handle it—I'm sure of that.* She shook her head, closed her door, and walked back to her desk.

Quinn stopped as soon as she exited the Chief's outer door. She felt her gut tighten and tried to keep her face from turning into a scowl. Billy was talking to an officer in the hallway outside the Chief's office. *Am I jealous? He's just talking to another officer.*

Officer Evans had her back to Quinn. "Yeah, nice seeing you, too. Catch you later."

Billy stood straighter when he saw the look on Quinn's face. He walked toward her.

"If you have time to join me in my office..." Her tone was formal and she walked straight ahead.

"I'm with you, *ma'am.*" The emphasis was not to be missed.

She stopped. "Guess I deserved that."

"I'm just following you." He leaned in and whispered to her. "And, I'd follow you to the ends of the earth."

She exhaled a big sigh and chuckled "Yeah, I definitely deserved that."

"The respect of calling you, 'ma'am?' Absolutely." He wiggled his eyebrows and stopped behind her as she put the code in the door to the main forensic lab and her office.

"Morning, Chuck." Quinn spoke to her lead forensic tech.

"Hey, Quinn. I thought you were off today? Oh, hey, Billy."

Quinn opened her office door. "Duty calls. You know the routine."

"That's why I'm here." Chuck laughed and turned back to his microscope. "Let me know if you need me."

"Thanks. Will do." Quinn flipped the light switch, quickly turned on her desk lamp, then reached and flipped off the switch to the ceiling light.

"Got a thing about lighting up the place?" Billy pushed the door without closing it completely as he moved and sat in the chair against the wall.

"Prefer less glare—always have."

"I love learning new things about you."

"So what did you learn by the meeting with my Chief?"

"About her? Or about you?" He watched her carefully.

"Both."

"She's a no nonsense person who expects her folks to do their jobs."

"You already knew that."

Billy decided Quinn needed to decompress from the meeting. "Look, if my presence made it awkward, you..."

"It wasn't you." Quinn stared straight ahead. "It wasn't even her."

"Then what was it?"

Quinn took off her hiking boots and put on the loafers she left in her office. "The demon on my shoulder—my former boss." She sighed and pointed to her shoes. "My feet are killing me."

Billy leaned forward and caught himself about to say, "I'll massage them for you." Instead he put his elbows on his knees. "Don't have any experience with a bad boss. Both sheriffs I've worked for have been good leaders. Want my thoughts?"

Quinn leaned back in her desk chair, let out a slow breath, and felt her eyelids flutter slightly. "Billy, I always want your thoughts: personal and professional."

"Let the immigration guy go. He's history. You learned from his mistakes. You've got a new boss. She was a smart woman to hire you. Now don't disappoint her—or yourself."

"You're absolutely right! Shall we go talk to a woman we may learn just lost a loved one?"

"You're going? Woohoo!"

"I'm the lead detective here. I was at the scene of a young woman's death. My other detectives all have full plates." She smiled. "Now I've justified it to myself, so I'm ready."

Billy nodded, stood up, and managed to close her door the rest of the way. He pulled her into a tight embrace. "I've been wanting to do that for hours." He kissed her lightly on the cheek and pulled back. "Thanks for saving my life…and my shoulder on that mountain."

She kissed him long and slow. "My pleasure. Purely selfish on my part." She stepped back from his embrace. "Now, Detective Williams, we have a job to do. First I need to check in with my detectives. Give me ten minutes?"

"Sure. While you're at it, might want to figure out how to get…" He watched as she picked up her desk phone.

"Dispatch. How may I direct your call, Detective Isaacs?"

"Sergeant on duty, please."

"Fishburn here."

"Sergeant, Quinn Isaacs here."

"Yes, ma'am. What's up?"

"I need an officer who can run me home. Both my vehicles are there."

"Yeah, heard you left the Falls in style today."

Quinn didn't participate in gossip. *Let it go.* "Nothing but the best for our fine citizens. Ten minutes work?"

"At your service. Pick up at the back door in ten."

"10-4." *I'd heard there was a sergeant who was a gossip. Now I know who. I knew it wasn't Sergeant Clark!*

Billy looked at her. "What's your plan, Detective?"

"Ask George to get a team to meet us at the parking lot at the Falls, go to my house, go pick up your vehicle, and in the meantime strategize figuring out who this young woman was."

"10-4." He winked at her.

Oh, yeah. We have a lot to figure out, Billy Williams. She picked up the phone and called the senior detective, George Marshall. Once she filled him in she listened. "Thanks, George. If you're sure you have time, we'll meet you and an officer at the parking lot at the Falls."

"Good enough, Quinn. What time?"

She looked at her watch and then at Billy. She mouthed, "an hour?"

Billy nodded.

"An hour from now work, George?"

"Yes, ma'am. See you there."

"10-4." She pointed as if to shoo Billy toward the exit and turned off her desk lamp.

She spoke to Chuck. "Headed to pick up my vehicle. Let you know if we've got a case."

"10-4." Chuck never looked up. He was totally focused on his microscope.

As the lab door shut, Quinn said, "See what happens when you give your technicians new toys."

"Shhh...Don't tell ours."

"Think I'll give her a call."

"I think she and Chuck have already talked. She's dropping not so subtle hints about how she wouldn't have to send so many things to Knoxville, if only she had...fill in the blank."

"Maybe we could figure out how to divide and conquer?" They were at the back door waiting on the ride to Quinn's house.

"How's that?"

"You buy 'this' and I buy 'that.' Elizabeth becomes our regional expert in 'this' and Chuck becomes our regional expert in 'that.'"

"Might have some possibility."

Quinn got in the front of the SUV with the officer.

Billy got in the back. "Well, well, Officer Evans. Who knew we'd see you twice in one day." Billy's quips were well known in the region.

"Privilege to serve, sir. Your address, ma'am?"

"1211 Sunrise, Officer. Thanks." They rode the short trip in silence. Quinn exited the SUV. "Thanks, Officer Evans. Have a nice day."

"You, too, ma'am, Detective Williams." *Wow, wonder why there's no chatter in the Station about her house?*

Wrong Turns

Andrew slowed about two miles west of Exit 407 on I-40. He pulled off the road and stopped. *What am I doing? Why don't I just call the police? I haven't done anything wrong—except to have learned the guys who rented my land are pretty bad fellows.*

An incoming text on his phone popped up on his dash screen. "Exit 407 NOW."

You don't have to shout. Then he saw the picture and gasped. He was glad he was stopped. Although it was blurry, he saw his wife and two young children; his son was four and his daughter two. They were in the back of a van with masks over their eyes and gags around their mouths. He pounded the steering wheel. *What the hell was I thinking? I should have sold that land years ago.*

There were only a few cars coming up in his side view mirror. He put on his left blinker and pulled out after the last car in his lane. One mile later he turned on his right turn signal in anticipation of Exit 407. A new text popped up. "Turn right go 2.2 miles. Stop." The rage was gone—he shook in absolute fear for his family—and himself. He refocused on the road and made the exit. *2.2 miles after I turn? Or* from *the Stop sign?* The trembling in his hands made it hard to reset the trip meter. He didn't dare rely on remembering the reading on the odometer.

As he started to make the turn, a large black SUV pulled off the highway behind him. *Oh, my God, are you going to trap me?* His heart was racing. He watched ahead for deer and behind for the SUV. The SUV turned left and sped off in the other direction. Andrew let out a sigh of relief. *No one has asked anything of me in the use of this land. I haven't even been out here in ten, maybe fifteen years. Why couldn't they just say what they want? Why do they have my wife and children?* He could feel every beat of his heart as he watched each tenth-of-a-mile tick over. At exactly four-and-a-half miles, he saw a black van on the right side of the road with its flashers on. He pulled in behind it.

Two men jumped out of the van and grabbed the front door handles on his SUV.

He was trying to unlock the doors. He rolled his window down. "Take your hands off the handles or it won't unlock." He unlocked the doors and completely forgot he had his pistol on him.

One man pulled open Andrew's door, snapped his hands behind his back, and handcuffed him. He slipped a black cloth over Andrew's head and forced him into the back seat of his own vehicle, pulled the seat belt, and passed it across him. Andrew felt a hand on his right click it into the seatbelt holder.

Andrew's head throbbed from hitting it on the door frame. *At least in the movies they push your head down. Well, at least now I know they aren't cops.*

The man's voice sounded altered—gravelly. "Not a word. They can hear us in the van and you want that pretty little wife of yours to be safe now, don't you?"

He could hear the second man clicking the other seatbelt on the passenger's side next to him. The one who cuffed him slammed the driver's door and pulled out.

What do they want? Why didn't I check them out when I realized their offer of rent was too good to be true? He dropped his chin to his chest and tried to concentrate on the time and distance they might be traveling. *I've watched too many cop shows. How would I possibly...stop! They've got your wife and kids.*

Who Was She?

Billy had started leaving a change of clothes at Quinn's last month. Both Quinn and Billy had changed their plaid shirts and jeans for slacks and shirts. Quinn had pulled the knot out of her hair and brushed out the tangles. Their respective blue nylon jackets with DETECTIVE on the back and the shield of their organization embroidered on the front were on the stools at the kitchen counter.

Quinn made two sandwiches and put an apple with each of them in a paper bag inside a small tote bag.

Billy refilled their Yeti's. "Sure hope the bears didn't eat the protein bars in my SUV."

"Me, too. And, guess what? We can eat on the run."

"Better to eat on the run, than to be on the lam."

"Ha. Ha. Let's go, Mr. Big Shot."

She opened her gun safe, took out her sidearm and shield, grabbed her jacket, and closed the door as she followed Billy into the garage. Quinn pulled onto her street and headed out for the second time today toward the base of the mountain they had climbed.

"Let's run through a plan. Thoughts?" She never took her eyes off the road.

"Forty-five minutes to get my car...well, maybe thirty at the speed you're driving."

"I can put on my emergency lights if it'll make you happy."

"No offense intended."

"None taken." She needed the banter with him. She was still unsettled by the meeting with Chief Hansen. *Is it because I could never trust my former boss to tell the truth? Maybe that's it. Chief Hansen has never lied to me. I have to trust that.*

"Quinn? Thoughts to share?"

She glanced over at him. "Seems to me, as far as we know, the young woman is ours to identify since she was found in our jurisdiction. The missing person call, which may or may not be our Jane Doe, is in your jurisdiction. Until we talk to the person who called it in, we have no further information unless we hear from our coroner or Chuck. That about sum it up?"

"Yes. Yes, it does." He nodded. *She's back in the game. Good.*

She was driving about fifteen miles over the speed limit, but it was a rural road, dry, and she knew it well. She decided to turn on her emergency lights for good measure.

"Something I haven't figured out to justify running your lights?"

"Road is clear, dry, and we have a dead body in our morgue of what appears to be an otherwise healthy young woman—age unknown. We have an apparently older woman who called in a missing young woman. If they are one and the same, then we have only to learn how she died. If they are not one in the same, there could be another young woman in jeopardy."

"Fair enough, Detective. Fair enough. Good thinking." He settled into the passenger's seat and slowly flexed his left shoulder. It hurt.

Quinn caught the movement out of the corner of her eye. "Billy, I'm so sorry. I should have gotten a bag of ice for your shoulder."

"I could have thought of it, too. I'll live. Don't like back seat drivers myself, but since I'm the copilot I'm going to suggest you slow down. We're almost to our turn off to the pull out at the base of the trail."

"So we are." She slowed and turned on her left turn signal as she saw a van turning in ahead of them. She switched off the emergency lights as she pulled into the parking area. "I did tell you George Marshall and an officer were meeting us here, didn't I?"

"Figured it out from your phone call."

She turned to look at him.

"I'm a detective, remember?" Billy flashed his impish grin.

Quinn laughed. "So you are." Quinn pulled beside Billy's SUV and they both got out.

George Marshall got out of the driver's side and Officer Evans got out of the passenger door of their van.

Officer Evans chuckled. "I know. Third time's the charm. Guess you figured out I'm the catchall cop today."

"Good for us." Billy walked to George and extended his hand. "Detective Marshall."

"Detective Williams. Good to see you, Billy. Thanks for sending the pictures. That should help when we get up there." George shook his hand and then slapped him on the back.

Billy flinched. It was his bad shoulder.

Quinn looked at her watch. It was eleven-forty. "We've had a busy morning. Thanks for coming, Detective. Officer."

"Yes, ma'am." Officer Evans stepped back.

"What do we need to know to find his place?" George looked from Quinn to Billy.

Quinn gave directions to the area near the falls and suggested they take their van as far in on the trail as they could. "It will leave you with about an hour hike to the falls."

"Know the area pretty well, Qui…" George caught himself. He generally didn't call Quinn by her first name unless they were alone or with their team. "..ma'am."

Billy felt the awkwardness and spoke up. "I left my blue and white handkerchief tied to a sapling at the base of the tall pitch pine where we found her. Hopefully no critters have found it yet."

"Thanks, that will be a big help." George nodded.

"Any questions?" Quinn looked from George to Officer Evans.

"Think we're good. Got a radio and we're headed up. I'll let you know when we finish."

"Thanks to both of you for the quick response. May not be needed, but don't want to lose any evidence if this turns out to be more than a lone hiker having health issues."

"On it, ma'am." George and Officer Evans returned to their vehicle.

"Ready to hit the road, Billy?"

"Indeed." He turned to look at her and winced as his left shoulder hit the side of his SUV. "I suggest we each take our sandwich and apple and proceed back toward the Valley at a normal pace. We'll be at The Mountain Villages by one at the latest."

"Sounds like a plan." She took one of the paper bags out of the tote and handed it to him. "Be careful eating as you drive. I'd hate to have to stop you for reckless driving." She smiled. "I'm okay, Billy. Are you?"

"I'll be fine. I just need to know you are."

"I am. Honest. Just needed to clear my head of the old and appreciate the new—especially the part that allows me to work with you from time to time." She leaned over and kissed him. "I'll follow you."

"Now there's an offer I can't refuse." He leaned in and kissed her. "We'll stop at the gate at the Mountain Villages and I'll inform the guard we're on a joint jurisdiction mission. Work for you?"

"Works for me. See you there."

Billy pulled out and watched Quinn in his rearview mirror to make sure she seemed to be driving okay. He wasn't hungry, so he left the sandwich and apple on the passenger seat. As soon as they were on the main road, he called his boss: Sheriff Chad Oliver.

Chapter 3

A bird is safe in its nest — but that is not what its wings are made for.
Amit Ray

Into the Valley

Billy pulled up to the gates of The Mountain Villages just outside the Valley township.

"Morning." Billy had his badge in his hand. The guard knew him. "Residence of Ms. Topping, please."

"Is she expecting you?"

"Sheriff Oliver's office let her know we were coming."

"One minute." The guard stepped away from the open top of the Dutch door and picked up the phone. "Ms. Topping, Detective Williams here to see you." There was a pause. "Yes, ma'am. I'll verify."

The guard returned to the door. "Ms. Topping said someone else is with you. Could you lower your windows?"

"I can, but there is no one in my vehicle." He lowered his windows. "Detective Isaacs of the Round City Police is behind me. She can show her credentials."

"Yes, sir. Please pull in and stop just inside the gate."

"Yes, sir." Billy pulled forward. *Nice enough guy, but he doubts I'd stop? Seriously?*

Quinn pulled up to the gate and had her ID and badge ready to show the guard. She had seen Billy lower his windows so she did too. "Morning, sir." She extended her hand with her credentials.

"Morning, ma'am." The guard looked at the shield and took her ID. He studied it and looked at her face. "Thank you, Detective Isaacs. Ms. Topping has given clearance for you and Detective Williams. Have a nice day."

Quinn was right behind Billy on the winding road toward the back of The Mountain Villages. *No front row seat for this woman.* The further back they drove the larger the lots until you couldn't see from one house to the other. Quinn followed Billy through an open, private gate. It closed as soon as she was clear of it. *Serious concerns about privacy or security—which is it? Both?*

They walked up the low narrow steps to the Tuscan style villa which stood in stark contrast to the deep greens of the trees and the dark high mountain behind it.

Billy rang the doorbell.

"Sir. Ma'am. This way. Ms. Topping is expecting you." They followed the woman in black slacks and a white blouse into the front room.

A woman in a wheelchair turned from the window.

"Detective Williams, thank you for coming. Detective Isaacs, nice to meet you." Each walked up and shook her extended hand. "I'm Marjorie Eldridge Topping. Please have a seat." As a retired attorney, she was practiced at meeting people in difficult circumstances. She gave an almost imperceptible nod to her assistant.

Quinn picked up on the nod as the woman moved to the coffee and tea tray in front of them. After all, she had grown up with similar help in her parents' home. She smiled at the woman. "Coffee would be lovely, thanks."

"Make that two, please." Billy watched the assistant carefully.

"I'll have tea, please." Marjorie Topping moved her electric wheelchair toward the coffee table. Drinks poured, she looked at the young woman. "Thanks, Maria, I'll call if I need you."

Maria shut the French doors to the hallway behind her.

"I'm grateful for your visit. My attorney told me that even though you can report a missing person anytime, most departments have their own rules on when they will open an investigation. Can I assume your presence means you'll look for my granddaughter?"

"Ms. Topping, unless there is suspected foul play, both of our departments have a forty-eight hour waiting period to open an investigation on an adult known to be healthy and capable of making personal decisions. Is that the…" Billy saw Quinn lift her finger and turned to see her looking at the photo Ms. Topping had handed her.

He sipped his coffee and then set down the cup.

"May I see that?" He reached for the photo.

Quinn had studied the photograph. *Now the Gucci loafers make sense.* "What is your granddaughter's name?"

"Angela. Angela Topping. She is my late son's only child. Harvey adored Janice, Angela's mother. He worshiped their child." She paused. "We're the last of the Topping family from Chicago." *You don't need to know we have a ne'er-do-well relation in Boston.* She had a slight shiver as she thought about Peter.

Quinn looked directly at their host. "Ms. Topping, I believe your granddaughter is the young woman we found on the top of a mountain this morning."

"Alive or deceased." Ms. Topping was calm and steady—her long cultured manners were apparent.

Billy searched through his phone and found the best picture of the young woman's face. "May I show you a photo?"

"Of course." Marjorie Topping leaned forward in her wheelchair.

Billy held out his phone, but she didn't touch it.

"Yes, that's Angela. Please tell me her condition. She looks like she's asleep."

"Ma'am," Quinn spoke softly, "I regret to inform you—your granddaughter is deceased. Her death happened in the jurisdiction of the Round City Police. As lead detective I promise you we will do everything we can to determine the cause of her death." Quinn was not willing to give her any specific details of finding the young woman or transporting her to the hospital until she knew the circumstances. *If this turns out to be a murder…* She knew everyone was a suspect.

"Where is she now?" Ms. Topping sat up straight in her chair and looked Quinn directly in the eyes.

"With our medical examiner, Dr. Walters."

"Thank you for your honesty."

"Ms. Topping, we need to know everything you can tell us about Angela's last known whereabouts, when you saw her last, any information you have on her residence, and how she spent her time." Quinn had her note pad out.

Billy pulled out a recorder.

Good thinking, Billy.

"I need a moment, please." Ms. Topping sat very still.

"By all means. Shall I get your assistant?" Quinn started to stand.

"No. I need you to find the person responsible for this."

"Detective Williams and I will step out into the foyer and give you a minute. As I'm sure you already know—if there is reason to suspect foul play, the sooner we have the information the better."

"I do. Thank you, Detective." Marjorie lowered her head as Quinn and Billy moved quietly into the hall.

Where Are You Taking Me?

Andrew Culbert III had driven and walked enough property in his life to have a good sense of distance. He had no sight through the hood over his head, but he could hear and count, so he would listen for any unusual sounds and try to keep track by counting. He had managed to get his fear under control and realize the very lives of his wife and children could depend on his memory. *Are they in the van those men jumped out of?* The two men in his SUV were completely silent except for the out of sync rhythm of their breathing. Andrew counted and listened. Listened and counted. He felt the SUV slowing and heard the blinker. They were going to turn. The SUV slowed, made a right turn, and drove a short distance before it stopped—he counted 1001, 1002...to 1032. *Thirty-two seconds east of the road off Exit 407.* The door beside him opened. The man on his right unclicked both seat belts.

"Get out and step back. Stand by the side of your SUV and don't move." The gravelly voice was like something from a bad movie.

"Yes, sir."

"Don't call me sir, and don't say anything unless asked. Got it?"

Andrew slid toward the back of his SUV and felt his arm rub against his revolver. *Lot of good that does me.*

He couldn't see anything, but he could hear the breathing of the two men a few steps away from him. He heard movement coming from the front of his SUV; someone stopped close to him and spoke.

"Mr. Culbert. Sorry for the inconvenience and subterfuge."

Andrew was listening for an accent, cadence, anything....

The man's voice was clear, crisp, and sounded well-educated. *He isn't from these mountains, though.* Andrew smelled the man's cologne. *What is that scent?* He was trying to make sure he had as much information as possible—if he got out of this alive.

Andrew swallowed hard but silently. "Not how I'm accustomed to doing business. How may I be of service?" *Is this the man who leased my land?*

"See, boys, I told you there were no worries with Mr. Culbert. Take a walk."

Andrew heard the breathing of the two men as they moved away from him. He was sure he could hear more than four feet hitting the road. *How many people are there?*

"Now, then. Let's make this quick and to the point. I need to buy the land you have leased out here and I need to close immediately. I also need you to arrange for me to buy the land on either side that backs up to the national park. You will have information for the name of the company doing the purchase when you return to your office. It will all be done by wire transfer and electronic signature."

"Where are my wife and children?" Andrew tried to steady the quiver in his voice.

"I have no idea. I assume you know their daily routine. Where do you expect them to be?"

Now Andrew's rage was creeping in. "Whoever you are, I want to know where my wife and children are. I was sent a picture of them with gags and masks in a van. Are they in the van that these men came out of?" He leaned toward the man's voice, but almost fell forward. He was off balance with his hands behind his back.

The man laughed. "Mr. Culbert, you are a very successful business man in a very small pond. In big lakes and rivers, things often require more...shall we say...manipulating in order to catch a fish; perhaps things you may not be accustomed to. I'm sure you'll find your wife and children are just fine, and I suspect my employees have some talented people at altering photos to make them believable. They just wanted to be sure you'd cooperate."

Andrew leaned against his SUV. "You could have just called and asked to buy the property."

"I could have. However, time is of the essence and I need this deal now. Apparently, you have indicated you were not interested in selling your family land. You need to be interested...am I clear? My men will return you to the highway and send you on your way. My people will be in touch with the terms of the deal and I need you to make it happen in ten days or less...less being better."

"But..." Andrew started but was interrupted.

"But, Mr. Culbert, you don't want to find out what's worse than that picture you saw. Good day."

Andrew had shuffled his feet several times and knew they were on a dirt road. He heard an occasional crunch as the man's foot hit something as he walked away.

Angela Topping

Quinn had taken in every inch of the foyer; she could draw it in detail from the fourteen foot wide floor to the Tuscan carved table just inside the door.

Ms. Topping's assistant appeared in the foyer. "Ms. Topping would like you to come back in, please." She opened the French doors.

Quinn and Billy entered and sat down again on the carved Italian Toscano chairs opposite Ms. Topping. *These are originals.* Quinn caught herself. She moved forward on fine upholstery and leaned toward Ms. Topping.

"I believe you had a recorder, Detective Williams?" Marjorie Topping's tone was authoritative, but not controlling. The grieving grandmother seemed to be tucked away.

"Yes, ma'am. With your permission, it will be helpful to record our talk to make sure we don't lose any details."

"That's fine."

Billy turned on the recorder and waited for Quinn; the death was in her jurisdiction.

"This is Quinn Isaacs, lead detective with the Round City Police on Friday, April 12, at one-fifteen PM This recording is voluntary on the part of..." She nodded to Ms. Topping.

"Marjorie Eldridge Topping."

"Also present is..."

"Detective Billy Williams of the Valley Sheriff's Station."

"The purpose of this meeting, in Ms. Topping's home, is to gather information related to the life of Ms. Angela Topping, granddaughter of Ms. Marjorie Topping. Is there anything you would like to add at this point, Ms. Topping?"

"Nothing other than I consent to this recording and will stop at any time I deem it necessary to consult my attorney."

"Ms. Topping, you may have your attorney present in person or on the phone now if you wish."

"Not necessary. What do you need to know about Angela?"

"Let's start with full name, next of kin, date of birth, and current home address."

Without further preamble, Marjorie gave all the pertinent facts about Angela, including her education, the real estate internship she had in college, and her current occupation. Then she looked down at the floor. "I am her only next of kin. Harvey and I raised Angela. Her mother died during childbirth."

"I'm sorry." Quinn spoke softly and watched Ms. Topping. "Do you know any of Angela's friends?"

"I think she talked to her neighbor from time to time, but she was a loner. Blame that on me. I always tried to keep her too busy to get into trouble."

Quinn nodded. "Has Angela had any health issues?"

"She's had allergies and asthma all her life. Her asthma appears to be well managed."

"Do you know the name of her physician?"

"I'll have Maria get it for you."

"How often are you in contact with Angela?"

"We talk...talked at least once a day." The catch in her throat was audible.

"And visited?"

"She came at least once a week to visit and she helped me with bills. It is important...was important...to me...for her to understand the family estate and trusts. I don't think I would have called you except for the fact she always let me know if she was going to be late."

"From your explanation of her education and current work, it sounds like she was very capable and reliable."

"She was. I don't know what I will do now." The steel reserve this woman had slipped as a tear ran down her face—unstopped.

Billy stopped the recording.

Quinn leaned toward her. "Ms. Topping, you need some time to process this loss. I will let you know as soon as we have information from Dr. Walters, our Medical Examiner. We will arrange for you to see Angela as soon as possible." She watched Marjorie Topping carefully. "I understand you will want to make arrangements—but it will likely be a few days before...."

Marjorie Topping nodded her head. "I understand." Then she looked directly at Quinn. "Detective Isaacs, I have a lifetime of dealing with people, including a career as an attorney in a major firm in Chicago. I consider myself a pretty good judge of character. I'm afraid that many who move to your lovely mountains assume you are all...well, less well educated; I know better. I appreciate the professionalism both of you have shown today and am confident you will follow-up, no matter where it leads, on the death of my granddaughter. I will wait for your call." She took out her phone and touched the screen.

Maria appeared in the doorway. "Yes, ma'am."

"Please get Detective Isaacs the name and contact information for Angela's physicians."

"Yes, ma'am." She stepped out of the room.

"Please, drink your coffee. Help yourself to the cookies. I'll excuse myself. Maria will see you out when she returns with the information."

Quinn and Billy both stood.

Quinn extended her hand. "I'm truly sorry for your loss, Ms. Topping. You have my word we will get to the bottom of Angela's disappearance and her death. I will be back in touch." She handed Marjorie her card.

"Thank you, Detective Isaacs."

Billy extended his hand. "We will support the investigation on this side of the mountains. If you need anything at all, do not hesitate to call." He handed his card to Marjorie.

"Thank you, Detective Williams. May I share an observation?"

"By all means."

"I am impressed with a male law enforcement officer who does not have a need to preempt a woman equally capable of running an investigation."

"Begging your pardon, ma'am. Detective Isaacs far exceeds my capabilities."

"Good man." She nodded her approval at Billy and pushed the button to move her wheelchair out into the foyer.

They watched her go. Billy sat down and Quinn walked over to the mantle.

Billy was intrigued by how Quinn's eyes seemed to constantly take in things around her.

Beneath the large professionally painted portrait of Marjorie Topping, there was an 8" x 10" framed photo of this small family—love among the three evident. "Look, Billy. They were a lovely family." She handed him the photo she had taken from the mantle.

Billy saw Marjorie Topping, a man he presumed to be her son, and her granddaughter. "Yes, a lovely family." *And lots of questions come to mind…not the least of which is whether Angela's mother really died in childbirth, and if so, what caused it?*

Quinn set the photo back on the mantle just as Maria entered. She had an envelope in her hand.

"I believe this will be all the information you need. Ms. Topping signed a release for these physicians to talk to you, and here is a copy of her Durable Power of Attorney for Angela."

Quinn reached for the envelope. She smiled. "Thank you." *Ms. Topping and I both know the DPA ended at Angela's death, but that might not matter to the physicians. Could save having to wait on a warrant if it comes to that.* "Thank you. We can see ourselves out."

Billy was already on his feet.

As they started down the stairs, Billy spoke quietly. "Good job, Quinn. Tough to do."

"Thanks for your support." She turned to look at him as they stepped off the bottom step. "And thanks for the compliment."

"Meant it."

"I know you did. Maybe the truth is some of my capabilities are just different than yours." She gently touched his forearm and squeezed it. "I need to get back to the Station."

"Figured as much. Maybe you could check in with Doc Walters and if he's not finished, we could grab some lunch at The Corral. It's close and I'm sure we don't want to eat your sandwiches, delicious though they would have been two hours ago."

"Great idea. Give me a minute." She took out her secure phone and dialed the ME.

Billy walked to his SUV and waited for her.

Quinn walked toward him. "He hopes to have COD soon. Nothing to share at the moment. So let's go have a late lunch and then I'll head back.

Told Doc I'd stop by the morgue." *Hmm...maybe I'm getting used to COD... actually seems easier now than saying Cause Of Death. Guess I'm settling into this work.*

"Lunch is my treat. See you there." Billy waved as he got in his vehicle.

What Next?

Andrew was forced into the driver's seat of his SUV. His shoulders shook as he followed instructions and threw the hood out on the ground. He took the dire warning not to look back seriously; he was careful not to even glance in his side or rearview mirror. He slowly pulled onto the road and prayed nothing was coming. He drove under the overpass and turned west onto the I-40 access ramp.

He dialed Kelly's number from his steering wheel.

"Hey, honey. Sounds like you're in your car?" Her voice was light and sounded normal to him.

"Yes. Had some business out east of the city. Where are you?"

"We're at home. Just got in from some shopping. Hard to buy Easter eggs with the kids. They're so excited."

He felt the tremble in his hands. *They're fine.* "You know, I've been thinking about Easter and maybe we should get away."

"Oh, honey, you know how hard holidays are with the kids when we're not at home."

He counted to three to calm his voice. "I do, but I promise we'll make it the most unique Easter ever. I'll tell you all about when I get home." He knew she'd agree to whatever he suggested.

"Okay, will I get details or will you surprise us?"

"Hmm...you know I love to surprise you."

"You do and I love it. When will you be home?"

"Need to stop at the club and change and then run by the office. I'll be home for supper if not sooner."

"Great. See you soon. I love you."

"Kelly, I love you, too." He had to keep his voice from cracking. "Give the kids a kiss and tell them I love them."

"Will do. Hurry home. We miss you."

"See you soon." *I hope I never have to miss you.*

He pulled into the garage at the club and all but sprinted to his private room aware of the cameras in the hallway. He walked to the closet and put his revolver in the gun safe. *What an idiot I am. I have no more business carrying a gun than flying to the moon. Come to think of it…flying to the moon might be better. Wonder if there's room on the next flight?* He showered, changed into his suit, and put his dirty clothes in a laundry bag; he knew they would be cleaned and ready the next time he came to the club.

Relieved he'd given his driver the day off, he was back in his SUV in the garage. He leaned his head back against the headrest. *Maybe I should just disappear—then Kelly and the kids will be safe.* He shook his head vigorously and backed out of the club parking garage. *I'm done watching cop shows.*

The Corral

Quinn followed Billy into the side parking lot at The Corral. She hadn't been over here since the end of the year. She backed into a parking space and Billy was waiting. He opened her door, leaned in, and kissed her on the cheek.

"That was nice." She pushed him back and stepped out. Then she turned and kissed him on the lips—longingly. She whispered in his ear. "Looks like your boss is here." She pointed to the Sheriff's SUV.

"Well, so it does. Do we accept his invitation to sit or…"

"Of course." She poked him in the ribs as she opened the side door to the restaurant.

"Thanks, ma'am." He stepped in and saw Sheriff Oliver at a back table. Quinn followed him in.

"Afternoon, Sheriff." Billy and Quinn laughed as their words were spoken at the same time.

"Well, afternoon to you two, too. What brings you to this side of the mountains, Quinn?"

She laughed. "Needed to escort this detective of yours to talk to a grandmother who filed a missing person report in both our jurisdictions."

"Oh, yes. I assume you know I talked to your Chief. Sit if you don't have other plans."

"Thanks." Quinn sat in the chair Billy pulled out. "Expecting anyone else, Chad?"

"No, ma'am. Wasn't even expecting you, but delighted to see you."

"Him, too?" She pointed her thumb towards Billy.

"Him, too." Chad chuckled.

Cheri took their orders and left.

Chad looked at Quinn and Billy. "Update?"

Billy nodded toward Quinn. "Her case."

Quinn filled him in on what they knew at this point. Their meals almost finished Quinn wrapped up the details as they currently knew them. "However this plays out, a young life ended too soon. We'll know soon if we have a criminal case."

Billy spoke before Chad could. "We'll do our part over here."

"Absolutely. Sounds like you've got it covered. Thanks for your work." Chad put money by his plate and stood. "Now, if you two will excuse me, I'm due back at the Station. Let me know if I can help in any way."

Quinn reached out to offer her hand. "Please give my regards to Bella. Maybe you two could come over to Round City for dinner one of these days. I'd love to visit with both of you."

"You've got a deal." He shook her hand. "I'll be in touch. Shoot, we might even invite this guy."

"Sheriff, don't get carried away." Quinn laughed and automatically reached over and squeezed Billy's hand.

The gesture didn't escape Chad's notice. "Been known to eat with him once or twice. Have a good rest of the day." Chad slapped Billy on the back.

Quinn could see Billy wince.

Cheri set their food in front of them.

As soon as Cheri turned away, Billy said, "Ouch."

"Oh, poor Billy. The biggest joker in these parts doesn't like being teased?" She pouted.

"Fair enough, fair maiden. Fair enough."

"Fair maiden?" Now she glared at him.

"Takes two to tango." They both laughed.

"However, the 'ouch' was because my boss hit my bad shoulder."

Her voice softened in sympathy. "I know—I'm sorry. I was just trying to distract you from the pain. Okay now?"

"I'll live."

"Counting on it." She smiled and stared into his eyes.

They talked about the turn of events in the day as they ate.

Cheri walked up with the coffee pot. "More?"

"No, just the check." Billy put his hand out.

"Checks." Quinn raised her left eyebrow.

"Yes, ma'am. Figured as much." She handed them each a check and picked up the cash from Sheriff Oliver and put it with his check. She walked away.

"I won't argue with you, but remember I did offer to treat."

"So noted, kind sir."

They both left money with their checks and stood up. Billy understood Quinn would have seen this as a working lunch.

"I'll stop by the ladies room before I head back."

"Meet you outside." Billy walked out the door and watched a pair of birds chasing a dragonfly with the blue sky behind them. *Are your lives complicated little birdies? Or do you really live a carefree life?* He turned when Quinn tapped him on his right shoulder.

"See, I remembered not to touch your left shoulder."

He turned and pulled her into an embrace. He didn't care who saw them.

Chapter 4

Only if we understand can we care. Only if we care will we help.
Jane Goodall

Round City Police Station

Quinn walked up to the back door at the Round City Police Station at the same time as her senior detective, George Marshall. "That's timing, George."

"Perfect. Sorry about you losing your day off."

"Hopefully we've both got something more to share. Your text didn't make it seem like it, though."

"Yeah? Not much up on that mountain, but hopefully you have something interesting?"

"How's your time?"

"My times your time. Outside the visit up the mountain, my other case is wrapped up and the report is already in your inbox."

"Good for you. Meet in the workroom in fifteen?"

"Works for me."

"Excuse me." She pulled out her secure phone. "Isaacs."

George stepped back for her to swipe her card first. Then he swiped his.

The ME was polite but brisk. "Have a preliminary COD for you when you get back."

"I'm back. Be right down." She ended the call. "Have time to go to the morgue?"

"You bet."

"I'll fill you in after we hear from Doc." They headed down the stairs to the morgue.

"Hey, Doc." George spoke first.

"Afternoon, George. Ah, two for one—deal of the day. Afternoon, Quinn."

"Hey, Doc." Quinn walked over to the body draped by a sheet. "May I?" She turned to Doc Walters.

"By all means." He watched as she pulled the sheet away from the young woman's face.

"This is Angela Topping. Angela, this is Dr. Walters. I see he took good care of you."

"Angela. Nice name. Not so nice death."

Quinn and George looked at the medical examiner.

"My office, okay?" Doc turned and walked the short distance to his office.

"Sure." Quinn led the way to the ME's office and sat down in a chair.

George sat next to her.

The ME pulled out his chair and turned his computer screen toward them. "Easier to show you with pictures." He pulled up a series of photos. "This one is her throat."

Both detectives nodded.

Quinn turned her eyes to the ME. "Not my area of expertise, but it looks pretty red and raw—like it's been burned."

"Give the lady the prize. You're absolutely correct, Quinn. She inhaled or ingested a very toxic chemical which burned her throat and lungs and likely caused her death."

"Do you know what the toxin was?"

"Still working on that. May take a while. No guarantees."

"How long before death would it have been inhaled or ingested?" Quinn was laser focused. She absently pulled her hair back into a knot.

George noticed her pull her hair back. *Something serious here—pulling her hair back seems to be her getting ready for action behavior.*

"Hard to be absolutely sure, but if I hazard a guess...no more than a day, and the time *is* only a guess."

"She had asthma and allergies." Quinn stated it matter-of-factly as she pulled the envelope from Ms. Topping's assistant out of her pocket and took out the papers. "Do you know any of these physicians?"

Dr. Walters studied the three names: a general practitioner, an allergy/asthma specialist, and a pulmonologist. "Don't know the GP, but the other two are at the university and top notch in their fields. Will this get us her records?"

Quinn shrugged. "Hope so. But Doc, if you think that someone other than Angela provided the toxin, I'll get a warrant if we need it."

"Unless she works in a chemical lab, it's highly unlikely she had access to it. Any idea where she's been the last twenty-four hours?"

George looked at the pictures on the computer screen and listened carefully to the exchange.

"I do not, but I am going to do everything I can to find out." Quinn stood up abruptly. "Come on, George. We may have a murder on our hands." She stopped in the doorway and turned back. "Thanks, Doc. Her grandmother will want to see her, but I don't want the body released until you have a definitive COD and we have a day or two to get a handle on this."

"We'll take real good care of her. When you want to bring the grandmother, just let me know. I'll let Dr. Scott know her name."

Quinn nodded. "Thanks." She was already headed up the stairs.

George shook hands with the ME and followed her. He took the stairs two at time and caught up with her at the top of the stairs.

"Conference in ten." Quinn said and kept moving.

"10-4." George shrugged and headed to his office area.

Quinn entered the lab and saw no signs of Chuck. She pulled off her nylon jacket as she entered her office and hung it on her coat tree. She turned on her desk lamp and then her computer. She sent a message to the Chief: "DB from AM is Angela Topping—potential homicide." The Chief had given them the missing person report, so she knew the connection. Quinn opened her secure folder and pulled up the report from the ME and printed it out. She saw a message from Billy Williams labeled: "Photos A.T." She opened it while she used her secure phone to call him.

"Williams."

"Hey, likely homicide on Topping."

"Cause?"

"Lethal toxin."

"Oh, sh…"

"Yeah, what you said—or didn't say. Will put out an All-Points Bulletin on her car. It's a silver Lexus LS hybrid. Shouldn't be hard to miss. Appreciate your help getting your folks to be extra diligent since it may be on your side of the mountain."

"You know it. What else do you need?"

"Right now? Time to put together a board and start trying to figure out what happened."

"Taking lead on it in your shop?"

"Yes. Marshall will back me up, so you could hear from him."

"Sounds good."

"Thanks, Billy. Talk to you soon."

"Let me know what you need." He wanted to tell her romantic things, to send her a hug, but he also knew how to walk the line between work and being in love—he hoped.

"10-4." She ended the call as she printed out several pictures of Angela Topping from the top of the mountain. *How did you manage to get to the top of the mountain with your body fighting a toxin that was capable of killing you. And why?*

She pulled out her notebook and the details on Angela Topping's car and submitted an "All-Points-Bulletin" to the statewide emergency alert system. She followed up with an alert to the sergeants in the Round City Station to make sure all officers knew to search off the beaten path and report immediately. Quinn turned at the tap on her door frame.

"Busy?"

"About to be. What's up, Chuck?"

"Kevin and I finished up that domestic abuse case. Just wanted you to know I'm more or less caught up. So, if you need me…"

"Just caught, so to speak, a case. Check with the ME and see if he needs anything related to the toxins that might be involved in the death."

"On it. Got a board started?"

She motioned for him to come in and turned her computer screen. "For now, just to give you a connection, this is Angela Topping."

"That the woman you flew in off the mountain?"

How does he know we flew her off the mountain? I didn't tell him. Word spreads fast around here. "One and the same, Chuck. George and I will start a board across the hall in a few minutes."

"Okay, I'm headed to the morgue."

"10-4."

Quinn sent the photos to the new high quality printer now installed in the conference room. She leaned back in her chair. *Four months into this job and I'm finally starting to believe I can actually function like a detective.* She stood and headed across the hall. As she put the code in the door, she noticed the lettering on the glass had been changed. It no longer read "Conference Room." She smiled. "Detectives Workroom" was the new precise lettering. George walked up beside her.

"Might seem like little things..."

Quinn turned her head. "What?" She saw he had something in his hand.

"Door with a code all the detectives know, not just new lettering on a door but inclusive lettering, equipment inside that will support us having a spacc to lay out a case and be able to examine it."

"Your point?" She raised her left eyebrow.

"It matters, Quinn. We all want to do our jobs to the best of our abilities. Too many folks move into lead positions because they see it as status—a promotion. It may be, but more than that, it's about making sure others can do their jobs and have what they need to do it right. You're doing that for us."

She stared at him and her hand trembled on the door handle. "Thanks, George. Thanks for being a part of the team." She stepped back and let him enter.

George handed her a small pale blue box as he passed her. She smiled at the words on the top of the box in pale silver lettering: "Sweet Creations."

"Oh, George. From your wife's bakery!"

"One and the same. Carrie asked me to tell you she hopes you enjoy them."

"Come on. I'll share."

"Nope. This one's for you. Better hide the box so no one steals it from you."

"In a police station?"

He laughed. "More than a few may think it's worth the risk."

She set the box on the table with her mug of coffee and the copy of the ME's preliminary report on Angela Topping. She walked over to the printer and picked up the photos.

"We have the basics of COD on this young woman. Here are some photos of her from the mountain when Billy and I found her." Both of them looked at the young woman. Quinn picked one photo and pinned it on their board.

"George, I haven't had time to enter my notes from the interview with her grandmother, Marjorie Topping. Let's refer to the deceased as Angela, and the grandmother as Ms. Topping, for convenience. Anyway, here are the basics:

Angela is the only child of an only child.

Age at last birthday was twenty-four.

Visited her grandmother at least weekly and helped with paying bills to learn family finances.

Called her grandmother every day, and let her know if she was going to be late, especially if she was coming over in the evening.

Graduated with honors from Sewanee: The University of The South.

Did an internship with a high-end commercial real estate firm in Knoxville, but didn't like the city." Quinn was surprised George could write on the whiteboard as fast as she talked. She took a deep breath and let it out slowly. *Whew, I raced through that!*

George looked at his notes. "So, did Angela have a job?"

"Her grandmother lives in The Mountain Villages."

"Well, that's pretty high end."

"Indeed. And, Ms. Topping, the grandmother, lives in the isolated estates with their own private gates at the back—up against the mountain."

George let out a whistle. "And, Angela's parents?"

"Not sure about the 'why' but the mother apparently died in childbirth..." She watched George put the information on the family tree he had drawn. "Her father...who was a Topping...is deceased."

"Okay, all of that needs looking into. Now back to Angela. Did she work? Boyfriend? Girlfriend?"

"Grandmother said she dated a young man in college, but broke it off before graduation. As for work, I'm still not clear on the specifics of Angela's work. She worked remotely in something to do with real estate. Ms. Topping is a retired attorney from Chicago..."

George interrupted her. "And she let you record her?"

Quinn nodded. "Even made a statement that the recording was voluntary on her part and she would end it if she had concerns. Of course, we offered her to have her attorney present or on the phone. She declined." She looked at George.

He shrugged. "Okay, no harm, no foul."

"Do we know where Angela lived and how she got to Ms. Topping's home?"

"She had a condo in Maryville in one of those new high-end complexes. Her grandmother wanted her to buy a home—which I suspect was so she could ensure her security."

"So why didn't she just buy one. Isn't that what rich people do?" George stopped abruptly and stared into Quinn's eyes. "Sorry."

"No apologies needed. It *is* what some rich people do. As you likely know, I am the only child of two only children; both grew up in wealthy families. I have my own struggles with the comforts money buys—and what I perceive as my lack of need for them. Yet, clearly you know I live in a home that is well beyond my paycheck as a law enforcement officer."

"Quinn, I wasn't prying."

"No problem, George. No problem. I'll just finish the story. My maternal grandmother was so pleased I didn't end up being sent to one of the coasts with my job in Immigration, she bought my home and paid to have it remodeled. End of story. So, back to the question, why didn't Ms. Topping just buy the house? I don't know. Another question for follow-up."

Trying to get them away from what he decided was uncomfortable for Quinn, George said, "Where's her car? "

"Don't know. Have an APB out on it including a call I made to the Maryville police who will let me know if it is at her condo. Also asked Billy Williams to have his folks keep a special lookout over there."

"Yeah, guess it could cross over jurisdictions."

"If it's a murder, it happened in ours. Could have started in theirs. We just don't know enough." Her secure phone rang. "Isaacs."

"Officer Kent in Maryville, ma'am."

"Thanks for your quick response, Officer."

"Ms. Topping has a garage with her condo and we'll need a warrant to enter as the management was not cooperative. However, one of her neighbors said she saw her leaving about five o'clock yesterday and hasn't seen her since. Is there something we should be checking over here, ma'am?"

"Not at this time, Officer. There is an APB out on the vehicle so if something turns up, we'd appreciate being informed. I can follow up with your detective unit."

"Feel free, ma'am. No need, though. I'll tell my sergeant. He'll pass it along."

"Appreciate it. We'll be in touch if we need further follow-up. Thanks, again, Officer Kent."

"Yes, ma'am."

"Good day."

"You, too, ma'am."

Quinn ended the call and looked at the photo of Angela on the board. "George, did you ever consider leaving these mountains?"

"No. You?"

"No. And the young man on that call just reminded me why."

"Why?"

"Civility. Simple civility. I don't need him to call me 'ma'am,' but I think he said it with every answer."

"We're losing it fast, though."

"Seems that way some days. Anyway..." She relayed the information regarding Angela's car and the woman who saw her leave the day before.

"Anything else? Thoughts on how you want to divide and conquer on this?"

"Give me a minute." Quinn sat down and sipped her coffee. She carefully opened the pale blue box. Inside were four perfectly shaped macarons. "Oh, George. The feet on these macarons are perfect. Carrie is an artist."

"That she is. She told me to make sure and find out which flavor is your favorite."

"All of them, I'm sure." She lifted the box to offer him one.

He patted his abdomen. "Gotta watch what I eat; the waistline you know. I get the benefit of the pastry wizard as a wife."

"You are indeed a lucky man."

"Don't I know it." He pulled out a chair and they both faced the board.

Quinn stared at the picture of a young woman who may have had macarons in France, but never would again.

Looking for Answers

Andrew Culbert pulled into his parking place in the basement of his office building and stepped into his private elevator. He usually used his driver and rarely came in this way. This afternoon was not a time to involve anyone else in his plans. The elevator deposited him in his private office. *Thank, God, Lee Ann can't hear the elevator.* He walked across the dense, deep beige, high quality commercial carpet knowing his footsteps would not be heard.

As he sat, he opened the safe in his desk, took out his secure laptop computer and the codes to his off-shore accounts. He would never risk anyone being able to find information on his work computer on his true wealth and assets. The first thing he did was send the pilot of his private plane a message with date and time of departure and the code for the location of his private villa in the Caribbean Islands—listed in the name of one of his off-shore accounts. He added a note for the pilot: "Destination a surprise for wife." *Big enough risk the pilot will know where we're going.*

The flashing light on his private desk phone caught his eye. Lee Ann, his administrative assistant, was the only one with that number—he hoped. He looked at his top of the line Apple watch and decided to wait until Lee Ann was gone for the day to listen to the message. She had already told him she had to leave at three o'clock. It was two-forty. He set his alarm to vibrate on his watch in fifteen minutes, walked over the leather couch and stretched out. He had to think this through—to make a plan.

At exactly two-fifty-five his watch vibrated and so did his private phone. It was the one the man had called on before. *How did he get this number?* He let it go to voicemail and decided he would listen after his pilot confirmed the flight plan.

Trust but...

Marjorie Topping moved her electric wheelchair into her home office and shut the door. She was confident Maria would not interrupt her. She opened the electronic rolodex on her computer and looked up two numbers.

"Ms. Topping, nice to hear from you."

"Thank you, Detective. Can you give me a few minutes of your time?" She knew the detective from the major crime task force in Chicago because of a case her late husband had handled in their family law firm.

"Absolutely."

"Thank you so much. I think I have an unusual situation and wonder if you can give me some guidance?"

"I'll do what I can; I certainly owe your late husband for his assistance in what could have been a sticky situation."

"That was years ago. He always spoke so highly of you. As you may know, my area of law was wills and estates...well, I feel a bit out of my element in a situation I have here in Tennessee."

"Oh?" *Tennessee? Hmmm…I didn't know your area of law but I'm not surprised. You don't make the front page of the social columns in every paper in the Midwest without having many connections.*

"Is that a problem?"

"I certainly don't know Tennessee law, but if your questions are of a general investigative nature, I may be able to give you some guidance."

"That's all I'm asking."

"Then how can I help?"

"This morning…" Marjorie Topping told the detective about her granddaughter's disappearance and the subsequent visit by two detectives. She did not share what she had told them. "My question for you is whether I should hire my own private detective?"

The woman on the other end of the phone sat back in her chair and tried to decide the best approach. After all, Ms. Topping's late husband had cooperated on a case which had helped build the detective's reputation as a no nonsense, get the job done, investigator.

"Ms. Topping, is Tennessee your permanent home now?"

"Yes. Does that matter?'

"Just helpful for me to think about the best way I might advise you. As I said, I don't know Tennessee law or law enforcement agencies."

"I understand. I just don't know if I should…"

"Trust them to do their jobs?"

"Well, I suppose. It does sound petty when it's articulated."

"Ms. Topping, I can only imagine you are struggling with grief in the loss of your only grandchild. It's natural to want to make sure the people trying to figure out what happened are competent to do the job. Do you have a local attorney?"

"I do."

"Maybe you should start there. While I have no doubt you have all matters related to your personal estate and that of your granddaughter in order, your reputation certainly speaks to your understanding of the need for objectivity in personal matters—particularly under the circumstances you describe. May I ask who your attorney is?"

"Mr. Gray Olson."

"If you wish to give me the names of the detectives, I'll try to see if I can learn anything about them. In the meantime, I encourage you to talk to Mr. Olson and see what he can tell you about these detectives."

"So you don't think I should hire my own detective?"

"I wouldn't presume to tell you that, Ms. Topping. As you know, I am a public servant and I always trust until I have a reason not to do so. I'm sure there are many fine detectives in Tennessee who are also public servants. Private detectives can certainly find out things, but some have been known to mess up an investigation on the part of the authorities. So, I leave that to your discretion."

"You've been most helpful. You're right. I should talk with my attorney and I will. The detectives are Detective Isaacs of the Round City Police Department and Detective Williams of the Valley Sheriff's Station. I live in the jurisdiction of the Valley Sheriff's Station. My granddaughter died in the jurisdiction of the Round City police."

"Please give me the best number to reach you. I'll call you as soon as I know something that might be helpful."

"I'm sure you're busy. I appreciate your advice and any help you can provide." She gave the detective her private cell phone number.

"My privilege, Ms. Topping. I'm sorry for your loss. We'll talk within a day—two at the most."

"Thank you. Have a good day."

"Good afternoon, Ms. Topping." The detective hung up the phone and pushed back from her desk. *Now to find out if these detectives are country bumpkins.*

Chapter 5

You can't live a perfect day without doing something for someone who will never be able to repay you.

John Wooden

First Steps

"You could eat one of the macarons to save me from myself." Quinn pushed the pale blue box toward him.

George pushed it back and patted his abdomen, but didn't speak.

"Look, Quinn." He pointed to the photograph of Angela Topping under the tree. "I don't know anything about clothes or fashion—just ask Carrie. I didn't look at Angela's belongings in the morgue. Did you notice anything unusual about them?"

"Well, I know more than I would like to know about fashion, but designer jeans and Gucci loafers aren't exactly hiking clothes. It's what I might expect a young woman of means to wear to see her grandmother."

George nodded agreement. "Anything you think we need to check for on the clothes?"

"Absolutely. Good call, George. I did ask Chuck to check with Doc Walters." She called Chuck.

"Yes, ma'am."

"Hey, Chuck. Have time to come across the hall?"

"Five minutes soon enough? I have something running in a machine."

"Five minutes works." She stood. "Chuck will be here in five. I'm going down the hall."

"See you back here in five." He reached over and closed the box from his wife's bakery. "No need to tempt Chuck." He put a piece of paper over the box.

Quinn shook her head and chuckled. She left the room and walked toward the back door of the Station for a minute to get some fresh air.

"Hey, Detective."

The male voice sounded disembodied; Quinn was startled as she hadn't seen anyone. She turned and saw an officer step from behind an SUV. "Simmons, nice to see you." He was walking toward the Station.

"Beautiful day to be alive, isn't it?"

"Yes. Yes, it is." She turned back to the door as he came up the steps.

Simmons reached in front of her to open the door. "Hope I wasn't inappropriate there, ma'am."

"No problem, Officer Simmons. I hope you have a good afternoon." She stepped through the door and headed back to meet with Chuck and George.

The two men were chatting when she entered the room. They stopped talking and looked at her.

Quinn sat down. "Chuck, we're looking at this from multiple angles at the moment. What's the word with Dr. Walters?"

"I've got her clothes and am running tests to see if there are any residual chemicals—might give us a clue to the toxin she may have ingested."

"And?"

"That's what I was working on when you called. First step completed from her sweater, but it will take time. The challenge with fiber analysis is clothes pick up odors from everything in the environment. If they aren't cleaned after each wearing, it can be difficult to determine the source even if we can figure out the chemical. Sweaters often have an added twist since they are generally dry cleaned which means multiple wears and chemical cleaning."

Quinn was nodding her head. *Would I have considered those things?* "That's helpful, Chuck. Thanks."

George walked to the board. "So why do the sweater first? Wouldn't the shirt or jeans be more likely to have been cleaned since last wearing?"

"Didn't say I wasn't working on them, you just happened to catch me when I got a hit on something on the sweater."

"Got a hit? What was it?" George studied Chuck's face.

"Chemicals take time to analyze. I don't have an answer for you, yet. Sorry."

Quinn spoke up. "No apologies needed, Chuck. We'll let you get back to your work and hope you have some answers that will give us a starting place."

"10-4." Chuck headed back across the hall to the lab.

"George, without her automobile or any evidence of how she got to the mountain, and less than twenty-four hours since she was last seen, I won't convince the District Attorney there's evidence for a warrant unless or until Doc Walters has a confirmed cause of death."

"Quinn!" The excitement in George's voice was evident as he jumped in at the end of her sentence. "We wouldn't need a warrant if Ms. Topping gives us permission to search Angela's condo."

"Brilliant, George. Just brilliant. It could help us rule out any chemicals in her home which might have caused her death." Quinn took a deep breath. "Okay, Ms. Topping is an attorney and I suspect she might be a bit wary."

"Wait." He held up his hand. "I must have misunderstood. I thought her husband was an attorney."

"He was, too."

"Got it. Okay, given that she's an attorney she might well appreciate your

thoroughness. Is Doc convinced enough about the COD, even though he doesn't have the chemical isolated either, that we could reveal to her if she pushes—at least we know it wasn't natural causes."

Quinn pushed back her chair and looked at her watch. It was just after four PM It would remain light for another couple of hours this time of year. She stood and walked over to the board. "Angela, what happened to you? Why did you say Billy's name?"

"What was that, Quinn?" George stood and looked at the board, too.

"Angela said 'Billy' as we approached her. Billy has never seen her in his life. He asked her if she needed help. She said, 'Save me.'"

"Does she know someone else named Billy? Did her grandmother give you the name of her ex-boyfriend?" George wrote the questions on the board.

Quinn walked back to the table to get her notepad. "Here it is. Walter Anthony Jones, Jr. He goes by Tony."

George wrote the information on the board. "Do we know where he lives?"

Quinn shook her head. "Ms. Topping thought he had moved out of state after graduation."

"Seems unlikely he'd have a nickname like Billy."

"True."

"Did you figure out the other word? Was it a name?"

"It sounded like 'cuss.'"

"Hmm...." He wrote 'cuss' on their crime board. "Were you and Billy talking when you came upon her?"

Quinn turned to look at him. Her eyes seemed distant. *Were we? Did I say his name? What happened just before we heard...* "Yes, that must be it, George. Billy had fallen and was still catching his breath when I went up to look over the flat top on the mountain. That's it. I heard a moan and turned around thinking he was hurt and called his name—then I saw him walking toward me. She was close enough, although we hadn't seen her, that she could have heard his name."

"Did he speak?"

"Yes, he answered me and then we both got quiet when we heard the moan again."

"Okay, we'll put a question mark by Billy Williams' name as a possible reason for her saying 'Billy,' but not eliminate that there may be someone named Billy in her life, or who was part of her being on top of that mountain."

"Good line of inquiry with any friends and neighbors...and with Ms. Topping, too. Thanks, George. Needed my brain jarred."

"Oh, I have no doubt you would have thought of it. It's one of the things I like about detective work."

"What's that?"

"The pieces of the puzzle. I always try to get as many pieces gathered as I can while sorting out the ones which clearly don't belong in the current puzzle." George looked at the board.

"That's because you are thorough and, more importantly, you care about serving others by doing everything you can to solve the puzzle."

"Why, thanks. Thanks a lot. I *do* care."

"It shows."

"Now, back to *this* case. Thoughts on calling Ms. Topping or dropping in?" George's voice carried a hint of excitement.

"I don't think she's the 'drop-in' kind of person. I've promised her I will do everything I can to determine where her granddaughter was and why—whether by her choice or otherwise."

"Would she meet you at Angela's condo?"

"She might. She's in a wheelchair, but I assume her car has accommodations or her assistant drives her wherever she needs to go."

"Thoughts?"

"I think asking her if she would meet us there and let us search the condo is the best approach. Saves the drive over, arranging a time, all that stuff."

George pointed to her phone on the table. "No time like the present."

Details

Andrew's phone vibrated. His hand shook as he looked at the screen. "C U Monday." It was from Lee Ann. She was gone. He let out a breath and knew he had to firm up his plans. First, he'd have to see what the request, offer, and deal was that this guy went to so much trouble to push him to make happen. *Is my lessee on my land a shell front? Maybe that guy was the one who is actually leasing it. How else does he know about it? What's so urgent that he needs almost ninety acres plus the privacy from backing onto the national park?* His laptop was on his desk next to his office computer. He scanned the emails on his office computer.

An email from Lee Ann was marked: "urgent." He opened it. "Mr. Culbert, there are details here for a land purchase, but I can't find any record of us negotiating anything on it. I will look into it further on Monday."

He clicked his mouse on 'reply.' "No need to follow-up. It was a prank by an old college fraternity buddy." His heart was racing as he read the details.

All the information on ownership on parcels, title searches completed two days before, sales price offers, and name of purchaser—*maybe...and who did title searches?* Andrew knew how real estate purchases worked and this wasn't it. He looked at the name of the owners of the properties adjacent to his and only recognized the name of one. *According to the title search this property was passed down just like mine was. Wonder if the guy has been paying the taxes.* He looked closely at the title search and it was free-and-clear and no liens—tax or otherwise.

Andrew stood up and paced the floor. *I could just send Kelly and the kids to the islands and tell her I'll join them. She wouldn't like flying without me, but she'd go; they'd be safe.* Although he kept a full bar in his office, he rarely drank. He opened the cabinet and looked at the selection of liquors. *Clear head. I need a clear head.* He walked over to his wall safe hidden behind a portrait of his father and removed twenty-thousand dollars. *Kelly can buy new clothes for herself and the kids and not put it on a credit card. Can't give her one from an off-shore account; she'll ask too many questions.* He turned back to his desk and put his laptop, two burner phones, and the money in his brief case.

The light still flashing on his desk phone caused him to almost drop the brief case. He set it on the desk, picked up the phone and pushed the button to play the message. "Don't go doing something stupid—like calling the police or leaving town. We've got eyes on that pretty little woman of yours." The message ended. Andrew dropped the phone in the cradle, leaned his elbows on the desk top, and lowered his head into the palms of his hands. *Should I call my brother-in-law? No...too many unanswered questions...What can I do?*

Advice

Marjorie Topping was once again in her living room when Maria answered the door. It was almost four o'clock.

"Ms. Topping is expecting you." Maria ushered Mr. Gray Olson into the living room and shut the door behind him.

"Good afternoon, Ms. Topping. I apologize I wasn't available when you called. How may I help you?"

Marjorie stopped her wheelchair in front of the coffee table. "Tea or coffee?"

"I'm fine, thanks. May I pour you some?"

"Tea would be lovely. Straight."

Gray Olson, an attorney in the Valley had come to the home of one of his wealthiest clients as soon as he listened to the message she'd left. He handed her the tea.

"Gray, I learned this afternoon that my granddaughter is deceased."

Gray looked across the coffee table at Marjorie and marveled at the calm and decorum she exhibited. He was aware she had negotiated some pretty sizable trusts and estates in Chicago and as an attorney was well experienced in keeping her emotions in check, but this was her granddaughter—her only heir. "Oh my, I'm so sorry to hear this tragic news. Had Angela been ill?"

"No. She didn't show up here last night and I called the local Sheriff's Station and the police Station in Round City. Both informed me about the time frame required for a healthy missing adult."

"I don't know the new Chief in Round City, but I do know the Sheriff and he would have at least taken the report and had someone talk to you."

"He did. So did the Chief in Round City. The lead detectives came this afternoon." She noticed the look of surprise on Gray's face.

"It's not because of my address, Gray." She saw him settle back into the chair. "They are the ones who found Angela."

"Detective Williams and Detective Isaacs? They found Angela?" *What's going on here?*

"Yes. They were apparently hiking on a mountain in Detective Isaacs' jurisdiction and happened to be at the same place Angela was."

"Does...did Angela often go for hikes? Was someone with her?"

"No. She wasn't a hiker. She had asthma and severe allergies. She was alone when they found her."

Gray leaned forward, rested his elbows on his thighs, and closed his hands together. "Did the detectives say her death involved foul play?" His voice was quiet and somber.

"No, they did not. Apparently, her remains are with the medical examiner in Round City."

"Dr. Walters is a retired physician and, in my opinion, a very competent medical examiner. While I thought it was unusual you had the two local lead detectives, given the circumstances I'm not surprised at all. Neither of them would pass this off to someone else."

Marjorie looked at him carefully. She had chosen him as her attorney because he had come highly recommended in the law community and she genuinely liked a man who stayed in his home town to try and make it a better place for everyone. "Detective Isaacs is the lead on the case. She gave me assurances that she would do everything possible to find out what happened to Angela—and whether she died from natural causes." Left unsaid was the possibility Angela was murdered.

"You can trust her, Marjorie. She would have some understanding of the risks that come with your personal circumstances. Her parents are from Knoxville—both teach at the university."

"I know."

Gray kept his eyes on her. *The social register still exists, I see. Why am I not surprised you had already checked her pedigree.* "Though she is new to the position in Round City, she's lived there for a decade or so and was an excellent agent in the Immigration Enforcement Agency prior to accepting this position."

"I know that, too."

"It's important to know the people who are investigating a situation like this. You won't have better anywhere. As surprising as it is to some who come to our community, not everyone has a need to live in a fishbowl."

"I know that, too." She smiled. "Relax, Gray. I did want your initial reaction to the two detectives, but mostly I need your advice on things related, and unique, to laws in Tennessee." Marjorie turned her head when she saw Maria at the door holding her hand to her ear. "Excuse me, Gray." She motioned Maria to come in.

"I'm very sorry, Ms. Topping, but the detective said it was important."

Marjorie raised her eyebrow and glanced over at Gray. "You may transfer it to my phone. Thank you, Maria." *Wonder which detective?*

The phone in the pocket on the side of her chair pinged twice.

"Marjorie Topping." She listened quietly and then said, "Thank you, Detective, I appreciate the information and your timely response. I don't think I'll need anything further." She listened. "Yes, of course. It was always his pleasure to be a part of your success. Thanks, again." She hung up.

Gray had watched Marjorie Topping carefully. Her expression didn't change throughout the exchange—calmness reigned.

"As my attorney, you should know that I reached out to a detective in Chicago who has a very solid reputation and worked with my late husband on a very major case."

"Marjorie, I would expect you to use every resource at your disposal to learn what happened to your granddaughter."

"Her primary advice was to talk to you, as my attorney, and as someone who would know the competence of local law enforcement officers."

Gray gave a polite bow of his head. "How may I be of service? You were about to ask me something related to Tennessee law."

Marjorie did not skip a beat. "Although I held Angela's Durable Power of Attorney, we both know that ended at her death. I am, however, her next of kin. I believe you are aware her mother died in childbirth and my son and I raised her."

Gray nodded.

"Angela, as you know, had a condo in Maryville and I need to…" Her phone rang. "Excuse me, Gray. This is most unusual." Then she saw the number. "Well, perhaps not."

"Marjorie Topping."

Gray stood and walked from the antique oriental rug onto the tiles that were in keeping with the Italian villa Marjorie Topping now called home. He looked out the large windows across perfectly maintained grounds which were still somehow in keeping with the mountain setting. There was not another house in sight.

"One moment." Marjorie turned her wheelchair while she muted her phone. "Gray, this is Detective Isaacs. She would like to visit Angela's condo."

"Why?"

"She says that they do not have a conclusive cause of death, but it was not of natural causes."

Gray was back across the room. He stood directly in front of Marjorie. "Are you inclined to let them?"

"I can't see any harm at this point, but my initial reaction is unless it is an official investigation under a warrant, I would prefer to be represented."

"Do you want to go?"

"No. I would rather remember her charming little condo with her in it."

"Fair enough, Marjorie. Fair enough. While I think you can trust Detective Isaacs to be respectful of Angela's things, I am available to accompany them, if you wish."

"Thank you, Gray. I would prefer that. Excuse me while I tell her."

Gray sat down and poured a cup of coffee. *This may be a long afternoon and evening.*

"Let me see what his availability is." Marjorie muted the phone again. "Gray, can you go to Maryville this afternoon?"

"Yes. Tell Detective Isaacs I'll call her and finalize details."

"Detective Isaacs, Mr. Olson can meet you in Maryville. He said he will call and finalize details with you." She looked at Gray. "He'll call you in the next fifteen to twenty minutes?" He nodded. "Thank you, Detective." She put the phone back in the pocket of her wheelchair.

"Thank you, Gray. I know this is inconvenient."

"Not a problem. This matter is an important priority."

"Maria will get you the keys to the condo and address. I will be available if you need to call me while you're there."

"Was there anything else related to Tennessee law you wanted to discuss?"

"It can wait."

"I have time."

"How long can they keep her remains before I can plan her...?" She stopped.

Gray Olson picked up immediately. "The medical examiner will not release the remains until he has a cause of death which can be substantiated. Sometimes that can take several days. Would you like me to make arrangements for you to go see her?"

"Not today. I'm not sure I can handle it." She dropped her head.

Gray walked over to her chair and squatted down beside her. He gently touched her arm. "Ms. Topping, we've only known each other a few years, but your love and devotion to your granddaughter was evident from the first time I met the two of you. You already know personal loss is never easy. There are too many unknowns at the moment to begin to bring closure."

Marjorie turned her head and looked into his eyes. "Gray, I appreciate the comforting gesture and words, I do. Right now though, I need you to make sure they figure out what happened to my granddaughter."

"I'll do everything I can."

The French doors opened and Maria walked in. "Please give Mr. Olson the keys to Angela's condo and the address. I will be in my room and do not wish to be disturbed unless it is Mr. Olson or one of the detectives."

"Yes, ma'am." Maria left the French doors open and went to get the keys.

Marjorie extended her hand, shook with Gray, and left without another word.

Gray waited until he got to his car before calling Quinn. Arrangements made to meet at five PM, Gray called his wife. "Hey, honey. Client needs my help. I have to go to Maryville. I'll call you when I'm on my way home. Might need to keep my supper warm." He listened to her quiet words of support. "Thanks, Honey. I'll let you know when I'm on my way home. I love you."

Chapter 6

If you want to conquer fear, do not sit home and think about it.
Go out and get busy.
Dale Carnegie

The Land

Again, Andrew read the email with the details of the land to be purchased and studied the proposed price. The offer for his land was fair market value, but the other two properties were more than fifty percent higher than their worth. There was nothing that made the sale seem unreasonable or unfair—except for his property. Still trying to figure out how they got his private phone number, he reread a text. "If it takes double the offer for the adjoining land, make it happen. You've made your profit on the lease. Be grateful. You know what the real cost could be." *How can I find out the number sending the text? I should call the police...or the SBI...Lance... I should have gone one more exit when I left and looked at my land.* He sat back in his chair and tried to decide if he should go have a look. His shoulders slumped. *They know where Kelly and the kids are. It's too big a risk.*

He sent a text to his driver: "Pick up 5:35 sharp."

"Yes, sir. Office or Club?"

"Office."

He found the number for the owner of the land on the east side of his—the man who had inherited his land, too; he had a passing acquaintance with Roger Gordon. He couldn't tell by registration who owned the other land, and wasn't sure he could find out. He stared at the ownership name as Roger Gordon's office phone rang.

"Good afternoon, Gordon and Associates."

"Good afternoon," he hoped his voice sounded normal. "This is Andrew Culbert. May I speak to Mr. Gordon, please?"

"Is he expecting your call?"

"I'm afraid this is rather spur of the moment. However, it is an important matter involving some property he owns."

"One moment, please." The male assistant was courteous and efficient in his tone.

Maybe I need a male assistant. No, I need a bodyguard...for Kelly and the kids.

"Mr. Culbert?" The man's voice exuded southern hospitality.

"Yes."

"I'm putting you through. Have a nice day."

"Thank you." He waited on the call to transfer.

"Gordon here."

"Mr. Gordon, Andrew Culbert, we met a few years back at the hospital charity ball."

"Oh, yes. I remember. My assistant said this had something to do with real estate."

Although Knoxville was a small southern city, it was big enough that social circles of the wealthy sometimes ran parallel to each other. Andrew was trying to think of someone who might be common to both of them. *I can't for the life of me...or my family...think of anyone.* "Yes, I deal mostly in commercial real estate, as you may know, but we actually own adjoining property out off of I-40 east of town."

"Really? That's been in my family for...gosh almost 160 years. It was passed down so many generations it got hard to keep track of who all the owners were. So, I just bought them all out about twenty years ago. What's up?"

"I've had an unsolicited offer for your land and mine." He gave Mr. Gordon the details and waited.

"Well, for starters, call me Roger, Andrew. I didn't get up this morning thinking about selling it, but truth is I'm not ever going to do anything with it. No one seems all too sentimental about it." He paused. "Listen, I'll sleep on it and touch base with you on Monday."

"Would really appreciate it. Forgot to tell you, I'm waiving my fee on this one to accommodate the quick sale and I'll just reiterate that the client will pay all closing costs."

"Almost makes it too good to be true." Roger chuckled. "And you know what they say about things that are too good to be true."

"Indeed I do. However, I have verified the availability of funds for the purchase and looks like we could have that money in your hands Monday week at the latest."

"Well, we also have a saying, 'Don't look a gift horse in the mouth.'"

Andrew tried to make his laugh sound genuine at an old southern saying. "Thanks for your time, Roger. If it's all the same to you, I'll call you…say ten on Monday?"

"I'll have a decision for you then. Have a nice weekend, Andrew." The call ended on Roger's end.

"You as well, Roger." *Funny how large sums of money make people chummy.*

Andrew stared at the portrait of his father, Andrew Culbert II. *What am I doing, Dad?* He knew he needed to do some background research on the owner of the second property. It was four forty-five PM.

Angela's Condo

Gray Olson was waiting in the driveway at Angela's condo when Quinn Isaacs pulled in beside him. She and George Marshall exited her SUV.

"Hey, Quinn. Nice to see you again. Sorry for the circumstances."

"Hey, Gray." She shook hands with him. "Gray Olson, this is George Marshall, senior detective in the Round City Police."

"Nice to meet you, George."

"Likewise, Gray. Thanks for meeting us here. I, too, am sorry for the circumstances."

Gray nodded. "Mind if we have a bit of a conversation—before we go through the condo?"

"By all means." Quinn leaned against her SUV. On the drive over, Quinn had spoken with the desk sergeant in the Maryville police and told her they were entering the property with Ms. Topping's attorney and had requested assistance. She was unsure when the Maryville Police chemical dog unit would arrive. "Shall I give you a rundown of what we know?"

A black van labeled "Maryville Police" pulled in front of the condo.

"George, could you ask them to give us a minute? Thanks." She turned back to Gray.

"I'd rather not have them in on my conversation with you."

"Why are they here?" Gray looked her in the eyes.

Quinn stepped closer to Gray Olson. "I will tell you what I can, which will be in any official report, but you will appreciate I may not be able to answer all your questions at this point."

"Appreciate any insights, Quinn." Gray looked over and saw the letter on the van: Trained dog on board.

Quinn gave Gray the details of finding Angela, suspicion of chemical poisoning not self-induced, and the need to try and track Angela's activities over the last few days. "Questions?"

"So, did I understand correctly that you have a witness who saw her leave at 5:00 PM yesterday?"

"We do."

Gray nodded. "Okay. I'm good with us entering and walking through the condo to determine if she was taken from here, although that seems unlikely. To be clear, however, I can't consent to opening anything personal, even a kitchen drawer and certainly not a computer."

Quinn wasn't surprised. "Understood. Should the need arise for any of that, we'll come back with a warrant. We're just trying to trace her activities as much as possible to try and determine if she was, in fact, taken against her will. I am not anticipating the chemicals were in her condo. Even if the dog in that van gives us the 'all-clear,' we've brought face masks, and each of us can decide if we choose to wear one."

Gray studied Quinn's face. He had only met her socially and knew Sheriff Chad Oliver spoke highly of her, but he was amazed at her attention to detail. "Then I'll open up for the dog."

Angela's next door neighbor drove up as they stepped onto the porch. She jumped out of her car.

"Hey, can I help you with something?" She walked across the grass toward them on her toes so her high heels didn't sink in the grass. "Angela's not home right now." The neighbor looked at the Maryville Police van and back at Quinn as she approached.

Quinn had her badge out. "Are you Ms. Thompson?"

The woman stopped and looked at her warily. "How do you know that?"

"I'm Detective Quinn Isaacs of the Round City Police Department. Officer Kent of the Maryville Police said he had spoken with you."

George stepped back and Officer Kent stepped out of the van and nodded at Ms. Thompson.

The woman appeared wary, but she visibly relaxed. "Oh, okay. Yeah, he did." She waved at Officer Kent.

Gray Olson was standing beside Quinn now and held out his card. He had a note from Ms. Topping, but decided he'd only show it if needed.

"I'm Gray Olson. I'm attorney for Angela and her grandmother, Ms. Topping."

"Marjorie knows you're here?"

"She does."

"Where's Angela?" The question was directed to Gray.

"She's safe. We just need to check on her property and make sure everything is okay."

Quinn admired Gray's calm demeanor. She watched Ms. Thompson carefully. *This woman is either the best neighbor in the world—or the nosiest.*

Quinn stepped up next to Gray.

"Ms. Thompson, I'd just like to verify when you saw Angela leave."

"Yes, like I told the other cop...sorry, police officer...she left about 5:00 PM yesterday which is when she usually leaves if she's going to see Marjorie."

"Do you know Marjorie Topping?"

"Met her once after Angela moved in. Seen her in passing a few times since. Seems a real nice lady. That's why there's a ramp to the porch." She pointed to the wooden ramp behind the shrubs.

Quinn gave her a reassuring smile. "We appreciate your concern and your time. We'll be out of here shortly."

"Well, go ahead. Angela and I just try to help each other since we both live alone. Thanks for showing me your badge." She turned to walk back to her car.

"Thank you, Ms. Thompson. Good neighbors are a real gift."

"Yeah, don't I know it." She mumbled as she walked away and entered her condo.

Gray opened the door and looked at Quinn. "Don't smell anything unusual. Sure you want to do this?"

"Best to let the experts decide." Quinn nodded to George.

Officer Kent walked up and introduced the dog handler who brought the dog forward and entered the condo. About fifteen minutes later the handler returned and spoke to the group assembled on the porch: Quinn, George, Gray, and Officer Kent. "Only chemicals appear to be for normal housecleaning found under the sink and in the laundry room. Nothing registers on my handheld chromatograph." He lifted a device just bigger than a sack of flour.

George looked at the man. "A chro... what? I though you used a spectrometer?"

The man chuckled. "The chromatograph measures chemicals, but you're right, it's attached to a mass spectrometer. Anyway, I think you're good to go in. Questions?"

Quinn looked at the group. "Thanks for your time and assistance. I think we're good." She turned to Officer Kent. "I appreciate your help. I think we're good for now."

"You sure, ma'am? We can hang around."

"Up to you, if you want to wait out here." She smiled.

"We'll just be in the van if you need help."

Quinn extended her hand and shook his. "10-4."

"Let's go see what we can see." Quinn opened the door, opting not to put on a mask—neither did Gray or George.

Gray stepped into the modern, spacious, great room. It was clean and orderly. Even the lap shawl on the sofa was neatly folded. Quinn and George walked in behind him.

They walked through to find the three bedrooms and two baths exactly the same as the great room: neat, orderly, no signs of distress, no notes lying around seeking help if someone happened into the condo.

They were back in the great room.

"Gray, do you know what Angela does for a living?"

Gray watched Quinn carefully. *Like you, Quinn, she doesn't need to do anything to make a living. Her trust fund might not rival what yours probably is, but she could have lived the rest of her life without working.* "She was interested in real estate. She was particularly interested in saving mountain property in land trusts so it could never be developed."

"Wow, that's impressive."

George spoke for the first time. "All the more so for a twenty-four-year old."

"Does her grandmother share her views?" Quinn raised her left eyebrow.

"Quinn, I suspect she learned it at her grandmother's knee." He stopped himself; he knew attorney-client privilege. He also knew it was something Quinn could learn through her own inquiries.

"Then, for now, we'll thank you for making the trip and allowing us to check her home off the list of possible places she could have been abducted."

The three shook hands in the driveway. George walked over and thanked the Maryville police then got in Quinn's SUV.

"Thoughts, George?"

"Nice condo. Clean, appears well-organized on the surface. Nothing to suggest a struggle of any kind."

"I agree. What do you say we go back and talk to Ms. Thompson and see what else we can learn about Angela." Quinn glanced over at him.

"You mean like is she just a do-gooder trying to save our mountains, or an activist tree-hugger?"

Quinn laughed. "Yeah, something like that."

"Works for me. Let's get a cup of coffee back there on the main road and give Gray time to be headed toward home. No sense upsetting the apple cart."

"Good idea, George. Good idea."

He settled in the seat at the use of her double statement. He loved their mountain speak.

They sat in the parking lot for ten minutes sipping very hot coffee and reviewing what they knew as fact and what new questions had come up for each of them.

"Maybe Ms. Thompson knows if someone named Billy is a friend or acquaintance of Angela." Quinn waited to see what George's reaction would be.

"Worth fishing for, don't you think?"

"Why don't you take the lead on talking to her. In fact, I'll stay in the car. She might be more amenable to one of us, and something tells me the one of us that is not a female."

"Now, boss." George only used "boss" when he wanted to jar her out of a thought she shouldn't be having.

"Okay. Point made. I do think it should only be one of us. Makes it seem more like we forgot to ask her something."

"I'll give you that. And since you're driving it seems more realistic if I hop out. Okay, Let's go do this."

Ms. Thompson stood in her doorway and answered all of George's questions. He left his card and turned back to wave and say thanks as he approached the SUV.

Quinn had been making notes while he was gone. She decided if Ms. Thompson noticed, it probably did make it seem more casual. "Any luck?" She backed out of the driveway.

"No current boyfriend for either of them apparently, in fact none that she has seen for Angela since she moved in two years ago."

"Okay, no one named Billy down the boyfriend line."

"Maybe, maybe not."

"Fair enough—online dating and all that." Quinn shrugged.

"I wouldn't know. Been married almost half my life and happy about it."

"Married at fifteen?" Quinn liked to spar with him.

"Good one. We just celebrated our twenty-fifth."

"Wow! Good for you!"

"My good fortune, for sure. Now, back to the case."

"Right." Ten minutes later, Quinn turned onto the highway and they were headed back to Round City.

"She didn't seem to have any idea what Angela did for a living. Knew she worked remotely, but they never talked about her work. Said it wasn't unusual for Angela to be gone for several days at a time. She tried to push on where Angela is right now."

Quinn knew George would not have told her. "Any word on what Ms. Thompson does?"

"Yes, she's a first year lawyer at an old established firm here in town."

"Ah, that explains the 'who are you?'"

"And the 'where is Angela?'" George said. "All in all, I don't think we have anything helpful—at least on the surface."

"Agreed. Would be good to corroborate Angela's departure time yesterday, though. I didn't notice cameras on either condo, did you?"

"Nope. I looked carefully on both porches, too." He took a sip of his coffee. "Ms. Thompson said the condo on the other side of her has been empty for months. Since Angela lives in the end unit on a cul-de-sac and wooded across the street, probably no one around there to ask." He turned to look at her profile. He knew she was probably wondering why neither of them suggested to talk to anyone else while they were there.

"You're right. We can always come back if the trail leads us back here."

"Oh, we'll be back." George was matter-of-fact in his response.

"Oh?"

"There's more to this than meets the eye."

"Is that experience talking?"

"Mostly. And, although I don't admit this to most folks, a bit of intuition that doesn't often fail me."

"I'm pretty good at the intuition thing, too. And, I agree. Shall we take bets on what will bring us back?"

"No bets." George feigned a righteous posture.

"You're right. On three we'll both say what our intuition is?"

"Okay. One, two, three…"

"Her computer." They both said it at the same time and then laughed.

"You're more fun to do an investigation with, Quinn."

"More fun than?"

"The guys."

"Why?"

"They love to posture and try to get the upper hand. With you, it doesn't seem it's about you and your ego—it's about the case."

"Quick assessment in four months, George."

"Detective. Remember, I'm a detective."

She laughed as she took the exit for Round City. "Yes, you're a mighty fine detective, George Marshall."

"Why thank you, ma'am. Back atcha."

They drove the rest of the way in silence. It was almost seven PM when they arrived at the Station, were cleared by the guard, and pulled into her parking space.

"I'll check in with Dr. Walters and write this up, George. You call it a day."

"What if Doc knows something more?"

"Then I'll let you know and we can decide if we need to work tomorrow."

"What? This isn't television? We can't solve a mystery in thirty minutes?"

"Not even sixty. Good night, George. I'll send Carrie a proper thank you for the macarons, but please tell her she's won my heart, too."

"Ah, our secret is out."

"What secret?"

"Fine pastries true love makes."

"Good night, George." She shook hands with him and headed to the back door and swiped her identification card. George turned and was on the phone as he headed to his vehicle.

Looking for Answers

"Ten more minutes." Andrew sent the fifth text to his driver. *What does he care? He gets paid well and gets huge bonuses for waiting around for me.* Andrew realized his irritation wasn't with his driver, it was the wall he kept hitting trying to find the owner of the land on the other side of his. He felt pretty confident that Ralph Gordon would take the deal.

In the tax and title records, *STELT* was listed with a private mailbox address in Bangor, Maine, and the taxes were up to date on the property. *STELT* had purchased the land for cash more than two years ago. *Hmmm...what does STELT stand for?* He sat back and ran his hands through his hair. *It's Friday evening. No one I can talk to until Monday.*

Andrew sent a text to Kelly: "On my way home." He took out his metal briefcase, put the twenty-thousand dollars in it along with his secure laptop. He looked around the office and decided on one more thing he would do.

When he exited his office building, his driver was standing outside the Escalade and opened his door. The driver didn't say a word, shut the door, and got in the driver's seat.

"Home." Andrew switched off the communication system and sat back. He leaned forward and switched it on again. "Lots going on. Sorry for being surly. I'll confirm, but may need you to take us to the airport early in the morning."

"No problem, sir. Whatever you need."

Andrew switched off the communication and leaned his head against the seat and closed his eyes.

Round City Police Station

Though Quinn was happy the elevator to the morgue wasn't noisy anymore, she took the stairs for the exercise.

"Hey, Doc."

Dr. Walters looked up from his lab table. "Quinn, why are you still here on a Friday night?"

"Same reason you are. A young woman died before her time."

"That she did. Pull up a stool."

Quinn sat down. "Any news?"

"Specific? Not yet." He looked up from his work.

"Time frame to knowing something specific?"

"Chuck and I both are making progress. We might be close to identifying the foreign toxin. Once we have her records from the physicians, I'll have a better idea how serious her asthma and allergies were. I can tell you, though, those are first and second degree burns in her throat."

"I've seen third degree on the flesh. I knew hers were bad, but to my untrained eye…"

"You've got a good eye, Quinn. Right for the job you have. Now here's some advice from someone who's more than twice your age."

Quinn cocked her head at him and waited.

"Go home. Take tomorrow for the day off you didn't get today. At this point I think we'll be another twenty-four to forty-eight hours before I'm willing to give a definitive COD."

"Doc, I respect your attention to detail and thoroughness. I know I can be accused of getting ahead of myself, but what if there's another young woman in danger?"

"There is."

She jerked her head toward him. "What? How do you know?"

"Because there will always be another one in trouble—another woman, man, child, family…well, you know the rest."

"Thanks, Doc. I think if we can find her car, we'll have a better chance of knowing where to look next. We walked through her condo and, on the surface, it gave us no clues."

"That, young lady, is the difference in guess work and detective work."

"Do tell."

"Surfaces give one picture, detective work, by definition detects what is under the surface. Now go home. We need you healthy and rested to serve this community."

Hmmm…George mentioned 'the surface'. Quinn had to catch herself to keep from kissing the ME on the cheek. "Thanks, Doc. Thanks for your fine detailed work and thanks for the advice. I appreciate it more than you can know."

"You'll be the first to know when I have an official COD."

"Thanks. Don't stay too late."

"I won't. Stay home tomorrow."

"No promises." She winked at him and went up the stairs two at a time.

Her personal phone buzzed in her pocket as she entered the code to her office.

"Isaacs."

"Williams."

"Find me a car?"

"Which phone are you on?"

"Oh, yeah. Let's start over. Evening. How's your day been?"

"Turned upside down. You see I had a date for a hike with…."

"Okay, okay. I know the rest of the story. What's up?"

"I'm finished at work and have a choice: drive home or drive to your home. Are you going to let my evening be something other than a lonely bachelor turning wood in his basement?"

Quinn plopped in her chair. It was the beginning of spring. The days were getting longer. It was still light. "I need to wrap up a few things here or I'd come turn wood with you."

"Okay, I stand rejected."

"I haven't rejected you—yet. Play your cards right and I'll let you pick up supper at my favorite restaurant here in Round City."

"And eat by myself?"

"Don't push it." She started laughing. "Seriously, I'll order from the Asian Deli and you pick up. We should both be at my house about the same time. If not, make yourself at home."

"Hey lady, you know something?"

"What?"

"Not only are you an intelligent beautiful woman, you are an ace detective—see how easily you figured out I want to see you tonight."

"Get on with you, mountain man. See you when I see you."

"Can't wait."

"Billy...please drive carefully."

"Always."

"Good. See you soon." The call disconnected and she immediately hit the speed dial for the Asian Deli and ordered.

An hour later she backed into her garage and was reaching for the kitchen door knob when it opened. She walked right into Billy's outstretched arms.

"I could become accustomed to this. How's your shoulder?" She kissed the front of his left shoulder.

"Glad you don't wear lipstick. This is a clean shirt."

"Trouble doing laundry at your house?"

"Wash, iron, and spray starch weekly."

She turned away from her gun safe, put one hand on her hip, and looked at him. "You wash, iron, and spray starch your shirts weekly?"

"Didn't say that."

"Okay, who does?"

"Ms. Jamison. She's done my laundry for close to fifteen years now."

"Well, well. Good to know."

She walked into the hall and put her jacket in the closet. "Give me a minute to wash up and I'll be with you."

"I'll get our plates ready. Thought the spring chill in the night air warranted a fire. Hope that's okay."

"Brownie points for you."

She went into her bathroom, pulled the knot out of her hair, swung her head left to right. *I love the feel of my hair being free.* She slipped out of her slacks and top and put on a sweatpants and t-shirt. *Oh, Mother, you would not want to see me dressed like this.* She smiled and ran the brush through her hair.

They sat at the small table in her great room and talked about their experiences today over the shrimp stir fry.

"That's all I know at this point."

"I think Dr. Walters was right. You need to take tomorrow off. There's no evidence anyone else is at risk and when you get his final report, you'll have solid information to use."

"With any luck the APB on Angela's car will yield some results." Suddenly she pushed back in her chair. "Oh, Billy. I forgot to call Ms. Topping." She looked at her watch. It was almost 8:30 PM

"Give yourself a break. I'm sure that Gray would have called her about the visit to Angela's condo. You can do one little bit of work in the morning and call her."

She let her shoulders slump. "Have I told you that you're good for me, Billy Williams?"

"How?"

She pushed her plate to the side, leaned across the small wooden table, and kissed him. "Let me count the ways."

"Name one?"

"I can do better than that..." She took his hand.

Leaving the last of their supper on the table, she pulled him down on the sofa in front of the fireplace.

Chapter 7

When I let go of what I am, I become what I might be.

Lao Tzu

Which Way?

Kelly was waiting at the front door when Andrew opened it. She threw her arms around his neck.

When he put his arms around her, she jumped back as his briefcase hit her square in the middle of her back. "Ouch, what do you have in that thing? Weights?"

He kissed her forehead. "Sorry, honey. Just so happy to see you I didn't think to set my briefcase down." He set it on the long table in the entryway and pulled her into a gripping embrace.

"I missed you." He held her tightly.

She looked up at him. "Are you having an affair?"

"What?"

"Just kidding. I was reading a novel and the husband became much more affectionate with his wife when he started having an affair."

"Leave that to the novels. I missed you, am excited about taking you and the kids away for several weeks..." He stopped when she stepped back from him.

"Several weeks? Oh, Andrew, do you know what it takes to be organized to leave for even a week? Clothes to pack, toys to choose, mail to stop..." She walked toward the kitchen.

He stepped up beside her as she moved to the stove to stir something. "Kelly, look at me, please."

She turned. "Andrew, what's wrong? You're acting so strange."

He sighed. "I'm tired. Lots of big deals lately and no time for you or the kids. We have a place starting tomorrow." He waited to see if she would react. "You'll love being on a sun filled island. They celebrate Easter, too, so the kids can experience a new Easter tradition. Just pack a change of clothes for each of you and one small suitcase of things you and kids can't do without. Then we'll pretend our luggage got lost and buy whatever we need."

In the ten years they'd been married, Kelly had never seen Andrew like this. "Andrew, please tell me there isn't something serious going on...like you're critically ill, or we're in trouble financially, something?"

"You always could read me." He hugged her close. "Really, I'm just tired. Tired of the rat race, and realized we have all this money and we go day to day like we couldn't afford to do something extravagant. So, I want to do something extravagant..." He smiled at her and kissed the top of her nose. "With the woman I love—now and forever."

"Then let's be extravagant. What time are we leaving?" She kissed him hard.

Andrew let out an internal sigh of relief. *That was easier than I thought.* His private phone vibrated in his pocket.

"How long til we eat?"

"Twenty minutes."

"Perfect. I'll confirm our flight time and be right down. Kids in bed?"

"Yes. Go kiss them, but please don't wake them."

"I won't. I promise." He headed for his children's room.

He stood just inside the door and looked at his two-year-old daughter curled up in her toddler bed and her four-year-old brother on his bed across the room. Kelly had the walls and the bed linens in their son's room decorated like a camping trip. They each had their own rooms, but always seemed to want to be together. He was grateful for that. He kneeled down beside each, kissed them on the forehead, and whispered. "I love you more than life, little one. I promise to always try and protect you." It was something he had said from the day they were born. Now he wasn't sure he could keep his promise.

As he reentered the kitchen and saw Kelly serving their plates, he became more determined than ever to protect his family. Kelly's brush with what turned out to be a benign uterine polyp had resulted in a hysterectomy after their daughter was born. She was healthy and with no need for birth control, he knew she didn't take any medications. He wouldn't have to worry about her health. "Honey, I just confirmed our flight and we'll need to be out of here at seven AM." He held up a finger. "Remember, nothing extraordinary, a change of clothes and whatever you can't do without."

He pulled out her chair at the small table overlooking their back garden. "Thanks for opening the doors and setting this table. I love this view."

"Me, too." She smiled at him and lifted her glass. "To my loving husband, who provides well for us, and is taking us on an adventure."

The text message vibrated again in his pocket. He ignored it.

I Want Answers

"Dammit, man, this is no joke. Doesn't that hick tycoon get it?" Gone was the polished, educated man who had presented himself to Andrew Culbert on the rural dirt road an hour east of this luxurious hotel suite. He hated overlooking the Culbert real estate building from the window where he was now sitting. *Did I think I could see into his office?* He slammed his fist on the table.

"Mr. S., I've left five text messages. He ain't answering. Want me to go to his house?"

"Did he leave his office?"

"Yes, boss. Went straight home. Maybe he ain't such a big tycoon. The hick don't have gates or guards on his house. Even looked like the little missus met him at the door—just like Ozzie and Harriet."

"How the hell do you know about Ozzie and Harriett? You aren't old enough." "Reruns." The answer was blunt. "Visit the house, or no?"

Mr. S. sat back. "No. I knew he'd need some time. You're sure he reached Gordon?"

"Yeah. Sounds like Gordon's in."

Mr. S. slapped his hand on the table again. "That isn't the one I need. It's the other piece. I just threw Gordon in to keep him from being suspicious."

"Look, boss. The operation on the leased land is running smooth. Ain't nobody been on any of that land for years—we check that regularly and keep our drones running, too."

Mr. S. nodded his head. "I know. I know. Okay, we'll give him til Monday, then I want pressure applied again. Got it?"

"Even if we get info that the deal is moving?"

"Insurance. Always need some insurance, right?"

"You're the boss. Now let me get you on your plane out of here. You don't take to these mountains too good."

"You got that right. Get me to the city." He walked to the main door of the suite. "Well, let's go. Make me a reservation for nine o'clock at my table at The View." He walked out leaving the door wide open and got on the elevator.

End of the Day

With her knees pulled up to her neck, Quinn pulled the shawl from the back of the sofa around her. "Mmmm...nice way to end the day."

Billy stretched his right hand over and touched her hands wrapped around her knees. "This could become habit forming." He pulled her hand toward him and kissed it. "Very habit forming."

She let out a long sigh. "Can we really make this work?"

"What? Time together on the sofa?"

She threw her head back against the luxurious pillow on the Miloe sofa her mother had insisted on buying for her great room. "Us, silly. Us!"

"Seems to me we work pretty well together."

She leaned over, stretched out, and laid against him on the sofa. "Yeah, we do: personally and professionally. I just keep waiting for the other shoe to drop."

"Has one dropped already? I missed it."

"How can you make a joke out of almost anything?"

"Practice, practice, practice." He pulled her up into a sitting position and they both sat cross-legged on the sofa. The shawl revealed the tops of her breasts. "Have I told you that in addition to being intelligent, beautiful, and a great detective; you are one sexy woman?" He reached over and ran his finger under her chin to the top of her cleavage and then back up again. Then he leaned in and kissed her long and slow.

Gently she pulled back. "Lots of practice at that, too, I see."

"You've taught me a lot in the last four months." He smiled at her. "What's bothering you?" The romantic mood was broken—for the moment, anyway.

"Billy, I love being with you and you're so easy to be around. My track record with relationships—well, men—has not been great. Don't give up on me."

He saw the pleading in her eyes. "Quinn, I'm not going anywhere. I've waited the last twenty years of my life to meet you."

She smiled.

"You. Not someone like you—You."

"And you keep coming back." She said it matter-of-factly but disbelief was under it.

"We can talk about this anytime you want—even right now. But here's what I'm going to suggest. Go take a shower, put on something comfy, and I'll clean up the dishes."

"Come shower with me." She reached for his hand.

"As tempting as that is, I think there's something eating at you. Maybe you can decide while you're gone if you want to discuss whatever it is when you come back."

"Are you going to spend the night?"

"Thought you'd never ask. Now, go."

Quinn stood with the shawl wrapped around her, gathered up her clothes, and headed to her bedroom.

Billy sat staring at the fire. *Dad, you always told me when the right woman came along, I'd know it and I'd know how to love her. You were wise enough to tell me that love and sex are great, but showing love always has to come first. I'm trying.* He put on his crumpled shirt and chuckled. *Well, Ms. Jamison, not even three hours wear out of this shirt—worth every minute.*

Twenty minutes later, Quinn walked back into to the great room in a long flowered caftan her mother had bought on one of the many trips her parents took abroad.

Billy whistled. "You look refreshed." Billy had slipped into his khakis and pullover shirt.

"I am. Thanks. Thanks for cleaning up the dishes, too." She kissed him on the cheek.

"My pleasure." He handed her a glass of sauvignon blanc and picked up his beer. He put his bare feet up on the coffee table and moved to slip his arm around her shoulder.

She noticed how slowly he lifted his arm. "Wait. I can sit on the other side." She moved to his right side.

"Much obliged. May have pushed the limits on the shoulder today."

"Should you have it checked?" She turned her head to study his face.

"I will if it's not better by Monday. It's not my dominant arm, so I can still do my sworn duty, but I don't want to be restricted in my movements either—at work or with you."

She loved his impish grin and his ability to take her out of her own musings. "Oh, I think you probably did push the limits today."

"Right...Well, speaking of work."

"Were we?" She raised her left eyebrow inquisitively.

"I think you need to speak of work, or a relationship, or something. What's eating at you, Quinn?"

She dropped her head back on his arm. "Nothing. And everything."

He waited.

"I don't know how I can be so decisive in the context of my work and so discombobulated in my personal life."

He waited.

"Can you see that?"

"That you are decisive at work and discombobu...whatever in your personal life?"

"Yeah, the latter...mostly."

"Maybe you should stop trying so hard to make everything make sense. You're in a new position in a new organization and, by all accounts, great at it. I have direct observation of your skills, and it's only one of the things I love about you." He paused. "Quinn, we witnessed the end of a young woman's life today. Training and experience aside, we're still human. I can only speak for myself, but I never deal with a death without thinking about my own life." He waited.

She stared straight ahead and spoke softly. "Thanks, Billy. I couldn't put my finger on it, but it's been a while since I was directly involved in a death—even though that one was at work. This one brought back the lives of girls I knew in high school—one I watched die a violent death. Somehow that makes me feel I owe Angela, more than most, every effort to find out why."

"And you will."

She nodded. "You sure you can put up with my weirdness?"

"Oh, you haven't even seen weird yet. I can be Dr. Jekyll and Mr. Hyde when I'm working a big case."

"I think I've been witness already."

"Yeah, guess you have." He gently lifted his left arm. He knew he was talking about one of their joint cases when she was in the Immigration Enforcement Agency.

"Thanks for your patience." She wrapped her arm around his chest and rested her had on his shoulder.

"We'll figure out how to navigate our jobs, the fact that we live in two different communities where our work..." He slid his arm from around her and sat up quickly. "I've got it. I've got it." He was jumping around like a silly school boy.

"Got what?"

"We can buy adjoining property on the county lines and build a house that crosses over them and then…"

"What?" She was laughing now. "Build a house over a county line? No zoning is ever going to allow that!" She was laughing so hard tears were running down her face.

"Ah…I have my ways." He rubbed his hands together and wiggled his eyebrows.

She was still laughing. "See, Billy Williams, you're so good for me. I get so serious about life, and work, and love, and you remind me it's good to be serious about all of those things, but it's okay to have fun, too."

"Hey, I *was* kind of joking, but the more I think about it, we could shorten the distance between us."

"Oh, really? How?"

"That idea about property that backs on the county lines. We could put a small cabin on each and then we could decide which one we want to be in—move back and forth between them to keep it legit. Great idea, right?"

She chuckled.

He pouted—a tactic he often used when he was trying to help her lighten up. "You don't like my idea."

She pulled him toward her and hugged him tightly. "I love your idea. That's not what scares me."

"Then what does?"

"What scares me the most is that I'm falling in love with you."

"I've already fallen in love with you." He kissed her gently. "Take your time. I'm not going anywhere. We'll figure it out as we go."

She ran her hand across his chest and rested her head against his.

"Let's call it a day." His voice was soft and reassuring. He stood and took her hand. They walked down the hall to her bedroom.

Finalizing Plans

It was almost eleven PM when Kelly stood in the doorway to Andrew's home office. "I've stopped the mail, sent my mom an email that we're going out of town for a while, and our bags our packed. Do you want me to pack for you?"

He sat looking across his large desk at his wife. She was a petite blond, with pale blue eyes, and always looked beautiful—even when she was frazzled. "Kelly Culbert, I love you. Don't ever forget that."

"I know, Andrew. I love you, too. Do you need me to pack for you? I need to get some sleep if I'm going to have two little ones ready to travel early in the morning."

"Thanks. I'm good. I'm serious about my pledge that we'll buy what we need. Shoot, we'll even buy what we don't need if we see something we want." He smiled at her.

She walked toward him. "Then I'll kiss you good night and head to bed." She was surprised when he stood up and held his arms out. Most nights over the last few years her good night kiss was a peck on the cheek. *What's wrong, Andrew? You're scaring me.*

"I love you to the end of the earth." He pulled back from their embrace, patted her on the backside, and turned her toward the door. "Now get some sleep. New adventures await."

"Good night, love. See you in the morning." She walked quietly across the large paneled room and closed the door gently behind her.

I pray to God that I can protect you, Kelly. I pray to God. He sat down and sent a text to his driver: 'will let u know next drive. No need for Sat. won't need B4 Mon.' Then he reread the text he was going to send in response to the five texts demanding to know what was happening: "Gordon looks good. Confirmation 10 AM Monday. Need STELT owner. Any leads?" He clicked 'send' and turned off the phone. *I am not going to have you track us or disturb me tomorrow. You'll get your pound of flesh from me on Monday.*

He took the metal briefcase to the bedroom with him, and saw Kelly already sound asleep on their California king bed. He put a change of underwear in a backpack, laid out a pair of khakis and polo shirt, and walked toward the bed. He'd thrown his cashmere suit across one of the wingback chairs and now it appeared to be someone sitting there mocking him. He tried to shake off the image. Normally very attentive to his clothing and grooming, he dropped onto the bed and lay staring at the ceiling. *Please, God. Protect my family.*

The Morgue

"Hey, Doc." Chuck walked into the morgue a few minutes after eleven PM.

"Hey, Chuck. Hope this means you're coming to tell me you're calling it a day."

"Only if you are."

"Let's look at what we have and see what's next."

"Works for me."

The two men sat at the lab table in the morgue and Chuck gave an update on his progress. "Nothing more I can do tonight, so I'm for heading home and back at it tomorrow."

Dr. Walters shared his current findings. "Sounds like we're at a good stopping place. I know Quinn is anxious to know if we have a murder on our hands, but they'll have to figure out that part. What we do know is some chemical was inhaled or ingested, and likely caused the death of Angela Topping. That's enough for today. Now go home."

"Come on, Doc. I'll walk you out."

"Thanks, Chuck. Appreciate it." He walked over and touched the door of the refrigerated unit holding the corpse of Angela Topping and whispered, "We'll do right by you, young lady. We'll do right."

Chuck was waiting to flip off the light switches in the morgue as Doc walked toward the elevator. "Too tired for steps tonight."

"Good plan, Doc. Good plan."

Chapter 8

Our ultimate freedom is the right and power to decide how anybody or anything outside ourselves will affect us.
Stephen Covey

The Morning Dawns

"How's your shoulder?" Quinn saw the grimace on Billy's face as he stepped off the stair trainer in her training room.

"Should have stuck with the simulated training." He gently worked his shoulder.

"Okie dokie, hot shower for you, and then ice and hot pad on that shoulder."

"Yes, ma'am. Headed to the shower."

Both of their secure phones rang simultaneously. They looked at each as they grabbed them and shrugged. It was six-thirty Saturday morning.

"Isaacs."

"Detective, dispatch here. Told to notify you the Topping auto has been found. Report in your secure server."

"Thanks. I'll read the report. Anything else?"

"No, ma'am."

"10-4." She ended the call and saw that Billy was responding to a text, not a phone call.

She waited until he finished. "That was my dispatch. I need to go read a report." She headed to her home office. *Why didn't I tell him it was about Angela's car?*

"I have to go. Truck with a body found near the county line."

"Your side or mine?"

"Not sure. I'll call you." They were both headed to her bedroom.

Showered and dressed, Billy had retrieved his service weapon from the safe he had brought over and put on Quinn's kitchen counter. He was drinking his coffee and had Quinn's ready when she walked in.

"Thanks for the coffee." She kissed him.

"My pleasure. I'm headed out. Need anything from me?"

"Yes, but not work—it'll have to wait." She winked at him. "My report was about Angela's car. It's been found. Let me know if your case intersects with mine. I'll let you know what we find with her car."

"Where was it?" He cocked his head.

"Halfway between here and Maryville; near Walland, I think."

"Who found it?"

"Highway Patrol. Looks like it was forced off the road...not sure. George is meeting me at the Station and we'll head out."

He kissed her and took her hand. "I'll let you walk me to the front door, and then we both need to get on with our appointed missions."

She sighed. "Yeah, so much for a lazy Saturday."

"I'm happy for a Friday night with you. There will be plenty of lazy Saturdays—one of these days."

Quinn watched him open the door. "I've decided that the emphasis on the days of the week are artifacts of the industrial age. Even different religions worship on different days of the week."

He kissed her. "Too philosophical for me at this hour. Talk to you soon. Take care of my detective." He was out the door before she could respond.

Your detective? Well, aren't you the slick one, Billy Williams.

She turned the lock in the door and walked back into the kitchen. At six fifty-five she pulled up to the gate at the police station.

"Morning, ma'am." The gate guard gave her a mock salute. "Any strangers tagging along with you today?"

"Only whatever insects managed to get into my vehicle during the night, Officer."

"Fair enough, ma'am. Fair enough." The gate rolled open.

Is it really the echoes in these mountains that caused people to say things twice? Whatever the reason, I love the familiarity it brings. She pulled into her parking space and George Marshall was leaning on the "Lead Detective" sign with his thumb out like a hitchhiker. It made her laugh. She rolled down her window.

"Trusting soul, aren't you?"

"It's a police station. If I'm not safe here, we're all in big trouble."

"True that. Ready to go?"

He was already at the passenger door. She saw he had a pale blue box between his thumb and forefinger in the hand with his field kit. He took it with his free hand and gave it to her.

"Carrie thought you might need some nourishment this morning."

Quinn patted her waistline. "She's a sweetheart, but..."

"Get used to it. You know the line, 'happy wife, happy life'?" He climbed in the SUV.

"Yes, I've heard it. Have no personal experience with it."

"Well, for us it is: 'Happy spouse, happy house.' So make us both happy. Enjoy it."

Quinn was laughing as she backed out of the parking space. "Know something, George, I like your version better. Too much pressure to think one partner can make a relationship work and make both people happy." *Am I putting that pressure on Billy?*

"My very modern wife let me know in no uncertain terms that it is not her job to make me happy—happy is on me. So we figured if we each work at being happy in ourselves and our work, it will make our home a happy place."

"Have you tried marketing your phrase?"

"Wasn't original. Carrie read it someplace."

"Ahhh...an educated woman who bakes. Lucky man."

"Lucky, yes. Smart that I convinced her to marry me—that's the real coup. Okay, enough talk about marriage. What's the word on the Topping auto?"

"You know what I know. The report was brief and the call briefer." They both waved to the officer at the gate as they exited.

"A highway patrol officer will meet us at the exit off 321 at the Foothills Parkway."

"I'll co-pilot once we get close."

"Thanks. I have the A-Team on standby."

"Worried it'll be more than we can do with my trusty little kit?"

"Just wanted to cover all bases. I don't know what we'll find and given that we know it's part of a likely abduction, I don't want to miss anything." She looked over at him. "No offense."

"None taken."

"I have a tow truck lined up, too." They settled into the drive which they knew would normally take fifteen to twenty minutes, but it was a lovely spring Saturday and folks would be out enjoying the mountains.

Up, Up, and Away

At this moment, Andrew was grateful his children were so young; no resistance to heading out early in the morning—other than normal morning wakeup. Kelly had dressed them without much to do about it. He secured them in their car seats.

"Ready, Kelly?"

"Ready." She climbed in the passenger seat.

He walked back to make sure the garage door into the kitchen was locked and double checked the alarm system. *I may be on a steep learning curve in finding out that even security systems can't keep you safe.* He climbed in the driver's seat.

Thirty minutes later they were at the terminal for private aircraft. After a brief conversation with the pilot, they did the cursory immigration checkout which occurred in many small private plane terminals: ID, passports... Andrew knew the real issue wasn't leaving the country, it was making sure you could get back in. They could. *But will we?*

The plane was fully equipped with a small stocked kitchenette. Andrew had insisted they not have any flight crew other than the pilot. His father had bought the Pilatus P-24 shortly before his death. At this moment, Andrew was glad it was capable of being flown by a single pilot.

"Kelly, as soon as we reach our cruising altitude, I will get breakfast for you and the kids. Just relax and we'll be on the way in a couple of minutes." They were all buckled in when the pilot made his pre-flight comments as they headed to the runway.

The little flyover Andrew arranged with the pilot last night was not something he shared with Kelly. The pilot had to alter his flight plan slightly, but not enough that it made for any likelihood of getting attention. It just wasn't the most direct route to the islands.

Andrew knew Kelly was not a big fan of takeoffs and landings, so he had made sure the shades were pulled by the facing seats she and the children occupied. He, however, sat further front so he could look out. They were in the air. He had to gather any information he could from this brief diversion.

Andy, Andrew's father, had owned a private plane for years, so Andrew had flown over their property in the mountains before. He knew the surrounding area and what could be seen from the air. *Why did I lease my property to anyone with an agreement that I wouldn't check on it?* Then he remembered it happened about the time they were dealing with Kelly's brush with cancer. He sighed. With a headset on he could hear the pilot and knew it wouldn't disturb or frighten Kelly.

"Coming up on the coordinates, Mr. Culbert."

Well, things have changed in that lease deal. I'm going to check on my land. Andrew already knew they were close because he saw the 1930s fire tower. He watched carefully. He hoped to see nothing but the evergreens and new growth on the sugar maples and hickory trees. He had his binoculars out and was stunned when he saw eight portable buildings. He hoped this was not his land. *Dear God, what are they doing down there?*

The pilot pulled up and headed south; they had a flight time of just over two hours.

Andrew sat back in his seat, removed the headset, and knew that something was very, very wrong. He struggled to stop his hands from shaking—

in fact, his whole body. He felt he was going to be violently ill—it wasn't air sickness.

A Truck and a Man

Billy pulled up behind the crime scene truck and saw a battered old red pickup truck—nose in against a large pine tree. Jeff Coleman, one of his detectives from the Valley Sheriff's Station, had been there since the early morning hours. It was Sheriff Oliver who had sent Billy the text to get to the scene.

"What's up, Billy?"

"Hey, Jeff. Sheriff thought…" Billy noticed the face mask Jeff and the others had on. "Got another one of those?"

"Yeah." He walked towards his vehicle and got Billy a mask. As he handed it to him, he glared at Billy. "Sheriff think I couldn't handle this?" Jeff said it partially in jest, partially out of concern. It wasn't typical of Billy to take over a potential crime scene.

"No, man, not at all. I'm working a case with Round City Police and he thought this might tie in. I don't plan to take over—or need to. You've got this and the boss knows it. Now relax. What's the word and why the masks?"

"The truck had stolen plates, Vehicle ID number scratched off, and there was no identification on the body. Damn truck smells like rotten eggs. I made everyone put on masks. Based on the tire tracks, it looks like the truck had slowed to almost a crawl; going off the road appears to be due to the lack of a live driver."

"How long before you move the body?"

"Well, guess that's something you'll need to decide."

"What do you mean? We have protocols. Have the techs done their work?" Billy's surprise was evident in the harshness of his tone.

"Yep, been out here for hours. That's not the problem. They're ready to move him. The question is, 'to where?'"

"What do you mean to where? The morgue, of course."

"Well, see, that's the problem. This little piece of land seems to be in the Round City Police jurisdiction."

Billy would prefer that his ME handle the body since they caught the case. *If it is tied to Angela Topping…*

"Oh, and Billy, the really odd thing is this ring which looks pretty expensive. It was on the floor under the passenger side of the seat." He reached out to hand an evidence bag to Billy. Then he stopped. He muttered, "Guess this is why the Sheriff called you."

Billy took the evidence bag from Jeff, but ignored the comment. He stepped back from under the tree where the truck had ended up. He wanted the sunlight. He turned the bag over in his hand. *Jeff obviously figured out the ring wasn't in keeping with the old truck.* The ring was simple, but elegant, and clearly very expensive. Inside the band was an engraving: 'J.T. 1990' with a heart. *J.T.? Not Angela Topping, the ring's too old. Her grandmother is Marjorie…J.T.?* He tried to remember Angela's father's name. He stepped over to his SUV, half sat with one leg on the ground and the other in his vehicle. He pulled up his files on his computer screen. He did a search on the report from the interview with Marjorie Topping. "Parents of Angela Topping: Harvey Topping and Janice Topping. Married June, 1990." He stepped out and walked back to Jeff.

"Here's what I know." He gave the information to Jeff. "Your call."

"Always the challenge of these mountains. Where are the jurisdictional lines? Sounds to me like the ring suggests we need to assume there's some connection to their case and technically it appears this land is in their jurisdiction. Send the guy to Round City."

"And the truck?"

"That, too."

Billy agreed but tried not to move his head. He wanted Jeff to feel confident that this really was his decision.

"If that's your decision, you can let them know what's headed their way."

"So we did the work and…"

"And…they get the heavy work. I'm sure their ME, techs, and detective handling the case will appreciate your efforts and call on you if they need you."

Jeff stepped back a few steps. "Yeah. Sorry I was such a grouch when you showed up. Been a long night and it just seemed to me this was going to be a whole lot more interesting than a drunk who ran off the road."

"You might be right—probably make us glad it's not our case." He slapped Jeff on the back.

Jeff smiled. "You've got a point there. We had our share of 'way too interesting cases' last fall. Guess the spring belongs to Round City."

"Buy you breakfast at The Corral?"

"Another time. I'm off duty when I get this dispatched. Bed seems like a good place for me to be. Thanks, though."

"Anytime, Jeff. Anytime." He extended his hand to shake.

"Really, thanks, Billy. I was an ass..."

"Enough of that talk. Go home and get some sleep. Call me if you need me to do anything." Billy walked toward his SUV.

"Sure will, Billy. Sure will."

Billy got in his SUV and took out his secure phone. He sent a text to the Sheriff: "Coleman sending DB to Round City Police morgue. Will notify Quinn."

The reply was immediate: "10-4."

Billy pulled out onto the road and dialed Quinn's secure phone.

"Isaacs."

"Williams."

"Hey."

"Where are you?"

"Just got to the location of Angela's car and looking over the scene. The Highway Patrol officer stayed with the car until we got here. It's inside our county line, so I've got the A-Team on the way. Looks like a deer went off her front bumper. I want a thorough search and record before we move the car."

"Did you find the deer?"

"We're still looking. It didn't do major damage but that's likely because Angela swerved to miss it."

"Good thing the officer saw the APB. Might have just had it towed."

"Seems like a good officer. She knew there was an APB and had been doing a little off road surveillance trying to help find it. Seems it's a common place to folks run off the road around here."

"No doubt—lots of deer in these hills."

"True. And you? What'd you find?"

"Coleman caught the truck and they've been out here most of the night." He told her what he knew at this point.

"So, he's calling us…Hold on." She switched calls. "Isaacs."

"Dispatch. I have Detective Coleman from the Valley Sheriff's Station for you."

"Give me a minute to end the call I'm on." She switched back to Billy. "Detective Coleman is on the line. Later."

"Later. Oh, and Quinn. Rather he didn't know I told you."

"Give me more credit than that."

"*Touché*. Later."

Why did he think he needed to tell me not to say anything to Coleman?

"Isaacs." Quinn responded when she switched calls.

"Detective Isaacs, this is Jeff Coleman. Did I catch you at a bad time?"

"Not at all. Been a while." She looked out to see the A-Team from her Station pulling up. "How may I help you?"

Jeff gave her the information and waited for her to respond.

"Have you dispatched folks to pick up the remains and the truck?"

"Got our morgue team here. Haven't called for a tow truck."

"If you're good with transporting the DB to our morgue, we'll pick up the tab. I can send a tow truck, if that's easiest for you."

"Sounds like a plan. Just have the driver call me for directions."

"Will do. Thanks, Jeff. Okay if I give you a call once we review what we have?"

"Sure, I'll help any way I can."

"Anything you need from me?"

"Officially, no. Just be curious to see what it turns out to be. Doesn't seem like a drunk run off the road."

"We'll keep you in the loop as much as we can."

"Thanks, Quinn. And, hey, congrats on getting the lead job over there. Word on the wind is that you're doing a great job."

"Thanks, Jeff. I appreciate the welcome to your ranks. I'm sure we'll have another joint project one of these days. You were a key in solving the case with the county commissioner."

"Thanks. I like the puzzles."

"Another detective recently said the same thing; I'm learning about puzzles myself. Thanks, again, Jeff. You'll hear from the tow truck driver."

"10-4."

Quinn sent a secure message to Chuck and the ME: "Male DB enroute, smell of rotten eggs in truck, may be related to yesterday's victim. Be back to Station soon." She finished the call for the tow truck and hopped out of her SUV. She headed toward Sergeant Steve Clark, head of their A-Team crime scene investigators.

Blue Skies and Sunshine

The plane seemed to glide in over the turquoise blue of the Caribbean waters. Andrew watched the white foam roll on top of the waves against the sandy shore. *Fascinating how it lays there til the next wave...* He heard the angst in Kelly's voice.

"What, Kelly?"

"How soon do we land?"

"Won't be long now, honey. I'll be right there."

At that moment, the pilot said to make sure their seatbelts were fastened.

Andrew slipped into the window seat so he could both see out and hold Kelly's hand. They had kept the kids entertained after breakfast and the two were playing with each other as the plane coasted onto the runway.

Kelly gripped Andrew's hand tightly and then let go as she felt the reverse thrust of the engines. "We're here." She smiled at him. "Wherever here is."

Andrew had been here many times on business and Kelly never knew he was not at his desk in Knoxville. Sometimes he felt guilty about it, but he knew flying was not something she enjoyed herself, nor wanted to know he was doing. *Thanks, Dad. A quick flight: that's the beauty of this plane.* He knew Kelly would be totally focused on the children when they disembarked and not looking for signs of where they were. There was only one hangar off the grass landing strip—Andrew's father had it built so the pilot could literally drive right into it. The pilot was booked in a nearby Bed and Breakfast and would be ready when Andrew needed to fly back to Tennessee.

An SUV with very dark windows was waiting for them. They stepped off the steps of the plane and right into the large SUV. He watched as the driver easily got the children into car seats in the middle row. He gave an internal sigh. *So far so good.*

"Doing okay, Kelly?" He kissed her as she sat down on the back seat and he moved in beside her.

"I'll be okay. Do we have a long ride?"

"We'll be there before you know it. You'll love the views of the ocean. Close by there is a place to shop that I may never get you out of."

"Right now I just want to get the kids settled." She squeezed his hand and rested her head on his shoulder.

He didn't tell her that he had made arrangements to have toys in the kids' rooms which he had updated a few months back—even though they had never been here. He always kept their rooms off limits when he was here meeting with clients. He was happy Kelly rested her head on his shoulder. He looked at his children who were each playing with a toy that had been in their car seats. He leaned his head against Kelly's and closed his eyes. He knew these moments counted—he didn't want to forget the importance of them.

Chapter 9

The simple act of paying attention can take you a long way.
Keanu Reeves

Mid-Morning

Quinn watched from a distance as Sergeant Clark and his team did their work on Angela's car—at least what they would do at the scene. Quinn focused on the meticulous work each of the techs did. *They will go over this with a fine tooth comb at the Station.*

"Detective Isaacs?" George called to Quinn.

"Yes?" As she walked toward him, she saw the paper map spread out on the nearby picnic table.

"Need to verify something with you."

"Sure." She stepped over to the table.

"You and Detective Williams were here on your hike, right?"

"Yes." She looked down and saw Indian Flats Falls with a red arrow pointing toward it.

"The call from Detective Williams on the truck with the DB put it about here, right?"

She saw another red arrow pointing to an area where the two jurisdictions met north of the Valley township and southeast of Round City. "Close enough without seeing it myself."

George pointed to a green arrow drawn close to where they were standing. "Seems a bit unlikely she was abducted here by the person in the red truck, taken all the way over here..." He pointed to the general area where Quinn and Billy had encountered Angela Topping, "...and the truck found here being involved in our case." The red arrow indicating the truck was located between Round City and Indian Flats Falls.

"Except...I didn't get to give you all the details about the truck."

"Ma'am?" George looked at Quinn and at the forensic tech standing with them.

Quinn heard some irritation in George's response. "First, good work mapping this out. I apologize for not having a chance to give you all the information. There was a ring found in the truck with the inscription 'J.T. 1990' and a heart. Angela Topping's mother's name was Janice."

He stared at her.

"Her parents were married in June of 1990. We will have to verify the ring as belonging to Janice Topping, but it's probably a safe bet."

George let out a long slow whistle. "The driver of the truck is dead, right?"

"He is. Should be in our morgue by now."

"Then maybe he was headed east and she escaped, so he started back to wherever he was from."

"Could be—we'll follow the clues." She pulled her hair back into a knot.

"That we will." George straightened up and started to lift the map. He saw her pull her hair back. *There it is. When she pulls her hair back like that, she's got something serious rolling around in her brain.*

"Detective Marshall," Quinn's voice was level and calm. "How long would it take to get from Indian Flats Falls parking area to the place the truck was found?"

George put down the map as he took out his phone. He entered the information, waited, and looked up at Quinn. "Twenty-five to thirty minutes—give or take. Why?"

"Just want to tuck it away. We'll be able to do some calculating once we have time of death for both victims."

"Yes, ma'am." George nodded. "We will." *She thinks Angela escaped this guy and he headed back west.*

"Detectives..." Sergeant Clark was halfway between Angela Topping's car and the picnic table when he called to them. "Over here."

"Coming." Both detectives stepped away from the table. George folded the map on the way.

"Got several sets of prints off the driver's window and dashboard." He pointed to the dashboard.

Quinn leaned in the window being careful not to touch anything. She noted the inside was very clean and well-kept. She studied the fine dust on the faint prints of four fingers on the top of the dashboard, but the very distinct thumbprint on the metal above the air vent just below the dash. "It looks like a left hand." She looked up at the sergeant.

"Yes, ma'am. My best guess is a male and that's a mighty fine detail on the thumb."

"Good work. We'll get Chuck on them as soon as possible."

"Can send photos shortly." The sergeant held up his secure phone.

"The sooner the better." Quinn stepped back. "Any sign of a deer?"

She knew the sergeant wouldn't speculate.

"We'll check it out thoroughly. The damage wasn't enough to stop her, but the shock of it may have been why she pulled off the road in the first place."

"Thanks, Sergeant. Once we know, we'll do our best to figure how she got from here to Indian Flats Falls." *Seems unlikely someone forced the deer in front of her. Opportunistic encounter?*

Quinn looked at George. "Thoughts, Detective?"

"Wondering if we could be so lucky with the prints?"

"Seems to me most cases are a lot of diligent work and a little bit of luck."

"True that, Quinn, true that."

Quinn turned her head and saw no one was near them. George's informality slipped back with ease. *Wonder how long it takes to change from the rigid hierarchical structure George had for so many years to one which gives some people more responsibility than others, but emphasizes teamwork as the best way of getting the work done?* She preferred it when George felt comfortable acknowledging their partnership.

Quinn moved toward the road and sent a text to Chuck to expect some fingerprint photos. She asked him to put one of the techs on it as soon as possible. She hoped the prints were in the system—or that they would find them on the man from the red truck headed to their morgue.

Blue Skies and Aqua Seas

On the balcony of the penthouse, Andrew and Kelly were drinking coffee overlooking the private cove on the Atlantic Ocean. It was a six story wooden building which resembled a large Victorian mansion although each floor was a single unit. Years ago, Andrew's dad had bought the entire building. Andrew had been in no hurry to lease or sell the other units; they had the entire property to themselves. The kids were excited about the toys in their bedrooms. The nanny Andrew had hired was playing with them.

"Andrew, I can't believe how quickly the children took to Suzanne. How did you find her?"

"Business acquaintance gave me the name of an agency which caters to families who require well-vetted, high quality help. I think she'll prove to be worth it. Smile, my love, this will give us some time to ourselves and help for you with someone who knows the island." He would not mention to Kelly that the nanny was a recently retired twenty-year veteran of the island police force—the real reason he hired her.

"Where did you say we are?" Kelly turned to look at him.

He caught her gaze out of the corner of his eye. "Kelly, look out there." He pointed to the right toward a large bird soaring just above the waters surface. "Nothing like that at home, right?" He pointed off to the left toward a flock of sandpipers landing on the shore just above the foam. He leaned over and kissed her—grateful for the distraction. He didn't want to lie to her, but the less she knew the better.

The diversion seemed to work. She changed the subject. "Are shops open tomorrow? It's Sunday, right?"

"Yes, tomorrow is Sunday and yes, the shops are open. Let's go shopping this afternoon though. Maybe get enough to get through the next week for clothes and anything else you want. Then tomorrow we can go out on a yacht."

"You really are being extravagant. I saw the washer and dryer; we can get by for a few days."

"We'll get new clothes. Nothing but the best for the love of my life."

"There you go again, getting all maudlin." She knew Andrew was like his father in some ways and didn't mix business with family. She hoped he would be different with their son some day; she thought it might be too much to hope he might include their daughter. She leaned toward him. "Andrew, do you promise me you're not ill? What has happened? It's not like you to be so off-kilter."

I know she settled for the life we live. She's smart and could have been a prominent CPA, but she also wanted kids—a family. I'm too much like my dad to bring her into the business…hell, no way I would now—I can't protect her as it is.

"Andrew." Kelly all but shouted his name. "Andrew, what *is* wrong with you? I have said your name five times. What is going on in your head?"

He stood and walked across the large lanai to the railing overlooking the sea.

She sat up straight as an arrow in her seat. "Now, Andrew. I want to know what's going on."

He headed back to the table trying to decide how much he would tell her when he saw a drone flying very close to their penthouse along the beach. He walked up to her, took her hand and said, "Come on, I promise, I'm just tired and I want to have some fun. Let's go get the children and go have a late lunch in a little out of the way place I was told about." He kissed her and shut the French doors behind him.

Round City Morgue

"Well, Sue, it looks like we're going to get busy shortly. A body is enroute from county line. The Valley Sheriff's Station techs estimate the time of death as late Thursday, early Friday morning."

"They just found the body?"

"Apparently found it late last night. I'm going to go read the report from their folks. I'll let you get things ready. Appreciate you coming in on a Saturday."

"No problem, Doc. Happy to help. I'll have everything ready." Sue, an intern from the best university forensic tech program in the state, wanted to learn all she could about doing autopsies so had asked to have part of her time with the medical examiner.

Dr. Walters walked into his office and pulled up the report and started reading. He made note of the report of the truck smelling like rotten eggs. *Could be a number of reasons for that, but we'll check everything.*

The elevator doors opened and a gurney was rolled in by two men. Doc stood up from his desk and headed toward them. He knew if they got in the building they had credentials, but he preferred to check for himself.

He looked at the clock and saw it was almost 11:00 AM. "Morning, boys. Don't think I've had the pleasure."

In a well-practiced motion, each man held up his badge and ID and introduced himself.

Doc gave the IDs a quick scan and nodded toward the remains they had on their gurney. "Fellow got a name?"

"Nope. Jenkins said they couldn't find any identification. Also there was a stolen plate on the vehicle and the dashboard vehicle ID number filed off."

Doc nodded. "Fingers have prints intact?"

"Yes, sir. Guess whoever goes over the truck will find the VIN. Probably stolen, so not much help except to help the owner stop looking for it."

"True that, gentlemen. Thanks for your work and for getting this man to us. Detective Isaacs will keep you folks informed."

"Appreciate it. Strangest one we've seen. The truck just kissed the tree. Like he died some distance away and just drifted toward it."

"Helpful to know. Thanks."

They transferred the body to the stainless steel table Sue had ready for them. The older of the two men turned to the ME. "Need anything else, just holler."

"Thanks. Sue, will you see these gentlemen out? They might like to use the facilities. Please get them a cup of coffee on me for their ride home."

"Will do. This way." She headed back to the elevator ahead of the gurney.

"Well, well, sir. What brings you to my table today?" Doc saw a gash and pooled blood on the side of his head. It wasn't the only evidence of trauma over the life of this man. He appeared to have had a hard life: scars, yellowed teeth and fingers from tobacco, leathered skin from too much unprotected time in the sun. "We'll see what we can do to find out who you are and what brought you here." He checked the tray on the rolling cart beside him and smiled to see the instruments were laid out in precisely the order he liked them.

Sue came through the door at the bottom of the steps. She picked up the camera from the counter and moved over to take photos and record the work of the ME.

Dr. Walters was grateful for the silence.

Headed to the Station

Quinn and George were headed back to the Station just before noon.

"George, I can update the board and see if we have the truck and driver in our custody yet; you go home. I appreciate your help this morning, but you've wrapped up a big case this week and should take some time off."

"All the same to you, I'll help out. Carrie's at the bakery until after four today, so I'd just waste my time watching television."

"Fine with me. Want to stop and grab a bite before we head in?"

"Sure. What do you have in mind?"

She turned off the main road to Round City onto a smaller road which ended at a small family restaurant where Billy had taken her last year. "Know this place?'

"I do. Glad to know you do. Wish I'd thought to ask if you'd been here."

"Billy Williams introduced me." She hesitated. "Actually it was right after Chief Nelson passed away. That's where I met Steve Clark."

George nodded. "That was a rough week for everyone. Never easy when you lose a fellow officer in the line of duty—harder yet when it's the Chief."

"I know." Quinn stayed quiet.

"Then, let's go have a toast to our former Chief."

"We're working."

"No problem. Strongest thing they serve is coffee and iced tea." George chuckled as Quinn put the SUV into park.

They ordered their lunches and made a toast. Quinn cleared her throat. "I'm trying to piece together how someone happened along at the time Angela Topping hit a deer causing her to stop on that isolated part of the road."

"Unlikely they put a deer in her path. Could be she was being followed and knew it and that's how she missed seeing the deer."

Quinn studied his face—his eyes were serious, but playful. She waited a few beats. "Fair enough. Did you see any evidence of a scuffle on the pavement?"

"No. She may not have resisted."

"I don't have much experience with assessing vehicles involved in crimes, although I've read plenty of reports. Will they be able to tell if there was a problem with her vehicle after hitting the deer?"

"Probably. This is why we have to follow the clues."

Quinn's brows furrowed. *Yeah, I know!*

"I think I see that little whip in your head. Stop beating yourself up. Experience—best teacher of all."

"Thanks, George. I need the reminder. And in case you're wondering, I also know there are some things we may never be able to answer."

The server put their food in front of them and they ate in silence.

Quinn picked up her glass of tea. "I don't know the last time I had a BLT. Thanks for the recommendation. It was wonderful."

"You didn't touch your French fries."

"Don't dare. Someone keeps bringing me pastries." She smiled. "And, trust me, I'll choose pastries made by Carrie any day over French fries."

"You just made brownie points with Carrie." George laughed and lifted his iced tea glass in salute. "By the way, the bread here is from her bakery. They used to make their own, but she got a contract with them at the beginning of the year." He beamed.

"Ahhh...that explains why it was extra delicious."

"Yep, pretty sure that's true."

The server put their checks down. They each put cash on the table and stood.

"Give me a minute, Quinn. I need to speak to someone."

"No problem. I'll stop at the ladies room and meet you outside."

Twenty minutes later they pulled into the Round City Police Station.

What's Up, Doc?

Scanned into the Station, Quinn and George headed for the stairs. They opened the door down to the morgue and saw Chuck was half-way down. He turned and looked up.

"Hey guys...uh...boss...uh..."

Quinn let out a soft laugh. "Relax, Chuck. I've been one of the guys most of my career. No offense taken. What's up?"

"Doc called me to come down and get prints off the guy the Valley techs brought in."

"Did you get the ones from Sergeant Clark?"

"Just about the time Doc called. Well, I should say I saw them then. Didn't check when he sent them." He held the door at the bottom of the stairs open for Quinn and George. "After you."

"Thanks." Quinn stepped into the morgue.

The ME turned and looked at them. "Wasn't expecting so much company." He looked back down at the corpse. "Be with you in a minute."

"Problem if I step over and look?" Quinn said.

"Not for me." The ME tilted his head to one side signaling she should come over.

Quinn stood and looked at the man's face. "Looks like a rugged life."

"Good observation, Quinn. What do you base that on?"

"Weathered skin, multiple old scars..."

George had moved in now, too. "Certainly suggests he spent a lot of time outdoors."

"Callouses. His hands are calloused." Quinn stared at the one hand that was lying palm up.

"Correct. But the finger tips are good enough for our fine technician here to get prints." The ME nodded to Chuck.

"On it, Doc." Chuck moved in and collected the prints.

"Let me know if you get a hit on them, please. I prefer to know the name of the person under my scalpel." The ME never looked up from his work. "If you're hoping for any information you can use, Quinn, it'll be a while."

"Sure, Doc. Figured as much. Just wanted to let you know I'm back in the Station. I do have a question, though."

"Ask away."

"Did anyone tell you there was a smell of rotten eggs in the truck?"

"Yes."

Quinn always admired how few words the ME used. "Good. Just want to know when you figure out if it has any chemical connection to Angela."

"You'll be the first to know."

Chuck headed for the stairs. "I'll let you know if I get a hit on his prints."

"Thanks, Chuck." Quinn turned to the ME.

"Doc, may I see Angela for a moment?"

"Sure. Sue, want to help Detective Isaacs?"

Sue walked over to the refrigerated unit and pulled out the stainless steel bed with the remains of Angela Topping.

"May I see her hands, please?"

Sue pulled the sheet away from her left hand first.

Quinn studied it carefully. "Thanks. Now the other."

Sue covered the left side of Angela's body and lifted the right side of the sheet.

Quinn studied the fingers on that hand. The middle finger had an indentation circling it—common when wearing a ring for a long period of time. "Thank you. That's all." Quinn turned and headed for the door to the stairs. She looked around. *Hmmm...didn't hear Chuck leave.*

See walked over to Dr. Walters. "Doc, I assume the ring is with Chuck?"

"Yes, ma'am."

"Thanks, Doc. Talk to you soon."

"Catch you later, Doc. George followed Quinn up the stairs headed to the door of the workroom.

Neither said a word.

Chapter 10

Every individual matters. Every individual has a role to play.
Jane Goodall

We Wait

"Let's get what we know at this point on our board, then call it a day." Quinn entered the code on their workroom door keypad.

"Fair enough. I could watch the Final Four in basketball this afternoon."

"Aha, the man does have an interest outside of work."

"You mean aside from my lovely wife?" George put a hint of sarcasm in his voice.

"Yes." Quinn gave him a glare and then laughed. She knew he was joking.

George walked to the board and picked up the dry-erase marker while Quinn turned on the computer.

"Okay, secure file open. Let's get this information on our board and see where we are."

George wrote the make of Angela's car, where it was located, and was recording the distance from where Angela was found and her home when Quinn spoke up.

"Do you have the paper map you marked-up?"

George took it out of his field kit. "At your service."

"Do you have photos of it?"

He took out his secure phone, took pictures, and sent them to her. "Now we do."

"Thanks, just wanted them electronically. Okay with you to put that one on the board?"

"Have a ready map anytime I want; thanks to the internet." He turned and put the map on the board.

"Steve said we should have a preliminary report on the A-Team findings no later than Monday. He didn't see a need to take Angela's car to Knoxville as the prints were clear and there was no evidence of external damage to the vehicle other than the possible deer—and that wasn't more than a dent."

"Normally, we pretty much do what we can here and short of something we can't process in our labs, or a bigger case than we think we have starting out, we don't use the state boys...and girls." He looked up at the ceiling like a soon-to-be chastised school boy.

"Glad you know women do this work, too. Now—to the red truck. Do we know if it's here yet?"

"I don't. Want me to check with the detective on this case...oh, that would be me." He chuckled. "I'll check my secure mail in a minute." He put the red truck and the ring found on the floor in the "questions to be answered" list.

"Let's make sure we have the damage on Angela's car. I want to see what the techs come up with...and if anyone finds a deer or evidence of one which she might have hit."

After a lengthy discussion on all the information they had at this point, George left to go to his computer in the bullpen as each of them took time to check their secure messages and emails.

Quinn was staring at the board when George came back in the room. He watched her take her hair out of the knot and put it back in again. *I wonder when she started doing that? Come to think of it, what tells do I have that reveal I'm concentrating? Or anything else for that matter?*

"George, Angela clearly didn't get to Indian Flats by walking. So, how did she get there? Why?"

"Puzzle pieces, Quinn. Puzzle pieces."

"I used to like television shows about detectives—neat, tidy, cleaned up, and done in sixty minutes."

"Yeah, no fun in that at all." He laughed. "There's a reason the old saying about being a detective persists."

"Which one?"

"Lots of foot slogging...well in today's world, more like digging in the dirt—even when it's using the internet."

"Got it. Tomorrow is another day. Anything else to add?"

George studied the board and shook his head. "Not at the moment. Let's call it a day and short of a call from some incredibly reliable source between now and Monday, try to actually have a day off tomorrow."

"Works for me." Quinn logged out of the computer and reached the door as George opened it.

"I like working with you, Quinn. Just thought I'd tell you that."

"Back atcha. Give my regards to Carrie and thank her for the goodies. Go watch basketball."

"You get out of here, hear me?"

"Shortly." She looked up and nodded.

"Talk to you soon." George headed toward the back door.

Quinn went across the hall to the lab and her office. Chuck was stooped over one of his new machines.

"Hey, Quinn." He glanced up and right back at his work.

"Hey. I'd like to see the ring they brought in from the truck."

Chuck pointed to the evidence bag.

Quinn picked it up. She could tell the quality when she looked at it: twenty-two carat gold—she knew the marking 916. She saw the emerald with occlusions that would make it worth a great deal. She set it down. "Chuck, I'm going to call it a day. I know this is a normal work day for you, but don't stay too late."

"Doc and I will keep at it so he can get the COD for you on Angela and this new guy, as soon as possible. We know it matters. About to run the prints and DNA on the guy in the morgue."

"Thanks, Chuck. Just call me if you need me. Otherwise, I'm going to try and stay away until Monday."

"Good plan." He stopped. "Oh, and Quinn, thanks for fixing my schedule so I can have Tuesdays and Wednesdays off. I appreciate it."

"I appreciate you and want to keep you. Do remember to step away—we must or we lose focus. Besides, you deserve to have some personal time. I'll let you know when I'm headed out." She walked in her office, turned on her desk lamp, and her computer. While her computer booted up, she sent a text on her personal phone: "Headed home. You?"

"Mine or urs?" came the reply from Billy.

"Will call in 30."

"OK."

Quinn smiled, focused on her messages and emails and had them answered in less than twenty minutes. She had written her preliminary summary on Angela's car as she and George completed the board; she needed only to let the Chief know where they were in Angela's death. She leaned back, closed her eyes, and sat up to reread what she was sending the Chief. *Okay, clear, concise, to the point. No frills.* She clicked "send" and closed out her computer.

Standing in her door she said, "Any luck on those prints yet?"

"Even computers take time, Quinn."

"Right. Outta here, Chuck. Call if you need me."

"Only if a life hangs in the balance. Go enjoy yours."

"10-4." Quinn closed the lab door behind her. She had her personal phone out ready to call Billy as soon as she got in her SUV.

"Hey lovely lady, I'm closer to your place than mine. That make a difference to you?"

"See you when you get here. I'll figure out something for supper."

"I could take you somewhere nice to eat."

"Then I'd have to change clothes."

"Well, we can't have that now, can we? See you shortly."

"Counting on it." She hung up and realized she was humming. *Maybe I am falling in love.*

Late Lunch and the Beach

Andrew Culbert III had made arrangements with the small open air café tucked into a cove near his condo building to be closed for a private gathering this weekend—just for him, Kelly, and the kids. The owner was only too happy to agree given the price Andrew was willing to pay—and the fact it was between tourist seasons. Locals didn't eat here.

"Andrew, the food was excellent. Why aren't there more people who know about this place?" Kelly watched the children playing in the sand just at the edge of the café.

"That's the joy of small island living in the Caribbean."

"What is?"

He realized he was working hard not to lie to Kelly, but at the same time he couldn't tell her what was going on; at least he thought he *shouldn't* tell her what was happening. *Why did Dad keep Mom out of anything to do with the business? What if something happens to me? Who will continue it? Kelly…* He felt her hand on his arm.

He glanced over. "What, honey?"

"Andrew," Kelly stood. He knew the tone of voice was meant to get his total attention. "I am taking the children back to the condo. Suzanne will watch them. Then you and I are going to talk." She leaned in and stared into his eyes. "I mean *really* talk. Whatever is going on affects all of us, and you need to be prepared to tell me everything." She pushed in her chair. "And, I *mean* it."

She moved over to the children, bent down, and brushed the sand off their legs and bottoms. "Come on, sweet children," she tried to put a smile in her voice. "Let's go." She hoisted her daughter to her hip, took her son's hand, and headed to the SUV parked outside the café.

The driver opened the rear door and secured the children in their car seats.

Andrew was on his feet. He walked to the owner, shrugged his shoulders, and tried to sound perplexed about his wife walking away—he knew the man had been watching them. "I'll send the driver for our evening meal around 6:00 PM. Then you go enjoy the evening off."

"Yes, sir. You can call anytime. Thank you, sir." The man shook Andrew's hand. His warm Caribbean smile of gleaming white teeth seemed to mock Andrew.

Andrew moved quickly out to the SUV and got in the front.

"Sir, the lady said she would like to return to the condo."

Andrew turned to Kelly. She was totally engrossed in the children and did not look at him.

Spring Afternoon in the Mountains

Quinn brushed out her hair, took a quick shower, changed into jeans and a polo shirt and had her head in the refrigerator looking for something to fix for supper when she heard three raps on the front door and the chirp of a code entered in the lock. She closed the fridge door and moved over to the cased opening between the living room and great room. She tucked herself back so she wouldn't be seen. As Billy's footsteps approached, she watched the floor. She saw the toe of his shoe step across the threshold, turned, and threw her arms out to hug him.

Billy jumped back and his hand automatically went to his sidearm before he processed what was happening.

Quinn saw the full alert look on his face and doubled over laughing.

He put his arms around her waist and twirled her in the wide doorway. "Hey! It is not nice...or safe, to fool with a cop like that." He grinned.

Quinn feigned kicking her legs trying to get loose.

Billy stopped and pulled her into a hug. "Playful this afternoon, are you?"

"Humor me. I was an only child."

"Me, too, but..."

"But, what? Tell me you didn't want to have someone at home to play hide-and-go-seek with?"

"I surrender, I surrender." He squeezed her hand. "I want a beer." He walked over and put his sidearm in the safe.

"Next I suppose you'll say you want to watch basketball."

He kissed her on the neck. "Or, I could think of other ways…"

"Slow down, fella." She pulled him to her and kissed him with a passion burning to get out of her.

He returned the kiss even more deeply. He pulled his head back. "*That is not the way to get me to slow down.*" He smiled at her. "Beer or…" He wiggled his eyebrows.

She moved over and opened the fridge.

He sighed. "Beer, it is. What can I get you?"

"Iced tea." *I am not a tease. Why didn't I lean into that moment?*

"Come on, I've wanted to sit on your front porch since the first time I saw it. Seems a perfect day." He took her hand and pretended he was pulling her against her will.

"Thanks, Billy. Have I told you how good you are for me?"

They headed for the front door. Settled in the rockers facing the park across the street, he reached over and put his hand on top of hers. "Okay, what's going on? This is not the detective I've come to know and love."

Quinn rocked, turned her hand up so her palm was facing his, and tightened her fingers through his. "Remember when I told you I think I have the ten-year-itch?"

"Yeah, like the seven-year marriage itch?"

"Yeah, I guess." She turned to look at him. "I've changed jobs and I love my new job; I just don't feel like I can get a rhythm to it." She watched his face in profile—he had a sharp angular chin and aquiline nose.

He turned toward her and smiled as he tightened his fingers in hers. "Quinn, I love you. I want to support you in whatever you need…"

"But…your patience is wearing thin?"

He leaned over and put his finger on her lips. "Shh…this isn't a contest. It's life. Life is messy; our work is messier." He saw her nod. "What's eating at you?"

She rocked…and rocked…and rocked. She felt the catch in her throat as she tried to speak. "I can't fix it. I want to fix things."

"Some things can't be fixed."

"Death. That's a big one." She rocked. "There's a twenty-four-year-old young woman lying in the morgue whose biggest worry three days ago was how long it would take her to transfer funds to buy mountain property she was trying to preserve."

They rocked in silence.

"Quinn," Billy spoke softly. "Want an observation from someone doing this for a while?"

"Anytime."

"We grow up being told that death is part of life. It is. What we learn in our line of work is that death can also be ugly, cruel, vicious and other adjectives most folks don't want to even think about. The Sheriff helped me learn you have to deal with the situation at hand, do the best you can to solve the crime or problem, set it aside, and move on. There will be another death, another day, and the ones *we* get—won't be pretty."

Quinn looked at him. Her hazel eyes showed deep sorrow.

Billy could see the pain behind her eyes—it made his heart ache. He leaned towards her. "And you lived the worst at an age no one should have to." He kissed her hand and then leaned back and rocked.

"Thanks, Billy. Perspective. Life is all about perspective, isn't it?"

Billy sat up straight in his rocker. "It is. So, here's some perspective. It's a beautiful late spring afternoon and the dogwoods are starting to bloom; we have this time—this moment. So, let's go find supper someplace."

She jumped up, pulled him to his feet, kissed him quickly and said, "Let's go."

On a Mountaintop

The portable buildings on Andrew Culbert's mountain property east of Knoxville had nondescript passageways connecting them. Each building had been roofed with shingles in multi-colors, like someone had bought them at a fire sale and slapped them on—they were intended to make the buildings blend into the trees.

"The boss ain't kidding. Get this production ramped up now." Mr. S.'s right hand man was wielding his power now that the boss had gone back north to the city.

"Yeah, yeah, working on it." The chemist never looked up from his lab table. Even with a doctoral degree from a prestigious university, he had lost one too many jobs for his substance abuse. He preferred to keep his head down at this point in his life.

"He paid good money to get all the mechanical things you need to do this work. He ain't getting no more people. Got it?"

"You get what you pay for." The chemist still didn't look up.

A fist slammed on the stainless steel table. "Dammit! Look at me, man."

"Yeah?" The chemist lifted his head in slow motion and stared through weary eyes at the man he considered a thug.

"Mr. S. wants you ready to triple the production as soon as he gets the land—and that's happening soon. Got it?"

"Yeah." The chemist looked back down at his lab table. He would walk the production machines in a few hours. The fine powder coming out at the end of the line ran into machines which put them into gel caps, which put them individually in plastic bubble packs—just like every other pill you could buy at your local pharmacy. The four folks now working in the last portable building putting the bubble packs in boxes thought they were working for a "mom and pop" vitamin plant. The part the chemist didn't want to think about was the chemicals in the aromatics he was producing as his side project—*death or personal fortune, which will I receive?*

"Alright, you bum, get on with it. When I check back, I want a plan. Got it?"

The chemist didn't respond. He did wonder where his brother had gone. He hadn't seen him since he tore out of here on Thursday.

Talk to Me

"Honey, I told you we could go shopping. Suzanne has the kids. What do you say?" The nanny had taken the children for a bath and playtime before she'd feed them supper. They would be asleep by seven PM and Andrew hoped Kelly would be less stressed.

"I don't want to go shopping. We have clothes with us, a washer and dryer, and no one other than Suzanne to see us even if we go stark naked. Please stop trying to avoid talking with me." Her tone carried an edge he hadn't heard since she was studying for her CPA exams.

He knew she meant business. *You didn't marry her because she was a dumb blond. You've let her desire—our desire—for her to be home with the kids make you act like you married a woman who couldn't think.*

Kelly propped her feet up on the coffee table—something she would not have done at home. She crossed her arms in a deliberate show of resolve. The tumbler of bourbon he had in his hand did not escape her notice. "Spill, Andrew."

Andrew leaned forward and put his elbows on his knees swirling the ice in his drink as he stared into the glass. "Kelly, I admit I've followed my dad's path in keeping you out of the business—I, too, wanted you to be with the kids, but I also miss those head-to-head business problems we solved together in graduate school." He glanced up at her.

Kelly continued to look at him; she said nothing.

"Up until now..." he paused, took a swig of his drink, slid back on the sofa, and looked out to the sea. "Up until now, business has been pretty routine and good. Folks buy mountain property for different reasons; some want an escape from the cities, some are moving out of cities...especially younger people who can work remotely, some like last year's intern, Angela, want to preserve..."

"Andrew, spare me the explanations. I know all that. I want to know what is going on with my husband."

He knew she was aware, even if the business had a downturn, they were set for life between his inheritance and her trust fund. "I'm being blackmailed..." He screwed up his eyes.

"For what? Are you breaking the law? Having an affair? Gambling? What, Andrew?" Her voice rose to a fever pitch.

Andrew expected Suzanne to come running to see if everything was okay. He stood and walked to the sliding glass doors. In a voice so quiet he could barely be heard, he said, "Kelly, I have never cheated on you...never will. I am not physically ill. I have never knowingly broken the law, cheated anyone, or even tried to make an outrageous profit. I don't know why this is..." He turned and saw she had moved to another chair and was watching him. He walked to the chair opposite her, sat down, put his face in his hands and shook from head to foot.

Kelly stood and moved over to him, pushed his hands aside, and sat in his lap.

He pulled her tightly to him and wept.

She held him and rocked slowly back and forth.

End of the Day

"This was a great idea, Billy." Quinn took a bite of a hushpuppy.

"Here to please." Billy and Quinn had set out with no destination and ended up at Pawpaw's Catfish Kitchen on US 321 outside of Pigeon Forge.

"You do it well."

He reached across the table and touched the back of her hand. "It will sink in sooner or later that I love you, care about you, and I am not going..."

"Away. I know. Thanks."

"Did you like the alligator bites?"

"Tasted like chicken." She raised her eyebrow. "Isn't that what folks say?"

"I suppose some do. Since I've never met an alligator in person, I don't know what they're supposed to taste like." A grin spread across his face. He watched her to see if she was beginning to relax. "I do know I like the alligator bites these folks make. How's the gumbo?"

"As good as I ever had in New Orleans."

"Spend a lot of time there?"

"From time to time. Worked for Immigration Enforcement, remember? Lots of regional meetings to attend—sometimes even in fun places."

"Yeah, I kinda like it when I get to go to a meeting in Nashville."

"Same difference, right? Good food and good music."

"Speaking of good music, let's go find some after supper."

She laughed. "You're joking, right?"

"Absolutely not. Night on the town, or in the country, as it were."

"You're on." She tipped her spoon towards him in a toast and then finished her gumbo.

It was close to midnight when they pulled into her driveway. Billy walked her to the door and stopped.

"Aren't you staying over?" She held onto his hand.

He leaned in and kissed her. "Fighting every impulse in my body not to go to the Valley, but duty calls early tomorrow."

"I'll get up with you, at whatever hour, to make sure you're home in time." The pleading in her hazel eyes belied the tough lead detective beneath; she didn't like admitting her vulnerabilities.

He pushed her in the door. "How about I help you get to sleep? Then I'll slip out and call you tomorrow?"

She wrapped her arms around his neck. "I'll take whatever I can get. I love...I'd love to have you stay for whatever time you can."

Her self-correction was not lost on Billy. *You'll get there, Quinn. I'm a patient man.*

Chapter 11

You can't do your job and be afraid.
Meryl Streep

Awake

"Isaacs." Holding her secure phone, she rolled over to see the edges of sunlight around her window shades and the clock face staring at her: *Sunday 11:14 AM*. She sat straight up in bed.

"Quinn, Chuck here. Got a minute?"

"Sure." She swung her feet over the edge of the bed as she noticed the left side crumpled, but no Billy.

"I know I told you I'd only call if a life hung in the balance; it doesn't, but solving a crime might."

"Give it to me." She tried not to sound agitated.

"We got a hit on the fingerprints on the dash of Angela Topping's car and the DNA from the guy in the morgue."

"Same?"

"No. The prints belong to a guy from Illinois with a rap sheet long enough to...well, he's a crook. The DNA..."

"Chuck, I'm on my way. Easier for me to see it. Be there shortly." She hung up, sent a text to George.

"Info: print and DNA hit. I'm on it."

There was an immediate response. "B there in 30."

Quinn set her phone down, double-checked that it was actually after 11:00 and her brain processed that it was Sunday. She headed for the bathroom to shower. *I don't know the last time I slept so well or for so long.* She turned to look at herself in the mirror—she saw a piece of paper taped to it.

"Morning, sunshine. Hope you slept well." A squiggly heart was drawn beneath it.

Oh, and you can be a romantic, too, Billy Williams. How can I resist? She had no idea what time he left, but she remembered him helping her get to sleep.

She was at the Station at 11:40 AM and headed in the back door when she heard her name. She turned to see George striding across what they fondly called "the flat." It was the empty pavement between the parking at the back of the Station for the Chief and lead officers and the outbuildings for the mechanics and storage.

"Anything to share?"

"I stopped Chuck mid-sentence. Told him it was easier to see and hear it than try to match up the information in my head. If you don't mind getting us coffee, I'll get the workroom and computer ready to go."

"On it." He held up a stack of blue boxes tied with a lovely ribbon each a bit larger than the one from the day before. "Carrie included Chuck and Doc in this little treat: croissants."

"Oh my gosh, be still my heart. See you soon."

Quinn unlocked the lab door and didn't see Chuck at his worktable. "Chuck?" Nothing. She turned to go across the hall and almost knocked him down.

"Oh, hey, Quinn."

"Hey, yourself. George is here, too. Workroom in five?"

"Let me grab coffee. I'll be there."

"Go get some good coffee...well, better than you'll get in the old coffee pot."

"Come hither, boss." Chuck stepped in and pointed to a new coffee pot sitting on the counter. "Pods and all. No more of my cheap coffee. Want some?"

She smiled. "George is bringing me some. A little birdie told me he has a treat too."

"Oh, goodie. Oh, goodie. From Carrie?" Chuck was bouncing like a school boy.

"Not for me to say. See you in five." She was across the hall entering the code in the keypad when George came down the hall. She held the door open for him.

"And who says chivalry is dead?"

Quinn paused. "Hmmmm...is chivalry a gender neutral concept?"

"Detective Isaacs, please. Not this morning."

"You're right." She sat and logged into the computer.

"Text from Doc. He's not here this morning. He can be in about two if we need him."

"Pretty sure Chuck is our source for now." Quinn entered the last digit of her access code in the computer.

"Did someone call my name?" Chuck swung the door wide open and was followed in by the Chief.

Quinn immediately stood. "Good morning, ma'am."

"Take it easy. Chuck's report suggested we might have some info on our two DBs. I was in the building so thought I'd stop in."

"Welcome anytime, ma'am." Quinn sat.

"If you pull up the following reports..." Chuck gave Quinn the identifiers.

"Got them. Ready, George?"

He held up his black dry erase marker.

Chuck walked over to the screen and pointed to the mugshot of the man whose prints were a match to the dashboard prints in Angela's car.

"Alfred Dunn, Also Known As 'Al, Lefty, Dunce,' AKA...Do you want the rest of the aliases read?"

They all shook their heads in a resounding "No."

George snickered. "Well, how much better can a Sunday morning in springtime be than when you have a suspect known as 'Dunce?'" He stiffened when he remembered the Chief was in the room; he glanced over and saw she was suppressing a smile.

"Last known whereabouts?" Quinn wanted answers.

"Unknown according to the report. Met his probationary period, well actually half of it, which got him off of probation four years ago." Chuck was reading the report aloud.

Quinn studied the mugshot. "Well, it doesn't look as if Mr. Dunn has changed his ways. You said the DNA belonging to the man in the morgue has been identified?" Quinn wanted to know who he was.

"Yes, ma'am. He's from Kentucky. Bunch of petty theft, drug use, but no assault, no felony, or deadly weapon records."

"Does he have a name?" George was poised to write the name next to the truck which he had moved from the "Questions" list.

"Sammy Patten, no current address."

"Prison time?" Quinn was scanning the report.

"County jail, nothing more than thirty days." Chuck pointed to the report.

The Chief opened the door.

They all stopped and looked at her.

"Keep up the good work. I look forward to your report." The door closed quietly behind her.

"George..." Quinn looked at the side-by-side reports on the screen and the information on the white board. "Think it's likely..." She picked up her cup of coffee.

"What?"

Chuck looked from one to the other.

"Not sure." Quinn stood and paced. *Two men from disparate places...*

"Chuck, where in Illinois is Dunn from?"

"Last known address was in a small town in southern Illinois—Cairo." Chuck furrowed his brow. "Isn't that like in Egypt?"

Quinn ignored his question. "Patten?"

"Rural route address in Kentucky across the river from Metropolis, Illinois. I looked it up."

Quinn pulled up a map of southern Illinois. "Well, not neighbors, but not so far as crime flies. Coincidence, gentlemen?"

"Don't believe in them, myself." George had pulled up a chair and was straddling it with the back of the chair to his chest. He sipped his coffee.

"Okay, let's make a plan." Quinn took one of the blue boxes and handed it to Chuck. She opened the other; she was starving.

Cloudy Day on the Island

"Andrew, why isn't anyone else staying here?" The afternoon sun sparkled against the blue-green of the sea as it splashed against the brilliant white sand, leaving trails of foam on its way out. They sat on the balcony sipping a glass of wine.

Last night he hadn't told her quite everything about the land offer, and didn't know if he could ever bring himself to tell her everything, but this he answered. "Dad bought this building years ago and had it completely modernized. It was finished just before he passed away. I never had the heart to do anything with it. He loved having the absolute seclusion here." *And now I'm grateful for it if I don't see another drone today.*

"Thanks for cancelling the yacht today." She smiled at him.

"Would you like to go tomorrow?"

"Not really. If this place was special to Daddy Andy, then let's just enjoy it."

"There's an indoor pool out back which you haven't seen yet. It's below the children's playroom. We could take the kids down there and wear them out. That should insure they sleep soundly." He winked at her.

"Why, Andrew Culbert, the third. Would you suggest some hanky-panky on vacation?"

He moved toward her and pulled her into his arms. "Let me count the ways."

Suzanne appeared at the sliding doors. "Excuse me, Madam. The children would like you to come see their artwork."

Andrew stood up immediately, took Kelly's hand, and headed toward the playroom.

"Daddy, look!" Little Andy, Andrew Culbert IV, pointed to a finger painting done by his little sister.

Andrew picked up Anne and twirled her around. "Look at the artist." He smothered her with kisses. They stopped and Andrew knelt in front of the easel. "It's beautiful, my Anne. Look, Mommy, isn't it beautiful?"

"Exquisite. What did you create, Little Andy?" She took her son's hand.

"It's a picture looking out the window." He pointed to the back side of the easel toward a window across the room. Almost four, Little Andy was small for his age, but very observant and his language was well ahead of most children a year older than he was.

Both parents walked around the easel and saw broad brush strokes representing the bottom three panes of glass a child would see. Inside each pane, using a finer brush, were stick figures of birds, trees, and a man. Andrew did not even see the trees in the painting. He walked immediately to the window and knelt down to look out at Little Andy's height.

The only things you could see from that height were inside the compound wall. He knew there were no men on the property; the driver lived nearby.

"Nice job, son. Proud of you." He tried to be quiet as he closed the drapes on the window.

Kelly stared at Andrew—and back at the picture.

"Suzanne, thanks for coming to get us to see the children's work."

He turned to his children. "Okay, kiddos. Let's go watch a movie. Then we'll have supper and soon it will be bath time." He swooped Anne up into his arms and saw Kelly take Little Andy's hand.

He looked over his shoulder. "Enjoy some quiet time, Suzanne. We'll feed the kids." He walked out the door and down the hall.

"This way, Kelly." He headed to a large set of French doors at the far end of the hall from the children's rooms. They entered a media room to rival any small town theater.

"Andrew, this is amazing: a real theater. It's far beyond our media room at home."

"You want this at home? We'll do it." He smiled at her and set Anne on the middle movie recliner seat. Kelly put Little Andy beside Anne and sat to his right. Andrew sat in the seat to the left of Anne.

Their children between them, Andy spoke into the remote and a list of children's movies appeared.

"*Dumbo*, Daddy, please."

"'*Dumbo*, it is, my son." Andrew lowered the lights as the movie started and leaned back holding his daughter's hand. *I am* the dumb one, son. *I have to figure out how to keep you safe.*

It All Takes Time

Quinn issued an All-Points Bulletin on Alfred Dunn and made sure his mug shot was clear. Then she contacted his last known probation officer.

"Certainly you may call me back." Quinn hung up her office phone.

"Isaacs."

"Detective, I have a call for you from Illinois."

"Put it through. Thanks."

"10-4."

"Isaacs."

"Detective, thanks for letting me verify. I'm not sure how much help I will be. You understand I am limited in what I can share without a warrant."

"We have a formal APB out for Mr. Dunn and a warrant will be forthcoming as a person of interest in the death of a twenty-four-year-old woman."

She heard the low whistle.

"That bad?"

"That bad." Quinn looked at her parents' photo on the wall.

"How can I help?"

"Worst offense known to you?"

"Assault with bodily injury."

"Weapons?"

"Never found, always suspected."

"Illinois is a long state. His last known address was in Cairo. Origin?"

"Birth certificate shows a suburb of Chicago, but he's long been suspected in running drugs down I-57 into the south. Are you anywhere near I-57?"

"No, but most of that traffic hits I-24 and some fans off on to I-40 which heads our way. I'm in east Tennessee."

"I suppose you can get most anywhere if you're motivated."

"That's true. As requested, I sent you the mug shot we have and I would appreciate an appraisal of the likeness to the last time you saw him."

"Pretty spot on. He's not bad looking if you can get past the mean. He's pretty good at keeping his mouth shut, and there's talk he's connected with a group out of Detroit, Chicago, and who knows where else, running home-made drugs."

"Like methamphetamines?"

"The word I heard was it's more lethal than that."

"Know a detective somewhere I can talk to about it?"

"Woman out of Chicago last I knew. I can get her name and send it to you."

"Would appreciate it."

"Don't know what I else I can tell you. Once they're released from parole, we let them go—got more than enough to manage right behind them."

"No doubt. No doubt. Thank you for your help and I'll be in touch if there are any further questions. Anything occurs to you, please reach out."

"Sure thing, Detective Isaacs. You have a good day now."

"Likewise." Quinn hung up the phone and realized she'd been pacing—a habit she had developed when she was thinking. *I acted like I knew what I was doing.* She promptly dialed the Sheriff's Station in the Valley.

"Detective Coleman, please."

"Coleman."

"Detective, this is Quinn Isaacs in Round City. Do you have a minute?"

"Yes, ma'am."

"Just wanted you to know we've identified the man in the red truck. He's got a string a petty crimes and drug use in southern Illinois and northern Kentucky. That's all we know at the moment."

"Thanks for letting me know. I'm sure you'll get to the bottom of it."

"We'll try. Thanks for your early work on this. I hope you have a good day."

"You, too. Ma'am." *She kept her word.* He started whistling.

Quinn stopped pacing and her look turned serious when she saw the buzzing phone was the District Attorney.

"Isaacs. Hey, Peggy. What's the word?"

"Read your secure message. Details to help me justify a warrant."

Quinn gave her the specifics including Dunn's criminal history and the location of the fingerprints in Angela's car. "It's all in the report I sent you."

"On it. Given a DB I don't think a judge is going to want to be bothered today. Your APB will get eyes out, and I'll work on a judge first thing in the morning. Mondays can be a slow calendar day for some judges."

"Thanks, Peggy. Appreciate it. Enjoy the rest of your day."

"Yeah, that's a thing in our lives, isn't it?" The sarcasm in Peggy's voice was evident.

"We're way overdue for lunch."

"Soon. Soon." She hung up.

Quinn looked at the phone and set it down. She felt a presence in her doorway.

"Quinn?" Chuck had his hand raised like a student.

"Chuck?"

"Ha! Well, I'm headed home and I just wanted to make sure you don't need me anymore today."

"Outta here, young man. Go home and celebrate a day of good work in crime fighting. We've identified one potential suspect, and may have one in the morgue in the death of a very young woman who to all appearances was trying to do some good in the world. Well done."

"Aww. Thanks, Quinn. Happy to help. See you tomorrow."

"That you will. Good night."

She saw it was a little after 5:00 PM She stood up and went down the hall to the women's room and stopped back in the workroom for one more look at the board. She picked up a green dry erase marker wanting it different from the ones George had been using. She stepped back and studied the crime board. *George is really good at mapping a crime. I need to make sure we get some pictures of these two men.* Next to Dunn's name she wrote to one side: possible interstate trafficking in narcotics. She set down the marker, made sure the technology was all turned off, turned off the lights, and went out the door. She had a satisfied smile at the click on the door.

George had left an hour ago. She knew he'd read her report on the call to the probation officer. Back in her office she sat in the visitor's chair in her small space and looked closer at the pictures of her parents and grandmother on her wall. She took her personal phone out of her pocket.

"*Hola, mi hija. ¿Cómo estás?*"

"*Hola, mi Madre.* I'm fine, thanks. You were on my mind and I wanted to say hello. Am I interrupting anything?"

"Not at all, my dear. How is your Sunday?"

"Busy, but good. Are you sitting down?"

"Oh, do tell me you're in love."

Quinn smiled. "I'm in a big like, that's for sure."

"That fine Mr. Williams?"

"Yes, Mother. Billy. That's not why I asked if you were sitting down."

"Then do tell."

Quinn knew her mother tried to have casual conversations; it just didn't come easily for her. "I slept until 11:15 this morning. Can you believe it?"

"And, darling, what time did you go to bed?"

Quinn decided not to answer the question as it was asked. "I was asleep by a little after midnight."

"Then I'd say you must have needed it. Good for you. Now, tell me. What's going on with your young man?"

"Mother, Billy is forty-two years old. Yes, young in the scheme of life, but not a high school boyfriend."

"When you reach my age, you'll understand the use of young in someone over thirty lessens the age you carry yourself."

"Good point, Mother. Hadn't thought of it that way. Anyway, Billy and I have managed to get together a few times recently. We went out to supper and out to listen to music last night. We both have busy jobs and time can be scarce." She paused. "He is a wood turner."

"A what?"

"He turns wood on a lathe. He makes bowls and he's helping me make a goblet."

"A wooden goblet? Whatever for?"

"A very tall glass of wine, Mother. A very tall glass of wine."

"Won't the wine stain the wood?"

Quinn could almost hear her mother's heart pounding.

"I suspect I'll use it as an art piece; you know, to admire my talent."

"That's better. Hold on, your father wants to speak to you."

"*Hola, Papa.*"

"*Hola, Quinn.*"

"How are you, Daddy?" Today she needed him to be her daddy.

"Always better for speaking with my talented and lovely daughter. How is the business of fighting crime?"

Quinn almost dropped the phone. Her father had never asked her about her work. Never.

"We take small successes in fighting crime with some satisfaction. Hard to nail too many big successes, but it happens occasionally. Thanks for asking."

"We care about your well-being."

"I know, Daddy. I know. I'm grateful. I see it's almost cocktail time, so have a toast to me. I love you both."

She heard her parents simultaneously tell her they loved her before the call ended. She smiled. *Well, Miss Quinn. Maybe you are the one who never wanted to talk to your parents about crime fighting. Maybe a little...* Her secure line rang.

"Isaacs."

"Doc here. Guess you didn't need me to come in earlier. I can come in now if you need me."

"We're good. Any chance we're close to a final cause of death of Angela Topping?"

"Putting it together now. Should have it for you in the morning."

"Thanks, Doc. I'll talk to you then about the man in your morgue. Stay home and enjoy the rest of this fine spring day."

"You, too, Quinn. You, too." The line went silent.

Well, one more call and the day would be complete. Wait, he's on duty today. Just go home, Quinn. You made a huge step in telling your mother you're in a 'big like.'

Chapter 12

It's not worthy of a human being to give up.
Alva Myrdal

Sunday Evening in the Islands

Kelly sat with her feet tucked under her on the sofa staring at the fire which took the chill off the early spring evening.

"Andrew, does this man have something on you to force you to execute the sale of your land?"

"No."

"Then why are you so worried about it? Everyone has the right to sell property at their own discretion. Did he make you an offer you can't refuse?" She couldn't imagine any offer they would need or want which would cause him to give up his family land—any of it.

"It feels that way."

"Why?" She turned on the sofa to look at him; he was stretched out with his feet on the coffee table swirling the ice in his tumbler of bourbon. "*Why, Andrew?*"

He hesitated. *It's her life. I'll protect her forever, but do I have the right to shield her from a threat to her and the kids?* He stared into the fire.

Kelly stood up and took the bourbon out of Andrew's hand. She moved his feet off the coffee table and sat on it facing him. "Now, Andrew. Or I swear to you even as much as I hate to fly, I will be on that plane home with the children faster than you can say, 'Stop.'"

He patted the sofa next to him.

She moved over beside him and sat cross-legged facing him.

He told her everything—only averting her gaze when he described the video showing her and the children. He stopped short of telling her he had worn a gun to the meeting.

She took his hands. "Look at me, Andrew. We are getting on that plane..." she looked out at the rapidly approaching night sky. "We are getting on that plane at the crack of dawn, and here's what we're going to do." She had always been very logical and methodical in everything she did. She outlined her plan and did not give him room to argue. "Questions?"

Andrew stood and walked to the sliding glass doors and opened them. The cove was on the west side of the island and the setting sun provided a brilliance of oranges and yellow against the blue-green of the sea. He saw the movement just seconds before the drone crashed into him.

The Mountain Villages

Marjorie Topping liked Sunday evenings when Maria stayed in her private quarters. She still had not seen the remains of her granddaughter and wasn't sure she wanted to. *Precious, Angela. Why? What happened to you?*

"Please leave a message..." She turned at the chirp of the recording on her home phone. She didn't use her landline except for the convenience of talking on the phone and being on her computer at the same time. With call blocking, she knew the only person whose number would ring through was her husband's nephew, Peter. She waited.

"Aunt Marjorie, it's Peter. Long time no talk. Give me a call. I'm trying to track down Angela. Have you heard..."

She picked up the phone. "Good evening, Peter."

"Auntie, how are you?" The feigned interest dripped from his lips.

"Well enough, thank you. How may I help you?" She didn't like Peter. Although he graduated from law school, she suspected someone got him through. He never passed the bar— she'd never said that aloud to anyone. Peter was fifty and never married, and now she and he were the last to carry the name of the Topping family of Boston and Chicago. She hated that he was her only living relative, even though he was legally no longer related to her—since her husband's death. *I choose to focus on being the last Eldridge from Chicago.*

"Heard from Angela lately?"

Marjorie's skin crawled. *I am not telling you anything about Angela.* "Is there something you would like me to tell her?"

"Yeah, sure. Have her give me a call at 617-555…oh, she has the number. Be good to catch up. Might have a land deal for her to look into."

"Oh?"

"Come on, Auntie. No need to bother you with her campaign to save the mountains. She reached out to me and I just wanted to tell her what I'd learned." *And no way you'll hear from me how often I'm in contact with Angela—you'd be real surprised.*

"Peter, please give me that number in full. Perhaps you haven't heard from her because she had the number written incorrectly. It can happen you know."

"Sure. Sure." He gave her two numbers. "Ok, Auntie. You take care now. Stay in touch."

"Good evening, Peter." She hung up and felt an urgent need to fumigate the phone and the room.

She was surprised when she jumped at the ringing in the pocket on the side of her wheelchair. She lifted out the phone.

"Marjorie Topping." She recognized the caller ID.

"Ms. Topping, this is Detective Isaacs in Round City. I'm sorry not to have gotten back to you sooner…"

"Not a problem, Detective. Mr. Olson informed me of your visit with him to Angela's home. I assumed you would call when you had information for me."

"Would there be a convenient time for me to come over tomorrow? Our medical examiner should have the final report for us sometime in the morning, and I would like to meet with you in person."

"I will make time, Detective. What is convenient for you?"

"Two o'clock?" Quinn wanted to make sure Dr. Walters would have time to get in and go over what they knew at this point. She was hopeful there would be a final cause of death statement so they could release Angela to her grandmother.

"I'll see you then. I'll notify the guard. Will Detective Williams be with you?"

It caught Quinn by surprise. "If I may, I'll let you know tomorrow if anyone is accompanying me."

"That will be fine. Anything else, Detective?"

"No, ma'am. I will see you at two tomorrow. Thank you for your time."

"See you then." Marjorie Topping ended the call, stared at the phone, and then back at her desk phone. *What is Peter up to?*

Sunday Evening in the Mountains

Quinn stretched, stood up from the desk in her home office, and walked into the kitchen. She was hungry, but couldn't decide what to eat. She looked up; it was already 7:30 PM She opened the fridge and shook her head. *You're pathetic. What is there here worth eating?* She opened the freezer and her eyes lit up. *Soup and toast.* She pulled out the frozen soup and whole wheat bread. She took a slice of bread and put the loaf back in the freezer. She hit "5" on the microwave to start the soup defrosting and reheating.

She grabbed a towel to dry her hands before she reached for her ringing house phone. Then she decided to let it go to voice mail.

"Hola, mi hija."

Quinn grabbed the phone. She could not understand why her mother insisted on calling the house phone. *Hmmm...maybe she just wants to leave a message.* "Hola."

"Oh, hello dear. I was trying not to disturb you."

"No problem, Mother. What's up?"

"After our call earlier, your father and I were discussing Easter. You do know it's next weekend?"

She didn't know. "Thanks for the reminder."

"Quinn, your father and I would love to have you and Mr. Willia...Billy, come for the weekend. Do you think that is possible?"

"Thanks for the invitation…"

"Oh, I know you can't always be sure of your schedule, but please try." There was a pleading Quinn wasn't sure she'd heard in her mother's voice before.

What's this all about? "I'll be there barring anything related to work. I will extend the invitation to Billy."

"Lovely. We hope to see you. *Te amo.*"

"Love you, too, Mother." Quinn held the phone out and stared at it. *Did my mother just tell me she loved me without me saying it first?* She pulled out a kitchen stool. *What is going on? First, Daddy asks about my work and now this?* Quinn shook her head from side to side. *It has to be me who is off-kilter.*

Without thinking she picked up the ringing mobile phone. "Isaacs."

"Williams."

"Hey! What's new?" She looked to see which phone she had answered. As much as she would like to have her personal and secure number on the same device, she knew it was not a good idea. She smiled at her personal phone.

"Minor crime, thankfully, but no less requirement for attention to detail."

"I hear you."

"How was your day?"

"I slept until after eleven this morning."

He whistled. "Really? Good for you."

"Really. Must have been the help I had getting to sleep last night." She smiled thinking of him.

"My pleasure."

"Mutual, I hope." She tried to make sure her voice didn't sound desperate.

"Yes, ma'am." He dragged out the 'yes.'

She smiled. "Found a note on my mirror. My ace detective skills identified the handwriting."

"Oh?"

"Yes, but the drawing was a bit elusive."

"Can't have everything. Does the line, 'it's the thought that counts' serve in my defense?"

"No defense required. I'll take any drawing you want to leave. It was sweet. Thanks, Billy."

"Tell me what you're doing."

The beep on her microwave caused her to turn her head. "I'm stirring some chicken soup and I'm going to make a piece of toast. Have you eaten?"

"I'll rustle up something when I get out of here. I have an interrogation of a teenager who cleverly got into an empty cabin, but wasn't clever enough to know the owners had an alarm linked to a system which notifies our Station."

"Oh, don't be too hard on him."

"Her."

"Her? Well, shame on me." She laughed. "I want gender neutral pronouns. It takes too much thinking to have a conversation."

"Not really. I just didn't want to miss the chance to catch the master at her game."

She laughed. "Fair enough. Fair enough." She put three more minutes on the microwave and sat down again. "Have I told you lately how much I enjoy your company?"

"Just did." The smile in his voice carried through to her.

"Oh, by the way, my mother just called. We're invited for Easter weekend in Knoxville."

"When is that?"

"Easter?"

"Yes."

"Next weekend. Haven't you put in your order with the Easter bunny?"

"I can't remember the last time I had an Easter basket." He paused. "So, are we going?"

"Can you?"

"I'm not on duty, unless..."

"Duty calls. I get it and so do my folks." She hesitated. She had never really talked about her parents to Billy...really anyone. "I had the surprise of my life today."

"What's that?"

"My daddy asked about my work."

"He did?"

"Yes. Nothing specific. Just 'how's the crime fighting going?'"

"Is that a first?"

"In ten years. Yes."

"How do you feel about it?"

There was silence.

"Quinn, are you okay?"

"Yes, yes, I'm fine. I was thinking about my reaction when he asked me, and my response to your question."

"And?"

"And, I think I've kept them from asking me. Kinda that control freak thing I'm working to abandon."

"Control freak? Are you serious?"

"Yes." Her voice was flat.

"Listen to me, Quinn. I don't know you well personally yet, although I am eager to know more, and maybe in your personal life you compartmentalize and are a control freak, but everything...do you hear me—everything I've seen in your professional life, you are the consummate team leader and team player—that is not a control freak."

"Billy Williams, you are so good for me. I love that you take the time to actually have a conversation with me."

And I'm looking forward to you saying 'I love you'—instead of 'I love that...'

The microwave beeped.

"Sounds like soup's on. Want to eat and call me back?"

"You okay with that?" Quinn opened the microwave door.

"Anytime. I'll finish up what I'm doing here and head home; most likely it'll be an hour- and-a-half or so. Call sometime before you go to sleep. I love you." He said it naturally, without making a declarative statement of it.

She noticed. "Thanks, Billy. Talk to you soon."

In the Lab

The chemist knew everyone else was gone from the buildings. He had set up a small lab in the building closest to his official laboratory. It was locked to keep others from stumbling on the aromatics he was trying to develop. He was headed there. The thug had left, and it was none too soon as far as the chemist was concerned. He looked for his phone which he was always misplacing; he found it and dialed his brother's phone.

Come on, Bro. Answer. His brother did not have voice mail set up and the chemist knew why. After ten rings, he touched the red button to end the call and set the phone down.

He unlocked the double locks on the passage into his private lab. He had the front of it set up as a storage for chemicals—harmless ones, but no one else knew that. He loved seeing the biochemical hazard sign on the outside door; it made the thug and his boss move past the door with lightning speed the few times they'd been here.

He stepped down on something when he opened the inner door. *What the hell?* He heard the crunch. The lights on now, he looked down and saw a phone. He picked it up and saw he had all but crushed it with his heel. *Well, Bro, guess this is why I haven't heard from you. How the hell did you get in here?* He threw the phone against the wall. *Dammit, how do I reach you now?*

Will Sleep Come?

Soup and toast finished and the dishwasher running after several days of dishes being left in it, Quinn showered and put on her nightgown. *I'm happy for spring and not needing a robe.* She stretched her arms high over her head, let out a long sigh, and headed for her home office.

She leaned her head back on her desk chair and laid out a plan for how she would try to simplify what was currently known about Angela. *Lots of data points need to be connected, but what is the simplest line to connect them?*

She started making notes on the information they currently had; a sort of review test for herself.

Angela:

Buys land and puts into conservatorship

Last known sighting 5:00 PM Thursday

Found Friday morning at Indian Flats Falls

Likely COD—chemical inhalation

Car found Saturday morning on Parkway

Ring with JT 1990 in red truck found near county line

How will I approach Ms. Topping about the ring?

Patten:

Found in red truck at county line

Truck belongs to whom

Cause of Death?

Dunn:

Prints in Angela's car

Connection to Patten? Angela Topping?

She looked at the list and picked up her secure phone and dialed.

"Williams."

"Isaacs."

"Work call?"

"For the moment. If you can spare one."

"Been home about thirty minutes. Even ate a salad. What's up?"

"Need a lesson."

"On?"

"Puzzles."

"I'll try."

"We have a board which has lots of detail and when I distill it, I come up with a few points of known information and many more questions. Is that typical?"

"The information or distilling it?"

"Either one? Maybe both?" She sounded like an apprentice unsure of which button to push on a machine.

"Are you able to give me a specific example without violating any privacy concerns?"

"You were in on the beginning of the case when we found Angela, and your Station has a finger in the pie, so to speak, with the grandmother—not yet ruled out as a suspect, finding the truck—so as far as I'm concerned, you can know it all. Guess I'll find out from an attorney down the road if I'm wrong."

"If one ever finds out you told me." His voice was professional and flat.

"Right. There's that."

They spent the next few minutes going through each of the elements she had put on her notes.

"Sounds pretty thorough to me, Quinn."

"I'm impressed with the graphic connections George put on the white board and it does paint a picture, but this list helps me to see what I know at the moment and where I might need to go."

"Then go with your gut."

She hesitated. "Is it just gut?"

"No. It's logic, and missing puzzle pieces, and a whole lot of still un-known."

"Billy, something tells me this is going to be a whole lot bigger than a twenty-four year old woman with a rich grandmother who died from inhaling chemicals."

"Could be. That said, you're part in it might not be."

"Come again."

"Not big on hypotheticals, normally, but let's play 'what if?'"

"Okay." She leaned back in her chair wishing she had a glass of wine instead of a glass of water.

"Angela meets Patten someplace, then they meet up for whatever they meet up for, and both tried some inhaler to let off a little tension. Seems that's the simplest hypothetical, right?"

"True." She dragged out the word. "Then how are Dunn's finger prints inside her car?"

"What do you think?"

Quinn sat quietly for a few minutes. "If I connect your hypothetical dots, *our* case could simply be drug overdose. Dunn could have come upon the car after Angela left it. It doesn't mean there isn't a dealer, distributor, network, behind the drug, but *our* case is the overdose."

"That's the simple hypothetical. Want another?" He rolled his shoulders. *This, Quinn Isaacs, is but one of the many reasons I am in love with you. You are smart.*

Quinn cleared her throat. "Can I take a bird-walk for a minute?"

"Sure, anywhere you want to go."

"I just realized one of the reasons I feel like I can't get a rhythm to this new job."

"What?"

"Information. In my job in Immigration Enforcement, for the most part, we had advance reports on movement of illegal immigrants. Sure, we might not have known the people moving them, or exact timelines, but by the time they got to east Tennessee we had some idea of what was headed our way. Granted we weren't always ready for things that happened—like with Chief Nelson, but we knew the caravan was enroute."

"Makes sense to me."

"The difference now is the crime has happened, or is in the process of happening, and we are going back trying to put together the pieces."

"Give the lady an A+! That's why it's called detective work."

She laughed. "Thanks, Billy. I'm good for now."

"Hanging up on me?"

"Yes, sir. If my gentleman friend wants to call me back on my personal phone, I'll answer it in five minutes. I want a glass of wine."

"Five minutes it is."

"10-4."

Feet propped up on her foot stool and a flick of the remote to start a fire, Quinn sipped her glass of Kim Crawford sauvignon blanc. She leaned her head back against the easy chair she loved to sit in; she could see the fire and the setting sun on her back garden. It was almost dark.

"Hello, there." Quinn all but cooed when she answered the phone.

"And to you. Comfy?"

"I am. Glass of wine, fire, setting sun, and a fine gentleman on the phone."

"Flattery will get you everywhere."

"Not trying to flatter. Stating facts. I'm a detective! Remember?"

"Ah, indeed I do. And a fine detective, I might note to the list of facts."

Quinn laughed. "How was your day?"

"Interesting."

"Anything you can share?"

"Just an observation."

She stayed quiet.

"The young woman I interrogated earlier isn't from our neck of the woods."

"Lots of that going on."

"True. That's not the curious part."

"Do tell.

"Straight up, blond hair, blue-eyed, all-American girl to all appearances."

"Ahhh...that surface stuff again."

"What?"

"Oh, nothing. Just a conversation George and I had about the difference in what appears on the surface and what we find when we dig deeper."

"Another fine detective."

"That he is."

"Anyway, I'm thinking I may have a trafficking ring on my hands."

Quinn sat up straighter in her chair. "If you do, then we do, or will, too."

"Maybe, maybe not. Anyway, I'll keep you in the loop if something tugs your way."

"Thanks. Guess that means she's spending some time in your fine facility."

"For now."

"Then tell me something Billy did for Billy today."

"Not much. But, it's early and I'm thinking I might go do some fine sanding on those chairs in my basement. It's spring and there's a lady I'd love to have come sit on my back porch and enjoy the sunset with me."

"Anyone I know?"

"Intimately."

"Ahh...then by all means finish the chairs."

"What do the last hours of your evening hold?"

"As much as I hate to admit it, having slept until almost noon, I'm going to bed...alone I might say."

"I'm sorry to hear that. Wish I could accommodate you...which I can if you can come over here."

"Early morning. Sorry."

"See, we need to buy property on the county lines."

She laughed, and laughed, and laughed.

"Quinn, I love you. Sleep on that."

"Billy, I'm getting there. Thanks for your patience. I'll leave you with a true confession."

"Oh, I love gossip."

"Not gossip. Truth."

"Not surprised."

"Earlier today my mother asked me if I was in love." She could hear his breathing: level, even, calm. "I told her I was for sure in a big like." She smiled, hoping it would carry through the phone.

"I'll call you right back."

The phone went silent. Then it rang.

"Are you okay, Billy?"

"Turn on your camera."

She realized he had called on FaceTime. She turned on her camera.

"That's better. Tell me what you said to your mother, one more time, please."

She looked directly into the phone and wondered why they hadn't looked at each other on the phone before.

"I told her I am for sure in a big like." She blew him a kiss.

"I'll take it. I love you, Quinn Isaacs. Take care of my detective and sleep well. I will sleep like a baby now. I love you." He grinned from ear to ear.

"Sweet dreams, silly man." She blew him another kiss and ended the call.

Part II
Follow the Clues

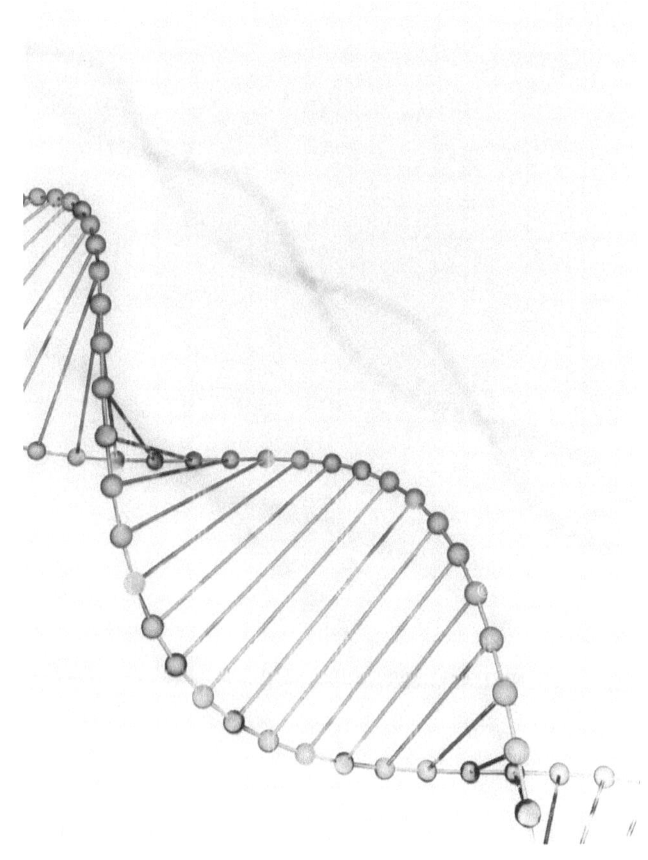

Chapter 13

I learned that you have to push away the demand of people's expectations by believing in your instincts.

Stefano Pilati

Morning Has Broken

Quinn stood with her finger on the pulse of her left wrist. *Good workout. That south sea island video was perfect for this morning's run.* She walked around her in-home gym as she cooled down. It was five twenty-four AM.

Thirty minutes later she was about to enter the combination on her gun safe when she heard a dripping noise. Her head jerked up. *Not again? I checked the upstairs bathroom last week.* She stood still. Her head turned and she watched drops of water fall from the kitchen faucet. She walked over, turned the handle, and the water stopped. *One of these days I have to get someone to come do an inventory of this house and make whatever repairs are needed.* She leaned against the counter and surveyed the spacious kitchen which opened into the great room. *I've been in this home for ten years already; guess I'm lucky nothing more than the upstairs shower has been a problem.* She expelled a long slow sigh. *Okay, get moving.*

She pulled up to the gate and lowered her window. She realized she hadn't met this officer yet. She pulled out her ID and held it up.

"Morning, Detective."

"Morning, Officer."

The gate guard walked around her car and stopped at her window.

"I cleaned the garage this weekend."

"Good for you. Have a nice day." The guard on the gate gave a mock salute with his finger to his forehead.

She looked in her rearview mirror and saw George pulling in. She parked and waited for him. Although his parking space wasn't right outside the back door like hers, he wasn't in the 'back forty' lot where most employees had to park. He took long strides to meet up with her.

"Morning."

"And to you."

"Did you clean out the garage this weekend?"

"Yep." He chuckled.

She shook her head. "Who knew the internet would make all our '10' codes known to the world?"

"I remember my dad talking about code words when he was in the military. Never thought I'd have to check my secure server each morning so I could let the guard know I'm not under duress."

"Yeah. Imagine what it is for me coming from a strip mall parking lot in one job to a gate, a guard, and a code in this one."

"Why weren't you in a more secure location at immigration?"

"Never had more than five people in this branch office and we were just a cog in the wheel. I suppose most folks in Immigration Enforcement management never thought we needed more than the bolt on the front door. Anyway, how are you this morning?"

"Ready to get on with solving this case."

"Me, too. Doc called me late yesterday…"

"Yep. Saw your report."

"He's usually in around eight unless he's working on an autopsy. Nothing came in last night, did it?"

"You mean a new body?"

"Right."

"None in early morning report. I can stop by and talk to the sergeant."

"No need. Someone will let us know. I need some time to deal with management issues…" She hesitated when he interrupted her.

"Better you than me."

"I'll call you when I set up a time to talk to Doc."

"Works for me. Need to catch up with everything else going on in our little shop. Later." He headed away from Quinn's office toward the detectives' bullpen.

Quinn entered the code on the keypad to the lab and switched on the lab lights. Chuck wasn't due in until 8:00 AM and she wanted the quiet. *I should have gotten coffee...* She glanced over at the new coffee machine and smiled. *Way to go, Chuck. Now how to pay...* She heard the chirp of the code in the door and turned.

"Morning, Quinn."

"You're early."

"Yep. Things to do." He put his bookbag in the cabinet below the counter. "Coffee?"

"Was just about to help myself." She stood there for a moment. "Chuck, how about I help out with the cost of this machine?"

"No way. It was a gift from my mom. She was so happy I now actually have two days off in a row she gave it to us."

Quinn studied the face of this bright, energetic young forensic tech. *How have we lost work life balance in this country?* "Does that mean you can help her out now?"

"Yeah, right. Cleaned windows last week." He rolled his eyes.

"You're a good son. Tell your mom thanks for me. Next box of coffee pods is on me. Let me know what kind of coffees you like."

"10-4."

Quinn smiled. *At least in-house we can still get away with our '10' codes.*

The management side of being lead detective was easy for Quinn, but she loved the field work. She approved the technology purchase orders which would up the level of equipment in each of the labs, double-checked the time and day for the quarterly meeting with the forensic techs, and scanned the duty sergeant's log for the last twenty-four hours. *Nothing out of the ordinary. Let's keep it that way.* She logged out of the secure server and headed across the hall.

She saw George staring at the board. "Couldn't stay away?"

George turned from their board. "No, ma'am. Something just isn't right in all this."

"Like?"

"Like the old saying, 'things aren't always what they seem.'"

"Walk me through it."

"Okay, we have the names of our deceased, presently in the morgue, and the fingerprints in Angela's car. Here's what we don't have: Dunn. Where is Dunn?"

"We have an APB out on him." Quinn's eyebrows knitted as she looked at George.

"Right. Next question: Why did Angela get in the truck with Patten?"

"We don't know that she did."

George looked at her and nodded. "Right. We know there is a ring we think was hers...Wait, do we have the report from the A-Team?"

Quinn opened her secure files on the workroom computer. "Yep, just came in—Monday morning about two AM as promised. I assume we're looking to see if Angela's fingerprints are in the truck?"

"Yep." George had his black dry erase pen poised.

Quinn muttered as she scanned the report. "Here it is. Angela Topping fingerprints on passenger door, dashboard, window, and on a smooth flat rock on the floor of the truck. Wait...three of five prints on stone suggest her hand gripped the rock."

"Well, well. Seems to me she could have been trying to get away. Any evidence of the rock connecting with Patten?"

Quinn continued to read. "Large bruise on upper right arm of driver, one inch below the shoulder to be confirmed by autopsy." *Wonder if there were any fibers on the rock?* She scanned the report. "Says no fibers or tissues on rock to connect to Patten."

"Any information on any soil or debris in the tires?"

"Analysis underway apparently." She looked up at the board. "George, if Patten drove from Indian Flats to the county line between here and the Valley Township, wouldn't any debris he might have picked up come off on the highway?"

"Sure, but once they have time to really analyze every particle, you'd be surprised what the techs find. You see, we just think we're the detectives, but they are the real detectives with their microscopes, chemicals…all that stuff they use to get to the molecular level."

"Seriously, the molecular level?" Quinn rolled her eyes.

"Give me a break. I don't know if they always do, but they could." He gave her a wan smile.

"Focus. We know Angela was in the truck." She wrote a note on her pad: *Does Marjorie Topping know Patten?*

George was walking back and forth in front of the board. There was a knock on the door. Quinn looked up and walked to open it.

"Morning, Doc. Thanks for coming up."

"Here to serve, Quinn. Here to serve."

Early Morning Flight

"Quiet, baby, it's okay." Kelly pulled Anne closer in her lap and tried not to look at Suzanne poised over the gurney in the back of the plane. Little Andy was in the seat facing her and waving his arms with a small model replica of their plane in his hand.

"Look, Mommy, we're ready to fly."

Don't remind me. She kept one eye on the children and one on the gurney where Andrew lay—still alive, but in a chemically induced coma. The nurse with him happened to be a traveling nurse who had been at the local medical facility and was scheduled to fly home to Louisiana later today. He was now flying with them to Tennessee. Kelly had been relieved when she found out the man actually had a degree as a nurse practitioner.

He approached her and whispered softly. "Ma'am, I've told the pilot we're good to fly."

The color drained from Kelly's face.

"Ma'am, are you alright?"

"Not a big fan of flying…we need to get him to the university hospital."

"There will be an ambulance at the airport and I will go with him. It's not a long flight. I can give you something to calm…"

"Absolutely not..." her voice was stern but calm. "Sorry, no. I need to be fully alert. I'll be fine. Let's get this plane in the air."

"I'll check in with the pilot. Do you wish to know anything else?"

"No. Thank you for coming with us and making sure my husband can make it to Knoxville."

The man looked at her. He didn't want to tell her that the bruise from the hard impact of the drone on Andrew's chest was so bad he might not make it to Knoxville.

Suzanne approached when the nurse moved away.

"Madam, do you wish me to travel with you? I can help with the children."

"Suzanne, you have been great, but I think we'll be okay. My mother will meet us at the airport and take the children while I go to the hospital." She tried to smile through the lie. She knew it would not be her mother meeting them at the airport.

"Very well. I look forward to being of service on your next trip to the islands."

"Suzanne, one quick question. Was this your first job as a nanny?"

Suzanne hesitated a moment. "Officially? Yes, madam."

"What work have you done?"

Suzanne had been told Mr. Culbert did not want his wife to know she'd been a police officer, but she decided the current circumstances warranted it. After all, there were lots of questions to be answered. She glanced over at the box holding the drone that plowed into him. "Madam, I'm retired from the island police force; I was an officer for over twenty years."

Kelly slumped in her seat. *Andrew Culbert, you better survive this; I have a lot of questions. No more playing the protective husband role.*

Autopsy Report

"Morning, George."

"Morning, Doc. Coffee?"

Dr. Walters held up his mug. "I'm good, thanks. Quinn, want to pull up the autopsy report on Angela Topping?"

"Done." She projected it on the screen. Her eyes focused on the entry: <u>Cause of Death: Pulmonary Edema: non-cardiogenic</u>. She waited.

"COD is, as you can see, pulmonary edema non-cardiogenic, likely caused by the inhalation of chemicals...some known, some unknown, and exacerbated by a history of allergy and asthma. Her heart was not a contributing factor."

Quinn and Doc jumped when George slapped the table. "Dammit." He looked from one to the other. "Sorry. Some high fallutin' lawyer will get the killer..."

"The one who might be the other body in my morgue?"

"Oh, yeah." George settled into his chair. "And *his* COD?"

"He died of pulmonary edema, likely caused... you get the picture. However, his lungs and bronchial tubes do not suggest a history of asthma. There is evidence of drug use in his nasal passage—without his medical records we don't know."

Quinn studied the report. "Doc, I see Angela's physicians in Knoxville were cooperative."

"No real reason not to be. Turned out Ms. Topping, the grandmother, had Angela's entire medical history sent to me. Just needed verification which is easier for a colleague to do than give new information."

"Lawyers." George shook his head.

Quinn ignored him. She already knew from her work in immigration the frustration law enforcement officers have with some lawyers; she was only beginning to learn how much more so it was when you were a detective.

She looked at the medical examiner. "Doc, what do you know about the chemicals?"

"We've isolated several which do not naturally occur in the same environments, nor do they generally end up in the same environment. What's important here is inhaled toxins of smaller particle size get into the lower respiratory tract delaying reaction, which suggests things like oxides of nitrogen, phosgene, chlorine..." He paused. "It's hard to tell the source of the chemicals and the concentration, though it was sufficient to burn Angela's esophagus."

George interrupted. "Any explanation for the rotten egg smell reported in the truck?"

"The techs are still working the chemicals in the truck, but sulfurs and methyl mercaptan can cause it."

"What is methyl mercaptan?" Quinn waited.

"Technically it's produced from methanol and hydrogen sulfide, but more commonly folks know it as the emission from paper mills and gas fields."

"Not a lot of that around here is there?"

"Not right in our back yard, Quinn. This is about the chemicals, though, not what is producing them. To determine where and how they were combined, and the method used to dispense and distribute them will take more work than comes with an autopsy."

Quinn and George looked at each other.

This was Quinn's case. George deferred to her. "Thanks, Doc. Anything else we need to know?"

"Nothing significant from my end. We can release Angela's remains. Do we know where Mr. Patten belongs?"

"There's no known address. We'll be working on his last known address now that we have a bit more information. Thanks for your help."

"Sure, Quinn. Anytime. Well, unless you need anything else, with no new DBs in my morgue, I'll clear up some paper work on my desk and head home. Call if you need anything." As a retired physician, Dr. Walters only worked when they had a death.

Quinn stood and extended her hand. "Sure, thing, Doc. Thanks. Enjoy your day."

"Later, George."

"Take care, Doc."

Quinn remained standing. "Let's take five. I need to walk down the hall and I need to think."

"Let's make it fifteen. I need to go outside and get some fresh air."

"See you in fifteen." Quinn suspected George was upset with himself for his outbursts—she was not. It was in-house, all three present understood the frustration, and besides, tough cases brought raised tension. She looked at the screen with the autopsy report. *How did you end up in that truck, Angela? Where was he taking you? Did he know?* She picked up her phone and called the ME.

"Doc, two quick questions."

"Sure."

"Did you find anything significant in the bruise on Patten's arm?"

"He had on long sleeves, so there was no visible evidence on the rock found in the truck. But if it was thrown hard enough, it could account for the bruise."

"Okay, thanks."

"Second question: I understand the COD and have a basic understanding of the effects of the chemicals. How would they affect cognitive functioning?"

"Depends."

Of course, it depends. Quinn refocused as she paced.

"Most likely brain response is short term memory loss..."

"Like being disoriented?"

"Well, sure you could lose your sense of direction, not remember something just experienced or heard."

"Thanks, Doc. Thanks a lot. Go home, now."

"On my way."

Quinn sat back and looked at the map on the board. *So, you might not have been headed anywhere near Indian Flats, Mr. Patten. Where were you going?*

Private Air Terminal

The Pilatus P-24 pulled into the private hangar in Knoxville and the ambulance backed up to the stairs. The nurse talked with the EMTs and they were ready to move Mr. Culbert as soon as the children were out of sight.

Kelly walked down the stairs with Little Andy and Anne to the waiting black Suburban. The woman inside strapped the children into car seats and was playing with them. Kelly talked with the driver and watched carefully as her husband was moved into the ambulance. She already knew he would go into the private wing at the hospital; Andrew Culbert II had funded it years ago.

"Ms. Culbert?"

"Yes?" She turned back. "Sorry. I just needed to see him off. Could you review the plan for the children with me?"

"Absolutely." The man told her the details of the plan.

"Most of that works for me. Did you say you have already picked up my mother?"

"Yes, ma'am. She's waiting for the children to arrive."

"Good. Then let's go get them settled. I need to get to the hospital."

"There is someone waiting for your husband to arrive at the hospital. He will be, as you know, in a private suite with round-the-clock care."

"Of course. However, he needs me there, too. I will get the children settled and then go directly to the hospital."

"Yes, ma'am." The man straightened his suit jacket and put away the identification she had insisted on seeing—a second time—before they left the airport.

Kelly climbed into the Suburban, fastened her seatbelt, and started a mental list of the things she would need before she went to the hospital: the first was two new phones.

Andrew had stressed the importance of the 10:00 AM phone call.

Who's going?

"Quinn..." George had come into the detective workroom with a bottle of water in his hand.

She looked up from the computer.

"Apologies."

"Not needed."

"Needed. I don't know why I had to rant about lawyers—hell, I even know one or two good ones."

"Me, too." She laughed and tried to show it in her eyes and with a smile.

"It just gets old afterwhile."

"I'm sure. I don't have as much direct experience in having diligent work derailed by lawyers, but I've seen the effects on cases I've worked: this one gets off, that one gets a slap on the wrist. That the issue?"

"Yeah…sorta. It's also about being under-resourced."

"What do you need?"

"No, I don't mean here…I mean the system. We're plodding away trying to solve a potential crime and there are ten more folks out there plotting new ones."

"George, don't get upset with me when I ask this question." She looked into his eyes.

"I'll try."

"When was the last time you had more than two days off in a row?"

He started laughing. "Great question. Well, there's time off and there's time off, right?"

"Meaning?"

"I can have two, even three days off, but I never leave the job."

"May I ask how Carrie feels about that?"

"She's worse with her work."

"Maybe all three of us need to figure out how we can actually be away from work when we aren't at work."

"Let's try to make it a priority." He extended his hand to shake hers.

"Deal. Unfortunately, time off is not the only problem of the moment. You good to get our day planned?"

"Absolutely. Thanks, Quinn. I'm back on track."

She nodded. "Now…" She pulled her hair into a knot at the base of her neck.

George smiled. *She's in her serious mode.*

Twenty-five minutes later they had a plan. Quinn would see if Billy could go for the interview with Marjorie Topping so as not to introduce anyone new into the interactions with her. George would work on the APB on Dunn, the updates on the truck, and Patten's last known address. They had checked and Dunn's prints were not reported as being anywhere in or on the truck.

"That work for you, George?"

"Good to go. I'll be in the bullpen if you need me."

"Touch base at four PM unless needed earlier?"

"Four PM, it is." George headed out.

Quinn took her secure phone out and called Billy.

"Williams."

"Isaacs."

"Morning."

"And to you. Got a minute?"

"Always...okay to be honest, almost always."

"That's better."

"What's up?"

"We have a COD on Angela Topping and I need to go talk to her grandmother. I know this isn't technically your case, but you were on scene and part of the initial interview. Seems best not to introduce anyone new to the situation with her."

"I'm all for inter-agency cooperation. We're in good shape here, but I'll run it by the Sheriff. Any concerns, I'll let you know."

"Thanks. We can go over the plan once you know if you can make it."

"Give me five. I'll see if the Sheriff is free."

"10-4." She ended the call, turned off the computer in the workroom, and headed to her office.

Her phone rang as soon as she sat at her office desk. "Isaacs."

"Williams. Sheriff is all for it. You said two PM, right?"

"Two PM."

"Want to have lunch at The Corral? Or I could throw together something at my place."

"The Corral has ears. How about a compromise? I pick up something over here and meet you at the Station?"

"That works. Make sure it isn't something that smells outrageously good or you'll never make it to the conference room."

"See you around 12:15, Detective."

"Yes, ma'am. You're welcome in our house, anytime."

"Later." She set the phone down and stretched. She slowly pulled the knot out of her hair. *Billy, Billy, Billy. How can you throw a pass in a professional conversation and not expect it to be seen as one? Lunch at your place—ha!*

Chapter 14

An effective leader is also an effective listener.
Artika Tyner

A Decision

Andrew would be in an induced coma for some days to come. He was safe in the secure private wing of the hospital and Kelly knew she would be there shortly to check on him. She had to try and manage the phone call he was scheduled to make this morning at ten. *Andrew, I don't know whether to be angriest at you for keeping me out of the loop or myself for letting you.* She had her plan laid out. The man with the earbuds seated by the door of the house seemed to look past her—her mother played with the children in a room set up with toys.

Lee Ann answered her work mobile as she picked up her purse. "Morning, Mr. Culbert."

"Good morning, Lee Ann."

"Oh, good morning, Ms. Culbert. How are you today?"

"I'm well, thanks. I apologize for the early hour..." It was just after seven-thirty AM.

"No, problem. I was just about to leave for the office. Is everything alright?"

"Well, actually, we had a little weekend getaway and we aren't back home yet." It wasn't a lie. They were in town, but not at their home. "I'm calling for Andrew to tell you to take a couple of days off." She waited a beat. She had no idea what kind of time off Lee Ann got. "He said there was nothing pressing. Is there anything you're aware of?"

"I don't know what to say, Ms. Culbert. Are you sure?" She looked at her phone to make sure it was Mr. Culbert's phone number. The number was blocked.

"Yes, I'm sure. Now, is it accurate there's nothing pressing?"

"No, nothing. We don't have any deals to close this week. Oh, wait a minute. I sent him an email…ma'am, is something wrong with Mr. Culbert?" She had never talked to Ms. Culbert about anything to do with the business.

"He caught a bug on our trip. Now, you said something about an email?" Kelly was sure Andrew kept things in secure electronic files; she had heard him talk with her brother, Lance, about cybersecurity. She also stayed up-to-date with current business practices through the "CPA Advisory" trade magazine.

Lee Ann hesitated. "Ms. Culbert, are you sure Mr. Culbert is okay?"

"Lee Ann, I don't mean to be rude, but I have many things to do today. What was it about that email?" Kelly saw the man seated by the door nod.

Lee Ann hoped this wouldn't cause her to lose her job. "There was information about a land sale." She hesitated. "It's just we haven't done any research on it."

"What land?"

"Ma'am, are you sure it's okay if I tell you?"

"Lee Ann…" Kelly's voice softened to a buttery southern drawl. "While it's true I am not generally involved in the day-to-day operations of the business, I am going to need to handle things for a few days."

Lee Ann filed Kelly's CPA license renewal for her—she relaxed a bit as she remembered. "Yes, ma'am. It included the acreage in your family east of Knoxville."

"Okay, thanks. I'm aware of it. There are two other parcels involved as well, right?"

Lee Ann let out a long breath. She wished she had a recording device. She had read the email from Andrew telling her the information was a prank from an old fraternity brother. "Yes, ma'am. Do you need the email?"

"Not at the moment." Kelly took a shallow breath. "If I need anything, I'll be in touch. I've been meaning to make some changes to the décor of the office for a while, so there will be some folks there working on it; don't plan on coming into the office until at least Thursday. I'll let you know as soon as I can when to come back."

"If you're sure, ma'am."

"I'm sure."

"Okay."

"One last thing, Lee Ann."

"Yes?"

"Please turn off your business phone and leave it off. If I need you, I will call your personal phone and ask you to call me back."

Lee Ann shivered. "Yes, ma'am. Tell Mr. Culbert I hope he feels better soon."

"I will. Now you go find a fun way to enjoy your time off. Lee Ann, hold on a minute." Kelly looked at the note the man held up for her. "I'm so sorry. I didn't even think about Easter being Sunday. You have Good Friday off, anyway, so just take the week. You'll be paid. Now, turn that phone off as soon as we hang up. Have fun." She ended the call and jumped at the knock on the door.

The man seated by the door stood up and opened it.

No Answer

"Mr. S., no calls from Culbert's phone in two days. No one spotted coming or going to the house in two days..." the thug was a hardened man, but he flinched when his boss yelled. He held the phone away from his ear.

"What do you mean he hasn't been seen? I told you to keep surveillance on him. Are you sitting on your thumb?"

The thug just ignored the comments; they didn't really matter. "Mr. S., I've called his private phone. I'm leaving messages." *And the man who fell asleep in surveillance is swimming with the fishies.*

"Did you try his secretary, assistant, whatever? Is that so hard?"

The thug rolled his eyes. *I ain't dumb.* "The man who answered said Mr. Culbert and his assistant were out of the office. He wanted to take a message."

"You didn't leave one, did you?"

"No, boss. I ain't dumb. Just don't know where Culbert is. It's like they all went into one of those black holes."

Mr. S. could be crass and was an opportunist but he wasn't stupid. He knew the thug wasn't too bright—but he was the best of the lot they had on this little project. He allowed himself a smile about the 'black hole' comment. *You don't know how black a hole you could end up in, dumb ass. I've got a boss, too.*

Mr. S. sighed. "Alright, alright. Let's give him the rest of the day. Meantime you get those boys you know to do some film doctoring so we can show Mr. Culbert, *the third*, what could happen to that pretty little wife of his."

"On it, boss. Took care of the guy who should..."

"Don't waste my time with petty details. Just get the job done. Where is the chemist in amping things up?"

"Don't seem like he cares one way or the other. Want me to work..."

"I will tell you when I want something done. In the meantime, do your job while you still have one." *I'll give Culbert until tomorrow. Then may have to call myself.*

"Yes, Mr. S. On it." The thug hung up and wondered how much longer he'd have to be in these mountains. *I want the wide open spaces of the cornfields and soybeans where you can see folks coming down the road. Get me outta these winding roads.*

Sheriff's Station in the Valley

Quinn held up her Round City Police Department credential.

"Afternoon, Detective Isaacs."

"Afternoon, Officer. Detective Williams is expecting me."

"Yes, ma'am. He's on his way up." The officer looked her up and down. She was a tall, very attractive woman with streaked blond hair shining like a hand-polished table top. He didn't know much about fashion, but was smart enough to know the quality of the suit Quinn was wearing had to be expensive. *No wonder everyone is talking about her.* He pushed the button to unlock the door between reception and the hallway. He kept his gaze on her.

"Thanks, Officer. I believe Detective Williams said to meet in the conference room."

"Hey!" Billy stepped up in front of her.

"Afternoon, Detective Williams." Quinn turned to the officer and smiled. "Thanks."

"This way." Billy reached out to take the bag with food. He gave her fingers a gentle squeeze as he did so.

"Thank you." She squeezed his fingers, too, let go, and followed him into the conference room.

Billy pushed open the door and went in ahead of her; the door was awkward to navigate in the small space. He purposely did not turn on the lights. When she entered, he closed the door and kissed her.

"Billy Williams," she hissed.

"Not to worry. New technology in town."

She stepped back and turned on the lights herself. "Oh?" She wanted to sound mad—she wasn't. She started laughing. "What's going on?"

"We now have a control panel for screen, camera, recordings, the whole nine yards. Means the camera isn't recording empty space 24/7." He waved to the panel on the conference table.

"Wow, Sergeant Whitehorse has been seriously working on the technology. I need to see what you have so we can look at our own. Hey, is that a digital whiteboard?"

Billy shrugged. "I think so, but not sure what that means."

"It means, Detective, that you can capture digitally what you write on it. I want one."

"Then I'm guessing you'll get it?" He raised an eyebrow.

"It's on my list." She groaned. "We just managed to go from a chalkboard to a dry erase white board."

"Well, progress is progress." He shrugged again. "Let's eat. What do you say? I need to hear what you want from me on this interview."

"I'll be back in a minute." She stepped out and went to the ladies room.

When she returned Billy had their food on paper plates. "Thanks for picking up lunch. Looks delicious."

She pulled the plate toward her. "You're welcome. Okay, here's what we know." She updated the cause of death information on Angela and Patten. "Trying to think through best strategy for asking Ms. Topping about the ring." She put the pictures of the ring found in Patten's truck on the table. She knew Billy had seen the ring in person.

Billy put down his plastic fork. "I don't know the last time I had tuna salad. Good choice."

"One of my favorites." She tapped the picture with her nail. "The ring?"

"Tell me what you're thinking."

Quinn outlined her strategy to address Angela's cause of death and how to try and figure out of Ms. Topping knew Patten or Dunn. "Wait. I just thought of something. Dunn and Patten both have ties to southern Illinois; Marjorie Topping lived in Chicago. Coincidence?"

"Don't believe in them myself. But hey, I do know geography and Chicago is probably about as far from southern Illinois as we are from Memphis." Billy grinned like a school boy trying to impress his fifth grade social studies teacher.

"Yeah." She took a bite of the cracker with some tuna fish salad as she flipped through her note pad. "Dunn was born in a suburb of Chicago." She clicked the end of the plastic handled fork on the table.

Billy watched her—fascinated. *Oh, Quinn, I would love to be able to see a movie reel of your thinking at the moment.* He ate without saying a word.

"Okay, threads to be tugged. At this time we don't know if we actually have a murder, right?"

"Right. Although it appears Angela may have been taken against her will, we don't *know* that and we don't know how she was exposed to the toxins that killed her."

"Right. So, how do I get Ms. Topping to let me have access to Angela's computer?"

"Get a warrant?"

"Based on what?"

"Yeah, well, there's that." He winked at her. *You'll figure out a way. Keep thinking.* Billy knew this was technically not his case. He also couldn't figure out how to get to Angela's computer.

Quinn put her napkin over her empty plate and stood. She reached for Billy's and put both in the plastic bag the food had come in. "I'll take these with me…"

"I'll put them in the dumpster. Nothing worse than the smell of tuna fish sitting in a trash can or a hot car."

"Okay. Thanks. Here look at this." She opened to a blank page in her pad. She considered the diagram George had on their board in Round City and drew a less complex one with the specifics related to questions they needed answered—by Ms. Topping, hopefully.

"Satisfied?" Billy looked at the diagram and nodded his head in approval at the web she'd drawn.

Quinn nodded her head. "Yeah…it's coming together." She looked at her watch. It was 1:30 PM She took out her secure phone and called Ms. Topping.

"Marjorie Topping speaking."

"Quinn Isaacs, Ms. Topping. I'm calling to let you know Detective Williams from the Valley Sheriff's Station will accompany me to your home."

"Thank you for letting me know. I'll inform the gate." She looked at her watch. "I'll see you in a few minutes.

"Yes, ma'am, We'll be there at two o'clock." Quinn heard the phone call ended by Ms. Topping.

At the Hospital

Kelly sat at the table in the suite with Andrew in a hospital bed on the other side of the glass partitioned wall. *Daddy Andy, when we sat with you here in your last days, I never expected to be back here trying to keep Andrew alive.* She looked at her notes on the call to Mr. Gordon. His assistant had apologized about having to delay the call. She took one of the phones she had bought as soon as they landed and dialed the number again.

"Gordon and Associates."

"Mr. Gordon, please, this is Kelly Culbert."

"Yes, Ms. Culbert. One moment, please."

She heard the click and then the voice of Roger Gordon. "Kelly, nice to hear from you."

Kelly? I only know his wife from charity functions. "Hey. How's Mara?"

"Fine, just fine. I was expecting to hear from Andrew."

"I know. He caught a bug over the weekend and really can't talk. He asked me to follow-up with you."

"Well, you folks, just like me and mine, have been in these hills a long time. I've done some real soul searching about letting go of our history with that land."

Kelly held her breath. She knew Andrew was afraid something bad would happen if Gordon didn't agree to sell. She put on her best southern charm. "Why, Roger, I certainly do know how deep your roots go here. I'm sure it wasn't an easy decision."

"No, ma'am. It surely wasn't."

Come on, Roger. I don't need the dramatics—just your decision. Of course, I may lie about your decision if I think it's going to put my kids at risk. She looked at the man seated on the sofa.

"So, I flipped a coin. As good a decision maker as any, don't you think?" He guffawed.

"Can come in handy, that's for sure." She tried to keep her voice light.

"Well, it was heads."

Seriously, just give me an answer.

"You win." He laughed with a such a belly laugh Kelly shook her head in disgust.

"Well, Roger, I think that's a win-win for sure." Her drawl dripped like honey.

"Now, just to be clear, Andrew told me he was waiving his commission on this. That right?" His drawl became more pronounced.

"Absolutely. We'll be working the details over the next day or so and let you know about closing."

"Andrew thought I might have my money by Monday next week, but hey, it's Easter week, right. Don't want folks working on Good Friday. So, I'm good anytime next week."

"Thanks, Roger. We appreciate the flexibility. I'll be sure we keep your assistant informed."

"That's perfect. Well, thanks, Kelly. Nice doing business with you."

"You, too, Roger. Give my regards to Mara."

"Sure thing." The phone call ended.

Kelly looked through the glass at Andrew—machines were breathing for him and she saw the steady rise and fall of his chest beneath the sheets. *What have you gotten us into, Andrew?*

The man rose from the sofa and came over to the table.

"You handled that just fine."

She looked past him. "Good." She prayed her children would stay safe.

Looking for Answers

Billy followed Quinn through the gate at The Mountain Villages and up the winding road to Marjorie Topping's home. She and Billy stood on opposite sides of the door. As she reached to ring the bell, the door opened.

"Detectives. This way. Ms. Topping is expecting you." Maria did not wait for a greeting. She stood back as they entered, closed the door and moved to the French doors where they had met with Ms. Topping before.

Quinn walked right up to the wheelchair and extended her hand. "Good afternoon, Ms. Topping. Thanks for seeing us."

"Certainly, Detective Isaacs." She took Billy's hand. "Good afternoon, Detective Williams."

"Ma'am." Billy nodded.

"Tea or coffee?" Ms. Topping extended her hand toward the drinks.

"Water will be fine. What may I get you?" Quinn waited.

"I'm fine. Thank you for serving yourselves."

Perrier poured in Waterford crystal glasses, Quinn took a sip, set down her glass, and took a silent breath before she started.

"Ms. Topping, again, I am sorry for your loss. I'm sure you want to know the report from our medical examiner, Dr. Walters. He has given us the cause of death on your granddaughter."

Marjorie Topping never took her eyes off of Quinn.

"The specific cause was pulmonary edema likely brought on by inhaled chemicals—the source of which is unknown at this time."

"Chemicals? Plural?"

"Yes, ma'am." Quinn waited. When Ms. Topping said nothing else, she continued. "Dr. Walters has filed for the death certificate and you may make arrangements for Angela."

"Thank you, Detective. I will do so immediately."

"Mr. Olson can advise you on Tennessee law regarding the legal disposition of remains in this state."

Ms. Topping nodded.

"Do you have any questions?"

"None at this time."

"May we take a few more minutes of your time for some things we'd like to clarify?"

"Yes. Do you want to record them?"

Quinn and Billy had already decided they would both take notes and not use the recorder having just told Angela's grandmother the cause of death.

"It's not necessary. We'll just take notes." Quinn looked up at her. "Unless, of course, you would like it recorded."

"I have no need for it to be recorded. What are your questions?"

Quinn handed Marjorie the picture of the ring. "Can you identify this ring?"

"Of course, Angela always wore it. It was given by my son, Harvey, to his wife when they were married. The stone has passed down in my husband's family for generations. Harvey had a new setting made for Janice. When may I get the ring back?"

"In due course, Ms. Topping." Quinn had given considerable thought to how she had asked the question. It worked. Ms. Topping assumed the ring had been on Angela at the time of her death.

"How long was Angela involved in land acquisition?"

"As I told you before, we have always had an interest in conservation in our family. Angela interned with a prominent real estate company in Knoxville which heightened her interest. She had her own funds which she was free to use any way she chose."

"What would be the largest land purchase she made in Tennessee?"

"Together we've bought approximately 1000 acres which are now in conservation. She did the legwork; I provided the funds."

Quinn nodded as she made a note. "Was the land bought in both names." Quinn could see irritation starting around the eyes of this resolute woman.

"It's easily found, Detective Isaacs. The Topping Family Land Trust is used for these projects."

"Thank you. Has Angela bought property independent of your joint ventures?"

Marjorie Topping studied Quinn's hazel eyes. "Perhaps. I'm not sure I'd know."

"Could she have purchased in her own name?" She was hoping Ms. Topping wouldn't answer.

"I have no idea." Her gaze hardened.

"Thank you. I appreciate your honesty." She turned to Billy. "Any questions, Detective?"

"Just one. As an attorney, you mentioned you did wills and trusts. Were you clients primarily in the city of Chicago?"

Marjorie turned her attention to Billy. She gave a short laugh. "Oh, heavens no, Detective. There are people of means in many suburbs and towns outside of the city. I had clients in many communities. What does this have to do with Angela's death?"

Billy ignored her question. "How old was Angela when you came to Tennessee?"

Marjorie Topping smiled at Billy. "We came here often when she was a child. At that time, we owned a cabin outside of Pigeon Forge. After my husband passed away, I began to think about retiring here. I like the locale, the people, and I wanted Angela out of the city. However, we didn't come here permanently until after my son...Angela's father...died five years ago. Angela was already here at the university in Knoxville and was devastated by her father's death. I was no longer in practice, so it seemed logical. When I found The Mountain Villages; it provided everything I wanted."

Quinn's voice was soft and quiet. "And may I ask what you were seeking?"

"Peace, quiet, and tranquility."

Quinn nodded. "Something we value in these hills." She smiled and decided not to ask about the man in the red truck. There would be back to talk to Marjorie Topping—and this time it would be with a warrant—she hoped.

Chapter 15

*We delight in the beauty of the butterfly, but rarely admit the changes
it has gone through to achieve that beauty.*
Maya Angelou

Looking for Answers

Kelly Culbert had Andrew's laptop computer and the stainless steel brief
case. She had no idea he had left twenty-thousand dollars in a safe at the
island. She turned to the man at the table with her. "Are you sure you can
get into this computer?"

"I can. That isn't the problem."

"Then what is?"

"The legal ramifications of doing so."

Kelly glared at him. "I don't care about the legal ramifications. My
husband is lying right there…in the room next to me… in an induced coma
fighting for his life! I'm trying to protect our family."

"So are we, Ms. Culbert. You asked for our help and we are here to help."

"Then get into this computer."

"Do you have your husband's Power of Attorney?"

Kelly took three deep breaths. "I do."

"Then as soon as I can see it, we can get into this laptop."

Kelly stood and paced. *I don't dare go to the house; they could be watching.
There's a copy in the bank box. Wait.* She turned to the man who she knew
was an agent in the State Bureau of Investigation even though she didn't
really want to acknowledge his connections. "If our attorney verifies it, is
that sufficient?"

"He can fax a copy to the secure account we discussed."

Kelly picked up the phone and went to contacts. None listed. *This isn't your phone.* She did not want to turn on either her phone or Andrew's. She turned back to the man who was on his own laptop. "Please look up the number for Hassleman and Associates, Attorneys-at-law."

"865-555-1212."

"Thank you." She dialed and walked over to the window overlooking the well-tended gardens at the hospital; her father-in-law had paid for them, too.

"Hassleman and Associates, how may I direct your call?"

"Mr. Charles Hassleman, please."

"May I tell him who's calling?"

"Kelly Culbert."

"Yes, ma'am. Please hold." The receptionist sent the call to Mr. Hassleman's assistant.

"Charles Hassleman's office."

"This is Kelly Culbert, I need to speak to Charles, please."

"Ms. Culbert, he's..."

"Interrupt him. It's urgent." Her patience was running thin and she hadn't slept well or eaten in hours.

The assistant was accustomed to the demands of clients who paid large sums to the firm.

"By all means, ma'am."

"Kelly, Charles here. How can I help today?"

Kelly tried to keep her voice low. "Andrew is in the hospital in an induced coma."

"Kelly, I'm sorry to hear that. What do you need?"

"I need a copy of his POA now. I do not plan to leave the hospital."

"Of course, Kelly. I'll need to have my assistant call you back to verify. She'll send you a release to sign for the Power of Attorney. I assume you're in Andy's wing at the hospital—the staff there can help you."

"That's fine, Charles. Have her call the hospital wing, not my personal mobile number. They'll put it through to me. I will expect a call in the next ten minutes and the documents immediately after."

"Of course. Anything else I can do at this time?"

"No, just please get it done." She had settled a bit.

"Immediately. I hope Andrew will recover quickly. If we can help in any way, don't hesitate to call."

"Thank you, Charles. I'll be in touch." She ended the call.

The man at the table nodded.

Next Steps

Quinn was driving back to her office from the Topping residence.

"Detective Isaacs, how may I direct your call?"

"Detective Marshall, please."

"Marshall."

"George, it's Quinn. I'll be back in about twenty minutes. Meet me in the workroom. Would you please see if you can schedule a call with the district attorney in thirty?"

"On it. Drive safely."

"10-4."

So, Marjorie Topping, your granddaughter had her own money and could make deals without your knowledge or consent. She watched the blossoming dogwoods and oaks as she drove toward Round City. *Well, for that matter, I could buy property and my parents would never know. Maybe conservation is something I should do with my trust fund. I could help preserve this land for others to enjoy forever.* She started humming. "This Land is Your Land." She pulled up to the gate. A different officer was on duty and he knew her.

"Good weekend, Detective Isaacs?"

"Cleaned my garage. Hope your weekend was good."

"Yes, ma'am." He nodded as he closed the gate behind her.

Quinn swiped her ID at the back door and went straight to the workroom. She punched each number of the code to the door lock with force.

George looked up from the computer. "Guessing the interview either went really well or bombed."

"Both."

George waited.

"Peggy O'Haire available?"

"Yes, ma'am. She'll talk to you in…" He looked at his watch. "seven minutes from now."

"Good. Here are the basics for the board."

Quinn pulled her hair into a knot at the nape of her neck, looked at her notes, started pacing, and launched into her list. "Need to find: Topping Family Land Trust, any property in the names of Marjorie Topping, Harvey Topping, Angela Topping, or all three—specifically in Tennessee. We'll expand it later if the need arises."

George made notes on the white board as she typed into the computer.

"Have you ever used an electronic white board?"

"What?" George scrunched his eyebrows and stared at her. *Where is this going?*

"Sorry. Random thought. The Valley Sheriff's Station has some cool new technology tools."

"Like what?"

"Like an electronic white board. I digress. Next point: Death under suspicious circumstances."

George pointed to Angela and Patten's names simultaneously.

"Probably both—but at the moment our focus is Angela."

George made a note by Angela's name. "Plausible."

"Plausible? What does that mean?"

"It means it is plausible her death was under suspicious circumstances."

"Yeah. Fine." Quinn sat down and typed furiously on the keyboard entering her notes. Her secure phone rang.

"Isaacs."

"Peggy O'Haire. You needed me?"

"I do. I need a warrant to search Angela Topping's home in Maryville and to pick up and access her computer or computers..." she took a breath, "...may need her grandmother's computer, too."

"Whoa. Slow down. I told George I only have a few minutes but I'm not going after a warrant without more information than that."

Quinn explained the COD on Angela Topping, the ring found in the red truck, that Patten's death was from the same cause and the similarity in the chemicals was verified but the source of the chemicals is unknown. Then she told her about the interview with Marjorie Topping and her concern about land deals and who might be involved. "That's why we might need Marjorie Topping's computer, too."

"Do you think she'll go get Angela's computer?"

"Personally? Hard to know. It won't be easy; she's in a wheelchair."

"Someone could take her."

"True. Does that help in getting a warrant?"

"Makes it easier to cross jurisdictions if I have something to suggest we're at risk of losing pertinent information in a possible homicide."

How willing would I be to stand in front of a judge and say with all certainty we are at risk of losing pertinent information? "Yes, Peggy, I think we could lose pertinent information."

"Okay. Let me run through it."

Quinn had her phone on speaker. She looked at George. He was nodding his head.

"Did I miss anything, Quinn?"

"No, Peggy. Do you need anything else?"

"No, I'll give it a shot without the grandmother's computer. I hate to go back, but I'd rather do it with justification. Back to you as soon as I can." Peggy's tone was clipped and serious.

"Thanks. You're awesome."

"Could you put that in writing?"

"Gladly. Thanks, Peggy."

"10-4." Peggy ended the call.

Quinn looked at the clock on the wall. It was three-thirty. *It's light until after seven...come on Peggy. Make it happen.*

George was doing a soft clap. "Good job, Quinn. Now, do you know what we're looking for?"

"You didn't buy the piece when I told Peggy we need to rule out that she was personally involved in dealing drugs?" Quinn gave a small pout.

He chuckled. "Sadly, that statement could be true of millions of people in this country. Might not be so far-fetched given she died of a chemical overdose."

"Exactly. Time for coffee." She stood and stretched.

"Come on. I'll buy."

"No need. Let's cross to my office."

"No, thanks. I've smelled Chuck's coffee. Never wanted to taste it."

"Times have changed." She entered the code to the lab. "*Voilâ*, real coffee." She pointed to the new coffee machine.

"Well, I'll be. Nice job, Quinn."

"Not my doing. Chuck did it."

"Not being an interloper, am I?"

Chuck came around the corner. "Nope. Help yourself. Drink too much and we'll let you buy pods."

"Deal." George headed to the coffee machine as Quinn opened her office door.

"Fix one for you, Quinn?" George lifted a pod toward her.

"Sure. Dark Roast. Thanks."

Coffees in hand, they sat in Quinn's small office space. "Does this space make you claustrophobic, Quinn?"

"I think you either have claustrophobia or you don't. I don't. It serves the purpose. Make you uncomfortable?"

"Only the memories."

"Well, I'm all for building new memories."

"Fair enough. I like what you've done with the place." He pointed to her photos on the wall and her coat tree.

"Thanks. Now, I want to divide and conquer on looking at land acquisition."

"I can do it. I'm sure you have plenty to do."

Her secure line rang.

"Isaacs."

"O'Haire. You're in luck. A judge was available. Warrant is in your secure folder."

"You rock. Thanks."

"Happy hunting. Later."

Quinn turned to her computer while saying, "Got the warrant. Have time to go to Maryville by way of The Mountain Villages?"

"Wouldn't miss it for the world."

They walked out of the office with the copy of the warrant in Quinn's hand.

Mr. S's Demands

The thug had been chattering for minutes. "So, Mr. S. Still no one at the house. You want me to go to his office?"

"Do you have that video done?"

"Yes, sir. It'll get his attention."

"Give me a minute." Mr. S. sat back in his chair and stared out the window overlooking his city; a real city, not the hick city in the south where his thug was.

The thug clicked his tongue against his teeth; it sounded like a mouse squeak.

"Stop it, already."

The thug stopped.

Can this guy go into an office without acting like the thug he is? Mr. S. had never given the thug this kind of assignment. He didn't have anyone else to do it, and he needed Andrew Culbert III to know he better get the third piece of land signed, sealed, and delivered. Then he considered the risk of having the thug seen. *Bad enough that the chemist has seen him. The chemist better be ready to move.*

"No, it's fine. I'll take care of it. Keep surveillance on the house and take a ride out to tell that chemist I want specifics on his production ramp-up by tomorrow." Mr. S. ended the call and looked up the Culbert Real Estate offices.

"Culbert and Company." The man's voice was even and unremarkable, but not southern.

Mr. S. knew the assistant to Andrew Culbert was a woman. "Andrew Culbert, please."

"Who's calling, please?"

"Name's Sampson." He almost choked trying not to laugh at his joke. "He'll know who I am. We talked last week."

"One moment, please." The man answering the phone wanted to keep Mr. Sampson on the line.

Mr. S. drummed his fingers on the desk. He looked at the city skyline. He didn't know which he liked better: Chicago or Boston. *Definitely not Detroit.*

"Sir, sorry to keep you waiting. Mr. Culbert asked that I take a message." He had already seen that the phone number was blocked. "May I have the best number for him to reach you?"

"No problem. I'll call later. When do you expect him?"

"He has a very busy schedule this week. I could try to find a time that works for both of you if you give me some options."

"Not necessary. Thanks." Mr. S. was as polite as could be. He ended the call. *You better hope your assistant is out sick and you have temporary help, Andrew Culbert the third—I will find you.*

Executing a Warrant

George drove out of the Station and headed toward the Valley.

Quinn took out her phone and dialed Marjorie Topping. "Ms. Topping, this is Quinn Isaacs."

"Detective." Ms. Topping's voice was flat in acknowledgement.

Quinn strained to hear over the road noise: theirs, or hers, or both?

"Ms. Topping, I left my pen on your table. It was a gift from my parents. May I stop by in twenty minutes or so and pick it up?"

"It is a lovely pen. I was going to call to let you know you left it. Unfortunately, something has come up and I'm not at home. Could you come another day?"

"Certainly. Perhaps tomorrow or the next day. I'll call. Thank you, Ms. Topping." She ended the call.

"Not home?" George glanced over at her.

"Not home. If I were a betting woman, I'd bet she's on her way to Maryville."

"I wouldn't take that bet."

"Nothing ventured, nothing gained."

"Lights?"

"Is there a reasonable expectation that she could destroy evidence?"

"Seems that way to me. I'd swear to it in court."

"Me, too. Lights." They both knew they couldn't use the siren. It didn't involve life or death—Angela was already dead.

As they approached the road to Angela's condo complex, George turned off the lights. He turned onto her street in time for them to see Maria, Ms. Topping's assistant, step out of the mini-van. As she took the wheelchair out of the back passenger door, they pulled up beside her leaving room for Ms. Topping to exit.

Marjorie Topping turned her head and stiffened. She almost snarled at Maria. "Head for the ramp, Maria."

Quinn was at Angela's front door as the two women arrived from the ramp which they had to enter from the far side of the condo. "Ms. Topping, this is a warrant to search these premises and take any and all computers and any supporting evidence into custody."

Marjorie glared at her. She did not extend her hand to take the warrant.

"We've notified the Maryville police that we're executing this warrant. I expect an officer from their force at any time."

Just then a Maryville police SUV pulled behind Ms. Topping's mini-van. Quinn was glad to see it was Officer Kent.

"Afternoon, Detectives." He strode up toward the door. "Ladies." He nodded to Maria and Ms. Topping. "Need assistance?"

"Thanks for coming, Officer Kent. Nice to see you again. This Ms. Topping, Angela Topping's grandmother. I was just informing Ms. Topping of the warrant to enter these premises and to take any and all computers and supporting evidence into custody."

"Problem with that, ma'am?" He looked at Marjorie Topping.

Ms. Topping grabbed the warrant out of Quinn's hand. She took her time reading it.

"Open the door, Maria."

"Thank you. I'll ask you to wait out here and enjoy the beautiful day." Quinn looked at Officer Kent who was between Marjorie Topping and the door.

He nodded.

Maria unlocked the door and stood back. Quinn and George entered.

"Angela used one of the bedrooms as an office. I'm most interested in the computer or computers. Since we weren't allowed to open any drawers or doors with Gray Olson, let's see what we see."

Quinn and George pulled on gloves. George turned on the light as he entered the room. Quinn walked directly to the laptop on the desk and began disconnecting it from the power source. She took the external hard drive sitting next to it.

Outside Marjorie Topping looked at the officer. "Sir, if you don't mind. I'd like to call my attorney."

"Sure thing, ma'am." Officer Kent walked out on the sidewalk.

Gray Olson answered. "Marjorie, everything alright?"

"No. It's not." She told him to make arrangements to have Angela's remains taken to the local funeral home and she would be in touch with them to finalize plans. "Now, Gray. I am at Angela's condo. I was met here by Detective Isaacs who served a warrant to search Angela's belongings and take her computer and supporting evidence into custody."

"Did you voluntarily meet her there?"

"I did not. I simply decided I needed to see the last place Angela was as a vibrant young woman."

"Are you satisfied the warrant is legitimate?" He knew Quinn would not have given her anything else.

"I am." Her response was blunt.

"Tell me what I can do for you."

"Can she keep me from going inside?"

"It could be tricky. Granted you have a key, but given that Angela is deceased, they could keep you out until the court satisfies your right to the property."

"I have the right. My name is on the deed, isn't it?"

Gray had been putting Angela's documents in order. He had not yet told Ms. Topping Angela executed a new deed with only her name. The signature looked like Marjorie's but he wouldn't want to swear to it.

"Did you sign to change the deed?"

"No. Well, not to my knowledge." She thought of the many documents she signed each week when she and Angela were together. Angela always gave her an overview of what they were doing. She had quit reading those documents several years ago—she had trusted Angela. Her shoulders slumped. "Are you telling me the deed only has Angela's name?"

"Yes." He waited.

The front door opened. "Ms. Topping, Oh, I'm sorry." Quinn pulled off her gloves and stuck them in her pocket. She saw Marjorie Topping on the phone.

"Hold on, Gray."

"Ma'am, I regret to inform you we will need to seal the house and have our forensic team conduct a thorough search." She was not about to tell her they had found a false panel in the office room wall; behind it was another room filled with computer equipment.

"Gray, did you hear that?"

"Marjorie, may I speak to the Detective? Or you can have her call me."

Marjorie held out her phone. "It's Gray Olson."

Quinn took the phone. "This is Quinn Isaacs."

"Hey, Quinn. Could you repeat what you just told Ms. Topping?"

Quinn told him.

"May I know the name of the judge who signed the warrant?"

She told him.

Not just 'A' judge. The senior judge in the county. "Thanks, Quinn. Any problem with you if Ms. Topping leaves?"

"No sir. I will inform her we need her to remain in the area. I will need to talk with her further. We also need access to Angela's home; I'd rather not replace the lock. My techs should be here within the hour. I don't know how long it will take."

He sighed. "Thanks. Please let me speak to Marjorie."

Quinn handed her the phone and stepped back into the house. A knock on the door and she opened it.

"Ms. Topping would like to speak to you." Maria stepped back.

"Yes, Ms. Topping?"

"I am going home. Maria, give her the keys. Mr. Olson has reiterated what I heard you tell him. You can reach me at my home when you need to do so." She turned toward the end of the porch and the ramp. *Peter must be involved in this. I miss my husband's intellect and analytical mind in times like this.*

"Ms. Topping, I will need to give you a receipt for these keys. Please give me a minute." Quinn walked over to Officer Kent.

"I'm going to write a receipt to Ms. Topping for these keys and I would appreciate it if you would witness it."

"Yes, ma'am. Anything else?"

"There will be. Let's do this first."

Officer Kent pulled back in the driveway after Ms. Topping and Maria left. Quinn was standing on the porch waiting on him.

"Thanks. I've spoken with your sergeant and she said you could stay until our forensic team gets here."

"Yes, ma'am. She notified me. What do you need me to do?"

"At the moment, just enjoy the beautiful afternoon in our hills. I'm expecting our forensic team within the hour." She looked at her watch. "Well, now the half-hour. They will have their credentials. Other than that, please keep anyone else off the property."

Angela's next door neighbor pulled onto her driveway at that moment. She stopped and got out.

"What is going on? Where is Angela? You don't just come to a house—is her attorney in the house?" She had walked over to the driveway.

Quinn took out her ID. She had already made sure her badge was visible. "Ms. Thompson, I'm Detective Isaacs."

"I remember. Where is Angela?" The anger in her voice was barely controlled.

"I regret to inform you that Ms. Angela Topping is deceased."

"What? You're kidding?" She gasped. "You're not kidding?"

"No, ma'am. I am not." Quinn's face was impassive but her eyes revealed compassion.

"Is she in there?" She nodded toward Angela's condo.

"No. To the best of our knowledge, she hasn't been back here since you saw on her Thursday afternoon."

Then the first year lawyer kicked in. "Was she murdered?" Ms. Thompson looked around the yard and then toward her yard.

The death certificate was filed, so Quinn knew this woman could get it. "She died under suspicious circumstances."

"That's all. That's all you're going to say? Suspicious circumstances?" Her tongue darted like a venomous snake.

"That is all I know, Ms. Thompson."

The woman looked from Quinn to Officer Kent and back to Quinn. "Am I safe here?"

Officer Kent stepped up. "We have no reason to believe there is any risk to you or the community."

"Yeah, sure. I went to law school. I know the pat answers." She looked at Officer Kent. "No offense." She turned and went back to her car, got in, and drove off.

Chapter 16

Whatever the present moment contains, accept it as if you had chosen it.
Eckhart Tolle

What does the future hold—in this moment?

Kelly scanned Andrew's Power of Attorney sent by their attorney. She put it in front of the SBI Agent. "Now will you please get into this laptop?" She was not about to tell him Andrew had said time was critical. She looked at her watch, the afternoon was escaping. She turned toward the glass window which allowed her to see into Andrew's hospital room. His chest rose and fell a beat after the rhythm she knew accompanied the machines keeping him alive. She stepped away from the table and moved to the bedroom in the suite to wash her face and compose herself.

"Ma'am?" The man called out. He had not heard her return and sit in the arm chair behind him.

She jumped up quickly and moved to the table—all but pushing the Agent out of the way. "I can take it from here."

He pushed the chair back and stood up raising his hands as if in surrender.

"Sorry. I didn't mean to sound so curt. Time is critical."

"Ma'am, I can help with whatever you need."

"I just need to see who owns the other parcel of land near ours. That's all." She pulled up the chair and the man moved away. She thought she could hear someone speaking into his earbuds. She shook her head as if to clear it and entered the last password she knew for Andrew's email; she prayed he hadn't changed it. It opened. She breathed a sigh of relief. She quickly scanned his inbox for any emails from the end of the week before. She saw the one to Lee Ann and read it and his response: "…fraternity prank…" Her gasp caused the man to step forward.

"Ma'am, I know we're here at your request but I *can* help you."

She counted to ten in her head, slowed her breathing, and shut her eyes momentarily. "Thank you. First, I would need to know why I need help. Please—just give me a few minutes."

"Yes, ma'am." He walked over and looked out the window and saw the agent here to relieve him being dropped off by a van. The markings were clear: State Bureau of Investigation. He knew Ms. Culbert's brother was a top ranking SBI official in Nashville—they were here to protect her and her husband, not run an investigation.

The A-Team

"George, I want to be here while the A-Team does their work. If you want to go home, please feel free to take my vehicle. I can get a ride with the team, or if it's going to stretch into days, I'll call for someone to come get me."

"Seriously?" He squinted his eyes and pursed his lips trying to make a ferocious frown. "Detective Isaacs, you are my boss and you can order me home. I'm going to trust you meant it when you said, 'if.'" He stared at her but couldn't keep his face from turning to a smile and then he chuckled. "I'm in for the duration."

She grinned. "Didn't figure you'd want to miss out. At some point we'll need something to eat, and so will these folks. So, maybe you could talk to Officer Kent and get the low down on what police officers around here eat."

"Say what? We have to eat what local cops eat? We're out of town. I vote for the best in Maryville."

"Nice try." She cocked her head at him and then shook it. "Just ask the fine officer for some guidance. We can figure out the details later." She laughed and sat down in one of the rockers on the porch. *Spring is such a beautiful time of new growth…from the flowers to the trees, to baby birds, and insects. Wonder why it also seems a perfect time for crime? Are the criminals like the bears in our mountain? Stretching from a long winter's nap?* She saw the

A-Team van pull into the cul-de-sac. She stood and stretched before walking out to meet Sergeant Clark.

Steve Clark was the first one out of the van and his long stride had him meeting Quinn half-way up the driveway.

"Detective Isaacs…" Steve nodded to George who was walking over from the Maryville police officer, "…sounds like you have some interesting stuff here."

"Could be. Could also be a very private young woman who was on the up-and-up and tried to keep her business transactions from snooping eyes."

"Does it really look like a mini stock trading space?"

"Well…" Quinn hesitated. "It certainly is no stock exchange in scope, but there are plenty of monitors and what appears to be a mainframe computer which in my limited knowledge must be really fast and have enough capacity to search at pretty good speed."

"Then let's go have a look." Steve nodded to Officer Ruth DeLoach and then followed Quinn into the house.

Although the lot lines were narrow between the condos, they were individual units. Deloach organized the other members of the A-Team and did a perimeter surveillance of the outside.

Inside, Quinn opened the door to the hidden room.

Steve stared at the refrigerator size mainframe, monitors, and keyboard. He felt the frigidly cold temperature which had to have been an added air conditioning unit to reduce the heat generated by this computer. He gave a low, slow whistle. "That's a pretty sophisticated secret door to a very curious room of sophisticated equipment. How old was this young woman?"

"Twenty-four."

"Did she graduate *summa cum laude* at MIT when she was twelve?"

"Not that I'm aware but we'll check it out. As far as I know at this point, she went to UT-Knoxville."

"When we found her car, you mentioned the family has money. Most folks at twenty-four aren't driving a Lexus LS."

"Right. So, I'm guessing the cost of this wasn't a concern either. Any idea what all this costs?"

"I have no idea. I'm sure Gilbert will know but I'd hazard a guess that it's more than a hundred grand."

"What do you think it will take to sort this all out?" Quinn pointed toward the desk in the room which they had thought was her only work space. "There's a laptop which we've secured." She pointed. "Didn't expect to find this separate room."

"Need some time and Officer Gilbert to give us an assessment."

"Is he with you?"

"At your command, ma'am." Officer Horable Gilbert walked into the office space. Everyone in the Station called him by his last name—they couldn't say his first name with a straight face.

"Evening. Thanks for coming." She pointed into the interior room.

Officer Gilbert stepped into the opening and immediately turned back to look at Quinn. "Somebody running book on horses from here?"

Quinn laughed. "Thanks. I needed that. It never even occurred to me it could be a gambling front." She laughed again. "Well, Sergeant Clark, you were right. You never know what a day will bring."

Gilbert looked from one to the other.

Quinn didn't miss the look. "Gilbert, tell me what you need in order to figure out what we have here."

"Time." Gilbert was quick with his response as he headed toward the desk chair in the inner room while he looked around at the monitors. "And, much as I hate to say it, more equipment and help than we have."

"State folks?" Clark asked.

Gilbert nodded.

Quinn looked from one man to the other. "I'll need a few minutes. While I'm making a couple of calls, could you check out the laptop?"

"That I can handle." He picked up the briefcase he had put on the floor when he came in the room. "Want to check for prints first, Sarge?"

"Yes, sir." The sergeant went to get one of his techs.

Quinn walked out of the room and called the Agent-in-Charge at the SBI, Ralph Jackson.

He answered on the first ring. "Detective Isaacs. To what do I owe the pleasure?"

"Agent Jackson, I'm back asking for help."

"Here to serve. What's up?"

Quinn informed him of the situation, the warrant, and what they had found.

"Any problem working in that space?"

"Not that I can see. The owner is deceased. Her grandmother will inherit according to her attorney—unless something unusual turns up."

"Grandmother likely to get possession anytime soon?"

"Not if I can help it. She doesn't need the house or anything in it. Besides, I'm not yet convinced it isn't a crime scene." She told him what she knew of Ms. Topping at this point.

"Then I think we start on site. We can bring it into our labs if we need more."

"Any chance of getting anyone to Maryville this evening?" Quinn had her fingers crossed. She really didn't want to prolong this.

"I'll call you back."

"Thanks, Agent Jackson."

"It's Ralph. And you're welcome, Quinn." He ended the call.

Quinn immediately called Chief Hansen's secure line.

"Detective."

"Ma'am. Sorry to bother you, but felt you'd want this update immediately."

"I'm listening."

"On the recommendation of Officer Gilbert, I've called in the SBI on the Angela Topping residence." She proceeded to tell her what they had found and the earlier interactions with Ms. Topping, who may or may not know about the room. "Given the size and scope of the equipment it would be best to try and do a preliminary investigation here."

"Quinn, I'll reach out to the Chief in Maryville and see how he wants to handle this. We may need to send our officers to provide the security surveillance there." Chief Hansen always cut to the chase.

"Thanks for the follow-up with the Maryville Chief. Their duty sergeants have been very helpful; their names are Kent, Johnston, and Newsome. Officer Kent has been of assistance since our first call to Maryville on Angela. Once I have confirmation on the arrival of SBI techs, I will leave it in the capable hands of Sergeant Clark and head back. Detective Marshall and I need to pull on some threads around Patten and Dunn."

"Sounds like a solid plan. Thanks for the update. I'll let you know after I talk with the Maryville Chief and I'll follow-up through your reports unless you need something immediately."

"Yes, ma'am. Good evening." She ended the call and answered the incoming. "Isaacs."

"Quinn, Ralph Jackson. I have a tech team on the way as soon as you verify the address."

Quinn gave him the address. "Thanks so much. Sergeant Steve Clark will be in charge. I can be reached at any time."

"Good enough. Have a good night."

"You, too. Thanks, again." She ended the call and looked out the front window. Steve Clark was talking with his team. She had not seen him walk out.

Chemicals, Photos, and Ire

Mr. S. stared at his phone waiting to see the doctored photo of the lovely Mrs. Culbert. He tapped the screen as if that would make it arrive sooner. "Come on, dumb ass. Send the picture." His phone rang in his hand.

"What?" His tone was worse than a dagger to the heart—sharp and to the point.

"Mr. S., the file is too big to send by text. I sent it to that secure email."

"Why didn't you know that...oh, never mind. Stay by your phone." He ended the call and turned to his laptop. He opened the secure file and a slow grin spread across his face. *Well, well, dumb ass. You did alright. I might just like a piece of that action myself. She's a looker.* He closed the file and hit redial on his phone.

"Yes, Mr. S.?"

"Any answer on Culbert's phone?"

"No, sir. No one's home either."

Mr. S. slammed his fist down on the desk so hard his bottle of beer almost fell over. "I want this video in front of him now. I don't care how. I care when. And when is now!"

"Yes, sir." He chuckled.

"What's so funny?"

"I bet Culbert's still trying to figure out how we got into his secure phone."

"How did you?"

"Best you don't know if you end up in front of a judge."

"Don't get smart with me." Mr. S. took a deep breath. "Okay, you're right. That's your business."

"Yeah."

"What did you say?"

"I said, 'yes, sir.' Must have been a bad connection, sir." *You better remember you hired me cause I'm willing to do things you don't want to dirty your hands doing. I can include you, too.*

"Send it now. Report back to me as soon as you get any response. In the meantime, did you talk to that chemist again?"

"Called him, sir. Couldn't be in two places…"

Mr. S. slammed his hand again and this time he hit the beer bottle. It flew off the desk. "Damn it. I don't want the details. I want the results. What's the timeline?"

"He says he'll need two to three weeks minimum, and that's if you get him some packing help."

"No more. Those illegals will work twenty-four hours a day. Get out there! Make it happen." He made an arc with his arm like he was going to throw the phone against the wall. He dropped it on the desk and stood up.

The thug looked at his phone. "And goodbye to you, too."

Computers

Quinn and Steve walked out into Angela's great room. Quinn turned on a table lamp and sat down. Steve sat across from her.

"Steve, do you need to keep your team here?"

"We'll wait on the SBI folks and then decide. Once the tech finishes checking fingerprints on the laptop and the keyboard on the computer with the mainframe, we'll go from there. We'll want to search the rest of the house."

"We have a warrant. I'd say it's a good idea; we sure didn't expect to find that room."

"Then we'll get that done."

"Can't afford to miss anything."

"I agree. The team did a perimeter search when we got here and there are two HVAC units and a whole-house generator at the back of the condo. While generators are not unheard of in these mountains, they're rarely found in town. Additionally, there are multiple internet entries into the house. In the room with the mainframe, there is a separate thermostat likely tied to the additional HVAC system, and there's a UPS..." He stopped when she raised her hand.

"What's a UPS?" *I know HVAC is heating and air-conditioning. UPS?*

"Uninterruptable power source. Sorry."

"No need. Just don't find a lot of computers or their paraphernalia on the highways of immigration enforcement. Thanks for the information."

"Sure. Ask anytime. Anyway, bottom line is this is a well-designed and thought out system. It wasn't put in here to play video games."

Quinn nodded.

Steve knitted his brows. "Did Angela have a roommate, boyfriend, girl-friend?"

"No evidence we've found, but I want to reinterview the next door neighbor. Earlier she told George she wasn't aware of anyone coming over other than the grandmother."

"Doesn't mean there wasn't."

"True. Back doors on cul-de-sacs offer some protection. I noticed the one in this unit actually opens toward the end away from other units."

"Yep. My team reported that. Could provide some cover. That's why I sent them to check for any evidence of..." He looked up as the front door opened.

"Sarge, got a minute?"

Steve beckoned Officer DeLoach into the room. "What's up?"

"There's a path through the woods off the end of this unit that seems pretty well worn and possibly designed to be a walking or running path."

Quinn stood up. "Does it lead directly to the door of this unit? Or out to the street?"

"Both, ma'am."

Quinn looked at Steve and then back at DeLoach. "Any outside cameras in the area?"

"Looking now, ma'am."

Steve nodded to the officer. "Good work, DeLoach."

"Teamwork, sir. I'll pass it on." She turned and went back outside.

Steve stood. "I'll check with the tech about fingerprints."

"I'm sure Gilbert is itching to get into the laptop."

"Oh, I'm sure, too." Steve headed to check with the tech.

Quinn took out her secure phone and sent a text to Billy: "Tied up in M'ville. More later."

There was an immediate reply: "10-4."

She smiled, looked up at the fading light in the sky, and pulled the knot out of her hair.

Off to the Island

Kelly's brother, Lance Macklin, had some investigating to do. He could have used an SBI plane, but the paperwork to fly out of the country would have taken more time than he wanted to wait; he was worried the work-related things he'd had to deal with the last few days meant he'd already waited too long.

He wasn't as wealthy as his sister and brother-in-law, but like Kelly, his trust fund gave him toys his salary would never afford. He owned a share in a private plane, but before he could go anywhere, he had to talk to the pilot who knew where he needed to go. He was in Knoxville in the hangar of Andrew Culbert's private plane. He presented his official SBI identification; he did not mention the family connection.

"I've checked the flight plan and that island is pretty remote. Are you sure my plane can land there?" He knew how to sound official without being demanding.

"Yes, sir. It's a small landing strip, but wide enough for the wings on this P-24. It can handle…" He stopped midsentence when Lance held up his hand.

Lance answered his phone. He'd sent a text to the SBI agent with Kelly to call when his sister was available to talk.

"Kelly?"

"One moment, sir." The agent handed the phone to Kelly.

"Lance, did Momma tell you…"

"Yes. Now please just listen, I don't have time for chit-chat. You're welcome and we've got you covered. But we have to justify the services you're getting, so I need to fly to that island and find that drone."

"Lance, the drone was on our plane. It crashed on the balcony after it hit Andrew."

"I still have to find out who was flying it." He mouthed to the pilot. "The drone?"

The pilot turned and headed to a cabinet in the hangar.

"Lance, it was on an island and I don't even know where. Why do you need to go there? Did you send agents to protect us without authorization?"

"Kelly, listen to me. Now." He walked away from the pilot. "You are my baby sister and someone sent that drone to fly into your space. As a former mayor, your husband was a government official who unfortunately lost his most recent run for governor and we don't know if this was related." He knew when she called him it may not have been a random act. "I have a short window to learn as much as I can. I'm standing here with your pilot and it would help if he could fly me down. I was going to take my plane but yours will be faster. All I need you to do is tell him to take me. Then I need you to tell me where you were staying." He knew the Pilatus P-24 would get him there faster than his small private plane.

Kelly took a deep breath. *Well, if he's on the island I'll have more time to verify who STELT is.* "Let me speak to the pilot."

"Mrs. Culbert?"

"Good afternoon. Sorry to have to ask you to take another trip. I need you to take Lance to the island and call the driver Andrew uses there." Just because she hated to fly didn't mean she hadn't paid attention to the pilot's interaction with the driver.

"Mrs. Culbert, ma'am, I know this is sounds like you, but I'd feel a whole lot better if you could fax or text me permission."

"Sure. I should have thought of that. I'm at the hospital and don't have access to print out anything official. But I can write a note, take a picture and have it sent to you." She had no idea the number on the agent's phone was blocked. "You can ask my brother to show you his official identification if it will make you feel better."

"Ma'am? Your brother?" He glanced at Lance. "Yes, ma'am. He showed it to me."

"He's Associate Director of the State Bureau of Investigation." She wanted that to sink in.

"Yes, ma'am." The pilot looked at Kelly's brother. "It'll be just fine, ma'am. Just text the picture of your note. Hope Mr. Culbert is better soon."

"Thank you. I'll send the note in a minute." *I should have gone to law school—then I could figure out who's going to ask me for what kind of permission. Are so many people dishonest that no one trusts anyone anymore?* "Now if I could speak to my brother again."

The pilot handed Lance the phone.

Lance had heard the pilot say brother so he decided to emphasize it now. "Okay, baby sister, we all set here?"

"I'm going to text him a note that he has permission to take you. He has the number for Andrew's driver down there. Just so you know..." She described the house, what she remembered of the road and the little open air café. *That should keep him there for a day or two.* "Lance, did you show him your SBI ID? I'm sure he'll fly more safely knowing you're legit." She tried to laugh.

"He'll fly safely, Sis." *Of course I've shown him my official ID. Do you think he would have talked to me otherwise?*

"Lance..." The angst in her voice came through loud and clear.

"Kelly, he's seen my ID. Now get some rest and take care of Andrew."

Lance called for his driver to come inside. He took his business card out of his pocket and wrote a note for the drone, held it in front of the plastic bag and took a picture. He turned to the pilot, held out his ID, and handed him the card.

"Yes, sir. I saw it before."

"This card will have to act as a receipt for the drone. If you want the picture with my card and the drone, I'll text it to you."

"No problem, sir. The card will do."

"Fine. While my sister is sending you permission, get the flight plan filed and this baby ready to go."

"Sir, this plane is always ready to fly. I'll file the flight plan right now."

"Good."

Lance's driver, a state highway patrolman in uniform, came through the side door. Lance handed him the drone which was in a large clear plastic bag. "Need you to get this to the lab here in Knoxville and I want to know everything they can find out about it: make, serial number, any registration, where it was bought...they'll know the drill. I'll call the local in charge. I'm going to take a little trip and will be back..." Lance looked at his watch. "I'll be back tomorrow. I'll call when I know my ETA."

"Sir, not to overstep, but shouldn't someone go with you?"

Lance stopped himself before he spoke. He knew he was second in command at the SBI, but he had spoken with the Director and they agreed the best thing for him was to try to figure out what was going on with as little attention to it as possible. He had started as a rookie agent just like everyone else and risen through the ranks. *I am not a political appointee or an administrative desk jockey…I know what I'm doing—even if I don't know what I'm getting into.*

"Appreciate the concern. Got this covered. Thanks for taking care of the drone."

The highway patrolman knew a dismissal. "Yes, sir. On it." He turned and left.

The pilot stood at the bottom of the stairs of the plane. "Ready when you are, sir."

He held up his phone. "I assume I can make a call from this baby."

"Yes, sir."

"Good. Then let's go." Lance jogged up the stairs and the pilot moved out of the hangar to start his preflight check.

Lance called Assistant Director Elliott Nelson who was in charge of the local SBI office.

"Nelson."

"Hey, Elliott. Lance Macklin here."

"Afternoon. What's up?"

"Need some help from your techs. I'm sending my driver in with a drone that was involved in an incident I'm looking into. Don't have anything else to share at the moment. Just need them to get any and all information they can about the drone, any prints…whatever you can find and identify."

"Yes, sir. Priority?"

"Top."

"We'll get on it."

"I'm headed out on another aspect that may involve the drone. I'll check back with you late tomorrow. If they find anything significant, you can send it to me by secure server."

"Got it. Good luck with your search."

"Thanks, Elliott. Later." Lance ended the call and leaned back in the plush chair on the Pilatus P-24 just as the pilot lifted off. He looked out over the pops of green which had started to appear as spring took over the mountains.

Chapter 17

Ideas are like fish...if you want to catch the big fish, you've got to go deeper.
David Lynch

In Good Hands

Quinn saw the SBI van pull up and met the agents at the door. "Agent Franklin, nice to see you again."

"May have to put you on the SBI payroll if you keep finding these unusual cases for us." He smiled as he shook her hand.

"You remember Sergeant Clark?" Quinn stepped to the side as Steve moved in and extended his hand.

"Thanks for coming. This one doesn't include all the old bones like the last case."

"Can't always have fun." Franklin grinned.

Quinn and Steve knew that Ed Franklin was a forensic bone expert.

"Understand you've got some high powered computing going on here, though. Is that right?" Franklin looked around the great room.

Quinn pointed down the hall as Steve led the way. "Come see for yourself." She introduced herself to the technicians with Ed Franklin. *Glad one of you is a woman. Might need someone who might think like Angela did.*

"Hey, Sarge. Just finished." The Round City technician who had been gathering prints looked up. Then he saw the others.

"These are SBI folks. What'd you find?"

"Same prints on laptop as some of the ones on the keyboard in there."

"Some?"

"Right. Found four that don't appear consistent with the ones on the laptop. I'll head out and get a run going on them."

"Good plan. Need some elbow room in here, too." He slapped the tech on the back and the others let him exit the room.

Ed Franklin walked in while the two techs stayed in the hallway. "Hey, Gilbert. Finding anything?"

"Hey, Ed. Just got started. You'll want to see the stuff in there." He pointed toward the open wall panel.

Ed turned and walked toward the opening. He surveyed the finishes on the hidden door. "Wow, someone went to a lot of trouble to make that disappear."

Quinn looked at Steve and then Ed. "So it appears. Inside you'll see why."

Ed stepped into the room and turned his head from side to side. "Whoa! Running book in here?"

Gilbert called out. "My bet is horses."

"Could be a lot more than that." Ed replied. "Well, no time like the present. Glad you got prints off the keyboard. Seems he lifted a few here, too." Ed pointed to the worktable and the access door on the mainframe.

Quinn was standing in the doorway. "Tell us what you need."

"Time. I'll get these two going on this and see if we can get in. They both have magic fingers."

Quinn noted how young the male tech looked. *If I were to bet, I'd bet this young man is a genius hacker working for the good guys.* "I'll wait in the great room."

"Be there in a minute." Ed Franklin turned to his techs. "Let me know what you need. I'll be in the front." He walked out. Steve followed him into the great room.

"Quite a setup in there, Quinn. We'll be here for a while, I'm sure. Unless you have a big need to hang around, I'd say head home. I'll call you when I know something."

"I'm going to go next door and see if the neighbor is home yet. Then George Marshall and I will head back to Round City. Steve's going to have his crew do a sweep of the rest of this place if it won't disturb you or your team."

"Nope. We're good."

Steve said, "Somebody on our team will stay when we're finished. That is, if we finish before dawn."

"I'll see if I can talk to the woman next door and then George and I will go get some food for all of you. Steve, I'm still waiting on the Chief to let me know if we need to relieve the Maryville officer. Need anything from me, Ed?"

"Not at the moment. I've got your number. I'll call." He shook her hand.

Quinn smiled. "Thanks for coming. I've got other threads to pull on this case."

She headed toward the door.

"I'll walk you out." Steve followed her. Once outside, Steve stopped her. "Quinn, even if Maryville wants someone here, I think we need our own folks here. We know Angela isn't coming back, but we don't know if someone else may try to enter. I think we need more than a front yard sentry."

"Good point, Steve. Since you and your team are here, at least for a while, I'll get it sorted out when I hear from the Chief and let you know. That work?"

"Sure. You and George don't need to get food. Saw a sub shop on the road out on the main road. We'll take care of the SBI folks, too. You can head on back."

"Thanks, Steve."

George walked up.

"Hey, George. Is the neighbor home?" Quinn nodded toward the Thompson residence.

"She drove up about ten minutes ago. Need anything?"

"Let's go have a talk with her." She turned to Steve. "Thanks for taking care of the food, Steve. Bill it to my unit."

"Oh, you bet." He laughed. "Thanks, Quinn. Glad you're on board." He turned and motioned to Officer DeLoach.

Quinn and George stepped over to the condo next door. She rang the bell.

"Yes?" Ms. Thompson was in jeans and a starched white shirt with the shirttail out.

"Ms. Thompson, I'm sorry to bother you, but I have a few questions I need to ask."

"You remember Detective Marshall. I'm Detective Isaacs." Both held out their IDs.

"Yes, I know. What are your questions?"

"May we come in?"

Ms. Thompson let out a long sigh, swung the door open further, and stepped back so they could enter.

"Thank you."

"Have a seat." She pointed to the furniture in the same open space that Angela's unit had.

"We won't take much of your time." Quinn smiled at her. George took out his note pad.

"How long have you lived here?"

"Little over three years. Since the complex opened."

"What amenities are provided with the complex?"

"Are you serious? What does that have to do with Angela's death?"

Quinn just smiled.

"Okay. Okay. There's a clubhouse, pool, workout room, walking trails, and there are supposedly plans for some retail space. Although I haven't seen any indication of that happening."

"Do you use any of the amenities?"

Ms. Thompson squinted her eyes. "Look, I went to law school. Graduated in the top five percent in my class. I've been through interrogation training and observed more than a few. Just ask what you want to know."

"Do you use the walking trails at the end of the cul-de-sac?"

"No."

"Did Angela?"

"I doubt it. Her asthma was pretty bad. She never opened up her house and to my knowledge didn't use the trails."

"Have you seen others use the trail?"

"Occasionally. Mostly notice it on weekends. During the week I'm pretty much focused on backing out of my garage and getting to work—determined to be the youngest junior partner." She smiled in a way that showed both confidence and ambition.

"Many folks use the trail on the weekends?" Quinn returned her smile—equally confident though not ambitious in the same dog-eat-dog way.

"Couldn't say. I've seen one or two. I walked it once when I first moved in. It winds through the whole wooded area this complex encircles. I'm sure it's great for folks who have time to use it, but I'm not a big fan of dark woods." She stopped abruptly.

"Thanks for your time." Quinn feigned walking away and stopped. "One more thing. Did Angela's generator get used much?"

"Her what?"

"She has a whole house generator behind her unit. Just wondered if you had much problem with loss of electricity."

"Really? She did? I had no idea. I never heard it. Why would you have a generator here?"

"Some folks just feel more secure. We do get some ice storms from time to time. Thanks, again, for your time. We appreciate it." Quinn and George headed for the door.

"I thought you said Angela didn't die here. Why the questions about the trail? Do I need to be worried?"

Quinn spoke with quiet authority. "No reason to be concerned. If that changes, we'll let you know."

"Well, I guess as long as half of the police in the region and the SBI are here, I'm safe."

Quinn smiled noting that the young woman paid attention to the vehicles parked in Angela's driveway. "We'll be in touch if we have any other questions."

"You know where to find me." Ms. Thompson held the door open and then shut it—barely missing George as he took his last step across the threshold onto the porch.

As they walked to Quinn's SUV, she pointed to her watch. "Have time to grab a bite on our way or do you need to get home?"

"I can always eat. Carrie's used to the hours. Anything you were fishing for with Ms. Thompson?"

They got in Quinn's vehicle. "Sorry, should have talked with you before we went in."

"No need. I was able to follow your questioning."

"If I had some evidence to pursue, I'd have kept at it. Just trying to get a feel for foot traffic around here." She paused and spoke in a much quieter tone. "Sometimes I feel like I'm taking this job in stride—sometimes I feel like I have no idea what I'm doing."

"Open confession of a fear every cop has...but is generally unwilling to admit. Of course, it's those who don't admit it to themselves who generally don't succeed."

"Thanks, George." She exited the condominium complex. "So, take me out of my pity party and tell me what you've learned in the last few hours here."

On the Island

They landed just before sunset and Lance was mesmerized by the brilliant yellows, oranges, and reds dancing across the horizon. "Nice place."

"Yes, sir." The pilot had not spoken other than to give safety directions. "Some of the nicest sunsets I've seen."

"Been here a lot?"

"Several times." The pilot knew his boss was Mr. Culbert. He was not about to say any more than he had to say. "I've notified the driver on the island. He should be waiting for us."

"Someplace I can stay around here?"

"Well, sir, I assumed you'd stay at Mr. Culbert's." He looked at Lance. "I stay at a small B&B near the landing strip. I can see if she has a room."

"I'd appreciate it."

"Yes, sir. I'm sure it'll be no problem. This isn't a big tourist area."

May or may not stay there, but want a plan. Lance stepped off the plane and noticed there was no other plane here and only this hangar. *Own this, too, Andrew? Your daddy probably did.*

The driver pulled up in front of the stairs. "Sir." The driver nodded and opened the back door.

"Problem if I sit up front with you?" Lance extended his hand to shake. "I'm Lance Macklin. I'm Mrs. Culbert's brother."

The driver looked at the man who was six foot three and would have towered over the tiny woman he knew as Mrs. Culbert. *If you say so.* "No problem at all." He shut the back passenger door and opened the front one.

Lance turned to the pilot. "Come on. We'll drop you at the B&B."

"Thanks. It's right over there." He pointed to the edge of the water on the southwest side of the island. "I'll walk. The driver can get you back here. Hope you find what you're looking for."

Lance looked at him with the eyes of an investigator. "Thanks." He turned to the driver. "The Culbert's home, please."

The driver pulled up at the gate to the wall around the Victorian building. *The façade reminds me of the Carson Mansion in California.* "Someone here?"

"Yes, sir. The housekeeper. I also took the liberty of calling Ms. Suzanne, the nanny."

Lance wondered why. *Any information is better than none.*

The gate opened and the driver pulled in. The housekeeper was standing on the back porch. She generally stayed out of sight when Mr. Culbert was here, but the driver had told her to be available.

Lance hopped out, asked the driver to wait, and walked up the steps.

"Evening, ma'am. I'm Mrs. Culbert's brother, Lance. Pleased to meet you." He knew his southern drawl and manners would go a long way.

"Pleased to meet you, sir. I'm Evelyn. Ms. Suzanne is in the kitchen. Come on in."

Updates

Kelly stared at the screen on the laptop. *Why did you tell Lee Ann it was a fraternity brother's prank?* She looked toward the window separating her from the room where her husband was fighting for his life. *I'm fighting for your life and ours. What were you thinking?* If the SBI agent could have seen her face he might have thought she was delusional.

There was a soft knock on the door. Kelly turned toward the door.

The agent stood to open it. He stepped back and a woman walked in. He spoke so quietly to her that Kelly couldn't hear. Then they both walked toward her.

"Ms. Culbert, this is Agent Sandy Davis."

Kelly extended her hand. "Nice to meet you. Thank you for coming."

"Nice to meet you, too. Sorry for the circumstances, ma'am."

"I'll be leaving now, ma'am. Agent Davis can assist with anything you need."

"Thank you for your patience and for being here, Agent. Have a nice evening." She shook his hand. As he left the room, she turned to Agent Davis. "I assume this means there are new agents with my mother and children."

"Yes, ma'am. Would you like to speak to them?"

"Yes. Is it possible to speak to my children on the agent's phone?"

"Certainly. I'll make sure the shift in agents has occurred and then you can talk to your children...and your mother if you wish."

"Thank you, I would like that." She turned and walked to the window between the sitting room and where Andrew lay in a hospital bed—tubes, machines, blinking lights overshadowing him. A tear ran down her cheek. She put her hand on the glass. *Please come back to me, Andrew. Please.* She took her hand off the cool glass and wiped her cheek.

"Ma'am. I have the agent on the phone." She extended it to Kelly.

"Good evening. Thank you for being there. Without alarming my mother or children, are they alright?"

"Appear to be enjoying a nice supper and I'm informed things are ready to put the children to bed."

She smiled. "Thank you. May I speak with my mother?"

The slow southern drawl of her mother's voice was unmistakable to her. "Honey, Kelly, are you okay?"

"I am, Momma. Andrew's in good hands here at the hospital and please pray he will show signs of improvement soon."

"Of course, dear. Of course. The children are happy and having fun playing with their toys. They love to play hide-and-go-seek, too. We're fine. Don't worry about us. You just take care of Andrew."

"I'm trying, Momma. Hopefully by morning I'll know more and can slip away to come see the kids."

"Kelly, they'll be fine. I know you miss them, but you stay there. Even if he can't tell you, Andrew needs you close by."

Kelly smiled. Her mother always dispensed southern wisdom. "You're right, Momma. May I speak to the children? Then I want to speak to you again."

"Hi, Mommy." Andy sounded so cheerful. "We had macaronis for supper."

She smiled, as she always did, when he tried to say a word that was still a bit challenging for him. "Sounds delicious. Is Anne being a good girl?"

"Yes, Mommy. Grammy plays with us like you do. My sister likes sitting in Grammy's lap."

A twinge of guilt, and maybe a little jealousy, pulled at Kelly's heart. "I know, sweetheart. Grammy gives good hugs."

"Yes, ma'am. I like Grammy's hugs, too." He paused and then whispered. "I miss your hugs, Mommy."

Kelly felt a knot tighten in her throat. Her voice almost croaked when she spoke. "I miss your hugs, too, sweet boy. Now finish your supper and be good for Grammy and the nice man there."

"Okay. I will. He's funny."

"That's good. Be polite." She knew the agent would be in plainclothes and she was grateful her mother understood that if her own son sent agents, she was not to question it. *What would I have done if my brother wasn't Associate Director of the SBI?* "Let me speak to Grammy and Anne, please. Daddy and I love you, Andy. We'll see you soon. Sweet dreams."

"Love you, too, Mommy. Tell Daddy I love him, too."

"I will." She had been watching Andrew the whole time through the window.

"Kelly, Anne's listening." Her mother's voice startled her.

"Hey, sweet girl. This is Mommy. I miss you and I'm so happy you're having fun with Grammy."

The two-year-old, Anne, smiled and stared at her grandmother. "K, Mommy." It sounded like she was saying, "mummy."

"Daddy and I love you and we'll see you soon. Be good for Grammy. Sweet dreams."

"Bye-bye." The sweetness in Anne's voice tore at Kelly—*Please, please be safe.*

"Kelly, it's me. The kids are fine. Now you get some rest and I'll be right here. We're all fine."

"Thanks, Momma. If you talk to Lance, please tell him I appreciate the support and love."

"He knows, Kelly. He knows."

"Please, Momma. It's important..."

"Of course, dear. I'll tell him. Get some rest. I love you always, you know that, right?"

"I do, Momma. Love you, too. Thanks, again. Good night." She ended the call. *Will Lance believe me that I just wanted protection because of the drone on an isolated island? I didn't think he'd take off and go to the island. At least it may mean he won't find out about the land sales.* Her hands trembled.

When she turned, she saw Agent Davis had moved over to the far corner of the room giving her privacy. She walked over and gave the phone to her. "Thanks."

She walked into the bedroom of the suite, sat on the bed, and wept silent tears. Within minutes, she sat up straight, stood, and went to wash her face. She was close to figuring out who STELT was—the ones who owned the third piece of property. *Wonder what Andrew will say when he finds out I know how to navigate the dark web?*

She walked back into the sitting room. "Agent Davis, have you had supper?"

"Yes, ma'am. Is there something I can order for you?"

"That would be nice. A Caesar salad with chicken and I think we need fresh coffee and tea. Please get whatever you'd like. Thanks."

"Happy to do it." Sandy Davis called the service desk in the wing. She'd been informed they would get the food and have a volunteer deliver it to the desk. The agent outside the door would get it. She jerked around when she heard Kelly scream.

"Oh, my God." Kelly was ashen white as she stared at the computer screen.

Sandy moved with speed to the table.

Kelly closed the top of the computer. *I hope she didn't see the picture.*

The Chemist

The chemist had the production of the capsules running smoothly and he only needed to periodically check the machines to make sure they didn't jam. He didn't care whether the folks in the last modular unit got them boxed and ready for shipping; the thug could worry about that. He was worried about his brother and couldn't figure out why he hadn't heard from him. His lifelong fascination with chemicals and their powers had absorbed the last three days as he continued to resolve the best delivery mechanism for his special project: nasal spray, powder inhale, or dispensed through the heat of a burning candle. He was currently testing each of them. *This project is only a little safer than cooking meth. I'll either figure out how to make a fortune or send myself into orbit.*

He'd been more diligent about keeping his phone close at hand, hoping to hear from his brother if by some miracle he remembered the number without his phone. His brother's crushed phone sat next to his as a reminder to be available. He saw a text flash on the screen: "Boss ain't joking. Ramp it up."

Yeah, yeah. Do you think your text message carries any more weight for me than that stupid phone call earlier? Kiss my... A pounding on the outside double doors broke his concentration. He rushed to the door.

"Mister. Need help. Problema." The short man, who the chemist suspected was an illegal immigrant, waved his hand toward the modular unit where the capsules came off the machines.

The chemist rolled his eyes. He was so close to solving his real problem. "Okay, okay." He locked the double doors and almost tripped over the short stride of the man in front of him. The explosion threw them both to the ground.

Chapter 18

It always seems impossible until it's done.
Nelson Mandela

Back to Round City

Quinn took the last bite of her sandwich. "Thanks, George."

"Officer Kent did us a solid. Good food!"

She nodded. "So the part of the walking trail that leads to Angela's back door seems more worn that the part leading to the street?"

"Without precise measurement, and not knowing if it was lower than the original path to start, it's only an observation."

"Seems to me a lot of what we do is observing—then putting the pieces together from those observations."

"That it is, Detective. That it is. Ready to hit the road?"

"Let's do it. When we get back, I'm going to update the board and then see if we have any hits on the prints from Angela's computers. Tomorrow, we need to see what we can find on Dunn and Patten and be prepared to pay another visit to Marjorie Topping if the SBI folks give us something we can work with."

"Well, for sure you need to go get your pen, right?"

"Oh, yeah, I'm saving that little ace in the hole if I don't get to go in with a warrant."

"Well, well. The new detective learns quickly. Good job, *Lead* Detective Isaacs."

Quinn heard the respect in the inflection he gave to her title. It boosted her confidence.

They both left money with a tip on their checks and stood to leave the small café. They wanted to be on the road back to Round City.

George held the door open for Quinn. "When I retire, I want to look at statistics on the longest APB on record."

Quinn gave him a puzzled look. "Seriously? Given the hands-on nature of Carrie's business, I'd think you'd want to travel."

"I'm sure we'll travel. We actually do get away from time-to-time now. Anyway, retirement is a long way off. Our current APB on Dunn is *now*. I can help update the board."

"Nothing critical, just want to have a look at it. We'll regroup in the morning."

"You're the boss."

Back at the Station, they scanned their IDs at the back door and Quinn turned to say good night to George.

He nodded his head toward their workroom. "Come on, let's get the board updated and then we can both go home."

She headed down the hall. In short order, Quinn was logged into the computer and George was writing on the dry erase board.

"George, we've got some information on the prints."

He turned from the board and looked at her.

"Angela's prints matched the laptop and accounted for some of the ones on the keyboard in the inner room."

"No surprise there. The others?"

"No hits yet. I'm guessing the speed on Angela is because she's in our system." She sighed. "I was hopeful we'd have a plan of attack for the morning."

"Still may have when we come in. Now let's finish up the board and get out of here." He turned to Quinn.

"Nothing on the APB on Dunn." She sat back in the chair. "Okay, run me through what you've put on the board."

The new information they had was in Quinn's written report and George had printed the photos of the outside of Angela's house and the trail and put them on the board. He turned to Quinn. "We have some things we didn't have before, but we have no idea if they're related to Angela's death or not."

"True." Quinn felt her secure phone vibrate. "Isaacs."

"Detective," the Chief's tone was crisp. "Just heard from the Chief in Maryville and we've agreed he'll keep a presence at the condo since we're in his jurisdiction. He also offered any assistance we need."

"Thank you, Chief. Sergeant Clark and the A-Team are still there doing a search of the rest of the house."

"My preference, given the unusual nature of this case, is to have you send a detective and an officer to be on scene until tomorrow when we can sort out what we need there going forward."

"Yes, ma'am. I'll get it done. Our report is in the system. Detective Marshall and I are in the workroom wrapping up for today."

"Okay. Good work, Quinn. Now go home."

"Yes, ma'am. Have a good evening."

George was watching Quinn and gathered they'd been given a directive.

Quinn sat her phone on the worktable. "Maryville will keep an officer there and we need to send an officer and a detective to relieve the A-Team. I'll set it up and Steve can notify dispatch when he expects his team to be headed out."

George nodded. "Sounds good to me. Need anything?"

"No. I'm good. You head out. I'll be out of here within fifteen."

He stared at her.

"I promise."

"Let me see your hands."

Quinn raised them and turned them back and forth.

"Still promise?"

She cocked her head and looked at him. Then she started laughing. "George, I didn't have my fingers crossed. Nothing more I can do tonight and I need to let this percolate."

"You're learning. I'll do a quick check in my office. Then I'll walk you out."

"George, go home." She tried to sound authoritative.

"Yes, ma'am. As soon as I check the office and stop by to make sure you walk out, too."

She laughed. "Thanks, George. I've never had a regular partner in my work. Nice to know someone's got my back—even when it's about making sure I get out of here!"

"Back shortly."

Quinn studied the board. *Something's missing. Who was Angela's contact in the land sales? Was it a partner? Financial backer? Just a friend? I can't help but think there's something we're missing here. Her death may truly be straightforward a result of exposure to the chemicals. But...*She flipped off the light switch in the workroom and walked across the hall. It was dark since Chuck was gone for the day. She made arrangements for coverage in Maryville and talked with Steve Clark so he could contact the replacements. She scanned the administrative email inbox and didn't see anything that couldn't wait until tomorrow.

She took out her personal phone and sent a text to Billy: "Headed home. Call later?"

She heard the outer door of the lab open. George called to her. "Ready to go?"

"Yes." She closed her office door and walked through the lab door George held open. They exited the Station and headed for her parking space. "Night, George. Good work today. Give my regards to Carrie."

"Night, Quinn. Get some rest. Might be a big day tomorrow."

"Whoa, whoa, whoa." She turned and headed toward him. "What does that mean? Something percolating in your brain you haven't shared?"

He stopped and looked at her. "Been at this a long time. Let's just call it the gut feeling that we're in the lull before the storm."

"Then we better be ready to batten down the hatches."

George started laughing. "Didn't know you had a nautical streak."

"Can't reveal all my secrets, right?"

"Right." His voice softened. "Now go home, Quinn. Act like you have a life outside of work."

She smiled. "Back atcha. Night." She turned back to her SUV, got in, and drove out of the Station parking area. Her personal phone pinged with a text: "Now?"

She touched Billy's number. It rang once.

"Guess now works." Billy's voice was soothing.

"Hey. Yes, now is perfect. Working?"

"Nope. I know it's after seven but have you eaten?"

"Yes, George and I stopped to get something on our way back from Maryville. Have you?"

"Headed home to do that. Of course, I could do without eating and head to the big city."

"Nah, Knoxville's too far. Why don't you come to Round City? I can probably even fix you an egg or something."

"Be there in thirty. Love you." He ended the call.

She backed into her garage, stepped out of her boots, put on her slippers by the kitchen door, and secured her service weapon and badge in the safe in less than two minutes. She opened the fridge. *Time for a grocery order. In the meantime...what can I fix him?*

Her secure phone rang. "Isaacs."

"Detective, I have a call from a probation officer in Illinois—Mr. Hodges."

"Thanks." She heard the low click as the call was switched to her.

"Isaacs."

"Detective, I told you I'd call back with the name of the detective in Chicago who had worked Dunn's case."

"Thank, Mr. Hodges."

"Well, seems she's no longer with the force. Tried to find out who else had worked on Dunn, but no luck. Afraid you'll have to go through channels with the police to get the report. Best I could do."

"No problem, Mr. Hodges. I appreciate your efforts. No signs of Dunn in southern Illinois are there?"

"No. I've got pretty good contacts and I'll let you know if I learn anything."

"I really appreciate it. Nothing new here. I'll let you know when we find him."

"Okay, thanks." *Confident, isn't she?* "Illinois judges aren't too happy about repeat offenders."

"Neither are Tennessee judges. Thanks, again for the effort."

"Anytime."

The call ended. She realized the chirping noise was the fridge door still open.

The Hospital

The blood had drained from Kelly's face. She stared at the screen.

SBI agent Sandy Davis was by her side and checking Kelly's pulse. "Mrs. Culbert, I'm going to turn your chair toward me." She had glanced at the computer screen as she focused on making sure Kelly was okay.

Did I get the lid closed in time? Did she see it? She looked at the agent. "I'll be fine."

"Mrs. Culbert, it is pretty easy for us to protect you from physical harm here, but I think your concerns are beyond that. I saw the screen before you closed the computer. If someone is stalking you, I can help."

There was a knock on the door. Sandy knew it was the agent with the food. She also knew he'd enter the room if she didn't answer.

"I'm fine now. Please get the door." Kelly nodded.

The door opened and the agent looked in. Sandy pointed to the small table with two chairs used for dining. He walked in and set the food down. "Something I can do to help?"

"We're good. Thanks." Sandy looked at him but turned her eyes toward Kelly.

He nodded understanding. "I'm just outside the door."

Sandy turned back to Kelly. "I'm going to get you some water and then you should eat. It will help."

"Thank you. I can walk to the table." Kelly stood and sat right back down.

"Just sit, please. I'll get you water."

As she handed Kelly the water, Sandy saw medical personnel moving with purpose into the room where Mr. Culbert was. She eased over and closed the curtains over the glass window dividing the suite from his room.

Kelly sipped the water she'd been handed and leaned back in the chair. "May I ask if you have children, Agent?"

"No, I don't. I understand you have two—a boy and a girl, right?"

"Yes, Andy is four and Anne is two. She's just starting to talk. I think it's because Andy always talks for her."

Sandy chuckled. "I have nieces and nephews. It seems to me the older ones always want to talk for the little ones. I always wondered if it was because the older one liked having control over someone else or if it was because they could anticipate what the other one wanted."

"Maybe a bit of both." Kelly's color was returning and she gave a sad smile. "If I share something with you, do you have to report it?"

"That depends on whether it involves a crime or not."

"I wish I knew."

"Mrs. Culbert..." She stopped when Kelly interrupted her.

"Call me Kelly, please."

"Sure, Kelly. I'm Sandy."

"Sandy, I know you know who my brother is. At first, I thought he sent protection because he's my brother and I asked—maybe that's part of it. He reminded me this afternoon that my husband just lost his run for governor and that could be a factor, too."

"Kelly, given what I know of your brother, he is an upright cop who has lots of talent which is why he was put him in charge of cybersecurity for the SBI. Some folks end up in director positions from political appointments, and they may or may not know anything about what we do. You already know your brother came up through the ranks. I worked a few cases with him several years ago and I deeply respect him. So, you can quit worrying about why we're here." She took a breath. "We can be a protective detail when it's required, but my first observations of your situation suggest you have some pretty weighty matters on your mind beyond the concern for your husband."

Kelly moved her fork around the plate with the salad on it, having only taken a few small bites.

"Kelly, you need to eat. I'm going to sound like the proverbial mother here, but you need your strength. At least eat the chicken, it will give you some protein."

Kelly laughed. "That's exactly what my mother would say." She looked at Sandy. "No offense." She guessed the agent was close to her own age. Kelly took a bite of the chicken. She took another.

Sandy let her eat. *I don't think that nude photo was something she put on the screen.* She watched Kelly as she took another bite.

The Chemist

The chemist realized he was on top of the man who was in charge of the group who packed the capsules being sold on the street. Fighting his own addiction every minute of every day, he wondered when anyone would figure out half the pills were sugar. He shook his head and turned it from side to side to make sure he still could. *What made me think of the capsules with sugar? Thought I'd forgotten my own little rebellion in making them.* He looked over his shoulder as he moved and then he looked down at the man on the floor. He wasn't moving. *Oh, shit. Did I kill him?* He reached down and touched the man's neck. *He has a pulse. Must have hit his head when he went down.*

He stood and walked to the door they had just shut before the explosion. The door handle was hot. *Dammit, there's a fire.* He didn't think he should move the man, but he also knew his phone was on the table next to his brother's in his special lab. *What set off the explosion?* He heard a moan.

"Hey, man. You, okay?" He bent down to the Hispanic man who was trying to sit up.

"O...K..." His voice was halting, but he was sitting up with his back against the wall. Then as if by magic, he stood. "Must go. Problema." He turned toward the next doorway which lead to the portable with the packing machines. He wobbled as he started to walk.

"Okay, let's go." The chemist planned to go to the exit door from the packing room and look back and see what was happening. "Phone?"

"*No hay telefono.*" The man answered in Spanish.

I guess that means no phone. Shit. He moved through the door into the last portable and saw the others standing by a non-functioning packing machine. He could have sworn the workers cowered back.

"*Señor, el problema.*" He pointed to the packing machine indicating the problem.

"Okay. One minute." He held up a finger and shut the door to the portable. He went down to the end of the appended hallway. Out the exit door he turned back and saw the smoke and flames coming from the building housing his special lab. Each of the portables was concrete, so he hoped the fire was contained. Then he heard the sirens in the distance. He took off for his jeep and hoped to be down the hill before they came up it.

The man who had come to him for help followed at a distance. When he saw the chemist run, he called to his coworkers, "Vamos, Vamos." They ran toward him, out the door, and disappeared into the woods.

Only Twenty-four Hours in a Day

Billy arrived at Quinn's home as the sun was setting. He knocked on the front door before he entered the code.

Quinn opened the door just as he turned the knob. "Welcome." She leaned toward him and kissed him—with a longing that surprised her as much as it did him.

Billy leaned into the kiss and then pulled his head back. "Hold on, I need air." He laughed. Then he tightened his arms around her in a bear hug.

Quinn rested her head on his shoulder. At just over five feet-nine inches, she didn't miss his six-feet one inches by much. "Come in." She stepped back and took his hand.

Billy shut the door and tugged her hand back toward him. "Let's try that again. I had just taken the stairs two at a time."

"Yeah, yeah. Any excuse...wait!" She squinted her eyes at him. "Have you been skipping out on your training regimen?" She wagged her finger at him.

"Are you kidding? I used to train because I'm an officer of the law. Now I train to keep up with you."

Quinn dropped on the living room sofa and laughed. She patted the seat beside her. "Come on, I promise to behave."

"No fun in that." He gave her cheek a light pinch as he moved past her to sit. "So you missed me."

"Was that a question?"

"Nope. Statement of fact—if that kiss is any indication."

She put her arm around his neck and leaned close to his ear and whispered, "Depending on how hungry you are for supper, you could find out now how much I missed you."

He turned his head and kissed her—supper forgotten.

At the Hospital

Kelly pushed the plate away and looked at the SBI agent. *She may not be a direct report, but she works in his agency.* A tear gathered in the corner of her eye. *I'm in over my head.* She felt a hand on hers.

"Kelly, I'll help you however I can." Her head turned at the quiet knock and soft opening of the door. She gently patted the top of Kelly's hand. "I'll be right back."

The two agents stepped in the hallway and Sandy saw the physician. She knew it was probably bad news. She introduced herself.

The physician introduced himself. "I need to speak to Mrs. Culbert."

"She's just had a severe shock. I think she's settled now, but I wanted you to be aware of it for whatever you might have to tell her."

"This one will likely be worse."

Sandy nodded, opened the door, and they entered.

Kelly was standing at the glass window with the drapes on their side open and the ones on the room with Andrew closed. She didn't turn when Sandy walked back in.

"Mrs. Culbert." Sandy was by her side and her voice was low. "This is Dr. Richards."

Kelly turned to look at the man. He extended his hand. "We met earlier."

"Yes, I remember. Please have a seat." Kelly pointed to the couch as she walked toward the side chair. Every fiber of her southern charm kicked in.

Dr. Richards put his elbows on his knees, clasped his hands, and leaned forward. "Mrs. Culbert, we did everything we could to save your husband."

Kelly sat ramrod straight, her mother's southern manners taking charge. "Thank you for coming to tell me, Dr. Richards. Did he suffer?"

"The research over time in these conditions shows no pain activity in the brain during an induced coma."

Kelly knew it would be a clinical answer. "Do you know the cause?"

"In all likelihood an embolism, but there will have to be an autopsy given the injury he sustained prior to coming here."

Kelly nodded. "Thank you, Dr. Richards. I don't have any more questions."

"If you need anything, or have any questions later, please let me know." He handed her his card.

Kelly stood. "Thank you. I will." She shook his hand and walked him to the door. She turned to Sandy and the professional behaviors she had mastered as a CPA before her children were born kicked in.

"Kelly…" Sandy spoke softly.

Kelly held up her hand. "Sandy, I'm aware it hasn't sunk in yet—and it will. Right now I need you to get hold of my brother. Then I need to go be with my mother and children." Kelly moved to the computer and picked it up.

"Yes, ma'am." Sandy took out her phone.

The Mountain Villages

Marjorie Topping had sent Maria to her quarters after they had supper. She wanted to look through documents she had signed with Angela and see if there were others—besides the deed to Angela's condo, which she had not actually signed. She picked up the ringing phone on her desk. "Yes." She knew it was Peter and held the phone away from her ear in anticipation.

"Auntie," his boisterous voice echoed around the room.

She felt her skin crawl. "Peter, while we have legally been aunt and nephew, none of our mutual connections are with us any longer. I would prefer you address me as Mrs. Topping going forward."

"What? Who ever heard of such a thing. You're my aunt. And what do you mean our mutual connections...has something happened to Angela?"

"Yes, Peter. To Angela, your father, Janice, and my dear husband—your uncle. Now I want the truth from you about your involvement in business dealings with Angela."

The line went dead.

Marjorie Topping hung up the phone and picked up her mobile phone—the one she used for business. She dialed the detective her husband had helped in Chicago only to learn she was no longer with the force.

Chapter 19

You are never strong enough that you don't need help.
Cesar Chavez

Dawn on The Island

Lance was planning his next steps as the plane headed for Knoxville early Tuesday morning. He needed more information. *Who had the drone?* The call from Agent Davis last night telling him Andrew had passed away had put a halt to the interviews he'd planned for today, but not to the questions. The pilot had been insistent they had to wait for first light to fly. Lance had spoken with Kelly and his mother and assured them they would get to the bottom of this. *I sure hope Kelly understood she could not disclose Andrew's death yet.*

Lance watched the morning sun rise over the horizon of the Caribbean and marveled at the diamonds dancing on the surface of the crystal clear blue water. *Nothing like this in Nashville.* He turned back to his notepad, determined to make as much sense of the information he had as he could. Four hours of talking to people on the island had been fruitful, but not completely satisfying. As the plane flew higher above the earth, he reviewed his notes:

- Housekeeper – never saw drone, quiet, not visually observant

- Suzanne – uses ex-cop attention, never saw drone before she saw it on the floor of the balcony. Focus was on help for Andrew.

- B & B Owner – friendly, knows local residents. Not heard any talk about Andrew. Knew old man Culbert.

- Pilot – knows more than he's telling. What? Somebody he met here?

- Café owner – likes Andrew. Thought Kelly was uncomfortable. Kids well-behaved. Sent supper to house.

- How much land does Andrew own here? Banking business here?

- Whose fingerprints on the drone?

- Who had opportunity & knowledge of Andrew's business and his whereabouts?

He continued his notes and did a few sketches of the area of the island where the house was as they flew up and over it. Because he didn't want to be tracked going to the island, he had taken a burner phone. As they entered US airspace, he turned on his personal phone. No one had called and he didn't expect anyone would have. Agent Davis had been the only call on his secure phone. He knew agents were with his mother and sister so they were safe. He needed this time: It might be the only two hours he had for the next day or two to think through what he knew at this point. He looked out the window and his brain begin a slow whirr of data—just like the computers he oversaw for the SBI.

Morning Dawns

Quinn rolled over as the alarm on her phone notified her it was five-thirty. She jumped when Billy reached over and stroked her face.

"Sorry. Didn't mean to startle you." He moved closer to her in the bed. "We could skip a workout in your in-home gym." He looked into her rich hazel eyes as she rolled over and looked at him.

"We could. But we won't." She kissed him on the nose, rolled to the side of the bed and said, "The one who finishes thirty minutes with maximum cardio for twenty minutes wins." She jumped out of bed, pulled on her exercise clothes, and was running down the stairs as he stretched and pulled on his sweat pants.

Thirty minutes later, Quinn was finishing her cool down on the tread mill. "I win."

Billy stepped off the incline trainer and looked at her. "Says who?"

"Says me." She smiled and took the towel off her neck and wiped her face. "Twenty-three minutes at optimum heart rate and finished in thirty minutes."

He put his hands on his hips, his towel still around his neck, and smiled. "You didn't say we had to do the same thirty minutes. I'll finish my thirty minutes and I've already done twenty-four minutes at optimum heart rate. So there." He winked at her as she stepped off the treadmill and he stepped on. "I'll let you shower and dress while I finish up here. Don't want to tempt you with any other heart elevating exercise." He wiggled his eyebrows.

"All kindness you are, sweetheart." She intoned the last word with a drawn out New York brogue. She snapped her towel, being careful not to actually hit him, and headed for her bathroom.

Billy continued his cool down and smiled. *Doesn't get much better than this. Unless of course we could be together every night.*

Wearing a pale-pink, silk shell and pink silk panties, Quinn was stepping into the black slacks of her suit when she saw Billy's face in the mirror of her dressing room.

He let out a low whistle. "Do you have any idea how sexy you look?"

She whirled around. "I'll accept that from my lover. But it better not be from the detective." She raised her left eyebrow and leaned in and kissed him gently on the lips. "To the shower with you. I'll have coffee ready. Eggs and bacon that you didn't get for supper last night work?" She grabbed the black jacket to her suit and threw it over her shoulder.

"Did I miss supper last night?" He stared up at the ceiling rolling his eyes playfully. "I don't recall that at all." He looked down and saw that she had already left the room. *Well, there you go, smart aleck. Joke around and the girl gets away.* He headed into the bathroom.

Ten minutes later he walked into the kitchen, opened his gun safe on her counter, and put on his service weapon and shield. He saw her jacket on the back of a chair and saw that she already had on her shield and service weapon. "Busy day?"

"I hope so. Didn't get a chance to catch you up on the Topping case last night." She looked over at him.

He gave her his school-boy impish grin. "Don't know why."

"Hmmm...well, if you can't remember, then I guess we don't need to do that again."

"Whoa, whoa, whoa." He walked over and turned her away from the stove top.

"The eggs are almost finished." She feigned turning back to the skillet.

"Let them burn." He kissed her lightly. "I remember exactly what happened last night, including missing supper. And, I'd do it all over again." He kissed her deeply. "Shall we skip breakfast?"

She gently pushed him toward the counter. "Not today, sweet man. Thanks for the offer, though." She pointed to the carafe on the counter. "Even made a carafe of coffee this morning. So pour our poison and let's eat." She turned back to the stove and finished scrambling the eggs.

"Smells delicious. Thanks, Quinn. Have I told you lately that I love you?"

"Yes." Her voice was soft and sweet. "And I love to hear you say it."

Billy took a deep, silent breath. *Progress. You'll get there, Quinn. I'm a patient man.* "Bacon, eggs, and toast." He lifted the lid on a small bowl. "Grits, too? You rock."

"Don't get used to it." She laughed. "Let's eat. I'll catch you up on the Topping case and I need you to see if you can go to Marjorie Topping's if things come together today."

At six-forty, they were standing at the living room door. "Thanks, Billy. Thanks for staying over. Please drive carefully."

"Winter's gone and the birds are singing and I'm in love with an amazing woman who happens to be one fine detective." He kissed her. "Let me know if we need to visit Ms. Topping today. Take care of my detective. I love you."

"You take care of my detective. Talk to you soon." She blew him a kiss as he trotted down the front stairs.

I'll take it, Ms. Quinn. I'm very fine with being your detective.

The Chemist

The chemist had managed to get his jeep across the road where he could see what was happening and not be seen. He always made sure he had an escape plan. He hadn't flinched at the noise from multiple sirens because he knew the locals who were part of the volunteer fire department jumped at any chance to run their lights and sirens on their pickup trucks. As soon as they made the curve up the hill, he continued down to the highway.

He reached in his pocket for his phone. Then remembered he'd left it in his lab. *Why in the hell do I have such an aversion to carrying that damn mobile phone? What difference does it make? My knuckle-headed brother's phone was right there with it. Not like there's someone I could call.* A slight smile crept across his face. *If what I could see is any indication, my little private lab is gone and I know all the folks in the packing room were safe….* The smile stretched across his face. He thought about how inconsequential he was in the rush of fire fighters and law enforcement to get to the scene. Two firetrucks equipped with water tanks had pulled onto the rough-cut road to the buildings. The chemist had watched them unload from their trucks then pulled out to the road as innocently as a local resident headed to town to get milk. He'd been half-way down the mountain when he pulled to the side of the road to let the sheriff's vehicles headed up the winding mountain road pass him. The chemist had given them a mock salute— unseen in the darkening sky. He let out a long slow breath, pulled out, and headed for the highway.

The early morning light was in his rearview mirror as he approached Memphis. *Not the shortest route to southern Illinois, but less chance of being picked up quickly.* Exhausted from driving all night and knowing he'd taken a risk staying on the interstate, he decided to find an out-of-the-way motel on one of the old highways and sleep. *I've got to ditch this jeep. Those workers could probably tell the cops.* He chuckled. *As soon as they found someone who could speak Spanish.* He took the next exit and pulled into the side of a gas station. Time for a bathroom break and another caffeine drink.

Safe House

The pilot had lowered the stairs on the apron outside the private hangar waiting for the local customs officer to check their credentials. Fortunately it was early enough in the morning there were no other private planes awaiting check-in.

"Hope this hasn't inconvenienced you, Director." The customs agent looked at Lance's SBI credentials.

Lance patted the man on the back. "Always expect a law officer to do his sworn duty. Just did my sister a favor. Went to check something at their property in the islands. Brother-in-law's in the hospital."

"Sorry to hear that, sir."

Lance nodded and was pleased when the customs agent turned for the door. "Won't detain you any longer, sir. Have a good day."

"Thanks."

The pilot raised the stairs as soon as the customs agent was off and turned the plane toward the private hangar and rolled it in.

Lance stepped up to the cockpit. "Thanks, man. I may need to go back in the next twenty-four to forty-eight hours, so stick around."

The pilot looked at him and gave a slight nod. "Yes, sir."

Lance wanted to sound casual. "Until we're sure there was nothing out of the ordinary with the drone hitting Andrew, I'm having an agent hang out here with you."

The pilot looked at him. "Sure. There's an extra bunk in the apartment. He'll be fine there. I may need to run into town."

"No problem. He'll be happy to take you."

The pilot turned toward his tablet and ignored the comment.

"Just want you to be safe." Lance bounded down the stairs and saw his Highway Patrol driver walk into the open bay of the hangar. An SBI agent was with him. Lance stopped to talk to the agent who was staying here to make sure he knew not to the let the pilot out of his sight. Five minutes later he was in his SUV and headed to the safe house where his mother, sister, nephew, and niece were being guarded.

Gut Feelings

It was almost eleven and Quinn had received nothing from the SBI techs. She was trying to find a link she could use to get a warrant for Marjorie Topping's computer. She couldn't figure out why she thought she needed her computer. *There's more to this than two dead bodies in our morgue.* She stood up and started pacing. She stopped, pulled her hair into a knot, and leaned against the wall as she used her secure phone to call the medical examiner.

"Morning, Doc."

"Detective."

"Won't take much of your time. Has Ms. Topping made arrangements for Angela's remains?"

"Yes, well actually her attorney did. The local funeral home will pick them up this morning."

"Okay. Thanks. Have a good one."

"You, too. 10-4."

Quinn put her phone in her pocket; her eyes were fixed on the crime board.

George had watched her every move without a word. Then he spoke in a soft voice. "Quinn, remember when we talked about the power of your gut in detective work?"

She stared at the information on the board. Without turning her head, she spoke with a quiet authority. "I do." She turned to look at him. "And slogging through all these minute details has my gut telling me there is some link to Marjorie Topping and the…" Her secure phone pinged.

"Isaacs." She listened. Her eyes widened and she nodded her head as she looked at George. She mouthed, "Got something!" Her eyes stretched wide as saucers. "Thanks, Steve. Tell the SBI folks they can take whatever they need to their lab. This is enough to keep things moving for now. Thanks a bunch."

She plopped onto the chair at the conference table. "A thread. A little thread." She logged out of the computer.

"What? What?"

"Let's go get coffee."

"What?! I have to wait til we get coffee?"

She simply nodded and walked to the door.

George decided not to interrupt her. He whispered, "On it, ma'am." He pulled the door to the workroom shut and checked that it locked. He turned, expecting to walk across the hall to the lab door. He saw Quinn had turned down the hall and headed toward the back door. He stepped up the pace to catch up with her. "Hey, I thought you liked the coffee from that machine with the funny little pods?"

As she opened the back door, she said, "Notify dispatch we'll be available but out of the building."

George shook his head as he took out his phone. *So, Quinn, you* can *give directions like a boss. Good for you.* "Isaacs and Marshall out of the building. Available by phone." He listened and responded. "Yeah, that's all you get." He opened the door to Quinn's SUV.

Ten minutes later they pulled up in front of Sweet Creations, Carrie Marshall's bakery.

George had not said a word nor had Quinn. She stepped out of the SUV and headed for the door. "Come on, let's have some good coffee. I need one of Carrie's croissants."

Carrie was at the register finishing up with the only customer in the shop. "Detectives. I'll be with you in just a minute."

The man turned from the register. "Well, hey, George." They shook hands. "Didn't know your lovely wife had to call you 'detective.'" He looked Quinn up and down. In a slow southern drawl filled with mountain twang he spoke to her. "Ma'am. You must be the new lead detective. I heard you were a right bit better looking than the last one. Word is you're smarter, too."

"Quinn Isaacs." She extended her hand. "I didn't catch your name." She smiled.

"Xaque. Pleased to meet you. Well, keep stomping out crime. Isn't that what you say?" Xaque chuckled as he walked out.

Quinn watched him go and turned to see George and Carrie shaking their heads.

"Nice to see you, Quinn. Been a while."

"Too long, Carrie. Thanks for all the treats you've sent me recently."

George snorted. "Yeah, and you get fresh treats. I get day old."

Carrie tapped him playfully on the arm. "Stop it."

"Not complaining. Day old bakery from you is still divine." He kissed her on the cheek.

"You're forgiven." She kissed his cheek. "Now, what can I get the two finest detectives in Tennessee?"

"Coffee black and croissant for me, please." Quinn pulled out her wallet and put a ten dollar bill on the register.

Carrie ignored it.

"George?"

"Same, honey. Thanks." He pulled out his wallet and put a ten on the register. Then he pointed to the table in the back corner. "Back there work for you, Quinn?"

"Meet you there." Quinn walked to the door marked "Restroom."

Carrie served them and went into the kitchen.

"Is she here by herself?" Quinn looked around.

"Wednesdays are usually slow. She has a high school student who comes in at 3:30 or so. They start prepping for the end-of-the-week baking."

"Makes sense." Quinn sipped her coffee. "Okay, Steve's call may have given us a gold nugget to have a serious talk with Marjorie Topping."

"What's got you so fixated on the grandmother? Think she had something to do with Angela's death?"

"I don't know. My gut tells me if she's connected in some way it's not directly."

George sipped his coffee and let her talk.

"So, we don't have enough to get a warrant, but the identification of three coded accounts buying conservation land gives us talking points." She stopped and took a bite of the croissant.

"That's what Steve called to tell you?"

"Yes. There are three trusts—TTLT, STELT and a TFLT—all registered in Bangor, Maine. The majority holdings are right here in these mountains."

"Whose names are on the trusts? Marjorie told us about the Topping Family Land Trust. Is that TFLT? She never said where it was registered. Why Maine?"

"I have no idea, but we're going to find out. Let's divide and see if we can conquer. The SBI folks are busy pulling the information. Steve asked if we wanted SBI help to research it."

"Do we?"

"I'd like us to try first. What do you think?"

"Fire away. What's your plan?"

The bell above the door in the bakery stopped their conversation. George was facing the door and saw four women walk in, likely coming to have lunch. Carrie's fresh sandwiches and salads were a big hit with folks who worked downtown.

Quinn and George stood and headed for the front door.

"Detectives, you forgot your change." Carrie waved their ten dollar bills.

Quinn waved. "Great as always, Carrie. Thanks." Quinn was out the door and headed to her SUV.

George stopped to give Carrie a kiss. He leaned in and whispered in her ear. "I'll take my change later." He winked at her and kissed her again. "See you at home."

"Take care of my detective." Carrie turned and walked to the women who had chosen a table in front of the window overlooking the city park. "How may I help you?"

Round City Police Station

Back in the Detectives Workroom, Quinn and George updated their crime board with the information from Steve Clark. Quinn finished entering the information into the computer and looked up at George's new diagram.

"Don't think I've told you, George, but you do a good job of making connections with those visuals. Must have been good at Venn diagrams in school."

"Ha. So long ago I don't even remember. Thanks for the compliment, though. I like the visual connections. Sometimes we get too deep in the words trying to understand connections— and a simple line from here to there can help us connect the dots."

"That's it. George, you're brilliant." She hopped up and with her long stride was at the board in three steps. "That's it, George. I've been trying to make all of this about Angela's death—which we do need to solve. But look at the lines that connect and the ones that don't."

"Yet." George said as he looked at the board.

"Right...yet." She followed the lines from the computers to the trusts. "Okay, I'm going to get Detective Williams to meet me at Ms. Topping's and you can get on with that computer search on the trusts. Need anything from me?"

"Nope. I'll go back to the bullpen and get our ace hacker...uh, techie guy to help me out. Together we can divide and conquer. Good luck with Ms. Topping."

"May need it." Quinn was already half-way out the door and headed across the hall to her office.

"Later." George called after her. He turned back and looked at the red line Quinn had drawn on the board.

Chapter 20

Keep your dreams alive. Understand to achieve anything requires faith and belief in yourself, vision, hard work, determination, and dedication. Remember all things are possible for those who believe.
Gail Devers

Safe House

Lance hung up from his call to the SBI Director in Nashville and dialed Assistant Director Elliott Nelson in Knoxville. The agents currently assigned to protection duty with his family members and Andrew's office were in Nelson's jurisdiction.

"Nelson."

"Elliott, it's Lance. Got a minute?"

"Anytime."

"I'm officially on leave but acting with the approval of the Director. Just need to share a few things and let you know I'm in Knoxville."

"Got it."

He filled him in with what he knew on the death of Andrew Culbert, III. "Given Andrew just lost a bid for governor, the Director wants the remains at the lab in Nashville. Nothing against your shop." He waited but Elliott said nothing. "We're going to keep his death under wraps. See any problems with that?"

"None. The two agents in my shop who know will never tell anyone."

"I'm sure of that. Worked with both of them back in the day, Elliott. You've got good folks. Comes from good leadership. Keep up the good work."

"High praise from the silent agent, thanks."

"Silent agent, eh?" He chuckled. "Goes with living in the computer world, I guess...or maybe we seek out the computer world cause we're not as good with people."

"You've got both skillsets. Now, anything I can do here for your family?"

"Nothing more than you're already doing. Appreciate it. I've upped the private security at Kelly and Andrew's home. Looks less suspicious than having our people there. I'd like to keep our SBI folks out of the neighborhood unless we have to be there for some reason. I'll be in touch soon."

"We're here for whatever you need."

"10-4."

The SUV pulled through the gate of the walled perimeter around the safe house. Lance took a deep breath; he knew his mother and sister needed him to be son and brother, not the SBI Associate-Director in charge of Cybersecurity. The family role just didn't come easy to him—ask his ex-wife.

The door opened and four-year-old Andy ran toward him. *Well, this will help.*

The agent seated in the corner stood. Lance motioned him to sit back down.

"Uncle Lance." Andy took a flying leap toward Lance who stepped quickly to close the gap.

"Hey, my man. How are you?"

"I'm good. So is my sister, Anne."

"Glad to hear that. Where is she?"

"She's with Mommy." He pointed toward the bathroom door.

"Ah. Got it." Lance saw his mother step from the kitchen. Boy in his arm, he stepped toward her.

"Hey, Mom." He put his other arm around her and held her close as he kissed her on top of the head. "I'm here now."

"Sure you are, Uncle Lance." Andy cocked his head to look at his uncle and grandmother. "You're holding me. You couldn't do that if you weren't here."

Lance chuckled. "Well, Mom, I can see we'll have to run fast to keep up with this one."

"Sure, Uncle Lance, I can beat you in a race. Wanna see?" He wiggled to work his way out of Lance's grasp. His feet touched the floor as Kelly and Anne entered the room.

Kelly ran to Lance.

He took her into his arms and held her tight. "I'm here, Kelly. I'm here."

The tears she had held back in front of the children flowed.

"Mommy, don't cry. Uncle Lance will stay. Right, Uncle Lance?"

"I'm here, Andy. We're all here."

"Not Daddy. Right, Mommy?"

Lance bit his tongue. *This is why I knew I could never have kids. Can't predict what they'll come up with next.*

"Daddy's with us in spirit just like he is every day when he goes to work." Kelly bent down and kissed her son on the cheek. "Now you go play with Anne so I can talk with Uncle Lance."

"Sure, Mommy. Come on, Anne." He took his sister's hand and headed toward the room where toys and art materials had been set up for them.

Lance watched them go. *And this is another reason I knew I couldn't have kids. Sure glad Kelly has them. She's a great mom.* He took in a sharp breath. *I'm the only man they'll know in the family now.* He looked from his nephew to his sister.

Kelly turned back to Lance. "Can we talk in the bedroom?" She headed toward the room she was sharing with the children.

Lance followed Kelly; their mother watched her children walk down the hall—her heart aching for both of them.

Mr. S.

The thug was biding his time calling Mr. S. *Why in the hell did I drive out here today anyway?* He had been lost in thought on all the switch-backs up the mountain road and had almost missed seeing the lineup of official vehicles along the side. He couldn't tell what might be going on so he decided to just keep driving past them. As he approached the turn into the road to the buildings where the chemist was, a patrol officer stopped him.

The thug rolled down his window. "Morning, officer. Looks pretty serious here."

"Live up here, sir?" The officer looked carefully at the man in khakis and navy blue golf shirt.

"Want to. Been looking at some land around here and was supposed to meet a realtor to discuss the property across the road." He pointed to the rough cut drive into the acreage on the road opposite the Culbert's land. "Seen him?"

"No, sir. Don't see any signs the property is for sale either. Sure you got the right place? Easy to get turned around if you're not from here."

"Well, maybe I am turned around. Sorry to bother you. I don't want to stop your work. I'll just turn around and go back to where I have a signal and try calling the realtor."

"Good luck. Careful turning around." The officer watched the man turn the jeep and memorized the license plate as the thug made the final turn to head back down the hill. As soon as the car was around the first switchback, the officer was running the plate. An unmarked car pulled out slowly headed down the mountain behind the jeep.

The thug took turns faster than he normally would but he knew he had to tell Mr. S. He got to the main highway, drove to the next exit, and pulled in behind a gas station out of sight of most folks entering. He didn't see the unmarked police vehicle stop at a gas pump.

"Yeah?" Mr. S. sounded sleepy.

"Mr. S., got some bad news."

Mr. S. sat up on the edge of his bed. He slapped the woman in the bed with him and growled, "Get out of here. Now."

She grabbed her clothes and left the room.

"Spit it out."

"Looks like the chemist is gone."

"What do you mean he's gone?"

"I didn't see his jeep."

"So what! Was he in the buildings? Maybe someone had his jeep."

"Couldn't get to the buildings. Looked like there was a fire. Couldn't tell how bad. Lots of official vehicles all around."

"Official? Like cops? Did they ID you?"

"Nah, hick cop. Told him I was meeting a realtor about the piece of land on the other side of the road. Didn't even ask for my driver's license." The thug grinned.

"Did you find that damn realtor? I haven't heard from Culbert. Go back to his house."

"No sign, boss." *And I ain't going up to his house.* The thug thought he heard sirens. He scanned the area. *Must be up on the highway.*

"Dammit, man. Find him. Do you hear me?" He heard the call drop.

Mr. S. touched the number on his screen to redial. *Stupid mountains. Give me the city any day.* The call rang, and rang, and rang.

The thug put his jeep in reverse, looked in the rearview mirror, and decided against backing into the police vehicle.

"Alfred Dunn, step out of the vehicle. Hands in the air."

Dunn, the thug, saw the five vehicles which had him pinned against the back of the gas station and the lineup of cops with their weapons drawn. He wasn't the brightest man on the planet, but he didn't have a death wish. Besides, he always made sure he worked for bigger fish he could rat-out— and ones who would bail him out.

Round City Police Station

"Williams."

"Hey, up for a surprise visit to Ms. Topping?" Quinn looked at the notes on her pad.

"Did she give you a time?"

"Not asking for one."

"The guard will want to know if we're expected."

"We are."

"Thought you didn't have a time."

"Told her last night I'd need to talk to her again. She might not like the timing, but I don't care."

"Well, well. Tell me when."

Quinn heard the beep signaling an incoming call. "Have to take a call. Can you hold on or want me to call back?"

"Call back."

"10-4."

"Isaacs."

The dispatcher was calm. "Highway Patrol. Says it's urgent."

"Thanks." She heard the click transferring the call from their dispatch. "Isaacs."

"Detective Isaacs, this is Sergeant Adams with the Highway Patrol."

"Yes, sir. How may I be of service?"

"Calling about your APB on Alfred Dunn."

Quinn felt her pulse quicken. "Find him?"

"Yes, ma'am."

"Alive?"

"Not expecting him to be?" The sergeant sounded curious.

"Just hoping he's alive. Have some questions for him."

"He is. He's on his way to you. Have someone to let him cool his heels until you can get to him? Or do you need my folks to take the long way round the mountain?" He chuckled.

"Timing couldn't be better. I'm here and will let him cool his heels while I watch. Then we'll try to get him talking. ETA?"

"Should arrive in less than thirty minutes. Let me know if you need anything else."

"Thanks for your good work. Look forward to hearing the details."

"Officer bringing him can fill you in."

"Good enough. Appreciate the support. Let me know when we can return the favor."

"10-4." The line went dead.

Quinn was pretty good at keeping her comments to a minimum, but she was intrigued at how many male law officers were short, sweet, and to the point. *Might need to work on that—or maybe they need to change.* She smiled as she called Billy.

"Williams."

"Successful APB on Dunn. He'll be delivered here in thirty minutes. You can come observe if you want. I want to team up with George on the interview."

"As you should. Be there in twenty."

"Whoa. I know this is an official call, so none of my business—technically. But personally...twenty minutes?"

"Lights. No sirens. I promise."

She laughed. "Okay, see you soon."

She headed to the bullpen to tell George. He deserved the news person-to-person.

George's head was buried in his computer screen. Officer Gilbert, the geek, was next to him just as absorbed in the screen. She had hoped the beep on the door lock wouldn't distract them, but both men looked up.

"Sorry. Didn't know your lock beeped like a trumpet."

"Keeps us safe." George grinned when he looked at her. "What's up?"

"Got Dunn." She said it with no emotion.

Officer Gilbert blinked. "Come again? Got dung?"

They all burst out laughing.

Quinn got the hiccups. "Well, Officer Gilbert, I've stepped in my share of it literally and figuratively, but I was trying to say, 'D-u-n-n,' Dunn. As in our APB."

George jumped up from his chair. "Yippee. Where is he? Let's go get him."

"On his way. Highway Patrol bringing him in. We'll let him cool his heels while we talk to the officer and then plan our interview strategy. Detective Williams is coming over to observe."

"Why?" George sat down deflated.

Gilbert stood up. "Need a break. Back shortly." He left the room.

"George, you and I will strategize the interview and conduct it. This case crosses over to the Valley and Detective Williams' team found the truck with Patten."

"Yeah, but not with Dunn. That was on Angela's car up on the Parkway."

"True. But if it's in the interest of finding out if her death was a crime, teamwork can help."

George looked up at her. "Sorry, Quinn. I was out of line."

"No, you were reacting to what I'm coming to understand was a way of operating in this department which didn't give you much input. I've been there. Immigration office here works a lot like that. But working cases with Sheriff Oliver in the Valley, I learned how much I like being on a team: competition in a healthy way toward solving a crime, not focused on outdoing each other."

George sat up straighter. "Was that your answer to one of your interview questions?" He raised his eyebrow.

She laughed. "Close enough. Chief wants us to be a team, too."

"Yeah. Like my Carrie. I'm finding out I have a lot to learn about healthy competition...and letting go of the kind that eats your soul."

"Then let's keep at it. Get Gilbert back on whatever you were doing and I'll see you in the workroom in less than twenty. Okay?"

He thrust his hand out to her.

She took it. "Same team, George. Same team."

He relaxed with the mountain double speak. *She's one of us.*

Quinn turned and walked out the door.

We Want to go Home

Kelly sat down on the bed and Lance sat in the chair at the foot of the bed.

"Did you learn anything on the island?"

"Kelly, look at me. I'm sorry about Andrew. I can't imagine...."

She held up her hand and turned toward him; her legs curled up under her on the bed. She gave him a wan smile. "Hey, big brother, not ready to talk about it. Okay?"

"Okay."

"Thanks for being my hero and coming to my rescue—again."

"Again?" He hoped she might relax and let loose of whatever had thrown her into the formal mode he recognized she and their mother always used when they took charge—or were worried.

She smiled. "Oh, many times. The first I remember is when that bratty little boy down the street took down the ladder I had used to climb up in the tree."

He laughed. "Yeah, falling and breaking your arm would have been less painful than what would have happened if Mom and Dad had found out you went up in that tree from a ladder."

She laughed, too. "And so many small things you probably do so naturally you never realized they were saving me. I love you, Lance."

"I love you, too, Sis. Now tell me everything that's going on. I've got a large contingent of folks covering this. We'll either have to reimburse the state for the service, or I'll have to have pretty good justification for them being here."

The take-charge Kelly didn't hesitate. "I'm fine if we have to reimburse the state. Mom and the kids have to be safe." She looked down at the bed. "Me, too." A tear slid down her cheek.

Lance slid the chair closer to the bed. "Listen, Sis, you know I'm not good at the small talk—major contributor to the end of my marriage."

Kelly reached over and took his hand. "I know. I know. It's okay." She swung her legs around to the side of the bed and sat up straight. "Here's what I know."

When she finished telling him about the hurried trip, Andrew finally confiding in her about the real estate deal he didn't understand, and the drone, she let out a long slow breath.

Lance had watchful eyes on her the whole time as he took in every detail. "Okay, that's a start. The agents on this detail are all based here in Knoxville, as are you, so I need to talk to the Assistant Director here."

"Oh, Lance, do you?" Kelly's voice trembled.

"Elliott Nelson is one of the good guys. He'll have to be brought in on this and besides he knows this area like the back of his hand. He's from these mountains. So, you'll just have to trust me to make a plan. I'll try to get things figured out so you can make an announcement about Andrew, but for now...."

"Oh, Lance. You don't think the people at the hospital will say anything do you?"

"Can't. HIPPA. Besides the team that serves that wing knows full well who donated the money for the building and they live in this community, too. I'm not worried about it."

She nodded her head. "Okay. Makes sense."

"Then let me get on with it."

"Can we go home?"

"Not yet. I've got some private security on your home and there's no evidence of anyone approaching it other than the postal carrier." He looked at her. "Any online shopping lately?"

She laughed. "No, not expecting any packages." She stared at him. "Oh, Lance, Sunday is Easter. The kids need new clothes, I don't have all their Easter gifts..."

Lance squeezed her hand. "Kelly, you were always great at detail and planning. We'll wing it. It's only Tuesday." He winked at her.

She stood up. "Come on. Mom needs to know what's going on."

They walked out holding hands swinging them like they did when they were little. Lance smiled. *Just like Andy did with Anne.*

The agent in the room averted his eyes.

Dunn Arrives

Quinn hung up the phone in the workroom and looked at George. "Matron says Dunn is in holding and the Highway Patrol officer has been offered our hospitality. We'll meet the officer in the matron's office. Ready?"

"You got it."

Quinn picked up her Yeti and headed out to get fresh water. They walked into the matron's office four minutes later.

"Quinn Isaacs." She extended her hand.

"Brooks, ma'am." *Wow! She's a looker.* The officer extended his hand as his eyes moved up and down her tall fit frame. He finally focused on the pin on the lapel of her expensive black suit.

"This is Detective George Marshall." The two men shook hands.

"Can't wait to hear how you caught him." George pulled up a chair.

"It was a dark and stormy night…" the officer caught himself, looked at Quinn, and blinked, "sorry, ma'am."

Quinn was laughing. "No apology needed. Humor gets us through many a day. Get you something to drink?"

The officer held up the coffee the matron had given him. "Thanks, been taken care of."

"Good. Where did you find him?"

Officer Brooks did not embellish his responses. He gave them the number of the exit off the main highway where Dunn had shown up. "We had a number of folks up that mountain dealing with a situation. He claimed to be meeting a realtor about property on the other side of the road from our scene."

Quinn and George nodded.

"Seemed pretty cocky—you know how city…" he stopped and looked again at Quinn. He'd grown up with a mother who read fashion magazines. He wasn't interested, but he learned his lessons at her knee. He had heard Quinn's southern accent. "…folks from the north can be."

"We have our share of newcomers." Quinn smiled.

"Well, anyway…" He told them about following Dunn down the hill and the capture.

George slung out his hand in a high-five. "Good job! Good job!"

The officer smiled. He, too, knew the double-speak of mountain folks. "Thanks. Got any questions, I'll try to answer. Otherwise, I'll let you get on with this jerk." He glanced at Quinn. *I hate having to watch what I say because of all the women cops.*

"Well, we're going to find out just how big a jerk he is, Officer Brooks. Thanks for the delivery. Safe travels getting home." She stood.

He stared at her. *Did she really say, 'jerk?'* "Thanks, ma'am. The matron signed off on the transfer, so I'll be headed out."

George stood. "Come back, anytime. Thanks." He shook the officer's hand.

Quinn shook hands and the officer left the matron's office.

George sat down and looked at Quinn. "Good comeback on the 'jerk' comment. Some of them will never learn."

Quinn sipped her water. She looked at George. "Oh, figured out long ago I don't have to change the world. Sometimes it's enough to just give it back to them." She went quiet.

George waited.

"Looking at property...hmmm..." Quinn tapped her pencil on the table.

"Yeah...I bet. Do *you* think it's coincidence he drove up on a scene with a bunch of law enforcement officers?"

"I think it's his bad luck." She looked at George. "That said, if I were a betting woman, I'd bet he had other plans up there and certainly did not plan on finding a bunch of cops. Let's make a plan to see what we can find out." She stood up and headed to the door.

"Right behind you."

Chapter 21

...you will not always be able to solve all the world's problems all at once. But don't ever underestimate the impact you can have, because history has shown us that courage can be contagious, and hope can take on a life of its own.
Michelle Obama

The Mountain Villages

Marjorie Topping searched through papers she had signed in the presence of Angela. She sorted them into three piles: Personal Residence, Topping Family Land Trust, Personal Assets. *When did I start letting important papers just stack up? Was it when...* She looked up at the knock on her office door. Maria would not enter without knocking.

"Yes, Maria?" She pushed her wheelchair back from the desk and moved toward the window to look out. She knew Maria could access most anything in the house, but she didn't need to put any of this right before her eyes.

"Ma'am, I'm going to Round City. Is there anything you need me to do before I go?"

"What do we need?" Marjorie seemed surprised about Maria being out of the house today.

"I have a dentist appointment, remember?"

Marjorie scanned the grounds of her property as she tried to remember. She didn't. "Oh, sure. Sorry. How long will you be gone?"

"Twenty minutes each way there and back, and probably an hour for the cleaning of my teeth. I was going to stop at the grocery store, too. A little more variety than we can get at the Valley Store."

"Sure. No rush. I have nowhere...what is the saying they have here?"

"Nowhere to go and all day to get there?"

"Yes. That's it. Drive safely. See you when you get back."

"Yes, ma'am. Your salad is prepared and in the fridge. Call if you need me to rush back."

"No need."

"Yes, ma'am. I'm leaving now." Maria turned and left as silently as she arrived.

Marjorie sat in front of the window—her focus was not on the yard. She reached her hand into the pocket on the side of her wheelchair and took out her personal phone.

"Office of Oliver, Olson, and Olson. How may I help you?"

"Gray Olson, please. This is Marjorie Topping."

"Good morning, Ms. Topping." Gray's voice carried the southern drawl she'd come to expect.

"Gray, how many times do I have to ask you to call me Marjorie?" She wanted the familiarity today.

"Just showing respect. Happy to oblige, Marjorie."

Marjorie struggled at times with her Midwest values which she viewed as equality focused and the deferential behaviors of so many Southerners— which she also liked. "Thank you, Gray. Have arrangements been made for Angela's remains?"

"Yes. Are you sure you don't want to visit the funeral home?"

"Absolutely. I want to remember her the way I last saw her. When the cremains are ready, will you please bring them to me?"

"Certainly, I can. I may be in court the next few days, so I could have them funeral home bring them...."

"No. I want you to do it. I can wait."

"No problem. I'll call as soon as I hear from the funeral director. Once my court schedule is finalized we can find a mutual time. Anything else I can help you with?"

Marjorie took a minute before she spoke. "Did you handle all of Angela's transactions in land trusts?"

There was silence on the other end. "Marjorie, you're an attorney. You know I can't discuss…"

"Was, Gray. I *was* an attorney."

He ignored her comment. "In either event you know I can only state that I handled any work Angela gave to me. I cannot be sure I handled all transactions of any kind for Angela and I can't betray client privilege." *Not to you without a court order, anyway.*

The cackle on the other end of the phone startled Gray. At first, he thought it was in the phone connection—he had never heard such a sound from Marjorie Topping.

"Marjorie, are you okay? Is Maria there?"

The cackle spread into a maniacal laugh with intermittent gasps for air.

Gray knew there would be an immediate response to the electronic pink note from his assistant. He typed with speed: Urgent-Call Maria to ck on M. Topping NOW.

As quickly as the cackle came, there was quiet. Then Marjorie, sounding as she always had, spoke in the soft unflappable voice he had come to expect. "Gray, there is little in life that is ever what it seems. Thank you for taking care of Angela's cremains. I look forward to your call. Have a nice day." The line went dead.

Gray did a quick walk out to his reception area in the small building housing this law practice for more than fifty years.

His assistant shrugged. "No answer from Maria. The phone doesn't even go to voice mail." She looked up at him.

"Okay, thanks. Try again in fifteen minutes or so." He turned and walked into his office—torn with his personal belief in his obligation to make sure another human was alright, especially one who just exhibited the most unusual behavior he had ever heard from her, and the reality that everyone has a bad day.

Detectives Workroom

"Send him back, please. He knows the way." Quinn hung up the phone from the front desk officer. "Detective Williams is here."

"I'll go meet him." George stood. "Need a walk down the hall."

Quinn heard the familiar click as the door locked behind him. She paced in front of their crime board. She picked up a purple dry-erase marker and drew a dotted line. Then she stepped back and looked at her additions to George's drawings trying to connect the pieces of this case.

She turned when she heard the door open.

"Detective, glad you could join us. How are things in the Valley?"

"Hey, Quinn. Fine. Just fine. Thanks." Billy Williams walked in ahead of George and winked at Quinn—unable to resist their personal connection.

George handed Quinn a cup of coffee. "Don't have to drink it. Billy declined."

Quinn cocked her head toward Billy. "Really? Our coffee's not good enough for you?"

"Already had my limit, thanks. Your fine detective here was nice enough to buy me a bottle of water." He nodded toward George and held the bottle of water up in mock salute.

Quinn nodded. "Southern hospitality. That's our motto. Okay, let's see...."

Billy was looking at the crime board. "Looks like you've picked up some new information." He squinted his eyes and cocked his head to one side.

Quinn looked at the board, too. "What's the matter? Don't you like my spider web?"

"I was about to ask about the color drawing. I like your spider web. Trying to make sure I don't walk into the middle of it."

Quinn stepped across to the outside wall and looked back at the white board. "Hmmm...it really does look like a spider web." She had meant her comment to him as a personal joke between them as he often misquoted the poem about "The Spider and the Fly." Then she shrugged, walked to the table, and picked up her coffee cup. "It's my scribbling. George is the Venn diagram guy." She sat down. "Okay, let's get to it. We need to think about our strategy for interviewing Dunn. Then I'd still like to get over to talk to Marjorie Topping today."

George started. "Here's what we know about Dunn." He listed the information they had on him from Illinois, mentioned the fingerprint on Angela's car, and explained to Billy the particulars of the Highway Patrol picking Dunn up today.

Quinn listened with rapt attention. There was nothing new to her in what was being said. It was the mental gymnastics she executed in trying to solve a problem that kept her focused.

Billy looked from one to the other but didn't speak. He heard every word George said, but he was also enthralled with trying to figure out what was spinning around in Quinn's head as another detective—and as the woman he loved.

When George finished, Quinn walked over to her purple lines. "Seems there was a fire at a portable on the land opposite the land Dunn claimed to be up there to buy. We've been promised a copy of the report."

"Want me to check and see if it's here?" George nodded to the computer.

"Sure. Fine." Quinn stared at the lines.

Billy sat without saying a word. He sipped his water and waited.

"Nothing yet." George clicked the mouse several times.

Quinn stopped pacing. "We can hold this guy for twenty-four hours, so let's go see what we can learn. We can go back if we need to. Any thoughts on any of this, Billy?"

"Lots of threads to sort here. You've been working this case, not me. So, the only question I'd have is do you see any pattern emerging?"

Quinn headed to the computer without saying a word. She went to the area maps on the computer and projected them on the screen. "Let's see if we can identify where Dunn was stopped by the officer. Brooks said the property was eight miles, give or take, up the road from the main highway."

George walked closer to the projection screen. "If we can find the distance on this map, we can pull it up on Google Earth and get the coordinates."

"Right, and then we run a property records check and see who owns the land." Quinn's pulse quickened. "Let's try to get the most accurate scale on the map possible."

Fifteen minutes later, all three of them sat back in their chairs, and smiled.

Quinn looked from George to Billy. "Andrew Culbert, III, property owner. I know that name. Big real estate in Knoxville. Is he the person Angela did her internship with while in college?"

Billy, who had been in the interview with Ms. Topping, spoke. "Marjorie Topping didn't name the realtor." He looked to the board to confirm. "Culbert is definitely a high end commercial real estate firm, though. He just lost his second bid for governor."

Quinn's typing on the keyboard was so fast both men looked at her.

"What are you looking for, Quinn?" George moved over behind her.

"If they stopped Dunn on the road, the only entrance I can see on Google Earth is off of this road." She pointed, sat back, and a smile spread across her face. "Look who owns the property on the other side."

Both men looked at the computer screen.

"Well, well, well." Quinn looked at George. "Let's go talk to Mr. Dunn."

The Interrogation

The matron escorted Billy to the observation room where he would watch the interrogation through the one-way mirror. He turned the chair around so he was leaning on the back of it facing the room in which they would talk to Dunn. *Wonder if all the high-tech stuff is going to make these old rooms obsolete? I kinda like looking-in knowing the perp is seeing himself in that mirror. Ahhh...the times are changing.* He watched the door to the interrogation room open and heard the shuffle of Dunn's feet joined by chains. *Wonder if Quinn's going to be good cop or bad cop?*

George pulled out the chair for Dunn. "Sit."

Quinn sat down opposite him and George moved to the side wall, put his foot against the wall, and leaned back like a cowboy in the wild west.

Billy chuckled silently; he knew the stance.

Quinn started the tape recorder knowing it was also being recorded on video cameras in the corners of the room. "This is Detective Isaacs of the Round City Police and..." she looked at George.

"Detective Marshall of the Round City Police."

Quinn gave the date and time as she looked directly at Dunn. "State your full name, date of birth, and current address."

"Alfred Floyd Dunn. Cairo, Illinois."

"Date of birth?" Quinn never took her eyes off of him.

Dunn winked at her. He stated his birthdate.

"Mr. Dunn, you have the right..." Quinn finished the Miranda warning. "Do you wish to have an attorney present?"

Dunn stared right at her. "Nah, sweetheart. I think I can handle this."

She stared at him but never changed her vocal cadence. "I need you to tell me if you want an attorney." She was well aware he knew the drill.

"Don't need an attorney. Good enough for you, sweetheart?"

While in the staring contest with him, Quinn had quietly picked up her leatherbound notebook—she dropped it on the table.

Dunn jumped and his eyes looked down at the table. "Holy shit." He looked back at her.

"That's *Detective* 'sweetheart' to you, *Mr.* Dunn." Her emphasis on 'detective' and 'Mr.' were in her deepest, slowest, southern mountain drawl.

Billy grinned from ear to ear. *Bad cop. You go, Quinn.*

"Mr. Dunn, you were picked up on an All-Points Bulletin as you have been duly informed." She leaned in and smiled.

"Yeah. So what?"

"So, I need to know your whereabouts over the last ten days. Be specific, please."

"Came down to enjoy the nice spring weather here in Tennessee. Been driving around."

"Staying where?"

"Here and there."

She had already verified there were no reported hotel or motel registrations in his name—didn't mean a thing, though. She had been disappointed when she learned the jeep was actually his and properly registered in Illinois. Nothing to tug on there. *Hopefully forensics will find a connection to some piece of this puzzle—this web...but who's the spider?* She didn't skip a beat in her interrogation.

"Who were you planning to meet about the property you want to buy?"

"A realtor."

"Name?"

"Can't remember." He grinned at her. His broken front tooth made him look like a loser in a bad bar fight.

She shifted tactics and leaned back in her chair. "A canvas top jeep seems an unusual vehicle to drive in the winter in Illinois."

"Ever been to Illinois?"

She ignored him. "Must have been nice driving on the parkway here in our fine state."

He grinned and flicked his tongue in the gap where his tooth once was. "Took the roof off. Real fine."

She softened the look in her eyes. "Nothing compared to that Lexus you saw on the Parkway, though, is it?"

He blinked and one eye twitched.

It was not missed by Quinn...or George...or Billy.

Quinn leaned back into the edge of the table and looked right at him. She put down the pictures of the Lexus, his fingerprint in the Lexus, and his FBI fingerprint. "Mr. Dunn, the woman who owned that beautiful Lexus where we found your fingerprint is currently at our local funeral home awaiting cremation. Something you want to tell us about that?"

"Whoa, whoa, whoa. What the hell?" He rattled the chains around his ankles. "What the hell are you talking about?" He looked down at the picture of the Lexus, his print, and the FBI print. "I didn't kill no woman. There weren't...wasn't nobody near that car. It was just sitting there pretty as you please." He stopped shuffling his feet.

"And that gave you the right to enter the vehicle?"

"Didn't en-ter it." He split the word. "The window was open and I touched the vent to see if was cool or hot." He got a self-satisfied smug look on his face. "You know, to see if I should go looking for the owner."

Quinn let a smile creep across her face. "Don't know how to touch a hood to see if it's hot?"

"Bitch."

"That's Detective Bitch to you." She pulled out a picture of Patten.

His eye twitched again.

Quinn hoped her breath didn't make the sound she felt when she saw the tell of recognition.

"Your friend, Mr. Patten…" She let that hang for a second. "Well, he has a different story."

"Son-of-a-bitch. Lies, all lies. He ain't nothing but a druggie. You can't believe nothing he says. Where is he?" Dunn had lost his cockiness and was looking around the room as if he expected Patten to appear.

"Oh, he's down the hall." *In our morgue. But I'm not telling you that.* "Here's your chance to tell your side of the story." She looked at George. "Detective, maybe Mr. Dunn would like something to drink?" She smiled at Dunn.

"What can I get you? Water? Iced tea?" George acted like a good food server.

"Nothing. I don't need nothing. I'm tired. Maybe I need some sleep…or a lawyer."

Quinn slapped her hand on the table.

Dunn turned his head and looked at her.

"Mr. Dunn, do you wish to have an attorney present?"

"Give me a minute."

"Sure. In the meantime…" She looked gave a slight nod of her head to George.

He took his phone out of his pocket. "Marshall." He pretended to listen. "Sure, I'll see if she can talk."

Quinn turned to look at him.

"Ma'am. There's a Mr. Hodges from Illinois."

Dunn jerked his head toward George as he recognized his former parole officer's name. He growled at George. "Get me some water."

Quinn looked at George. "Tell Mr. Hodges I'll call him back. Please get Mr. Dunn some water."

"Detective Marshall exiting interview."

Billy squirmed. *I will come right through that glass if that guy tries one thing.*

Quinn folded her fingers over her palm and looked at her nails as if she were trying to decide if she needed a manicure.

Dunn didn't even notice. His eyes were darting all around the room.

Quinn smiled inwardly. *You go right ahead and try to figure out how you're going to play this one. I've got you linked to Patten now.*

The door opened. "Detective Marshall reentering interview." George held the bottle of water in front of Dunn but did not set it down. He wanted Quinn out of range first. He was relieved he had a legitimate reason to send her out of the room. He didn't trust this guy at all. "Ma'am, that report you wanted from the Highway Patrol has come in. The matron said you wanted to see it."

Quinn stood. "Isaacs leaving interview."

George took the top off the bottle and set it in front of Dunn. *Don't give me a reason to regret giving you this.*

Gray Olson's Office

Gray Olson wondered what was taking his sister so long to answer when he heard, "Hey! What's up?"

"What's up with you? Must have rung twenty times."

"Nah, only seventeen. My, my, you're edgy."

"This is an office call—not one to harass your brother *or* your law partner." Gray let out a long sigh.

"Hey, seriously, I'm sorry. I was in the bathroom and left my personal phone on my desk."

"Why didn't it go to voicemail?"

"Because I don't have time to listen to work voicemail and personal. You know you can always reach me on my work mobile."

"Even in the bathroom?" His tone was lighter—the man she was accustomed to hearing.

"I'm guessing this isn't a social call. Are you okay? Family, okay?"

"Yes. Yes. Just need to talk to you about a client."

"Then why didn't you say so?" His sister preferred living in Knoxville to their home in the Valley of the Smoky Mountains thirty minutes from the nearest city—if you could call Round City an actual city. "Who?"

"Marjorie Topping."

"Haven't had any dealings with her."

"I know. But how about Angela Topping?"

"Daughter?"

"Was her granddaughter."

"Was?"

"Long story." They generally only talked about problem cases or ones involving major clients—which were sometimes one in the same. "Mostly interested in land conservation."

"Nothing I've dealt with. What's got you worried?"

"Marjorie is a retired attorney from Chicago. Up until this morning, totally unflappable in my experience with her."

"Including the death of her granddaughter?"

"At least on the official notification." He told her what had happened including the initial visit to Angela's condo, and then the warrant, and Ms. Topping's reaction to that.

"Well, dear sheltered mountain brother of mine, that's a lot for one person to handle. Sounds like hysterical laughter to me. There are clinical definitions for such outbursts, in case you aren't aware."

"Only if a psychiatrist calls it that on a witness stand."

"Have you reached her assistant?"

"No. We've tried several times. It just rings on her mobile and the house phone goes to voicemail."

"Did you try calling Ms. Topping back?"

He hesitated. "That's why I'm calling you."

"Why?"

"I'd like you to call her and tell her I'm due in court...relax, it's true. I had already told her I'd likely be tied up for several days." He sighed. "I did hear from the funeral director and Angela's cremains will be available before the end of the week."

"Can't handle making the 'here's your granddaughter' call?"

"No, no, no. I told her I was waiting on my court schedule and once I knew when the cremains would be available, I'd let her know."

"Okay, I guess I can do that for my brother and my law partner. I assume the real reason for my call is to make an assessment of whether we need to call for a wellness check."

"Yes, please." He gave her Marjorie Topping's mobile number.

"Done. Anything else?"

"Glad you're my sister *and* my law partner."

"Mom would be proud. Love you. I'll let you know."

Chapter 22

In the middle of difficulty lies opportunity.
Albert Einstein

Interrogation Room

"Detective Isaacs reentering interview." Quinn looked at George who had pulled up a chair and was sitting with his right ankle resting on his left knee and his arms crossed on his chest. She sat down opposite Dunn.

"Mr. Dunn, since we have interrupted this interview, I am going to reread your rights."

"No need." Dunn blurted spitting water between his teeth onto the table.

"You have the right to..." She kept her eyes on him the whole time. "Do you wish to have an attorney present."

"Listen, honey." He grinned. "Detective honey." His grin grew into a scowl. "I know my rights. You know my rights, and I'm betting that dude over there knows my rights. Hell, whoever is behind that crappy mirror staring at me knows my rights. Now you listen real careful."

Quinn did not bat an eye—or speak.

"I want a deal. I know stuff and I know how this little game is played. You want the big fish. For the record, I don't swim with little fish. And I damn sure don't want to be any kind of fish in some hick Tennessee prison." He sat back in his chair with a smug tug to his lip pulled between his teeth.

"I'm listening."

"Here's the deal I want..." he spouted several demands. "Last, I ain't serving no time."

Quinn looked over at George. "Detective, when's the last time we made a deal with anyone?"

"Never."

Dunn stamped his feet. The chain rattled. "Bull..."

"Detective Marshall, why have we never made a deal?"

"Because we can't, ma'am."

"See, Mr. Dunn. Even this fine detective in this little town in east Tennessee knows that only the District Attorney can make a deal. And even the DA needs a judge to approve it." She smiled.

George slid his chair closer but didn't get next to the table. "Ma'am, maybe the DA would listen if we had a good argument for making a deal."

Quinn looked at him. *How hard was that for you, George?* "Detective, I am the lead detective...your boss. Are you trying to tell me how to run an interview?"

"No, ma'am. I just think..."

She tried to give him the meanness glare she could. "Detective, when I want to know your *opinion*, I'll ask for it. This is *my* interview." She turned back to Dunn. "Give me one good reason *I*..." she threw a glance at George, "...should ask the DA to make a deal."

"You don't have to ask; you tell the DA what to do."

Both detectives laughed. Quinn stopped first. "Oh, if only that were true." She shook her head. She leaned in toward the table. "You see, Mr. Dunn. I'm much meaner than I may look and I promise you cops are not big fans of the deals that get made." She sat back. "But, today? Today, I'm feeling generous. You tell us what you know about the little operation up on that mountain...I mean naming names—and what you know about Mr. Patten, and we could be persuaded to ask our DA to give you a break."

"I need a break." He looked at her. "You know...to take a leak."

"Then you shall have it." She stood up. "Detective, take this man to holding. Detective Isaacs exiting interview." She slammed the door on her way out.

"Hey, wait." Dunn sputtered as she walked out.

SBI Safe House

Lance left his mother and sister playing with the children and went into the bedroom his mother was using. His call was answered on the first ring.

"Nelson. What's up, Lance?"

"Need to meet. Have time?"

"Here, there, someplace else?"

"Wherever we can do it soonest."

"I'm on the road. I can be where you are in less than ten. Save you driving into the city."

"Will your agent have a heart attack if you walk in the door?"

"Hope not. Hate the paperwork."

Lance laughed for the first time in a long time. "Right. Thanks, Elliott. Oh, and one thing. Do you have someone available who could verify ownership on some property?"

"Sure. Send me the details."

"10-4." Lance sent the details Kelly had given him on the three pieces of property including theirs out in the mountains. *Why doesn't Kelly know what is happening on their property?*

Detectives Workroom

Quinn and Billy walked to the workroom while George took Dunn to the matron. Billy brushed his hand against Quinn's several times on the walk. She didn't object.

"I'm going to step in here." Quinn stopped outside the women's restroom.

"I'll meet you at your workroom door. By the way, I like the new wording on the door." He winked at her.

"Thanks. See you shortly." She walked into the restroom and stopped to look in the mirror. *Sweetheart? Bitch? Honey? Detective Sweetheart to you. Did I really say that? Wonder what Billy will say about my bad cop?* She stared at her reflection. *I hope he'll tell me I didn't give George a chance to be good cop. I'll deserve that rebuke.* Her hands washed, she undid the knot of her hair and slung her head from side-to-side as she ran her fingers through her hair. She washed her hands again and headed for the Detectives Workroom.

Billy came up as she was opening the door with a fresh bottle of water in his hand. "Didn't ask you what you might want to drink."

She pointed to her Yeti on the table. "I'm good. Thanks." She walked in and took a long slow drink of water.

"Cameras in here?" Billy looked around the room as he shut the door.

"Better not be."

"Good." He walked over to her and pulled her into a long, slow kiss.

"Thanks. I needed that." She stepped back, straightened her shoulders, and looked at him.

"I know. I know. Work and personal." He gave her his school-boy impish grin. "What better way to tell the woman I love that I just watched her play a mighty fine 'bad cop'?"

"Easy, Detective. Words. Use your words." She smiled and was about to kiss him when she heard the beep of the code being put in the door. "Later."

George walked in. He felt the heat in the room. "Sorry. Interrupting something?"

"Not at all." Quinn pulled out the chair and pointed. "Have a seat. Let's talk next steps."

Both men sat.

She pulled up a report on the computer and displayed it on the screen. "Here's the Highway Patrol report."

Billy and George turned toward the screen.

She zoomed in on the detailed narrative in the report. "Local volunteer fire department called to the property at..."

They each read the information. Quinn had decided not to read it aloud so she could get the reactions of each of these men. Billy finished first and turned to the crime board. George stood up and walked over to it.

"Ready to write, George?" Quinn stood.

He held up the black dry erase marker at a clean section of the board. They started throwing out questions and comments.

"What was in that building to explain the smoke color reported?"

"Was the building a total loss?"

"Was it a licensed business?"

"Did the land owner have anything to do with it? Know about it?"

"Who was there? Any deaths?"

"Any connection to the land across the road owned by STELT?"

"Who is STELT?" Billy turned from the crime board to look at Quinn.

"We're working on it." Quinn told him.

"Can we get eyes on the land?"

"Any report on smells? Rotten Eggs?"

They continued on for several minutes and then the comments and questions slowed.

Quinn had been pacing her hair swinging as she watched the board. "No need to force it. Let's see if we have or can find answers for any of these."

George stepped to the table and picked up his water bottle. "I need to go talk to Gilbert. Maybe he's found out how, or if, STELT, TFLT and TTLT are connected."

Quinn nodded. She looked at her watch. "It's almost lunch time. I want to let Mr. Dunn cool his heels for a while. Might jog his detailed memory. If you can get an answer about STELT and it turns out to be one and the same as TFLT or related, I want to go see Ms. Topping ASAP." She turned to Billy. "And you, Detective?"

"I'm at your disposal. Cleared it with the Sheriff and I think that web of yours up there may be just the explanation for what we've got here."

She nodded. "That's what I'm thinking. What we thought was going to be the source of the chemicals that killed Angela Topping may be only the surface of a much deeper web." She paced. Then she clapped her hands together. "Okay, George. You check with our tech geek, Gilbert. Billy and I are going to pay Ms. Topping a visit. Call if you learn anything."

"10-4." George left the room.

"We can grab something to eat on the way," Billy offered.

"Sure. I want to put the windows down and get some of this fresh spring air. It always helps my ability to think."

"I agree. Fresh air is always good for sleuthing. I'll meet you at the back door." Billy walked into the hallway.

She chuckled. *Now there's a word—sleuthing.* Quinn watched him leave the room. She was both pleased and disappointed he didn't kiss her as he left.

The Mountain Villages

The land outside the window in her home office faced the rising mountains taking Marjorie's eyes up to the blue sky and the thin wispy clouds resting like a shawl on the shoulders of the craggy mountaintops. She jerked at the ring of her doorbell. Turning her wheelchair toward the hallway, she pulled out her phone to look at the image on the screen from the camera. She saw the delivery truck in the driveway, the uniform cap on the man's head, but she also knew the face. She dropped the phone into the side pocket of her chair and motored toward the front door.

Unaccustomed to opening the large door, she had to maneuver several times to get the door open without hitting her wheelchair. She stared out the glass at her husband's nephew. He reached for the doorhandle on the storm door which was locked. She glared at him. Twisting and turning the chair, she was able to reach the lock on the handle and clicked it. She moved her chair backwards so she was still facing him and let him step inside.

"Auntie," Peter feigned affection in his greeting.

"Mrs. Topping, Peter. I don't want to tell you again."

"Ahhh, you know the old saying, 'your in-laws are always your in-laws.' Lucky us, eh?"

Marjorie hated this man, her relationship to him, and most of all, the things that would keep them connected—at least as long as they were both alive.

"I see you've finally found honest work." She looked at the logo on the uniform. "I haven't ordered anything. To what do I owe this visit? I don't recall inviting you."

"You never do. However, as you are always quick to remind me, I'm the proverbial bad penny."

His menacing grin made her skin crawl. "What do you want?"

"How are you, Peter? Nice to see you, Peter. Boy, just like the gig in that chair you're still as stiff as a board."

She ignored his comments as she turned her chair toward the living room.

Peter followed her and waited until she had herself positioned. Then he walked to the chair facing her.

The doorbell rang.

"Who is that, Peter?"

"How would I know? Guess you want me to get it." He patted her cheek moving his now gloved hand across her face as he headed for the front door.

Marjorie felt the latex and tried to process him wearing a glove as she turned her head and reached up with her hand. She had an urgent need to wipe his hand off her face.

The storm door was being held open by a woman in a black suit. He looked her up and down; the quality of her suit did not escape him. "Looking for someone?"

Quinn held up her badge as did Billy. "Detective Quinn Isaacs. We're here to see Ms. Topping."

Peter held the large wooden door open and made a sweeping arc with his right arm as he gave a slight bow. He had completely forgotten he was still in a delivery uniform. "She's in her parlor."

Quinn stepped through the door and headed toward the living room.

Billy entered the house and took hold of the outside handle of the door pulling it toward him to shut it as he saw the man holding the other side angling to exit. "Maybe you could join us for a minute." Billy nodded to the man. "Pretty sure your company requires you to wear a cap. Must have taken yours off. Let's go see if you left in the *parlor*." Billy used his best southern drawl on the last word.

Peter turned ahead of him and walked into the living room—his eyes scanning for an exit.

Quinn's phone was on the table as she gave information to dispatch while she administered chest compressions to Marjorie Topping who was lying on the floor.

Billy moved closer to Peter whose head was now focused on a door in the far corner.

"Have a seat." Billy nudged him toward a chair.

Peter moved toward the chair, sidestepped it, and headed toward the door.

Billy had him on the floor, his arms pinned behind his back, and handcuffs on before Peter could take two steps.

Billy left him there and moved over to Quinn as he pulled on gloves. He saw the foam on Marjorie's mouth. "I can take over. Just slide to your left on the next compression."

The doorbell rang.

Quinn slid to the left and Billy immediately positioned himself to continue compressions. Quinn pulled off her gloves and had her badge in her hand as she ran to the front door.

She held up her badge. "This way."

The paramedics followed her into the living room. Billy was sitting on his heels. He shook his head.

Quinn looked at the inert form of the late Marjorie Topping.

One of the paramedics moved over and checked for a pulse in the neck. He immediately removed his hand, pulled the saliva covered glove off turning it inside out and put on another glove.

"Put it in an evidence bag, please." Quinn said without thinking about it.

The paramedic nodded.

Billy pulled Peter to his feet. "Come on, fella. You have some explaining to do."

Safe House

Elliott Nelson looked at Kelly Culbert who was sitting with her mother and brother at the table in the open kitchen in the safe house. The SBI agent on duty was with the children in the playroom.

"Ms. Culbert, I am sorry for your loss."

"Call me Kelly, please. Thank you. I'm still not processing it." She shrugged. "I guess you understand that."

"Yes, Kelly, I do. Sad to say."

Lance watched his sister and tried not to intervene.

"Lance has told you the threat made on my hus...my late husband." She said it with no emotion at all—just stating a fact.

"Yes. I'm expecting a call with verification of the STELT property. Do I understand you've spoken with Mr. Burton on the other property?"

"I did. He has agreed to sell his property and expects the closing to take place...well, he said he knew the end of the week was Good Friday, so he seemed fine with the closing taking place the first of next week."

"Good. Good." Elliott nodded his head. He saw Kelly's mother had her hand on Kelly's arm.

"I know this is not convenient, but we'd like you to stay here for another day or two. Lance and I are going to take a run out to this property and see what's up. Anything we need to know?"

Kelly looked from her mother...to Lance...to Elliott. She shrugged. "We haven't been out there in years. It's acreage Daddy Andy inherited from his great-grandmother—I think that's right."

Lance put his arm around his sister. "Doesn't matter. We can figure all that out. Right now we need to figure out why someone wanted that land so badly. You okay to stay here for another day or so?"

She looked at her brother. "I don't have to like it. I do have to protect our family. So go do what you need to do." She felt her mother squeeze her arm; a reassuring gesture she had always treasured.

Elliott and Lance stood and the two women did as well.

"Come on, Mom. Two little kids are being awfully good. I think there's some ice cream in the fridge, right?" Kelly took her mother's hand.

Mrs. Macklin looked at Kelly. "The agents..." she turned to Elliott, "I should say this to you, Mr. Nelson. Your agents have been the most unusual combination of totally helpful, available, and invisible. I don't know how they do it. Thank you." She turned and smiled at Kelly, "Now, yes, ice cream was on the shopping list." She smiled at her daughter.

Lance and Elliott were out the door and in the back seat of Elliott's SUV with the window between them and his driver closed. They headed toward downtown Knoxville.

"Thanks, Elliott. I'm sure my family is not your first priority today."

"Family, immediate and extended through work, are always first priority. Something tells me this is going to be about much more than family though. Tell me what you learned about the drone."

"Not much to tell. I ended up flying home because I knew my mother and sister needed me here. For the most part, the folks I interviewed who are residents there seemed pretty straight forward and none of them had ever seen a drone flying around there. It's on an island which is pretty isolated on the west end where my brother-in-law seems to own a pretty sizable chunk of land."

"Any other big pieces he owns?"

"Well, when you're in the commercial and land real estate business, I suppose you buy and sell a lot of land. Andrew, like his daddy before him, was smart and savvy when it came to knowing a deal when he saw one and making a deal when he wanted to."

"Always thought he had a pretty good business mind and was hopeful that would help get him elected to governor."

"Yeah. Gossip in Nashville was he didn't play ball with some of the folks who like to control things from back rooms."

Elliott almost snorted. "Probably wasn't all gossip."

"Yeah. Don't we know it. Anyway, there is one thread I want to tug from my visit to the island."

"What's that?"

"Andrew's pilot."

Elliott listened to Lance's observations about the pilot. "So, I don't have any hard evidence, but something just doesn't sit right."

"Smart to leave an agent with him. Sometimes things aren't always what they seem."

"Amen to that. What's the plan?"

"I told the driver we'd head for the office, but now I'm thinking we should just stay on the road and go check this land. What do you think?"

"Let's do it."

The Valley Sheriff's Station

The Topping home was secured and officers on site while they waited on the official COD to ensure it was a crime scene.

Quinn and Billy returned to the Valley Sheriff's Station.

Sheriff Chad Oliver walked into his conference room. Quinn and Billy stood.

"Sit. Sit." He shook hands with Quinn. "Good to see you, Quinn. Looks like the work might be agreeing with you."

"Mostly." She smiled. "Appreciate the help of your detective on this case." She sat.

"That would be me, Sheriff." Billy grinned.

Chad threw a glance Billy's way and turned to Quinn. "We can change that, Quinn, if necessary. We have other fine detectives."

Quinn was accustomed to the Sheriff's deadpan style. "Oh, he'll do for now."

"Good. Good. Hate to waste your time bringing someone else up to speed. What's going on?"

"As you're aware, Billy and I found a young woman up on the mountain near Indian Flats Falls..." She did a quick recap of what they knew at the moment. "There is a man in your holding who was present in the home of Mrs. Topping when we arrived. I was administering chest compressions while waiting for the paramedics when he attempted to leave and Billy cuffed him. This happened in your jurisdiction. Your support up until now has been appreciated. I am here, with my Chief's approval, to officially request a joint investigation of this case along with ours involving your victim's granddaughter, Angela." She took a deep breath and chuckled. "How convoluted was that sentence?"

"Relax, Quinn. We're good." Chad gave her a reassuring smile.

"I need to update the SBI. They're still working on Angela's hard drives. Since we share a district attorney, I think we need to get a warrant to confiscate Ms. Topping's computer, but she is your case."

"Quinn, you dealt with interagency jobs in Immigration Enforcement. This is no different. You're just in a different role. You'll figure out what you need. I'm sure you and Billy will get to the bottom of this."

"Thanks, Chad. Your support is helpful and your encouragement appreciated." She turned to Billy. "Well, Detective. Have a plan for the man in your holding?"

"Oh, yeah. I want to be good cop." His mischievous grin wasn't missed on the Sheriff.

"Lock this one up if you need to." Chad pointed to Billy as he walked out the door chuckling.

"Yes, sir. And, Chad. Please give my kind regards to Bella."

"Done." He closed the door.

Chapter 23

Spring is when you feel like whistling, even with a shoe full of slush.
Doug Larson

Interrogation in the Valley

Quinn was pacing in the interrogation room in the jail at the Valley Sheriff's Station. *Petersen Samuel Topping...who names a child Petersen? Peter, yes. Pete, yes. Petersen...Did Angela say cuss or cuz? How are they all related? Marjorie's husband? Will Petersen be surprised when he finds out we know his name even though he hasn't said a word since his cutesy gesture when he let us in the door at Marjorie Topping's home.* She made a mental note to congratulate the forensics team for finding his hidden driver's license so quickly. *I just hope the run Officer Gilbert is doing will tell us more about him.* She also hoped this preliminary interview would get them information. She stopped pacing when she heard the click of the door handle.

Petersen Topping entered the room in an orange jumpsuit, a waist chain with wrists cuffed to it, and ankle chains.

"Here, let me get that for you. Can't be easy in those." Billy pulled out the chair for him.

Really, Billy? Good cop pulls out his chair! Quinn had to catch herself to keep from rolling her eyes.

She knew the cameras were recording, but she and Billy had agreed they would use the small recorder placed on the table. *Love it when the out of towners think we're country bumpkins.*

"This is Detective Isaacs of the Round City Police, and..."

"Detective Williams of the Valley Sheriff's Station."

Quinn gave the date and time. "Mr. Topping, please state your full name, address, and date of birth."

Peter stared at her. "Petersen Samuel Topping." He gave his date of birth and address on Brookline Avenue in the Fenway area of Boston—both of which they already had.

"Mr. Topping, you have the right…" She finished reading him his rights. "Mr. Topping, do you understand these rights as I have explained them?"

"Yes."

"Do you wish to have an attorney present?"

"I am a lawyer."

"Mr. Topping, do you wish to have an attorney present or to represent yourself as a self-identified lawyer?"

"I don't need counsel."

"For the record, you are waiving your right to have an attorney…" she waited a few seconds on purpose, "…other than yourself present for this interview."

"Yes."

"Thank you."

Billy was leaning against the wall on his left shoulder and she saw him flinch. He shifted and leaned toward the table as he spoke. "Detective, perhaps Mr. Topping would be more comfortable…"

Quinn turned and glared at him. "Detective Williams, this is my interview and I will thank you to wait until I speak to you or ask something of you before you interrupt. Is that clear?"

Billy took the chair which was beside him, turned it so the back was facing the table, and sat down facing the back of the chair. "Yes, ma'am." His southern drawl was as thick as molasses on a sugar maple in the winter time.

She turned back to Peter. "Mr. Topping, what brings you to Tennessee?"

"Visiting my aunt."

"Who is your aunt?"

"Marjorie Topping."

Well, that answers that question. "You were dressed as a package delivery carrier to visit your aunt?"

"What difference does that make?"

"Just making sure we're clear in what capacity you were visiting Ms. Topping. Since you've indicated you're a lawyer, the uniform doesn't make sense."

"She's an uptight old...b...lady. Thought I'd give her something to make her laugh."

"Did she?"

"Never."

"Was she expecting your visit?"

"Never was part of our family rituals."

"To let someone know you'd come to visit?" Quinn tried to feign interest in such behavior.

"Nope. Always just seemed easier to show up."

"Did Ms. Topping visit you without notification?"

"Never visited me."

"Did she visit your parents without notification?"

"How would I know?"

"Given the date of her marriage to your uncle, you would have been a child and teenager while your uncle was alive. Surely, like in all good families, they came to visit." She put on her very proper well-heeled society smile.

"She was cold as ice even then."

Quinn shifted tactics. Her tone was low and slow. "We don't take too kindly to murder in these mountains."

"Unless you're killing an attacking bear." Billy chuckled at his own comment.

Quinn ignored him.

Peter looked at him with disgust. *Hick cop. You're even more stupid than this broad across the table.*

As if nothing had happened, Quinn continued. "Our forensic team has checked the registration on the van you were driving and it is completely unknown to the company whose logo is on it."

Peter didn't blink.

"Needless to say, that has made us very suspicious about the boxes inside that van. Anything you want to share about the van or its contents?" She didn't expect an answer.

Peter looked over to Billy.

She waited a few seconds, shrugged her shoulders, and slammed the palm of her hand on the table. She gritted her teeth not to flinch at the sharp pain.

Billy leaned back as if she had slapped him.

Peter Topping jumped and the chains rattled.

"Mr. Topping, I am the one interviewing you." She pointed to Billy. "This detective is here to learn something about conducting an interview. You need to pay very close attention to *me* and answer my questions."

Peter leaned his back against the chair. "Listen, little lady. I don't take orders from you or any other woman. You are holding me against my will, without cause, and I will own this hick village before the week is out. Is *that* clear?"

Billy pulled his chair up to the table.

Quinn pretended to ignore him.

"Hey, buddy."

"I'm not your buddy!" Peter almost growled.

"Sorry, just mountain talk. Sir, I think I can help us move this along." His face toward Peter, he glanced over at Quinn out of the corner of his eye signaling Peter—"Help me out here; she's tough. You know the type!" He leaned his elbows on the table. "I see your hands are pretty red. Is that why you needed those latex gloves we found in your pocket?"

Peter shifted his shoulders from side-to-side. "I don't have any latex gloves."

"I know." Billy chuckled. "We took them." He grinned his school boy grin.

Quinn leaned into the table. "Enough—I don't qualify for the boys club and I'm not a smart lawyer like Mr. Topping here. But even he knows they'll find his DNA on the gloves. So, cut the pal talk."

This time Billy nodded toward Quinn. "Tried to help, buddy." He turned to Quinn. "He's all yours."

Peter tried to sound like a lawyer. "I have nothing more to say. You can return me to your pathetic holding cell or we can sit here and stare at each other. I'm done."

Quinn stood. "Return him to holding. We'll be back when we have the final forensics and Ms. Topping's cause of death." This time she put her hands on the table and leaned across the table toward him.

Billy hoped the man would make some gesture toward Quinn. *Go ahead, bad boy. I'd go to jail to teach you not to ever do that again.*

Quinn shrugged. "Your cooperation would have been noted in our report to the district attorney but I can promise you this…" she leaned in closer, "that time has ended." She walked to the door and opened it.

"Williams returning suspect to holding. Interview over." This time Billy made a point of pulling out the chair under Peter a little too fast for him to be able to stand up without the risk of falling.

Peter caught himself on the table with his elbows. He righted himself and walked out as fast as his ankle chains would allow.

Valley Sheriff's Conference Room

Quinn sipped from the bottle of ice tea. Billy had a cup of coffee on the table.

"Well played, Detective." Billy lifted his coffee cup in mock salute.

"Not." Quinn let the word hang in the air.

Billy decided not to play into any qualms she had about the interview. "He's not a lawyer."

"I know."

"Do you think he knows we know?"

"He doesn't care. He's playing us for small town yokels." Quinn stood.

"So what?"

"So...we're not."

"You're not that insecure. Who cares what he thinks?"

Quinn paced.

Billy knew she was running something important through that brain of hers. *I wish I could see into your brain, beautiful lady.*

Quinn's secure phone rang. "Issacs."

"Jackson here."

"Ralph, what's up?"

Billy mouthed, "Ralph Jackson?"

She nodded.

"Got a minute, Quinn?"

"Of course."

"You remember our regional director, Elliott Nelson?"

"Yes, of course. We worked the case on..." She caught Billy out of the corner of her eye. It was the attempt on Billy's life they had worked together. She stopped.

"Right. Of course you did."

"Elliott would like to come and meet with you tomorrow morning as early as you can make it happen."

Quinn's eyes were dancing around the room. They landed on Billy.

"I'm in the Valley at the moment." She brought him up to date on Marjorie Topping's death, Peter Topping in holding, and her desire to move on getting a warrant for Marjorie's computer.

"I'm sending you something that will make your DA only too happy to go to a judge. Do you want Williams in on the meeting?"

"Absolutely. We've formally agreed to a multi-jurisdictional investigation. Are you coming?"

"No, but Associate Director Lance Macklin, the head of cybersecurity for the SBI, will be with him."

Quinn sat down. "I'll stay in the Valley until I get the information from you. If the DA can find a judge right away, I can bring the computer with me." *Do I need a warrant since it's an active crime scene? Is it a crime scene before we know the COD? No, wait. Billy has to get the warrant.*

"Quinn?"

"Oh, sorry, Ralph. Brain ran down another train track."

Ralph started laughing. So did Billy.

Quinn put her fingers to her lips.

Billy chuckled and stopped laughing.

"Eight o'clock too early in the morning?"

"Eight it is. Tell Director Nelson I look forward to seeing him and meeting Director Macklin."

Billy raised his eyebrows.

Quinn ended the call and immediately dialed Chief Hansen.

"Hansen."

"Chief..." She filled her boss in on the events to date and the impending visit from the SBI folks.

"Quinn, it sounds like you've stumbled into a hornets' nest."

"Could be the imperfect web, for sure."

"You could be right. Thanks for updating me. The SBI will be welcome as will Detective Williams. See you in the morning."

"Yes, ma'am." Quinn saw Billy watching her. She ended the call. "Problem, Detective?"

"Oh, no. None whatsoever." He showed her the text from the Valley medical examiner. COD: Cyanide poisoning.

She shocked even herself when she leaned over and kissed him.

Billy leaned into the kiss and then sat back and shook his finger at her. "No fair."

"Not at all." She put on a puppy dog look: *I didn't do it.*

"You're forgiven." He slapped his thighs. "Now, let's figure out who needs to request the warrant from Peggy, pick up that computer, and go get something to eat."

"Perfect. We can pick up something and eat at my place."

"You're on. Now that we have the COD, we don't need a warrant. The computer is in our jurisdiction..."

A few minutes later, the phone in the Valley Sheriff's Station conference room rang.

"Williams."

"Detective, it's DA O'Haire."

"Thanks."

Billy pushed the speaker phone button. "Williams."

"O'Haire, here, but you already know that. What's up?"

"Detective Isaacs from Round City is here on speaker phone."

"Hey, Peggy."

"Hey, Quinn. What's up?"

"We're on a joint case which has evolved from the death of Angela Topping." Quinn continued and filled her in on the latest developments.

"Billy sent you the information we received from the SBI. We want to pick up Ms. Topping's computer. Hold on a minute."

She turned to Billy who had looked at a text on his secure phone. "Peggy, I just got a text from the scene at Ms. Topping's residence. Seems her assistant is there pitching a fit that they won't tell her anything or let her in the house. We may need to put all computers in the house on that warrant."

"Do you have a cause of death on Ms. Topping?"

Quinn was quick but gave as much detail as they had. "ME here just confirmed cyanide poisoning. Waiting on the forensics on the glove we took off of her nephew."

"Took off?"

"It was in his pocket. Retrieved when we brought him to the Station."

Peggy said, "So, it's possible it was administered as opposed to self-injested?"

"Well, Quinn, you get all the cuties, don't you? Billy, I thought you were supposed to help a fellow officer."

"Ha, ha, Peggy. She does just fine on her own. We're treating the Topping home as a crime scene, but until we have the ruling on the glove, we can't go wholesale through the house."

"Good for you. Quinn, that is a good lesson to tuck away."

"Got it. Do you think you can get us a warrant so I can pick up the computer and bring it Round City?"

"Got two judges in the building this afternoon. Let me see what I can do."

"Thanks, Peggy. Anything else, Billy?"

He shook his head.

"Did you hear his head rattle, Peggy? That was a 'no' from him."

"Good enough. Hang tight." The call ended.

Billy watched the desk top phone go dark. "Now we wait."

"I don't do that part well."

"You'll learn." He smiled at her.

"Do you need to go check on Maria at Ms. Topping's?"

Billy shook his head. "Nope, she should be arriving here momentarily."

"Why?"

"Attempted assault on a law enforcement officer—a big mistake in our neck of the woods."

"Should be in any neck of the woods, or city, or…" Quinn shook her head. "Okay, I'm going down the hall. Are we going to talk to her?"

"As soon as she's in holding."

"Okay." Quinn walked to the door. She turned around. "Billy, what if she knows Peter Topping? Should we take that risk? Is she likely to see him?"

"Good thinking."

"On the other hand…"

Billy stared at her. *Oh, where is your brain now, Quinn Isaacs?* He finished her sentence. "We have five fingers."

"Ha, ha." She shook her head in mock disdain. "Maybe we want to find out how well she knows Peter Topping if she knows him."

He studied her face. "Go down the hall. I'm not as quick as you are; I need to think this one through."

Quinn winked at him and left the conference room.

Maria Arrives

Quinn reentered the conference room and saw Billy on the phone. She stopped.

He saw her and waved her in. "Okay, Peggy. Thanks."

"So?"

"So, we got our warrant. Keeps it clean."

"Good."

"Officer bringing in Maria is going to bring her here and go write his report. The officer she attempted to push, before the other one took hold of her wrist so she couldn't, agreed we might prefer the attempted assault as leverage."

"Whoa, whoa, whoa. I'm not going to bargain assault on a police officer for getting her to talk."

"We won't. We just present her with the facts."

"This is in your house and I'll follow your lead. How do you want to handle this?" Quinn respected Billy and knew this was in his jurisdiction.

"Relax. It's been a long day already and there are too many flies in this ointment."

"Web." She was looking at the table and startled herself when she spoke.

He laughed and spoke very softly. "Quinn Isaacs, have I told you lately that I love you. I love everything about you."

"Even when I blunder into situations."

"Even then." He blew her a kiss. "Now, let's get this strategized. They'll be here any time now."

The knock on the door came as they agreed on their plan and Quinn moved to the side of the table beside the door.

Billy went to the door which he opened with his right hand. "Thank you, Officer." He looked at Maria. "Please come in." He stepped back.

Maria stopped when she saw Quinn. "What are you doing here?"

"Good afternoon." They had decided not to use her name as they had not been officially introduced to her with a last name even though they had it from the officer on the scene.

"Please have a seat." Billy pointed to a chair at the end of the table which put Quinn to her right and him to her left.

"I'm sure you remember us, but since all conversations in this room are recorded, we'll just state our names for the record. I'm Detective Williams of the Valley Sheriff's Station…" He nodded at Quinn.

"I'm Detective Isaacs of the Round City Police. And you are?"

Maria looked from one to the other. "I'm Maria Parsons. Where is Ms. Topping?"

Billy ignored her. "Have you been out all day today?"

"Where is Ms. Topping?"

"We'll talk about Ms. Topping in a few moments. First, I've asked your whereabouts today."

The curt officious tone they had heard when she greeted them at Ms. Topping's home was on full bore. "If you must know, I had a dentist appointment today in Round City. Then I went to the grocery store."

"Did you go anywhere else?" Quinn smiled.

Maria looked at Quinn. "I'm not sure why any of this is your business." She turned back toward Billy.

"As you would have seen," Billy said in a matter-of-fact way, "there is police boundary tape around Ms. Topping's home. Since you are her employee and therefore responsible for many aspects of her welfare, we just need to know her condition the last time you saw her."

"Why? Has something happened to her?"

Quinn was intrigued with the calm. *That isn't the response of a caregiver who is concerned for her charge. Which is the real you? The demand when you entered to know where Ms. Topping was—or the cold calculating woman asking the question?*

"May I have the name of your dentist?" Billy had his pencil poised over his pad.

"Am I being interrogated? Don't you have to read me my rights or something?"

"I'm more than happy to read you your rights. You have the right…" Billy recited the Miranda warning. "Do you understand these rights as I have explained them?"

"Yes." Maria stared at the wall.

"Do you wish to have an attorney present?"

"No." Maria did not take her eyes off the wall.

"The name of your dentist?" Billy sounded more forceful now.

Maria didn't answer.

Quinn slid her chair closer and spoke softly. "Were you expecting someone to visit Ms. Topping today?"

Maria turned to look at Quinn. Then she lowered her head. "He told me he wouldn't be there long. I just needed to be out of the house for a couple of hours."

"Who told you?"

Maria lowered her head again. "Peter Topping. Ms. Topping's nephew."

"Why did you agree to leave?"

"He wired ten thousand dollars to my bank account." Tears ran down her face.

Billy stood up and took out his cuffs. "Maria Parsons, you are under arrest as an accessory to murder. Please stand up."

"Murder? What? Ms. Topping is dead?" Maria's tears became sobs. "No, no, no!"

"Detective Williams exiting Conference room with Ms. Parsons."

Quinn watched him leave the room. "Detective Isaacs ending interview." She clicked off the button on the console which now controlled the recording devices in this room. The door was ajar and she turned when someone walked in.

"Sylvia, how nice to see you."

Sylvia Whitehorse, the lead sergeant and second in command, at the Valley Sheriff's Station came in and extended her hand to shake Quinn's. "Congratulations on your new job as lead detective—well deserved. Haven't seen you in person to tell you. Thanks for your note about my dad and the change in our local tribe."

"Oh, Sylvia. I appreciated your note. It means the world to me to have your support." Quinn's eyes searched Sylvia's face. "I'm so sorry about the loss of your dad, but I honestly don't know the right protocol. Do I congratulate you on being the new tribal chief?"

"I'm humbled by the responsibility, but thanks for your good wishes."

"Puts a lot on your shoulders: tribal chief and lead sergeant."

"Here to serve, Quinn. Here to serve."

Quinn settled hearing Sylvia use the double speak many mountain folks uttered when they wanted to reassure someone or make a point. Folk wisdom suggested the echo in the mountains caused people to speak that way.

"I'm glad you stepped in. Billy should be right back."

"I'm here. Hey, Sylvia."

"Hey, Billy. Anything I can do?"

Billy caught her up on the events of the day. "We'll let Peter Topping and Maria Parsons spend the night in our fine accommodations. We'll be back to talk to them tomorrow."

Quinn looked at Billy. "Do either know the other is here?"

"No. We don't have men and women together anyway. I could have let her see him, but right now I don't want either to know the other is here."

"Good call." Sylvia nodded. "I'm headed to roll call. Let me know if you need me to do anything on this. Otherwise, catch you both later. All the best, Quinn."

"Thanks, Sylvia. You, too."

Sylvia pulled the door closed behind her.

Billy reached out and took Quinn's hand. "I'm going to go pick up the computers our guys found in the Topping residence, then I'll stop and pick up supper. Meet you at your house before seven. That work?"

Quinn flipped off the light switch, pulled Billy to her and wrapped her arms around his neck, and kissed him deeply. "Let me count the ways." She stepped back. "Thanks, Billy. See you soon." She turned and walked out of the Conference Room toward the front and out to her SUV.

"I'm counting. I'm counting." Billy smiled and walked to the back of the Station to his own vehicle.

Chapter 24

A lie can travel halfway around the world while the truth
is still putting on its shoes.
Jonathan Swift

Wednesday Morning

Quinn felt, more than heard, the soft steady breathing close to her face. Barely opening her eyes, she reached her hand out and stroked Billy's cheek.

"Good morning." The smile in her voice carried through her soft touch.

"Well, hello there. Have I told you I love watching you sleep?"

"Oh, my. I can't imagine why." She pulled the sheet up under her arms as she sat up and looked at him. "It must be boring to watch me breath in and out in slumber."

"I could watch you all day and night in any condition." He pulled himself up on his left elbow and leaned in to kiss her. He gasped.

"Billy, are you okay?"

"Shoulder. When will that shoulder quit catching?" He sat up straight with a slight pant of pain.

She moved over and kissed his shoulder. "There, there. It's all better now." She pulled her head back and looked up at him. "Seriously, Billy, I think you need to go see Doc Smith and maybe have him do an x-ray. You took a pretty hard fall up on that mountain."

He arched his shoulder and then reached over his head. "I'm good."

"Yes, good. However, you are not out of pain. Please?" She fluttered her eyes.

"Well, that's a new one. Haven't seen the eyelash flutter before."

"Careful or I'll give you a real pain in the shoulder."

He laughed. "Quinn Isaacs, I love you." He slid closer. He kissed her gently. "More and more every day."

"You're pretty special yourself, Detective Williams. Thanks for getting my pen at Ms. Topping's." She kissed him lightly. "Speaking of being detectives, we have a meeting in…" she looked at the clock. "Oh, my gosh, in fifty minutes. I'm headed to the shower."

"Great, I'll join you."

She wagged her finger at him. "You can have it right after I'm finished." She grinned and jumped out of bed.

Billy entered the kitchen as Quinn was putting on her service weapon. "You get ready in a hurry, ma'am."

"No makeup. Don't need much time to shower and dress—especially when your uniform-of-the-day is the same every day." She pointed to his Yeti. "Coffee's in it. Let's go."

"Hmmm…no makeup. So that's your secret. Must be why I take so long to get ready."

Quinn started laughing so hard she almost dropped her coffee. "That's a good one; you wearing makeup. Come on, lover boy, let's go."

Billy headed to the kitchen door, opened his gun safe, and put on his service weapon. "I'll follow you out through the garage. No sense traipsing through the house."

"Be my guest." She looked into the garage as she opened the kitchen door. "I moved my personal vehicle to the far side of the garage—you could park inside."

"What? And give the neighbors more to talk about?" He winked at her. "No problem. I'm fine parking outside. Beat you to your Station."

"I can ticket you. Don't speed." She kissed him and got in her official SUV.

The Meeting

George entered the Detectives Workroom with a large box of Carrie's pastries. He had insisted upon bringing them when Quinn had called to tell him they were meeting with the brother of the recently deceased Police Chief this morning.

Quinn looked up from the computer and smiled. "Thanks, George. I'm sure this is much more exquisite breakfast fare than our guests are used to. Thanks for getting the room set up, too. Ready?"

"Ready. Where's Billy?"

"He stopped to talk to one of the officers he knows. I'm going to head up front to meet our guests."

"10-4." He shrugged when Quinn pointed to his tie. "Haven't seen Elliott since the funeral. Guess I'm a little nervous. Things have changed a lot here."

"That's on me. So, relax. I doubt he'll even notice." She opened the door and walked toward the front as her secure phone buzzed. "Isaacs."

"Ma'am, Directors Nelson and Macklin are here to see you."

"Turning the corner now. Thanks." She reclipped the phone to the waist on her slacks as she stepped to the locked door between the main part of the Station and reception.

"Oh, here she is." Elliott Nelson turned toward Quinn.

"Director, welcome." She turned to Lance Macklin. "Director Macklin, I'm Quinn Isaacs. Welcome to Round City."

"Pleased to meet you, Quinn. Heard a lot about you."

Elliott stepped beside Quinn as they walked. "Seems your reputation precedes you, Quinn. Lance told me he'd heard about several of your cases in Immigration Enforcement. Imagine that—all the way to Nashville."

Quinn felt color rising and hoped it didn't show. "Thanks for your kind words. Just trying to find the truth—wherever it's hiding."

Both men nodded.

Quinn opened the door to the workroom and saw her Chief talking with George and Billy.

"Elliott, nice to see you. Welcome home." Jill Hansen extended her hand.

"Thanks. Always good to be home. Do you know Lance Macklin?"

Chief Hansen extended her hand. "Haven't had the pleasure. Jill Hansen."

Lance shook her hand. "Nice to meet you. Understand you've come home, too."

"Glad to be here. I don't want to interfere in the work you're here to do just wanted to meet you and let you both know you're always welcome in our house. Let me know if I can do anything to help." She nodded to Quinn. "Good luck."

"Thanks, Chief." Quinn watched the door close behind Chief Hansen.

George offered coffee and pastries and they were all seated.

Quinn pulled out her chair. "Gentlemen, thanks for coming. How can we be of service?"

Lance jumped in first. "Understand you have Alfred Dunn in holding."

Quinn nodded. "Just so you know, I have spoken with Dunn's former parole officer—twice."

Elliott raised his hand, palm out as a signal to slow down. "Lance, you have your back to the crime board. By the way, Quinn, like what you've done to create a workspace. Never could understand why my brother put up with your predecessor." He looked from her to George with a look which seemed to acknowledge he knew the situation under the former lead detective. "Sorry, out of line. Lance, you might want to look at their board."

Quinn studied Elliott's eyes. *Why was it important to you to tell me you didn't approve of my predecessor? Reassurance that you're okay with me being here?*

Lance turned around. He studied the board and turned back to the table. "My apologies. This is your house. I need to give you full disclosure. I am Associate State Director for Cybersecurity of the SBI. I'm technically on leave, but operating under the auspices of the Director for reasons which will become clear in a minute." He looked around the table.

Quinn, George, and Billy sat still and quiet. They waited.

Lance let out a breath. "My sister is Kelly Macklin Culbert. My brother-in-law, Andrew Culbert the third, died under suspicious circumstances and I have my sister and her children and my mother in protective custody. As you likely know, Andrew recently lost his bid for governor and we are not convinced his death is unrelated. It has not been made public and is not to become such until we know more." He leaned back in his chair.

Quinn, George, and Billy nodded.

Elliott took over. "Andrew owned land which had been leased from him and was, it would appear, being used for nefarious purposes. Mr. Dunn was picked up on your APB when approaching the property. We have reason to question his potential involvement in Andrew's death." He looked toward the board. "I see by the web you have outlined over there, that you already know about the land and at least one other parcel adjacent to it." He pointed to the STELT label next to the Culbert land on their board.

"In addition," Lance's tone now sounded like an SBI agent, not just a concerned brother. "Our computer folks have found evidence on the mainframe from Angela Topping's residence that all of the property in that area was being researched."

Elliott stood up. "For what reason, we don't know."

Quinn looked at George. "Perhaps we should start at *our* beginning incident and bring you up to speed. George?" She gave him a slight nod.

George stood and went to the board. "Angela Topping was found by Quinn and Billy up near Indian Flats Falls." He pointed to the map. "She died at the hospital of an inhaled substance only partially identified and as yet an unknown source of origin." He walked them through finding the red truck, Patten, Angela's ring in the truck, Angela's car on the parkway, Dunn's fingerprint. "...and just yesterday the death of Ms. Marjorie Topping and the arrest of her nephew, Peter, and Ms. Topping's personal assistant, Maria. Quinn or Billy will need to bring you up to speed on that. Any questions?"

Elliott was leaning against the wall facing the board. "The lines creating the web certainly make sense."

Lance stared at the purple inked web. "What's that line drawn to the Valley Sheriff's Station? 'Oh, what a tangled web we weave....'"

Quinn looked at Billy who nodded. She turned to Lance. "Detective Williams has been, with his Sheriff's approval, supporting the investigation into Angela's death. Yesterday Sheriff Oliver and Chief Hansen agreed to a joint operation since the Topping deaths cross over our jurisdictions. I had already invited the SBI, as you know. We appreciate your assistance with the technology. You mentioned finding evidence of searches related to the land. Were they on Angela's computer?"

"No, they were in a compartmentalized file which was being accessed from several different ISP addresses. We're waiting on our legal department to say if we need a warrant to track those addresses."

Quinn raised her eyebrows in surprise. "Doesn't our warrant to access the computers cover that?"

"No. Different ISP than Angela Topping's."

Quinn nodded. "Got it."

"Our primary thread in this web is the threat to my late brother-in-law and family by whoever was trying to pressure him to sell his family land and acquire the parcels on either side."

Quinn and Lance seemed to be in a private conversation. "Did he sell them?"

"No. Well, that is to say, he was working on it and had a verbal agreement from Roger Burton. Kelly, Andrew's wife...my sister, talked to Mr. Burton and he said he would sell, but no papers have been signed by him. Kelly was trying to track down STELT that is the registered owner of the land Mr. Dunn claimed to be interested in purchasing."

"So are we." George said without emotion.

Quinn stood and walked to the Board. "We know from our discussions with Marjorie Topping that there is a Topping Family Land Trust, registered in Maine as TFLT." She indicated the TFLT point on the web. "We have yet to figure out why it is registered in Maine. Mrs. Topping made clear that Chicago was their home before coming to Tennessee."

There was a knock on the door. George stood to answer it. Officer Gilbert walked in. He stepped back when he saw the SBI Directors. "Sorry to interrupt. I didn't..."

Quinn stepped up. "Come in, do you have something on the trusts?"

"Yes, ma'am."

"Officer Gilbert, this is Director Macklin of the State Bureau and I think you know Director Elliott." Quinn stepped back as the men shook hands. "Gilbert is our leading tech expert and he's been trying to track down the connection between the owners, if any, of these trusts."

Gilbert nodded. "I did."

All eyes turned to him.

"The STELT, TTLT, and TFLT are trusts registered in Maine. However, as part of their holdings they have conservancy easements in several states including Tennessee and Maine. The conservancy easements are registered in the state where the land is and held inside the trust in Maine."

"So, do we know who STELT is?" George momentarily forgot others were in the room sounding like one buddy talking to another. He straightened up. "Sorry."

Quinn smiled. "We're all anxious to know."

"First you might want to know that the TFLT conservation property is designated as Conservation Land which will belong to the state of TN at such time as there is no direct heir of the Harvey Topping or Marjorie Eldridge Topping line." Gilbert looked at Quinn.

She nodded. "Go on."

"On the other hand, TTLT and STELT have a clause allowing the sale of the conservation easements held in it 'to benefit the common good as determined by a majority of the living heirs of the family who meet the definition of an heir in the Trust.'"

"Whoa, whoa, whoa." Elliott stood up and raised his hand to stop Gilbert. "Does that mean if a single person is the sole surviving heir, they can take all of that land out of the Trust?"

"Sir, I'm not an attorney. I'm quoting the wording in the trust." Gilbert hoped he wouldn't get pressed on how he managed to get that deep into the language of the trust.

No one asked.

"Gilbert, do we know who the current members of the TTLT and STELT are and what those letters represent?"

"Yes, ma'am. TTLT is Two Toppings Land Trust and STELT is Save The Earth Land Trust."

"And the owners of the two Trusts?"

"TTLT is Angela Topping and Petersen Samuel Topping…STELT is Angela Topping."

The room went quiet.

Quinn spoke first. "Lance, does this make any sense in relation to your family and their land or your brother-in-law's death?"

Lance sat down. "One of the things we do in law enforcement, no matter what our role, is try to solve puzzles."

All the heads in the room nodded.

"I'm not ready to say my sister and children are out of danger, but if my brother-in-law was targeted so Topping could acquire the land on the other side of Andrews, it must mean he didn't know Angela set up another trust. As for Topping's actions, we just have to make sure we track down all his accomplices. If they weren't involved in Andrew's death, we're left with the possibility it was tied to Andrew's campaign for governor."

Elliott pulled out a chair at the table and sat. "Or someone or something totally unrelated to either."

Lance looked at Elliott. "True."

Elliott continued. "If Petersen Topping is the guilty party in all this and he already knew the land owned by STELT was actually Angela, why is it listed in the properties he told Andrew to purchase?"

Lance jumped right in. "Red herring. He assumed Andrew couldn't get access to figure out the ownership of the Trust and he'd bargain down the final price on the other two parcels as a threat. Seems logical to me."

Billy spoke for the first time. "Well, you're giving Peter Topping way too much credit if our observations from the interrogation yesterday are any indication."

Quinn whispered to George to go to the crime board. "Gentlemen, let's see if we connect this web any more solidly knowing what we know now. Then we need to go back and interrogate Alfred Dunn and Peter Topping based on what we know."

Heads nodded around the table.

"Ready, George?"

George moved to a blank part of the Board. "Fire away—so to speak." It broke the tension in the room—everyone chuckled.

As the names and locations of people, the unknown people, Culbert land site, and crimes and potential crimes were listed, Quinn watched carefully as the new web expanded. "Elliott, you said there was nefarious activity up on the Culbert land. Do you know specifically what?"

"Yes. They were manufacturing chemicals into drugs which were being put into capsules and packaged in bubble packs; we assume to be sold. Our lab is working on determining what chemical or chemicals are in those capsules."

"Do we know who was doing the manufacturing? Were there any people there working?"

"No, when the fire rescue teams arrived because one of the portables was burning, there was no one in any of the units they had placed up there."

"More than one portable?" George sounded incredulous. "We're used to the meth cookers up here. They rent old property cheap. Portables?"

Billy chuckled. "No limit to what they'll do. We had a case in the fall where the boy was cooking meth inside a stolen rental box truck."

Lance shook his head. "What? A box truck?"

"Yep. He blew it and himself from here to kingdom come."

"Didn't hear about that one." Lance was still shaking his head.

Quinn walked over to the board. "Based on the threads in this web, I think we need to interview Dunn first. His fingerprints were in Angela's car. She died of chemical inhalation inside a truck which might have been used in kidnapping her, and we have Mr. Patten linked to Dunn."

All five of the men were looking at her.

"Dunn's clearly a gofer for someone. I suspect he will sing like a canary given the chance to cut himself a deal." She saw everyone in the room bristle. "I don't like deals any more than you do. And, I'm not in favor of offering him one. But I can promise you our DA is going to want to fry the big fish in all of this."

"Okay if we watch?" Elliott looked at Quinn and glanced at Lance.

"Be my guest. George and I need a few minutes to figure out our strategy. Officer Gilbert, would you be so kind as to show our guests the facilities and get them fresh coffee? We'll meet back here in twenty minutes. George, meet in my office in five?"

The men all stood as Quinn walked to the door and left the room.

George took his time walking to the men's room. Four minutes later he was in Quinn's office.

"Quinn, do you think Peter Topping had anything to do with Angela's death?"

"I think we don't know enough. Maybe she did drugs and her grandmother didn't know. No evidence of that in her home, but she apparently didn't leave home to go to work every day so except for her neighbor, she didn't seem to have a lot of social interaction. We'll see where this leads us."

"Don't you think her neighbor, Ms. Thompson, would have been suspicious if she thought she was doing drugs? After all, she was all over us for being there."

"Good point. Let's see if Dunn can name names. What do we need to know?"

They strategized and looked up when they heard a knock on the outside door of the lab. Quinn forgot Chuck was off today.

George stepped out. "I've got it, Quinn. It's Gilbert." He opened the door.

"Just letting you know we're back in the workroom. Quinn, do you want me to stay?"

"Not sure there's anything at this point, but you're welcome. Good work, Gilbert."

"Thanks. I'm going to go back to my computers. May find some more in all this before the day is done."

"Go for it. Thanks, again, for your jwork."

Gilbert headed out.

"Ready, George?"

"Think I've got it. We may flip-flop good cop and bad cop."

"Yep. Let's see how he takes to that."

Interrogation Room

They retrieved Billy, Elliott, and Lance from the workroom and headed down to holding. The Matron had been notified to have Dunn ready.

Quinn escorted their visiting law officers into the observation room. "Make yourselves comfortable. The show is about to begin."

She watched as George brought Alfred Dunn into the interrogation room.

"Have a seat." He switched on the recording device to make a show of it for Dunn. The cameras in the ceiling were already running.

Quinn walked in and sat opposite Dunn. "Mr. Dunn, as you know I am Detective Isaacs and this is..."

"Detective Marshall..." he gave the date and time.

"Please state your full name, address and date of birth for the record." Dunn complied.

"To keep the record clean I will repeat your Miranda rights."

"No need."

"Let's just keep the record clean. You have the right..." She looked him in the eyes the entire time. "Do you understand these rights?"

"I do."

"Do you wish to have an attorney present."

"Only the one who can make me a deal."

Quinn tried not to flinch. "Mr. Dunn, you will have the opportunity to talk with our district attorney should you provide us with relevant information material to the death of Angela Topping. Do you wish to have an attorney represent you?"

Dunn leaned in. "To keep the record clean," he grinned as he gave her back the words she had used earlier. "I know how this little game is played. I'm only interested in my interests. Is that clear? I don't need no attorney to represent me. I need that *district attorney* to give me a deal." He dragged out the last sentence.

Quinn gave him a faint smile and was about to move on.

"Is that clear?" Dunn shouted at her and the spit from his mouth through his cracked tooth landed on the table right in front of her.

George came off of his chair. He reached the corner of the table and slammed his palm on it. "Hey, scum bag, here in the south we don't talk to ladies like that. Is *that* clear?"

In a very soft voice, Quinn said, "Detective Marshall, let's move on. Now, Mr. Dunn, please tell me how you know Sammy Patten."

"Didn't say I knowed him."

"Oh, maybe I misunderstood you before. Shall I replay that tape for you?"

George jumped in. "Let's just go get the jerk."

Quinn put out her hand as if to silence George. "Detective, please. I'll decide if we're going to get Mr. Patten."

Dunn leaned back in his chair. "Ran into him in the joint in Illinois. Loser that kid is. Sure as hell didn't expect to run into him visiting his brother here in Tennessee."

"How did you run into him?"

Dunn grinned and crossed his arms.

Chapter 25

Truth is proper and beautiful in all times and in all places.
Frederick Douglass

Observation Room

Lance turned to Billy. "Not easy to watch someone else do an interview you'd like to do, is it?"

Billy shook his head. "Oh, don't get me wrong; I like getting to the truth as much as the next cop. For me, watching this show is worth far more than the price of admission. How about you?"

"Been a long time, I have to admit. Guess I miss it more than I realized."

Elliott held up his hand for them to stop talking. "Listen."

Through the speakers in the room they heard Quinn's question.

Billy wished they had a camera on Quinn's face so he could see her staring at Dunn which he had full confidence she was doing.

They watched Dunn lean in. "Lady...Detective Lady, you ain't getting that name from me until I talk to your district attorney." He leaned back, grinned, and the tip of his tongue protruding through the gap in his broken tooth appeared to mock Quinn.

Even though they could not be heard in the interrogation room, Billy whispered, "She'll walk out on him."

Lance whispered back, "Ten to one she pressures him."

Elliott whispered, "Let's wait and see. I want that name." He leaned forward. "What did Dunn just say?"

The other two men shrugged.

Interrogation Room

"Mr. Dunn, sir." She smiled and softened her tone. "I know for a fact our DA will value the information on the little manufacturing project going on up on private land and that Mr. Patten's brother was the chemist."

Dunn chortled. "No kidding."

"Knowing where we can find the chemist would go a long way to..."

"How the hell would I know?"

"Now, now. Mr. Dunn..."

George slid his chair over to the table. "Listen up, Dunn. You've strung us along for..." he looked at his watch, "for over an hour. Nothing you've said convinces me you didn't kill Angela Topping."

Dunn stamped his feet causing his ankle chains to rattle. Quinn and George ignored it.

"You listen, jerk." He glared at George. "I done told you everything I know about that little drug...what'd you call it? Manufacturing? I told you Patten was a junky; his brother was too but at least he had skills. Even you can figure out he musta got something from his chem head brother who was running the show. This Angela was probably a junky, too. Hell, half the young people in Amer-u-ka are today."

Billy sent a text to Officer Gilbert to try and track down Patten's brother, the chemist.

Quinn cringed inside at the way he said 'America.' She waited. "Then let's talk about Andrew Culbert."

"What about him? I only saw him once."

"Oh, where was that?"

"On a country road when my boss talked to him." he stopped.

Quinn waited. *You may have only seen him once, but I bet you're responsible for getting those photos doctored.*

"Have you been to Mr. Culbert's home?"

"No."

"His neighborhood?"

"I told you I want a deal. No deal. No name. No more talk." Dunn sat back and crossed his arms again as he stuck out his chest.

Quinn did not bat an eye. "Detective, return Mr. Dunn to his cell. I have other fish to fry today." She stood and opened the door.

"Let's go, *Mr.* Dunn." George let the name drip from his tongue like he wanted to spit it on the floor.

"Hold on. Hold on. Get me your DA. I'll tell him the name." Dunn put his hands in his lap this time.

Quinn didn't want him to know she already had the DA ready to listen. *Worst of all I doubt the DA can even make accessory before the fact stick since the probability is very likely Patten took Angela against her will and Dunn had nothing to do with it. Best she might get is in the drug manufacturing and perhaps distribution. We need to know who's behind this.*

Quinn leaned on the door handle. "Detective Marshall, I'll see if the DA is available."

"Yes, ma'am." He plopped back in his chair and leaned on two legs of it against the wall and glared at Dunn.

"Isaacs leaving interview." She gave the time.

Observation Room

The three men stood when she entered.

"I've called Peggy O'Haire. She's on her way to the Station. Any thoughts on the likelihood of her going for accessory to murder?"

Lance jumped in first. "If Patten was responsible for making or even having the chemicals that killed Angela, whether she went with him voluntarily or by force, Dunn knew about the drug manufacturing. That should count for something."

"Not a lawyer, myself..." Billy spoke next. "As big an ass as I think this guy is, he's been in the system several times and they learn enough to be dangerous in prison. He's not going to give us a name on accessory charges. I think he was following Patten and stumbled across Angela's car on the parkway."

Quinn looked at Billy. "Interesting observations. Elliott?"

"Not much of a speculator, but I want the name. So will Peggy. I think she'll offer him a deal on drug manufacturing and trafficking and he'll end up getting a lawyer who will whittle down whatever sentence she offers."

"Thanks, gentlemen. Helps me to hear the thinking of experts. Now if you'll stay tuned, I'm going to meet our tenacious DA, Peggy O'Haire." Quinn gave a nod of her head and left.

Interrogation Room

Quinn met Peggy outside the interrogation room. She knew Peggy had been watching the entire interview. It was the blessing and curse of two-way video and audio. She didn't have to review what was said, but knew her every word and action had been monitored.

"Morning, DA O'Haire."

"Morning, Detective."

"Want to move this to a conference room?"

"Nah, You sat in here with him, so can I. Let's see if he lawyers up when I walk in."

Quinn opened the door.

Dunn jerked his head toward them. "Shit. Another dumb broad."

Peggy walked in and took the chair across from Dunn. "DA O'Haire entering interview."

"Detective Isaacs entering interview."

"Mr. Dunn, your Miranda rights are still in effect. Do you understand these rights and responsibilities?"

Dunn stared at Peggy. Later she would swear she thought he was going to stick his tongue out at her. "Yeah."

"Mr. Dunn, do you wish to be represented by counsel? If you can't afford a lawyer, one will be provided for you."

"I told you I know my rights."

"Yes, sir. You did. I need you to tell me, on the record, whether you wish to have an attorney."

"Ain't you going to say, 'to keep the record clean.'" He smirked and his tongue protruded through the gap in his teeth.

Peggy had watched the interview. *Well, well, Mr. Dunn. You do pay attention.* "I'm always in favor of keeping the record clean." She smiled. "Do you wish to have an attorney."

"Nah. Just wanted to see if you bitc…uh, ladies had the same routine. Actually, I kind of like having a purty woman in front of me. Ain't had a lady DA before—that's a new one." Then he tried to put his forearms on the table but the chains holding his wrists to his waist wouldn't let him move that far. He pushed his wrists against the table. Then he leaned back and held them up. "Think we could take off this jewelry and talk like we was civilized?" He rattled the chains.

"Unlock the wrist cuffs, Detective Marshall." Peggy never took her eyes off of Dunn.

George made a show of searching for the key. *I'm tired of his BS. Maybe this will give me a reason to…*He caught himself and knew the thoughts were not a good thing. *How'd I get so prone to violence myself?* He unlocked the cuffs as Dunn held his hands up.

His hands unlocked, Dunn made a show of shaking them and waving them around in the air. "Much better. Civilized. Isn't that a word you lawyers like? Civ-uh-lized?" He put his forearms on the table. "Now, lady DA, what 'cha offering?"

Ten minutes later, Peggy sat up straight and stared at Dunn. "Mr. Dunn, I have told you repeatedly. I will seek accessory to murder in the death of Angela Topping. While the common belief is you get to bargain, I'm sorry to tell you, I hold the only bargaining chip and I don't play the game in reverse. You tell me what you know and then I'll tell you what consideration I'm willing to present to a judge based on your information. So, you tell me what you know now, or I'm out of here and you're back in the cell on murder charges. Five, four, three…"

"Okay, okay." Dunn let out a long sigh. "My boss is Petersen Samuel Topping—fondly called Mr. S." His grin was wicked. "I prefer to think the 'S' stands for Shi…head." He laughed.

As soon as he said the name, Lance and Elliott stood. "Let's go."

Billy stood and headed for the door.

Quinn nodded at Peggy. "Isaacs leaving interview." She met the men outside the interrogation room. "Let's go to the Valley, gentlemen."

"Meet you there," Elliott and Lance were already at the door to the stairs.

Valley Sheriff's Station

Quinn and Billy pulled into the parking lot at the same time. Quinn was out of her vehicle and around the front of Billy's. "Why didn't you park in the back?"

"Want to welcome the SBI guys to our shop. Here they are." He nodded as Elliott pulled into the lot.

Billy had called the Sheriff as he drove to the Valley. Chad was waiting for them inside the front door.

"Elliott, Lance, welcome to our little corner of the world." Chad had his hand out.

Greetings exchanged, they all headed to the conference room.

"Upped your technology, I see." Lance pointed to the new white board.

"Can't let you cybersecurity guys have all the fun, Lance. This redesigned conference room is thanks to the talents of Sergeant Whitehorse."

"Round table, too?" Lance ran his hand across the top.

"Yes. That, too. Do you know the reason?"

"No."

"I believe you know Sylvia Whitehorse is a member of our local native tribe, and by the way, is now their Chief."

Elliott whistled. "Hey, I didn't know that. When did that happen?"

"Chief Whitehorse, her father, passed away in December and with the agreement of his tribal council appointed her Chief on his death."

"I'll stop by and see her."

"Please do, Elliott. She'd be glad to see you. Anyway, Lance, the tribal council sits in a circle because it makes all members equal in discussion.

The Chief is still the final arbiter, but is an equal member in discussion. I try to practice that with my folks."

Billy slapped Chad on the back. "And he does it well."

Chad gave Billy his look that meant "back pedal it."

They each got a drink from the counter on the far side of the room and sat.

"Chad, I've got to find out if this Topping guy had anything to do with the death of Andrew Culbert. If he did, we can take all the time we need. If he didn't, I've got to move on and figure out what happened."

"I understand. We've got Topping ready for interview. What's your plan, Williams?"

Billy sat up a little straighter. He couldn't remember the last time the Sheriff called him by his last name.

"Since we have multiple charges to lay on him, and they all started in Detective Isaacs jurisdiction…" He looked at Lance. "Well, they probably started on Mr. Culbert's land, but the actual deaths—or murders happened here." He stopped for a moment. "Detective Isaacs and I will interview him which we assume he will see as a follow-up to yesterday. He doesn't know we have Maria here. We will need a few minutes to strategize and then we'll begin."

"Okay if we watch?" Elliott directed his question to Billy.

"Fine with me. Want to impress them, Sheriff?"

Chad shook his head. "Comedian in every crowd, folks."

Elliott and Lance laughed.

Quinn tried to keep a deadpan look—the twinkle in her eyes gave her away, though.

Chad continued. "Our enhanced technology allows you to sit here in the comfort of this conference room and watch the interview live streamed. I suspect DA O'Haire will be watching, too."

"Then let's go, Detective Isaacs." Billy stood and headed toward the door.

Quinn stood. "Not sure if you'll be here when we return, so just wanted to say it's been good to see you again, Elliott. Thanks for all the help. Lance, a pleasure. If Topping doesn't get us the information to answer the questions about your brother-in-law, I'll be interested to know the outcome."

"Let's hope we solve it. A drone to the chest on an isolated tropical island doesn't bode well if this character isn't responsible."

"I understand." She shook his hand and exited the conference room.

"Elliott, Chad, where did Round City find her?"

Chad didn't hesitate. "Ten years with Immigration Enforcement in these hills. Don't be confused by the polish—good Knoxville family for generations. Good brain, quick thinker, and civic mindedness brought her to law enforcement. Good to have her on the local beat now."

Elliott jumped in. "Amen to that. Great work in immigration but underutilized. Now my hometown has a good lead detective. Loved my brother, but he was blinded by the big city yokel he hired before her." He took a breath. "Chad, guess you know. But, Lance, Quinn was the heroine in that high school shooting in Knoxville."

Lance let out a low whistle. "Wish I'd realized that when I met her. Nerves of steel and compassion bigger than life is what I've heard."

Elliott nodded. "Truth in that. Never heard her mention it once. Did you, Chad?"

Chad shook his head. Not one for gossip, he stood to refill his coffee cup. "So, catch me up on the latest in cybersecurity, Lance."

Sheriff's Station Interrogation Room

Quinn and Billy walked out of the matron's office and Billy signaled her to have Peter Topping brought to interrogation. A guard escorted him putting a little more pressure on his elbow than was necessary.

Peter tried to pull away. "Get your hands off of me. I can walk."

"Regulations, sir. Need to be able to keep you from hitting the floor if you fall." The guard kept his eyes straight ahead.

Quinn and Billy let them get to the door before they walked down the hall.

"Listen, Detective Isaacs, this is my house."

"And you listen, Detective Williams, this is my prisoner. Got it?"

"Mine, too. Remember one of the murders is in my jurisdiction."

Quinn's shoe caught on the floor and she tripped and did a side step. *That was close.* She gripped the folder in her hand.

Billy restrained himself from helping her. *Be careful, Quinn.* He looked down at the floor to see if there was something that needed to be cleaned up or fixed. He saw the tear in the floor tile. *Have to remember to tell matron to get that fixed.*

The guard was standing just inside the door. Topping was seated.

"Detective Isaacs entering interview."

"Detective Williams entering interview."

The guard stepped out.

"Good morning, Mr. Topping." Quinn looked at her watch. "Yes, it is still morning. I trust you slept well."

Topping glared at her.

"Today is..." she gave the date and time. "Detective Isaacs of the Round City Police and..."

"Detective Williams of the Valley Sheriff's Station."

"Please state your name, address, and date of birth for the record."

"You already know it."

Quinn smiled at him. "I do; but you see, these recording devices and the attorneys and judge who watch them are pretty particular that we have all this information recorded. Surely you know that; you're a lawyer." She cocked her head and at the same time turned her eyes from friendly to disdain.

"Petersen Samuel Topping..." he gave his date of birth and address. "For the record, I am being held against my will under false charges."

Tch, tch, tch, Peter. I have you lock, stock, and barrel.

"For the record, Mr. Topping, you are being formally charged in the murder of Marjorie Eldridge Topping, in the assault of Andrew Culbert the third, as an accessory to the murder of Angela Topping, and as an accomplice in the manufacture of illegal drugs for sale and distribution across state lines." She waited a beat. They had agreed not to mention the death of Andrew Culbert but wanted to get him in the record.

Peter couldn't help himself. "You can't prove any of it."

Quinn opened the folder in front of her with slow deliberation. "Let's see." She turned the picture of Marjorie Topping lying on her living room floor so he was looking at her. It was a close up with the cyanide causing bubbles around her mouth. Next, she put the picture of the glove taken from his pocket, and next to it the report indicating the cyanide, his DNA, and his fingerprints on the cuff where he pulled the glove on.

He stared at them. "So? You put my DNA and the cyanide on that glove."

She smiled and tapped her fingernail on the report. "I suppose you could find a *fine attorney* to argue that point." She looked at him. "However, these are your fingerprints." She pointed to the top of the glove. "That one will be hard to argue. I'm sure you had already figured that out...since you're a lawyer."

"Shut up, bitch."

"Detective bitch to you." *Do these guys ever quit?*

She turned to look at Billy. "Detective Williams, do you have any questions for Mr. Topping on the murder of Mrs. Marjorie Topping?"

Billy pulled his chair up to the table so he was on the corner to the left of Quinn. "Just one. Did you know that the property she and Angela bought in the Topping Family Land Trust is designated as Conservation Land?"

"Yeah, so?"

Quinn leaned on the table with her arms crossed. "Oh, I'm sure you know Mrs. Topping had a fine reputation as an attorney."

Peter snorted.

Quinn continued. "She set the land in the TFLT as Conservation Land to be held by the state in perpetuity at the death of *her* last direct descendant." She waited a beat. "And that brings us to the death of Angela Topping."

Quinn took out the picture of Angela and the death certificate. "The chemicals ingested or inhaled by Angela Topping were so unique our medical examiner had to do a national search to try and determine their origin."

She watched his face. "Imagine our surprise when we found your little drug manufacturing enterprise on the land of Mr. Andrew Culbert."

Peter couldn't help himself—his mouth and ego had always been his downfall. "You can't prove anything."

"We have a direct match to the chemicals found in a very secure vault at the site and the one's which cost Angela her life. We have witnesses and recordings of your calls to the office of Mr. Culbert and his private phone." She leaned in further. "And we've got you on the assault of Mr. Culbert, as well."

"Stop. Stop right now. I didn't assault that two-bit realtor. I only met him once and he'll have to tell the truth on the stand. I never threatened him."

"No, you didn't threaten him. Alfred Dunn did."

"Stupid SOB. I knew it. I knew it. Lying SOB. I want a lawyer and I want a deal."

Quinn turned to Billy. "Detective, I believe that's our cue. This interview is over."

Billy opened the door and nodded to the guard. "He's all yours."

They watched Peter Topping leave the room.

Billy chuckled. "Wait until he finds out the STELT land isn't his either."

"Might be fun to watch, but he won't need it—the best he can hope for is life without parole if Peggy doesn't go for the death penalty on Mrs. Topping—which I suspect she will."

Valley Sheriff's Conference Room

"Fine job, Detectives." Elliott was standing with his hand out when Quinn and Billy entered the conference room.

Quinn spoke with a softness and concern that couldn't be missed. "Thank you, Sir. Still don't think we have answers on Mr. Culbert."

Lance stood. "I agree. However, I have one more thread to tug. Ready, Elliott?"

"Yes. Let's see if we can find an answer on Andrew in Knoxville." He turned to Chad. "Thanks, as always, for your hospitality."

"Always welcome here, Elliott. It's home. Lance, nice to see you again. Hope you find the answer to your brother-in-law's death. Let us know."

"Will do."

Quinn's secure phone rang. "Thanks. I'll be in touch." She stepped to the side as she shook hands with Elliott and Lance. "Isaacs."

"O'Haire. Save me a trip to the Valley. Send Topping to me."

"Do you want Maria Parsons, too?"

"Not yet. She can cool her heels there. I've got bigger fish to fry first."

"On it." She hung up the phone.

"O'Haire?" Billy said.

"She wants Petersen Samuel Topping in Round City. She said Maria could cool her heels here."

Chad nodded. "We're on it. Maria can be held here. I'll take care of it. Good job, both of you."

"Thanks, Chad. I need to call my Chief."

Billy turned for the door. "Call me when you're finished." He walked out with Chad.

"She did a good job, Billy. Would never know she was a rookie."

"Oh, yeah, Sheriff. Glad I don't have to worry about her taking my job."

"Don't be so sure." Chad slapped Billy on the back and headed down the hall to his office.

Billy stood there. *What does that mean?* His personal phone rang. He looked at the caller ID. "That was quick."

"Chief is no nonsense. I want to go for a picnic. Let's get lunch at The Corral and go sit up at the lookout."

He walked in the door of the conference room and ended the call. "Let's go. I'll call for lunch and it'll be ready when we get there."

"Billy, I have to go back to Round City as soon as we eat." She watched his eyes.

"I'm glad we can have lunch. Time's a wasting. Meet you at the lookout."

She found herself, yet again, both happy and disappointed he didn't kiss her.

Lookout Point

Quinn's secure phone rang just as she arrived at Lookout Point. "Isaacs."

"Marshall here."

"What's up?"

"Just thought you might want to know we got the final report on Patten's truck. There were powder chemicals in a metal container which had been taped under the hood. Apparently, the lid wasn't tight and they escaped the container and were in the hoses of the HVAC system in the truck."

"Was that what the officers reported as smelling like rotten eggs?"

"Yes. It was reduced to a powder to mix with other chemicals. Anyway, the chemicals in the truck match those that killed Angela Topping and Patten."

"Have you seen my report on Petersen Samuel Topping?"

"Yes. Hope Peggy puts him away forever. Think Lance Macklin can find who was responsible for his brother's death?"

"Oh, I'm sure he'll do whatever has to be done to figure it out. Anything else?"

"No. Just thought it might help you to wrap things up."

"Thanks, for the call. Catch up with you tomorrow."

"10-4, boss. Good job."

"Thanks, George. Back atcha. 10-4."

Quinn sat in her SUV in the silence and felt a warmth, a sense of community, as she looked out over the tiny community known as the Valley. The word carved in the sign caught her attention: Valley. *Everyone puts 'the' in front of Valley when they speak, but it's not part of the title of anything.* Even though she couldn't see the sign on the grocery she knew it read: Valley Store. The same was true on the school: Valley Middle High School. *Wonder why this is just...Valley.* She heard the sound of a vehicle and turned to see Billy pull up next to her SUV. She stepped out of her vehicle and they walked together to the bench.

"This was a great idea." He put his arms around her, pulled her to him, and gave her a long slow kiss. "And, you, love of my life, are..."

She cut off his sentence as she returned the kiss. The she pulled back. "That was fun."

"Yeah, let's do it again." He started to kiss her.

"Yeah, that was fun, too. I meant the interview." She undid the knot she had put in her hair before the interview with Topping. She hesitated. "Fun? Not the best word, is it? It was—satisfying. Yes, it was satisfying."

"It was—is." He looked at her. "I like your hair loose like that."

She shook her head. "What do you mean?"

"You know, you pull it into a knot when you're highly focused and then at some point you untie the knot."

"I do." She turned from him and looked out across the valley. *Do I? Why?* She glanced at him. "Are you sure?"

"100%." He watched her.

She lowered her head and spoke so softly he could hardly hear her above the breeze. "The first time I remember pulling it back into a knot is after Eliza was killed and I was trying to calm Mary Sue and Tricia. My hair kept falling in my face so I pulled it back and tied it in a knot." Her voice trailed off. She put her head on his shoulder. "Is it a bad thing? Distracting to others?"

He whispered to her. "It's fine. Every good detective has a tell."

"They do?" She looked at him now.

"Yeah, like Columbo with his cigar."

Quinn broke into raucous laughter that carried across the mountain. She heard it echo. Then she got the hiccups. She felt Billy wipe the tears that were running down her face.

"I like your tell. It's a good one—sends a signal of no-nonsense; let's get to the work." He brushed his finger down the bridge of her nose.

"Thanks, Billy." She turned to him and smiled.

"Do you think Lance will figure out who killed his brother-in-law?"

"Oh, I'm pretty sure he'll figure it...." Her secure phone rang. "Isaacs."

"Lance here. Not even to Knoxville and just had a call from Elliott's team. I had sent them for a closer look at the hangar and quarters of Andrew's pilot."

"And?"

"And, they found a second drone. One with ninety-nine percent probability of having hit Andrew. There was also a large deposit in his bank account from what is likely an illegal PAC supporting the other gubernatorial candidate. Evidence was in the pilot's private quarters—I think we've found another killer."

"I'm glad to know that, Lance. And, I'm sorry."

"Yeah, me, too." *I shouldn't have accepted the drone he gave me as being the one from the island.*

"Thanks for letting me know. I'll tell the other folks here."

"Appreciate it. Thanks again for your work."

"We'll get all the loose ends wrapped up soon."

"I have no doubt about that. Now, I need to wrap this up and help my sister plan for the arrival of the Easter bunny for two really cute kids."

"Good luck." The call ended.

"What? What?" Billy panted like a puppy wanting a treat.

"Calm yourself, boy." She told him what Lance had said about the drone and the pilot. Then she opened the barbeque sandwich. "In the immortal words of Sir Walter Scott, 'Oh, what tangled web we weave, when first we practice to deceive.'" She took a bite of the sandwich and ate.

"Good sandwich." Billy said.

"It is. Thanks." She told him about George's call. "Even with an APB now out on Patten's brother—the so-called chemist, we may never know if Angela was taken against her will or willingly got in the truck with Patten."

"One of the hard things about this job is you can solve the crime and never know all the details."

"Yeah. I'm learning that. It's about trying to find the truth. I think the biggest difference between this new job and my old one is now I feel like I'm making a positive difference in my own community."

"You do—and you will."

"Thanks for your help and cooperation—as a detective."

He leaned over and kissed her. "My pleasure. I like being on the same team with you."

She smiled and looked into his eyes. "Me, too. By the way, Lance reminded me it's Easter. Okay if we go to my folks on Saturday?"

"Wouldn't miss it for the world. Will we get Easter baskets?"

"Guaranteed. You won't believe what my mother will put before you."

"Then let them know we'll be there with bells on...no wait that's Christmas...with bunny ears."

Quinn almost choked on her sandwich. "You are so good for me, Billy Williams."

Billy stared as Quinn. "I love you, Quinn Isaacs. Is there anything you can't do?"

She looked deep into his eyes. "Yes, Billy Williams, there is." She turned to look out over the mountains. She whispered. "I don't know how to tell you—I love you."

He put his arm around her shoulders, pulled her close to him, and whispered into her ear. "You just did."

About the Author

Jacque Jacobs currently lives in Vero Beach, Florida. With over forty-five years in education as a teacher and leader in K-12 education and universities, she and her late husband, Dr. John F. Jacobs, lived and worked on five continents.

She is a life-long story teller which she credits to her roots in the Smoky Mountains where both of her parents' families settled. She published in her academic life and still writes stories of her family's travels and time living abroad which spanned over forty years. She wrote her first novel in December 2020 in twenty-four days and wrote six novels in ten months in the series: *Love is a Cabin*. The first book in that series is *High on a Mountain*. The first book in her second series: *Detective Quinn Isaacs* is titled *The Almost Perfect Crime*.

Jacque can be reached at JEJLetters@gmail.com

Her website is https://www.LoveIsACabin.com

Author's Note

When people ask if I know my characters before they unfold in the story, I find it awkward to answer. Many years ago I was taught that you have to have a plot, know your characters, and figure out your setting before you can write a novel. As much as I enjoyed writing in my academic career, it was based on research and experience. Writing novels is different. My life has now spanned across nine decades (1940s-2020s) and in my seventy-seven years on this planet I have met more people than I can count—in places big and small across the five continents on which I've lived. I've read hundreds, if not thousands, of crime novels, detective stories, and spy novels. With my background in special education, I often worked with students who not only were challenged in learning new material, but were often on the extremes of the continuum of human behavior. Likewise I met teachers, administrators, and parents across cultures and work environments. All of them a gift to me in so many ways.

So, for the record, I don't know my characters until they appear on the page. Sometimes when I give a character a name and then go back on my first round of editing, I realize the personality of the character has something in common with someone I know of the same name. In this novel, I thank friends whose names, if not necessarily their personality, gave me inspiration for names for several characters: Dr. Roger Carlsen, Dr. Lance Curlin, Mara Buskey, and Xaque Gruber. Other times the name has no connection. Sometimes a name is a function of me thinking about the ethnic heritage of people who settled in the mountains of east Tennessee.

As for the plot, even I am sometimes surprised at what appears on the page. One of my daughters said, "Mom, how do you know all this crime stuff?" I jokingly tell her she should be worried. The one thing I can tell you is that once the crime appears, the charges and penalties are well researched based on what I can learn in Tennessee law before the final edits. I take the research of factual information very seriously.

Families and communities are complex webs when they are deep rooted in a place, and the increased mobility of our society bringing new people and customs to that place adds more threads to the web. I hope you've enjoyed *The Imperfect Web of Crime.*